SOL GATE
A.R. KAVLI

SOL GATE

First edition. September 24, 2022.

Copyright ? 2022 A.R. Kavli.

Written by A.R. Kavli.

Published by Long Shadows Press

Cover art by selfpubbookcovers.com/thrillerauthor

Chapter 1

SOL SYSTEM, 31AUG2319.

CMDR. EUGENE K. WALSH marveled at the ancient alien edifice highlighted in his display. The cyclopean nexus gate hung like an enormous, lidless eye. Its obsidian structure was nearly invisible against the expanse of deep space behind it. The gate was a ring ten kilometers in diameter and one kilometer across from the inner surface to the outer. Impossibly, the structure was only ten meters thick when viewed from the side.

Walsh activated a spectral overlay and traces of light highlighted the gate in his optical rig. "Amazing."

"What's that, *Capitan*?" asked Lt. Cmdr. Alejandro Portos as he floated into Flight Ops. "That it's a million years old or that we broke it so quickly?"

Walsh covered his irritation by swiping his hands in the air to alter the augmented-reality view of the gate being projected directly onto his retinas. It spun in his vision and changed magnification, but he wasn't paying attention now. The age of the gate, and how the colonies had disabled it and isolated Sol, were both monumental questions. Questions that had gone unanswered by Sol's best minds for centuries. But whenever Alejandro spoke of the gate, his tone was that of one asking a child if they still believed in Santa.

Walsh checked the time floating in his vision. "Bravo shift isn't due for pass-down for another half hour."

"I like to see what's going on early. Not that anything goes on early or late on these science escorts." He looked at Walsh hopefully. "Is anything going on?"

Walsh shook his head. "Nothing but studying humanity's greatest known mystery." With a flick of his hand, the hovering gate disappeared.

He'd finish his studies later. The science ship *Peruvian Angel* would be sharing its sensor feed and observations for another eighteen hours, then Walsh and crew would escort the ship back to Luna.

"Well, I hope there are no more ships heading out to the nexus when we get back," Alejandro said, offering Walsh a wry smile. "With all due respect, Capitan, I know you love the gate, but I'm a bit tired of this run. Please, for the sake of my sanity and career, stop volunteering."

Walsh looked at his executive officer and chuckled. "All right. I'll see if we can go find some Calies or Marties to blast."

"About time," Alejandro said. "You know that's why I signed up with you. The bigger the coattails the better."

"I'm flattered."

Alejandro smiled. "I hope so. I'm trying my best. Besides, we've been studying that thing for over a century with nothing to show for it."

Walsh rubbed a finger across his augmentation rig, known as an AugR, and brought up the status screen of the CAR *Thunder*. The AugR band ran between his temples and around the back of his head, clinging to the shaved flesh of his regulation fleet tonsure. Many, like Alejandro, just went bald. Walsh preferred to keep the hair on top as long, if not a bit longer, than allowed. He found the ladies liked it better that way, too.

Everything on the screen was green, as he knew it would be. There were other ships in the area: corporate researchers, university science vessels like *Peruvian Angel*, unmanned sensor and navigation satellites. And a European Caliphate cruiser. *Thunder* still had time on station and everyone was keeping their distance according to treaty.

Until they weren't.

A yellow glow filled Walsh's vision. "What is it, Yeoman?"

"Capitan," answered the ship, "one of the Caliphate's sensor drones has crossed the treaty boundary."

Alejandro snorted. "They must be eager to solve the mystery."

Walsh queried the local nav-sat and its time report matched that of *Thunder* and *Peruvian Angel*. "Local time is good. They know it's not their turn yet."

"They're just pushing," Alejandro said, unconcerned.

Walsh rubbed his forehead. It was impossible to know how the admiralty at Liberty Station would judge his actions. Especially that idiot Admiral Maconez. If Walsh gave, Maconez would say he should have held. If Walsh held, Maconez would say he should have given. On balance, given his history with the Calies, he preferred to avoid any further hostile incidents.

"*Angel*, this is *Thunder*. The Cali's getting pushy. Is your last data run finished?"

"Roger that, *Thunder*," answered the science ship's executive officer. "I don't like being pushed off. But I don't like being in the center of interplanetary incidents, either."

"My thoughts, exactly. We're ready when you are. Please burn at your earliest convenience."

"Burn in twenty, *Thunder*."

Walsh closed the connection and zoomed in on the offending drone. He considered issuing the standard ship stand-off warning to the Caliphate commander, but it would seem weak to challenge them and then leave anyway. Better to just let it go.

If they'd let him.

"Yeoman, did that drone just assume an intercept course with the *Angel*?"

"Yes, Capitan."

Walsh cleared his throat. "Caliphate cruiser *Gibraltar*, you are in violation of the Gate Accords of 2231 by sending a remote vehicle into the exclusion zone outside your agreed time allotment."

A red halo surrounded Walsh's vision.

"Capitan," Alejandro said. "The Combat Management System has flagged the drone as a possible hostile."

Walsh made sure he was transmitting a broadband, omnidirectional signal. "*Gibraltar*, your drone is now on an intercept course with one of our ships. You need to abort and recover your drone. Please respond."

Walsh's heart began pounding in his chest. His breath grew short. This was close to how the last incident had started. He opened the emotional damper system in his vision. Within a moment, he could feel his heart slowing and his breathing returning to normal as the AugR band introduced calming brainwaves.

Walsh took a slow breath. He looked over and saw Alejandro slipping into one of the control stations. "XO, sound battle stations. All hands to Ops."

Alejandro stared at him in disbelief.

"XO?"

"Yes, Capitan." Alejandro adopted the distant stare of someone in AugR. "Battle stations. Battle stations. All crew report to Ops."

The crew locator indicators in Walsh's display showed the remaining three crew members rushing into the operations compartment. They flew in and buckled into their stations. All eight of *Thunder's* crew were now connected to the ship's systems. Once everyone was in the armored operations pod, the remaining internal hatches sealed.

Walsh pulled up the tracking information on the Cali cruiser. It was holding station, but the drone was still closing on *Peruvian Angel*. "Flight, put us between the drone and the *Angel*."

The feeling that he was overreacting overcame him. Even at full speed, the drone couldn't do much to a full-sized ship in a collision. Unless it had some kind of bomb or other hidden surprise. But that would be stupid.

The ship's voice came over the operations channel. "Capitan, *Peruvian Angel's* computer is reporting the Caliphate drone is directing active, high-powered scans at the ship."

Walsh sighed. "Cease and desist your scans, *Gibraltar*. We are here under Confederation authority as per the Gate Accords. Back off. We'll be done soon."

"Capitan," the ship said. "*Peruvian Angel* has identified possible tactical software-intrusion programs injected among the sensor's scans. I have been provided with a sample and I concur the threat is possible."

"Confidence?" Walsh asked.

"Sixty-seven percent chance of ongoing cyber intrusion against *Peruvian Angel*, Capitan."

Walsh tensed again, but decided against another calming for now. This was going to turn nasty and he wanted to be on edge. "*Gibraltar*, immediately desist transmitting signals or we'll be forced to take action."

Alejandro's avatar appeared in Walsh's vision. He spoke on a private channel via the subcutaneous communicator, known commonly as a sub-q, implanted in his jawbone. "What would the *Angel* have that they'd even want, Capitan? This is a setup. They're goading us into firing first."

"They fired first," Walsh said. "A cyberattack is still an attack."

"Is it worth it for a bunch of useless data about the nexus?"

"We don't know what's on the *Angel*. Even if she doesn't have classified material, it's still a provocation. Looking weak could be just as bad as looking overeager."

The digital avatar generated by Alajandro's AugR perfectly recreated his worried expression. "I suggest we just leave."

"We were trying to." Walsh rotated the tactical display with gentle waves of his hand. There just might be time. He opened the ops channel. "Navigation, get us between that drone and the *Angel*. We should be able to make it with a LOX injection."

With a curt salute in AugR, the navigation officer acknowledged the order and pushed *Thunder* into a hard pivot. The crews' stations rotated to put the acceleration force on their backs. Walsh felt the force of the pivot correction and the heavy press of the fusion thruster, followed by the kick of liquid oxygen injection.

"Yeoman, fire up the ECM," Walsh said. "See if we can't jam up that signal."

"Electronic countermeasures activated, Capitan. Still no reply from *Gibraltar*."

"Any change in the drone's trajectory?"

"No, Capitan," the ship answered.

Walsh traced a line in the tactical display and looked over at Alejandro. "XO, bring accelerators online. If target Delta-1 crosses this line, destroy it."

Alejandro widened his eyes momentarily, then nodded once. "Roger, Capitan."

Minutes passed while Walsh watched the drone approach. "Yeoman, current confidence of drone hostilities?"

"Current confidence assessment is seventy-one percent, Capitan. Our countermeasure efforts are impeding that assessment, however."

Walsh had hoped the drone would employ some anti-countermeasures techniques such as shifting its frequency hopping or varying its signal generation patterns. Anything that would give *Thunder* a chance to capture more evidence of the drone's intrusion attempts. Instead, the drone continued towards the red line he'd drawn in space. Walsh brought up the Combat Management System in his vision.

The drone passed the line.

"CMS is engaging target Delta-1, Capitan," Alejandro blurted.

Walsh watched the burst of shells from the number one magnetic accelerator speed towards the drone. Thermal plumes erupted from several ships in the area as they fired their engines to clear what had just become a live-fire zone.

The drone made no evasive maneuvers as the incoming shells shattered it.

"*Gibraltar*'s fire-control arrays are powering up and targeting us, Capitan," said the tactical operator.

Walsh nodded. Everyone could still step back and stand down. He hoped they would. "Return the favor and paint *Gibraltar*. Designate target Alpha-1. Mount kinetic penetrator warheads and open missile bays two, four, six, and eight."

"That escalated fast," muttered Alejandro.

Walsh chuckled. "It always does. XO, get the *Angel* out of here and plot the *Thunder* a matching escort course. Keep us close enough to provide point defense."

"Capitan," the tactical operator announced, "*Gibraltar* has deployed four missiles. They've cleared the ship, but haven't fired yet."

"*Gibraltar*, this is Commander Walsh. You need to stand down." The comms systems registered a reply from *Gibraltar*. Walsh let out a slow breath. Someone was finally talking. If they could talk, they could keep from poking holes in each other's ships. He opened a visual channel and saw the glowering, tattooed face of a dark-skinned woman.

"This is Captain Sabira Bitat. I'm not sure how you plan on altering your records, Commander Walsh, but mine show you are the only one who has discharged weaponry."

Walsh furrowed his brow. "So your logs won't show the fact that your drone had not only entered the exclusion zone during our research allotment, but that it was transmitting actively hostile signals at a registered Confederation science vessel?"

"Those were standard scientific sweeps directed at the nexus, Commander."

"Assuming I believed that, or even that I believed you believed that, your drone was still in the exclusion zone and on intercept with our ship."

"You destroyed a Caliphate vessel, Commander." She stared at him with cool eyes. "Perhaps you should recalibrate whatever system identified the signals as hostile. They were not. I will be sure to send a copy of those transmissions when I file the complaint against you."

She was unflappable, Walsh had to give her that. A replacement drone had probably already been printed. "Be sure to include your refusal to respond to my calls."

"We had to reboot our comms system."

"That's convenient."

Captain Bitat sniffed. "Are you calling me a liar, Commander?"

Walsh shrugged. "Not at all. It's convenient because now you can thank me for taking care of your rogue drone."

"You have destroyed a Caliphate craft. You will bring down your firewalls and grant us access to your logs for the purposes of investigating your claims."

"You know that's not going to happen, right, Captain?" Walsh cast a level look at the woman. She was going to push it. He just wanted to leave the sector and Bitat seemed intent on turning this into an incident. That might be the whole point, though he couldn't see the advantage of that for either of them.

Another red flag appeared in Walsh's aug-view as the ship spoke over the operations channel. "Capitan, electronic intrusion attempts detected from *Gibraltar*."

"Well, shit," Walsh muttered. "Initiate counter-intrusion." He knew the ship had done so without human orders, but Walsh was performing for the investigation to come.

Alejandro's voice sounded over the channel, dulled with disbelief. "They're firing at us."

"They're screwing with us," Walsh answered. A group of five shells sped towards them on the display. The Combat Management System flashed red as it fired its own shells to intercept. One enemy shell evaded *Thunder*'s defensive, requiring another burst of shells to destroy it.

He'd had enough of this. The last incoming shell hadn't come close enough to be a threat. But it had come close enough to drive home the point that the Cali ship—the Cali captain—had just fired at them directly. He had to respond; Eugene K. Walsh had a reputation to protect.

Fingers dancing in the air, Walsh input engagement orders into the CMS. *Thunder* immediately fired ten shells from her mag-guns. *Gibraltar* shot them down and sent ten more back at *Thunder*. The ships in the area that hadn't already fled did so now. Walsh couldn't blame them. The remains of ships from the now-defunct Earth Protectorate League still drifted in the area. They had been destroyed by the energy released from the gate when the Colonial Defense Fleet killed the nexus and ended the war, severing Sol from Tau Ceti—and the rest of the galaxy. Their skeletal hulks, combined with the untold ages of the mysterious gate, gave this sector a certain brooding reverence, and acted as a reminder of how fragile spaceships really are.

The two ships continued to exchange fire while *Thunder* and *Peruvian Angel* made for the edge of the exclusion zone and what Walsh hoped would be the end of the fight. Neither ship was attacking in earnest, but if a shell slipped past a ship's point defense, people could die. *Gibraltar* wasn't pursuing, so range continued to open, making it easier to intercept the incoming attacks. It had become a fool's game Walsh wished to be done with.

The next string of shells from *Gibraltar* was significantly longer, appearing as an angry red line in Walsh's AugR. Apparently, Captain Bitat wanted to up the game. If the missiles didn't start launching, everyone could still disengage with hulls intact. Walsh directed part of the next barrage at each of the waiting missiles drifting around *Gibraltar*.

Walsh set the CMS to shift to full point-defense fire and ordered the ship to orient for incoming fire. *Thunder*'s main hull, like most of the ships in the Confederation fleet, was constructed of a series of interchangeable, cylindrical modules. The reactor and fusion thruster were set at the end of a 150-meter framework of armored girders to reduce the crew's radiation exposure. Four large, teardrop-shaped assemblies spread like the wings of a dragonfly—the ship class namesake—away from the hull. Magnetically circulated, liquid-metal coolant carried heat away from the ship to radiate it into space.

Thunder pivoted to point its armored nose cone towards the incoming fire. The four coolant wings rotated to present a flat profile to the attack. Bursts of shells reached out from *Thunder*.

Walsh's heart pounded in his chest. Regardless of how this battle turned out, it wouldn't be good for him. Just firing at the Calies, even if they had initiated hostilities, could kill his career. If he couldn't find a sympathetic patron, the Admiralty could take his ship. He'd worked too hard to give it up. Ironically, it was those skills and abilities that made him a good capitan that were going to get him in trouble.

He watched with mixed horror and satisfaction as several shells got past *Gibraltar*'s point-defense fire. The flashes of three impact points on her nose cone twinkled in Walsh's overlay. Two of the four missiles on station around *Gibraltar* crumpled and tumbled away.

Gibraltar was a tough cruiser and Walsh didn't expect much, if any, damage had been caused to the ship's forward armor. But he hoped it might make Captain Bitat reconsider playing this game. "Any indication of internal damage?"

"No, Capitan," Alejandro said. "Power levels and thermal signature show no significant change. They did pick up a wobble and corrected it, so we got them."

Walsh's shoulders grew tense as he waited for more return fire. After several minutes, he blew out a low breath and grinned. "Congrats, everyone. You're all combat vets now."

Alejandro shook his head. "This hardly counts."

"They fired at us, we fired back. Just because no one exploded doesn't mean it doesn't count." Walsh scanned his eyes through his overlay view until the tactical screen was to the forefront. "Any signs of damage or return fire yet?"

"No, Capitan," the tactical officer said, his voice quivering with excitement and nerves. "The *Gibraltar* has changed heading. I think she's taking her research position. They're keeping their nose towards us though."

Walsh zoomed in *Gibraltar*'s image. Three blackened craters were visible on her forward armor plating. "That seems reasonable. Keep us between the *Gibraltar* and the *Angel*. I think we can get our flashlight out of Captain Bitat's face now—defensive scanning only. And close all missile bays. But keep the warheads loaded. Hopefully, we can all go our separate ways now and everyone can keep the air in their lungs."

He left the crew at combat stations for another three hours. When *Gibraltar* finally turned her nose away to take up position around the gate, Walsh allowed himself a smile. "Bravo shift, you have the *Thunder*." As was tradition, the crew all made deep rumbling sounds in reply. He'd never heard it done with so much enthusiasm. The crew was full of nervous energy. Despite the veneer of professional modesty, the crew had accepted that they'd been in a real battle. Walsh loved it. "Alpha shift, dismissed."

WALSH LEANED BACK AND closed his eyes. "How bad are the scout's wounds?"

"You are doubtful he will survive without the aid of a priestess of Zara," the ship answered.

"They're not likely to help me."

"The comments you made at their banquet were certainly unappreciated."

Walsh chuckled. "They were funny, though. You have to give me that."

The ship's yeoman didn't reply.

"Nothing? Fine. What color is his tunic?"

"The color is irrelevant."

Walsh opened his eyes and leaned forward. It was a pointless, habitual gesture since he spoke to the ship via his overlay no matter his position. "I don't know that, though. If it isn't relevant, just make up a random color. It's the tiny details that can really make a story stand out."

"I must ask an out-of-character question. Why would the scout's tunic color matter, Capitan?"

"It might not. But say a certain sect, or warband, or gang all wear the same color. It could be a hint about his affiliation. Now, back in character."

"Understood, Araminix. The scout's tunic is blue and covered in blood," the ship continued. "He beckons you over..."

Walsh closed his eyes again and relaxed as the ship described the scene. Immersive role-playing had come a long way since his youth, but sometimes there was nothing like letting one's own imagination paint the scene. Walsh had been training *Thunder*'s digital yeoman for almost a year, teaching it the kind of adventures he liked, both in theme and genre. It was improving, but its storytelling routines weren't on par with its tactical abilities.

While the adrenaline had gone from Walsh's system, he was too jittery to go to sleep. It was hard to pay attention to the ship describing the fantasy scout's desperate plea to carry his urgent message to the city. Not the most original hook, but Walsh wanted to see where the ship went with it. If he could keep his mind on it.

Walsh was just getting ready to pause the adventure and drift to sleep, when the yeoman interrupted.

"Apologies, Capitan. We have received a priority one message from Fleet Command at Liberty Station."

Typical. He knew whatever was in it would probably keep him awake until his sleep shift was over. "Load to my overlay."

Walsh allowed the message to pop up without opening his eyes. It was close to what he expected. The European Caliphate had issued a formal complaint about the events near the nexus and the admiralty was reviewing his ship's logs. Standard bureaucratic protocol. He was sure they'd have filed against the Cali's cyber-intrusion attempt.

At the bottom of the file, Walsh's eyes popped open. It wasn't just notification of a formal complaint. They had already scheduled a board of inquiry. The trip back to Earth was scheduled to take three months—plenty of time to run a full investigation and play patty-cake with the Caliphate. Even if the Confederation was technically in the wrong, it usually put up a fight. This had Walsh picturing eager workers erecting a gallows overnight.

"What the hell?" Walsh muttered. There were flight orders attached. *Peruvian Angel* was to carry on alone and *Thunder* was to make maximum burn back to Liberty. The approved delta-v expenditure was unusual. Then he read the approval signature.

Vice Adm. Terrano Maconez.

Walsh forwarded the flight orders to the XO. After a moment, Alejandro connected via overlay, speaking on the sub-q. Probably to hide the tremble in his voice from the operations crew.

"What does this mean?" Alejandro asked.

"It means the good admiral can't wait to get his teeth into us."

"I knew it," Alejandro said. "We shouldn't have interfered. We should have just left."

Walsh took a moment to gather himself and keep the disgust out of his voice. "Don't worry, XO. He's mostly after me."

"How can you be so calm about this?"

The man was more worried about getting in trouble than having been shot at. Walsh couldn't blame him—didn't want to lose his command, either. One had to watch their six for backstabbers and bootlickers. Keeping a commission in the Confederation of American Republics required political acumen. And friends. Powerful friends.

Maconez was no friend. This wasn't Walsh's first shoot-out and he knew Maconez would paint him as the incident-causing warmonger. Walsh grinned at the thought that it might be true. But he'd fight that database jockey tooth and nail to keep his command.

"At least we'll get to enjoy some thrust gravity on the way home," Walsh said. "We can break out the pool table."

Chapter 2

WALSH SAT QUIETLY AT the large, silvered table that stood between him and the bureaucratic firing squad assembled against him. He glanced at the officers, advisors, senators, and undersecretaries sitting in their wood-paneled work stations. In the center was the chief orchestrator of this show: Vice Adm. Terrano Maconez. He was here to take away Walsh's command. Walsh was here to stop him.

The VIPs weren't looking at him yet. They wore the half-doze look of people in the overlay. Their pupils flitted back and forth as they accessed files and exchanged messages. Presumably about him or the proceedings. The officers were medically epilated from the top of their temples down, wearing a fleet regulation tonsure to accommodate the mandatory overlay crown. Many civilians wore a similar style, but some were only shaved in a thin band around their head, slightly wider than their crown. With long hair and creative use of nano-styler, the crown and bald stripe were barely visible.

He knew many of them, had served with a few. It was hard to gain an impression about how they might feel about him since they were all immersed in the overlay. A few throats twitched as they spoke on their sub-q comms. They might be talking to each other, but they weren't talking to him. Walsh grinned. The VIPs were making him wait. Probably at Maconez's request.

Resentment tightened his shoulders and shortened his breath. He was not some cadet, not some office commander. He was the CO, the *Capitan*, of a warship and a decorated combat veteran. Admirals and senators they may be, but he didn't deserve this disrespect. Of course, he wouldn't be a CO if he let his tongue go ballistic. With a slow breath, Walsh forced a smile and accessed his emotional dampener.

Having controlled his resentment, Walsh grew bored. With nothing else to do, he glanced at various people before him and started accessing their overlay profiles. Names, ranks, organizations, awards, voting districts, and other official statistics hovered above their heads. The accompanying official portraits were uninteresting.

Out of curiosity, Walsh passively scanned for social profiles. As he expected during duty hours and official functions, their social profiles were disabled. There was always someone who forgot, though. Often it went unnoticed because people knew better than to query. But Capt. Julianne Conrad's social profile blinked alive over her head.

Walsh allowed himself a grin. Julianne was a sexy woman in and out of uniform. Her irises had digital implants that swirled blue and green like ocean vortices when off duty. The social avatar smiled and tossed her hair to one side, revealing a slender shoulder. Their last tryst had been three years ago and Walsh remembered it fondly.

His reverie was interrupted when the social profile disappeared. He instinctively glanced down and met her glare. Julianne was still beautiful when she was angry, too. Her overlay must have informed her of the social query.

He considered flashing her a coy smile, but wasn't in the mood. Despite her loveliness and her combat record, Walsh was disappointed to find her here. His stare returned to the wall behind the VIPs' seats.

Flanking Adm. Terrano Maconez were Adm. Linda James and Sen. Marina Midland. He understood Admiral James being there. Senator Midland was influential but held no positions in any military-related subcommittees that he knew of. The members of the review board started to open their eyes as if waking from a dream. He'd find out why she was there shortly.

Maconez offered a polite smile before speaking. "Thank you for joining us, Commander Walsh."

Walsh heard victory in the man's voice. "Thank you for inviting me, Admiral." A water pitcher engraved with the stylized, five-pointed star of Liberty Station was on the table next to a matching cup. He filled the cup and took a sip. The cup smelled newly printed.

"Commander," continued Maconez, "this review board was instituted to address an incident occurring in the Nexus Gate sector on the thirty-first of August, 2319. The incident involves the CAR *Thunder*, then under your command, firing at the ECS *Gibraltar*."

Walsh fought to keep his face neutral in response to the gross mischaracterization of the incident. His face kept trying to twist into a wry grin, which he covered by stroking his beard. It wasn't a good start.

"The complaint filed by the European Caliphate has been verified by *Thunder*'s own logs, Commander Walsh." Admiral Maconez paused to glance somberly at those sitting on either side of him. "Do you have any opening comments concerning these accusations?"

"If we are going to be addressing the incident in further detail, Admiral, I'd prefer to keep my comments limited to answering point by point. Especially concerning the hitherto unmentioned hostile actions of the *Gibraltar*."

Maconez raised his brows and looked down, adopting a rueful expression. "If you wish, Commander. Let it be shown Commander Walsh has nothing to say for himself at this time."

Walsh narrowed his eyes for an instant before recovering. "Thank you, Admiral."

The next hour was spent listening to Admiral Maconez detail Walsh's errors without much opportunity for rebuttal. It was a thinly veiled diatribe against Walsh and those like him, so much so that even others on the review board began to lose interest or even look uncomfortable. A few, though, hung on every bitter word.

"This isn't your first hostile action against EC ships, is it, Commander Walsh?"

"This is not the first time I've had to defend my ship and crew against Caliphate aggression, Admiral."

Admiral Maconez waved a dismissive hand. "What led you to believe the EC drone was being aggressive?"

"I thought you had my ship's logs, Admiral."

"I do, Commander. Please answer in your own words."

"The logs are my own words."

Maconez raised his eyebrow.

Walsh refilled his cup of water and sipped it. "Of course, Admiral. The first aggressive act was when the drone crossed into the exclusion zone agreed upon by Gate Accords. We still had eighteen hours in our research cycle."

"And you immediately assumed it was aggressive behavior?" Maconez flashed a grin. "Space is a big place full of invisible lines. Why not assume a navigational error? Remotes do sometimes go astray."

"It seems I give the Caliphate crews more credit than you do, Admiral. I will, however, keep that in mind if I find myself accidentally crossing one of those invisible lines in the future." Walsh returned the grin. "And I hope you'll afford me the same consideration you give the Caliphate."

"Don't get smart, Commander," Admiral James said.

Walsh wiped the grin from his face. "Apologies, Admiral. It was not my intention. Back to the drone, the invading of our space was only the first warning sign. I immediately tried to contact the *Gibraltar* and received no reply.

"The next warning was when the drone started actively scanning the *Peruvian Angel*. Next, the ship notified me it detected possible cyber-intrusion signals embedded in the drone's transmissions."

Admiral Maconez frowned. "Possible?"

"Yes, possible, Admiral. Higher than sixty percent and later the ship determined an over-seventy-percent confidence," Walsh said. "As you know from the ship itself."

"So you destroyed the drone?"

"Yes, Admiral. After the *Gibraltar* continued to refuse to answer my calls. They sure answered quickly after that."

A couple of review board members chuckled. Maconez stared them down, then glared at Walsh. "Their ship logs show a comms failure that was also the root of the drone guidance malfunction."

Walsh raised on eyebrow. "Well, I'm glad I was able to clear up their technical problem for them. I hope the Confederation billed them appropriately."

A woman chuckled. Walsh though it was Julianne, but he didn't want to break eye contact with Maconez. The admiral was starting to lose the board members and that made Walsh feel saucy. But he couldn't afford to push it.

"So, Commander," Maconez said, "you felt it an appropriate response to destroy a European Caliphate spaceship. Assuming you actually felt it *was* a threat of some sort, how do you think a cyberattack on a science ship studying the same nexus everyone has been studying for over one-hundred years would be a threat?"

"Admiral, I have no idea what was in the *Peruvian Angel*'s databases. But that's not even the main threat. Implanted hostile programs could do anything. Harm the crew. Turn the ship into a giant kinetic weapon to be rammed into, say, a large space station like Liberty. And that would be a shame, wouldn't it?"

Maconez cast a preemptive glare around the review board before anyone could laugh. "You opened fire, without authorization, on a spaceship of another nation."

"It was an unmanned drone that the *Gibraltar* probably reprinted in an hour."

Maconez leaned back in his chair and sighed. One finger twirled as he manipulated something in his overlay. "Commander Walsh, would you consider yourself to have a violent personality or hold a grudge against the Caliphate due to past hostile encounters?"

"I'm only as violent as I need to be," Walsh said. "And no, Admiral, I don't hold a grudge against the Caliphate."

"That's not what your crew says." With a sly smile, Maconez motioned to the door behind Walsh. A moment later, Lt. Cmdr. Alejandro Portos sat down at the large table, though well away from Walsh. "Thank you for joining us, Lieutenant Commander Portos."

"Thank you, Admiral."

"Please characterize for us Commander Walsh's attitude during the confrontation with the ECS *Gibraltar*."

Alejandro glanced at Walsh and looked away. "Yes, Admiral. He was very decisive and—"

"Were you convinced of the threat, Lieutenant Commander?"

Alejandro hesitated before answering. "No, Admiral. The drone's behavior was erratic, but I didn't find it to rise to the level of firing on it."

"Did you express your concerns to Commander Walsh?"

"Yes, Admiral. But once I had I did as ordered. As XO, it's my job to support the Capitan."

Walsh almost laughed.

"Commendable, Lieutenant Commander," Maconez said. "The job of every officer is to obey their superiors, even if they dislike those orders. What was Commander Walsh's state of mind? How did he seem to you?"

"Certainly professional, Admiral. But beneath that, he was almost... gleeful. He seemed to be goading the Caliphate ship into a confrontation. When it was over, he congratulated us all, like it was some game."

Walsh slowly turned towards Alejandro, who remained staring straight ahead. Alejandro had always been a bit too eager to please, but Walsh hadn't figured the man for an outright backstabber. With pursed lips, he fought against the urge to tell the man off, to call him a coward. He lost that fight.

"You..." Walsh started. A priority overlay message flared to life in his vision.

Shut up. It's what he wants.

It was from Senator Midland. Walsh sensed a double-edged sword hanging above his head. He kept from glancing at the senator.

"... are welcome to your opinion, XO," Walsh continued. "And I'm sorry you got that impression."

Maconez smirked at Walsh. "Please keep your comments directed to the board, Commander. But he's not an XO anymore."

Walsh raised his brows at Alejandro. Alejandro looked away again.

"Lieutenant Commander Portos is now Capitan of the *Thunder*."

It seemed the floor fell away beneath Walsh's feet. His stomach flipped. Then came the anger, rising in waves from his neck. It had all been a big show, a stage for Maconez to justify his foregone conclusion by demonizing Walsh in front of the review board.

It would be nearly impossible to recover from losing a command like this. Especially when a flag officer with nothing better to do, working to destroy his career. Maconez had let him think there was a chance this could go some other way. And Walsh had bough t into that fantasy. He'd be flying a satellite, if that. Walsh would never get another command.

He cleared his throat and offered his former XO a thin smile. "Well, congratulations, Alejito." Walsh turned to Maconez. "It seems everything was already decided."

Maconez shrugged, wearing an expression that asked *What can you do?* "Firing on a ship without prior authorization from Fleet Command is a serious offense, Commander."

"Even when they fired first?"

"But it was you that fired first, Commander," Maconez said. "As you and your ship agreed."

"They launched an intrusion attack and fired at—"

Maconez raised his hand. "Commander, Commander. This squabbling doesn't suit you. And to return to your statement, not everything has been decided. Including your next assignment. Although, I have worked up a list of suggestions."

The battle was a decisive defeat. Maconez had managed to wheedle his way into being judge, jury, and executioner of Walsh's career. If he was done for in the fleet, Walsh was going to tell *Mamon*-ez where he could shove the rocket he rode in on.

Senator Midland flipped her hair, revealing her overlay crown as she did. "I was wondering, Admiral Maconez, if you would share that list of suggestions."

Maconez looked at her uncertainly. Then he nodded towards her, the shortcut gesture to share via overlay. "Of course, Senator."

The senator's eyes flicked as she read. "I see that none of the suggestions include giving Commander Walsh another command."

Maconez snorted. "I would say not, Senator."

"I understand that losing a command like that can be disastrous to a commanding officer's career."

"Commander Walsh has proven himself to lack the temperament to be trusted with the command of a spaceship. We can't have capitans that go around opening fire on their gut reactions."

Walsh opened his mouth, saw the senator glance at him dangerously, then snapped it shut.

The senator smiled. "Admiral, I'm looking at his record and it is exemplary. I'm no admiral, of course, but the previous engagements that prompted concern earned the commander commendations. His ratings are excellent when compared to other officers across the fleet. It seems a shame to lose that experience."

Maconez shook his head. "That's the point of this hearing. The type of experience he has to offer is not what the fleet needs."

"As a member of the review board *and* senior member of the Space and Science Appropriations Committee," the senator said, flipping her hair back again, "I disagree. I don't wish to interfere with fleet personnel decisions, but the commander has valuable experience he can pass on. We may need that experience in upcoming conflicts with Mars or the Caliphate."

"We do have other combat veterans in the fleet, Senator," Maconez said. "Including Lieutenant Commander Portos here."

"But most are deployed, yes? Do you want to pull them off their patrols?"

Maconez shook his head. "No, Senator. Nor do we need to. We—"

"Captain Alvarez of the *Amazonas* is ready to rotate out, correct?"

Admirals Maconez and James both stared at the senator. Finally, Admiral James answered, "Alvarez's rank is commander. Anyone commanding a spaceship has the title of capitan. But yes, he's waiting for a replacement."

"Excellent," the senator said, ignoring the rest of the admiral's explanation of military protocol. "We can keep Commander Walsh's expertise and free up Alvarez for his next, uh, what's it called? Billet, right?"

"Yes, Senator," Maconez answered. "I mean about it being a billet. I'm not sure—"

"That the Science and Space committee will approve your project requests?" Senator Midland finished for Maconez. "I assure you, they will."

Maconez stared at Midland, utter confusion written across his face. Walsh suspected his own expression was the same. The look of victory that had been riding on Maconez's face was gone, confusion changing to disbelief, which was in turn replaced with weary resignation.

Walsh shook his head. "The *Amazonas*?"

"Yes," the senator answered.

"*Tres Grande*?" Walsh asked.

Admiral James nodded. "That's the one."

Walsh tried to keep from whining. "She's a training ship."

Senator Midland stared at Walsh placidly. "'Ship' is the key word, Commander."

He rubbed his face. His cadet cruise had fortunately been on a deployed frigate. Not only was *Amazonas* a training ship, it was a dinosaur. Being a leftover from the collapsed Earth Protectorate League, it was well over one hundred years old. And it was huge. Plenty of room to fit all those cadets.

Walsh let out a breath. *Cadets.*

He forced a polite smile as he considered the senator. *Amazonas* might be his only chance to keep a command. And who knew what he might land after that tour. Surely a shipload of cadets couldn't be worse than flying a shipload of ultrarich tourists for Solar Transit Inc.—could it? Assuming they'd even give him a job if he got drubbed out of the service.

He wondered what the price would be for the senator's benevolence.

"I look forward to that opportunity, Senator, Admirals," Walsh finally said, sounding as genuine as possible.

Senator Midland clapped her hands once and beamed. "Excellent. Admiral James, I trust your office can arrange all the military stuff."

Admiral James glanced at Maconez before answering. "Yes, Senator. We'll have the orders written up before the end of the day."

Glaring at Walsh, Maconez raised a finger. A bell sounded in everyone's overlay. Maconez rose and the rest of the board did the same. Senator Midland cast a knowing glance at Walsh as she filed from the room.

He was reminded of the old story that ended "You knew I was a snake when you picked me up."

Chapter 3

CMDR. FELICIA DIAZ stood at attention in front of the crew and cadets of CAR *Amazonas* in drill and ceremony hall Charlie. The ship's formation stood at parade rest in their dress crimsons, waiting to officially meet their new capitan. Diaz was hoping to get back to business without a cadet doing something stupid that would in turn make her look stupid. There were enough black marks on her record already.

As XO, she had been required to attend the change-of-command ceremony and banquet the night before. The senators, of course, blathered on endlessly as they loved to do. The commandant of the academy waxed poetically about the cadets—who weren't even present—and entrusting them into the hands of the veterans of the fleet. Even Capitan Alvarez went on at length, spurred on by the joy of getting a *real* command and copious goblets of spacer punch.

Though the new capitan, Commander Walsh, kept his speech blissfully short, she recognized the resentment beneath the words. The admiralty had tucked them both away in *Amazonas*. He hadn't smiled once during the ceremony, not even when he left with the slinky admin lieutenant from the academy staff.

"Capitan Eugene Walsh is approaching," the Liberty Station virtual yeoman announced in crew's sub-q. The formation grew tense in preparation. Ten seconds later, the door slid open and Walsh entered.

Diaz snapped to attention. "Attention on deck!" She heard the sound of the ship's company coming to attention behind her. A quick glance in her overlay at the compartment's overhead camera confirmed everyone was in their proper position.

Walsh marched straight towards her and she kept her gaze beyond him. With a final heavy step, he halted in front of her.

She saluted sharply. "All hands present and accounted for, *mi* Capitan."

"Very good, Commander Diaz," Walsh answered as he saluted. His tone was flat. The anger from the ceremony was gone from his voice, but he made it clear he wasn't pleased about being there. He glanced at the white gloves she wore and spoke to her over the sub-q. "Why the gloves? They're not required for inspection."

"They are optional, *mi* Capitan," she said back over the connection. "Do you want me to remove them?"

Walsh pursed his lips as he considered her, then shook his head. Aloud he said, "Prepare for inspection, XO."

Diaz did an about-face. "Company, open ranks!" She made the announcement aloud and over the crew's sub-q connection. Each rank marched forward in unison, taking the required number of steps to leave walking room between them. Another quick glance at the overlay told Diaz each row was in place. She was pleased. Basic drill, aside from lining up for formation, was a skill set spacers quickly forgot after getting to the fleet. Most spaceships didn't have the room or need for such formations.

Something was out of place in the ordered lines of the formation. One female cadet was half a step too far forward. Diaz sent her a quick command to guide right, before turning to face Walsh. "Ship's company ready for inspection, *mi* Capitan."

Walsh nodded and stepped to the first rank, which contained the staff and officers of *Amazonas*. Dress crimsons consisted of a long-sleeved, knee-length crimson tunic, split below the waist in front and back. The trim and insignia were colored burnished gold. The accompanying slacks, soft shoes, and flight caps were black, trimmed with white. He gave each a cursory glance and nod before side-stepping to the next. Diaz followed, averting her gaze.

When the capitan made it to the cadet ranks, he inspected them more carefully, eyeing them closely up and down. This was a new batch of cadets and Diaz hadn't come to know any of them yet. But the academy had at least trained most of them how to dress themselves and Walsh found few demerits to mark.

The capitan continued, adopting an inspection rhythm of scanning, nodding, and stepping, with only a few comments. He came up short in front of the female cadet Diaz had ordered back in line. The look of disbelief on Walsh's face was apparent, even though Diaz wasn't looking straight at him. He turned his head toward her and his expression seemed to ask if this was some kind of joke.

Diaz's eyes went wide when she took in the disaster of military bearing before them. "*Dios mio*," she muttered. So much for not looking stupid in front of the new CO. She averted her gaze again. The academy couldn't teach everyone, it seemed. It wouldn't be the first shipwreck cadet to cruise on *Amazonas*. Fixing that shipwreck was part of her job.

Walsh glowered down at the cadet, who looked mystified, though not overly concerned, about the capitan's sudden displeasure. She looked up at him.

"Eyes front, cadet," Walsh ordered. "What have I done to you, cadet?"

It was obvious the cadet was struggling not to look up at Walsh again. "Sir?"

"Why do you hate me so much, cadet?"

"I don't hate you, sir," she answered with a smirk.

"Then why would you show up to my formation looking like you just rolled out of your rack the morning after your graduation party? Did you sleep in that uniform?"

The cadet started to laugh but choked it back when Walsh raised his voice.

"This is not funny. When did you print this uniform, cadet? It looks like it's a month old. Did you even use your profile when you printed it? Your tunic looks two sizes too small. Your ribbons are printed almost on your collar. You know the computer will put them where they belong, right? Did you do this on purpose?" Walsh flicked the top corner of the cadet's flight cap before she could answer. "And your damned cover is on backwards, for the cosmos' sake."

The cadet reached up to correct her cap.

"You are at attention, cadet," Walsh snapped. "You can wear your cap backwards for now."

Diaz could sense the anger rising in the capitan. Not the dramatic anger military instructors have rained down on their screwed-up students since time out of mind. It was the genuine anger of someone who's pissed and found someone to legitimately vent their wrath on. If the cadet was upset by the display, she didn't show it. At least she'd stopped smirking. Diaz might just have to drop the cadet out of an airlock if she saw that smirk again. She might do it anyway.

"What's your name?" Walsh asked, calm now.

"Cadet Sobella Midland, sir."

Walsh frowned and glanced at Diaz. He closed his eyes and turned back to the cadet. "Any relation to the senator?"

"She's my mother, sir."

Walsh grinned and nodded gently as if he'd finally understood a bad joke. He opened his eyes and turned to Diaz. "XO, how did this catastrophe get past her division officer like this?"

"These are new cadets, *mi* Capitan. They haven't been assigned to a division officer yet."

"Next time, if we survive this cruise, it will fall to the XO."

"*Si, mi* Capitan." So much for the first impression.

Walsh continued his inspection and Diaz followed. That was probably what the rest of her career would be—following people who still had a chance at saving their career. This capitan might still have a chance. But not her. Not *mano blanco*.

The new capitan made few comments as he finished the inspection. They returned to the front of the formation and Diaz ordered the ship's company to close ranks again. Walsh stepped forward and did an about-face to address the crew. His words came over the speakers hidden behind the room's walls.

"I'm Cmdr. Eugene K. Walsh, your capitan as of last night. It can be stressful to get a new boss that you know nothing about. Whether it's a section leader, division officer, or CO. Especially if you don't have much vacuum time. You never know what you'll get.

"It's the same for a new staff officer or capitan. There's a new set of technical specifications to learn and a new set of personalities. While this isn't my first command, it is different from what I'm used to. Different not only in mission, but in character. Even the sheer number of personnel aboard the *Amazonas* is new. The fleet doesn't focus on massive cruisers like the EPL did. This ship—our ship—holds a unique position in the CAR fleet."

Walsh paused to scan the ship's company. Then he nodded as if to himself. "Regardless of rank or position, we'll all have to figure out how to work together and get the mission done. That won't change when you get to the fleet, so to speak."

He paused again, looking as if he was going to add something else to the crew. Instead, he faced Diaz. "XO, get the crew on board and prepare for departure."

Diaz returned Walsh's salute and watched him leave the compartment. Then she did an about-face. "All hands will report to shuttle dock alpha. You'll be assigned to a division officer by Hector, *Amazonas*'s yeoman. Then proceed to your assigned shuttle for orbital transfer to *Amazonas*. Once there, change into working flightsuits and check in with your div-O ASAP. Dismissed!"

The crew fell out in ranks. Most of the cadets milled around, muttering in confusion, until one of the staff pointed them towards the exit. The screw-up, Midland, hesitated by the hatch. Diaz had seen that wide-eyed stare of disbelief on cadets before. But Midland looked as if she was getting ready to run. When the cadet looked again, Diaz caught her eye and glared until Midland stepped into the flow of people.

That one was going to be trouble. And a senator's daughter, too. Diaz hadn't liked the capitan's expression when he found out. "*Dios mio*," she muttered.

Lt. Cmdr. Robert Bovree sidled up next to her. "So, what d'you think of the new guy?"

Diaz kept her gaze on the cadets filing through the hatch. "I don't know yet."

"Yeah, he didn't say much last night, either," Bovree said, playing up his Louisiana drawl. "At least he talks Spanglish right well."

Diaz shrugged.

"Here's a bit of intel. He and Captain Correia of the *Calypso* are a hot item from my reports."

Diaz scoffed "Ooh, *que hombre*."

Bovree chuckled. "Well, the ladies seem to think he's quite the man. According to my reports."

"Reports?"

Bovree grinned. "As security officer, it's my job to gather intel."

"Sounds like gossip, not intel."

"That's only because you don't know better. They're not mutually exclusive."

Diaz raised her eyebrow. "Anyone who will talk about someone to you, will talk to someone about you."

"Sounds like you talk to a lot of gossips, XO."

She cut him a sidelong glance. "Aren't you supposed to be wrangling your cadets, Bobby?"

Bovree popped a saucy salute and headed towards the line of cadets, pantomiming whirling a lasso over his head. "He-yaw!"

The security officer was a goof, but he was a good instructor and took his job seriously—if nothing else. And she already knew the capitan's amorous reputation. Diaz was embarrassed for him. It wasn't professional at all. Yet he was the one they made capitan. As long as he didn't think she was going to be slipping off with him after any parties.

Not that she was his type. Her own "reports" said he liked them trim and sultry. Diaz was neither. And though he was definitely attractive for being so pale, vaqueros weren't her style, either. Even if she was looking for some kind of relationship, it certainly wouldn't be with her CO. Her granny warned her never to fish off the company pier.

At least Walsh had seniority over her. If the admiralty had assigned a junior capitan, *Amazonas* would become to her a true *casa de la vergunza*: a true house of shame.

Chapter 4

AMAZONAS was huge. Ungainly, even. Walsh shook his head as the ship grew larger in the view portal of the capitan's skiff. A Dragonfly-class spaceship like *Thunder*, sleek and modular, slid behind the behemoth, contrasting the difference in the spaceship architecture between the old Earth Protectorate League and the Confederation of American Republics. *Amazonas* had been designed to suppress the colonies and needed to be an interstellar fortress.

She was over three hundred meters long from cone to thruster. The forward section was a large cylinder containing all of the manned compartments. Four evenly spaced capsules slowly spun around the forward hull on long pylons to generate pseudo-gravity. At the other end of the ship were the nuclear-thruster array, power plant, and eight large tanks that held the reaction mass. A thick, circular plate just forward of the thruster array shielded the crewed compartments from radiation. The two sections were separated by a long, thin, cylindrical section of hull to keep the radioactive section as far from the crew as possible. Instead of the magnetically circulated, liquid-metal coolant loops used by more modern ships like *Thunder*, *Amazonas* used a series of large radiator fins set around the power plant area to dissipate waste heat.

It reminded Walsh of a medieval mace: heavy and primitive.

And old. Barring a few space jalopies still in use by the Junker clans out by Jupiter, the surviving Nova-class cruisers like *Amazonas* were the oldest ships in Sol. It had been almost two hundred years since colonies shut down the gate, and the ship that now filled the viewing port had already been on duty for decades before that. It was a relic, repurposed into a nursery, and he was her capitan. At least it would get him away from Liberty Station.

"What was that, sir?" asked Lieutenant Roberts, the pilot.

"Hm?" Walsh realized he must have spoken his last thought aloud. He hoped he hadn't been muttering a whiny stream of consciousness for the pilot to hear. "Oh, sorry. Just glad to be back in space."

"Roger that, Capitan. I start feeling cooped up on that thing."

"Liberty's one of the biggest stations in the system."

"Oh, it's not the space, sir. It's the people there." Robertson glanced over his shoulder at Walsh. "It's a regular den of vipers. I'd rather get grounded planetside than get stationed there again."

Walsh nodded but said nothing. They were approaching the ship's number-one dock, and he floated back to his seat and strapped in. He could barely feel the jolt from the docking and when the airlock seal glowed green, Walsh released his straps and pulled himself towards it. "How many trips does it usually take to get all the crew?"

Robertson spoke as he began the skiff's shutdown sequence. "Five total. Liberty lends us three and our shuttle will make two trips. Usually we use one of the large-craft docking rings, but they're full at the moment."

Walsh knew they were full—and why. When the requisition came through for the cost of using the station's shuttles from his operations budget, he found the remaining two docks had been filled just before *Amazonas* would have requested to dock to take on crew. The two ships had been approved by none other than Admiral Maconez; free of charge. It was the admiral's way of wishing him a fond farewell.

The inner airlock opened and the digitized whistle of the ship's bosun pipe echoed through the ship's speakers and the sub-q connections of the duty crew that had remained on board. Five officers were lined along the starboard bulkhead, bodies rigid in the zero-g and turned slightly to grasp handholds with their left hands.

Beyond looking sharp and professional in appearance and demeanor, Walsh was not one for ceremony and tradition. How had so many vestiges of the wet navy made it into space? On *Thunder* with its eight crew, it seemed almost ridiculous to adhere to some of them. Often they didn't while underway. But this was a training ship, and the teaching and observing of such things were part of every cadet's training. He usually relied on a protocol guide in his overlay; if he ever lost his overlay, he might not remember which shoe went on which foot.

He saluted the foremost officer. "Permission to come aboard."

The officer returned the salute. "Permission to come aboard, Capitan." The other four officers immediately saluted and the whistle sounded again.

"Capitan is aboard," announced the digital yeoman. "Capitan is aboard."

"The yeoman will show me to my cabin," Walsh said, dropping his salute. "Make ready for the cadets. Carry on."

Walsh floated from the dock into the main compartment, following the visual cues the ship's yeoman was providing to his overlay. He'd spent hours taking virtual tours of *Amazonas* but this was his first time inside. Fighting the urge to take off exploring, Walsh continued to the spoke tube that led to spin habitat A. The tube entrances moved slowly at the center of their spin, making it easy to grab. He began climbing outwards and flipped at the gravity-warning marker so that his feet were facing the direction of the increasing pull from the spin. Each habitat contained three decks; the operations center and crew quarters were on the outermost deck to get the most pseudo-gravity. The ladder exited near operations, but Walsh followed the overlay navigation points to his stateroom.

A clunky fossil the ship may be, but the capitan's cabin was the largest he'd ever seen. When he would finally be able to set aside his resentment at this posting, Walsh could definitely get used to having this much space. He was no aesthete, but the space seemed decadent. Wasteful, even. The desk that folded down from the wall was fabricated to make it look as if it was made from richly colored wood. Walsh ran his fingers along the desk, tapping its cool surface in places to make sure it wasn't made of wood. As he did so, Walsh felt a faint thrum from the table. He reached out and touched a bulkhead, feeling the same there. Closing his eyes and listening closely, he could hear the sound of the ship in the background. Each ship, even among those of the same class, had its own unique sound. The same components wore differently, developed different harmonics, experienced different levels of degradation due to varying levels of thermal shock and radiation exposure, based on where they flew and what they had been exposed to.

Amazonas had been in service for so long, and in extra-Solar systems to which Walsh had never been and would likely never go, there was no telling what made up this ship's song. Walsh shook his head. There was a lot of history here. This ship belonged in a museum.

Walsh focused on his overlay and flipped through his most recent notifications. "Ship, has all my data been transferred to ship local nodes?"

"Yes, Capitan," answered a voice in his overlay. "All service and trainings records, along with your personal media, have been transferred from *Thunder*. No physical item transfer was requested. As capitan, you are allowed an extra mass allotment."

"I like to travel light. And I don't want anything valuable I might have get blown into space."

"Hopefully, no one will get blown into space on this trip, Capitan. I have an exceptional safety record."

Walsh raised his brow and looked up from his tablet. "I?"

"I have adopted certain personality expressions for the sake of easing comfort among the crews of cadets. My internal data show that my adopting a more personal form of interaction reduces cadet stress levels by as much as twenty percent in some cases. I can revert to more standard interaction if you wish, Capitan."

Walsh believed it was best to get the trainees ready for what they'd see in the real fleet. But changing established processes without a good reason usually caused pointless confusion. Walsh hated the new-sheriff-in-town mentality. "No need to change for now, ship."

"Very good, Capitan. To continue along those lines, I am called Hector. Though I will of course respond to whichever designation you assign."

"Hector will be fine. Notify me when all hands are aboard."

"Yes, Capitan."

Walsh finished reviewing the day's logs, signing them off with his biometric signature via his overlay. The previous capitan hadn't left him much to work with. But given how much Liberty was charging for even proximity docking, Walsh couldn't fault the man. No wonder the station was so huge. He closed down his work files with a pinch of his fingers and stood.

Though he'd been studying the VR version of *Amazonas*, Walsh kept the internal information labels active. As his vision panned around the compartment, a small window would open in his vision to inform him what each object was. He could open it for more details or deactivate notifications on specific items. If he wanted, he could change someone's face or other aspects of their appearance when he saw them. That was strictly forbidden in the fleet as conduct unbecoming, but he knew it still happened. The superimposed visages were seldom complimentary, and often lewd. Walsh didn't mind lewd, but it was a safety and security concern. It was important to know who you were flying with.

He opened his locker. At the top was a small uniform-printer and at the bottom was a recycling chute. Standard operating procedure for dress uniforms in a fleet where the printers were ubiquitous was to print one before each inspection. Dress uniforms hadn't been a concern on *Thunder*, since they didn't bother with many inspections. But the academy required regular uniform inspections. And as the capitan, who needed to set a proper example, he was now required to perform regular uniform inspections. The division officers would be responsible for most of them, but not all.

Dizziness washed over Walsh and he stumbled, grabbing the door of the locker to keep himself from falling. "Whoa."

"Exercise caution when changing the elevation of your inner ear, Capitan," Hector said. "Due to the relatively short spin radius of the habitats, there are minute changes in gravity between the deck and the normal height of your head. Those changes, coupled with a Coriolis force, can cause dizziness and nausea if you change elevation too fast."

Spin gravity was something else he'd never had to worry about on *Thunder*.

"Noted." Walsh closed the locker, opened the head, and grinned. Now that was nice. He'd never been on a spaceship large enough for the capitan to have his own. A cluster of spray and vacuum nozzles protruded from the deck and the overhead, and a fold-up sink and flusher were set into the sides. "Nice."

Walsh toured the ship as the crew and cadets boarded. The tubes to the habitats were bustling with people trying to find their berthing, their division officer, or which way was up. After an hour, the activity died down as the division officers cornered their cadets and gave their introductory speeches. Walsh returned to his stateroom and an hour later Hector chimed in his ear.

"All hands present and accounted for, Capitan. They are assembling in the habitat-B inspection compartment."

"Why?"

"For the departure inspection, Capitan."

Walsh pursed his lips. "We just had an inspection."

"Yes, Capitan."

It seems it might take a computerized yeoman to keep track of all the damned inspections they were going to have. "I guess I should print up a new set." He opened the locker and stared at a brand new set of dress crimsons that hadn't been there before. The smell of newly printed material wafted from the locker.

"Taken care of, Capitan. I've also downloaded the traditional departure speech to your overlay."

Walsh dressed without further comment to the ship and made his way from spin habitat A to habitat B. The compartment wasn't as large as the one on Liberty Station, but it was still a monumental waste of volume. Even if they could reconfigure it.

The speech was bland and Walsh didn't add any excitement to it. He wanted to be done with it. At the end of the speech, he forced himself to at least pretend he was paying attention. He was happy to note that Cadet Midland was squared away, though her uniform still seemed—appreciably—a little snug. He resumed his position at the front of the formation. "XO, *Amazonas* passes muster. Let's get out of here."

"Where to, *mi* Capitan."

"Make best speed to the Nexus Gate Sector."

Chapter 5

WAKING UP IN GRAVITY was something Walsh could get used to—eventually. After being underway for five months now, his back was still stiff at the end of each sleep session. None of the military ships he'd served on had persistent pseudo-gravity, relying on doses of spacer's cocktail, thrust pseudo-gravity, and an extensive exercise regimen to fight off some of the deleterious effects of prolonged zero-g on the human body. While staying in a station, Walsh preferred to sleep in low or null gravity. The floating sensation comforted him. One ship's doctor he'd served with believed the effect was related to memories of being in the womb.

Walsh didn't know about all that, but he didn't care for the way his hip popped as he turned to make his bunk and fold it back into the bulkhead. A gold plaque that read "Velocity is Victory" was on the bulkhead opposite his bunk. It had been fused there before he'd been born and was innocuous enough to have survived the sensitivities of the ship's many commanders.

The head slid open when Walsh approached to do his morning necessaries. "Any red flags, Hector?"

A full-body avatar of a swarthy man with a thin mustache appeared in Walsh's overlay. He still wasn't used to seeing the life-sized apparition: cramped ships used simple icons or miniature faces to prevent visual clutter.

"No, Capitan. We're on station, matching orbit with the nexus gate about ten thousand kilometers inward. There are other ships present, but we are well outside the exclusion zone."

"Any inspections today?"

"Not for you, sir."

Walsh grinned. He'd grown accustomed to the constant inspections. They were part of the job. But he was glad when he had a day free from them. He was especially glad for days free of Cadet Midland. "Good. Tell

Diaz I'm heading to PT and chow, and that I'll call her for passdown in my stateroom."

"Yes, Capitan."

An exercise jumper was already hanging in his locker and Walsh slipped it on. The passages were filled with the yawns and morning-breath of the cadets and crew getting ready to go on shift. They shuffled through the passages towards the mess hall or the gym, rubbing their sleepy eyes. Chatter and laughter filled the air, along with the occasional clanging of actuating hatches.

He entered the gym and input his routine into an open treadmill. A progress-tracking window opened in his overlay and the belt started rolling beneath his feet. Two other crewmen were starting their regimens too; one running, and the other doing squats and presses with flexible exercise bands.

Working out was one of Walsh's least favorite things to do. As he understood it, some people reached the point where they enjoyed their exercise and a so-called runner's high. He hated it. It was a chore, a requirement. That it was mandatory and imperative to keep healthy were without question. But the only reason that really motivated him was that he enjoyed the ladies and the ladies preferred well-toned men, despite their objections. So Walsh pulled up the reports and ran. Reading the maintenance logs was more interesting than working out.

Perusing the logs proved Hector right: nothing interesting from silver shift. More crew and cadets entered, offering him furtive greetings. Walsh nodded in reply to some of them and turned away to avoid making further contact as he continued exercising. "Hector, is everyone up to date on their PT regimen?"

"We have had a few excused sessions among the crew and cadets, but the only one flagged as being unauthorized is Cadet Midland. It has been reported to her division officer and she was counseled. She has missed two sessions this week. Cadet Midland is assigned to gold shift."

Walsh shook his head. "Has she reported to Medical during those missed sessions?"

"I show no record of that, Capitan."

"Priority connect to her overlay, please."

A moment later, Cadet Midland's facial avatar appeared in Walsh's overlay. "Uh, Cadet Midland here. Sir."

Midland was a pretty Latina, lacking the cool eyes of her senator mother. She was someone Walsh would consider docking with under other circumstances. "I see you've missed some PT, Cadet. It's not just some makework for cadets. There's a reason it's mandatory. Your div-O explained all this during your last counseling session, I assume?"

"Yes, Capitan."

"Do I need to write up your div-O for not properly seeing to your qualifications?"

Midland's dark eyebrows shot up in alarm. "No, sir. It's not her fault."

"Then you'll report to gym one and get your PT done." The pace on the treadmill increased and Walsh struggled not to pant while he was speaking. "Before I finish, Cadet. Or you and your division officer will be on report." He dropped the connection and watched eagerly as the running routine counted down towards the finish.

The exercise routines were determined by Hector in accordance with the Department of Space Physiology directives. When Walsh finished with his run, he was directed to the strength bands by his overlay. The bands had the dual advantages of having little mass and being usable in zero-g. Walsh was halfway through his squats when Midland rushed into the gym.

"Cadet Midland reporting as ordered, sir."

Walsh offered a curt nod, sending a drop of sweat flying from his brow. Each habitat had its own gym. Midland was berthed in hab-B, but he'd made her report to hab-A to make a point. He wanted her to see that not even the capitan could ignore PT. And he wasn't going to let her off the hook if he had to do it.

Even if she was the senator's daughter.

"This is going to be a tough cruise for you, cadet, if you don't get your act together."

She looked back, her expression showing a clear lack of concern. "Yes, sir."

Walsh didn't know if her attitude was from a lifetime of privileged immunity from the rules or a lack of understanding of the chain of command. "And you realize that you can be barred from full-gravity environments due to medical reasons, right? I've know spacers that get so used to low-g they can't even visit the main rings on Liberty."

Her brow furrowed in concern. "I'll try to keep up with it, Capitan."

Walsh grunted as he strained through another squat. "It's all part of the price we pay to live the dream. Carry on."

Midland gave a mirthless smile, "Yes, Capitan."

She turned to an open treadmill and unenthusiastically plodded along. Walsh was not encouraged by the cadet's unwillingness to even pretend contrition. Especially after being confronted directly by the ship's capitan. But she was the hidden price to keep his command. What was one more less-than-competent cadet in the fleet? With his help, she'd get her commission, a cushy job on Liberty Station, and muster out at first chance. Then she could polish her medals while she ran for office like her mother.

Then he could get back to a real ship. Hopefully, they would both survive her cadet tour.

A projected hologram of *Amazonas* hovered in Walsh's quarters when he opened the hatch. The habitat modules spun lazily and a large "BCT-111" was stenciled along the forward hull. The designation was the reason for the ship's moniker, *Tres Grande*. It was big, to be sure, but that "T" in the designation wasn't so grand: Battle Cruiser, Training.

Walsh tossed his gym clothes in the recycler and stepped into the head. A fine mist sprayed from the nozzles and, seconds later, he was covered in an enzyme foam. He lathered his scalp, beard, and other hairy patches before the foam disappeared, leaving him clean and dry. Goosebumps rippled across his skin as the evaporating enzymes cooled him. Walsh shivered and stepped out of the head.

A fresh flightsuit hung in the locker and his breakfast ration carton had been set on the desk by the cadet. He'd resisted having his meals delivered, but it was part of the mess cadet's duties. Though he still went to the mess hall regularly, Walsh enjoyed being able to eat in peace. On *Thunder*, with its crew of eight, seeing the capitan during daily routines wasn't particularly noteworthy and most protocol was ignored. On *Amazonas*, the cadets were constantly tripping over themselves to snap the sharpest salute or call out "Attention on deck!" or shuffle away on sight.

But he was enjoying the convenience and feared it was making him soft.

The smell of warm oatmeal filled the room as he unzipped the container. A smattering of blueberries, fresh from the ship's aeroponics bay, lay on top. He pulled utensils and a spill-proof cup of spiced hot chocolate from the box and dug in. Fleet life sciences knew how to make delicious, nutritious food, but you couldn't beat fresh blueberries. Walsh savored the meal and wiped a dollop of oatmeal from his beard when he finished. He dropped the container and utensils into the recycler to be made into the same shapes for the next meal.

Walsh opened his overlay and scanned for any updates. "Hector, please ask the XO to come to my stateroom."

"Yes, Capitan."

The aroma of the spiced chocolate still filled the cabin when Lieutenant Commander Diaz entered a few minutes later. Walsh sipped at his drink while the XO walked to his desk and saluted. "Good morning, Felicia."

"Capitan."

With a flick of his eyes, Walsh made a seat slide out of the wall for her. "I'll stand, Capitan."

As he'd expected. He nodded and stowed the chair. She was a plain, flat-faced woman and Walsh thought he understood her standoffish manner towards him. She'd been assigned to *Amazonas* for screwing up, too, though her screwup had cost lives. And a ship. In her position, it would be foolish to ever expect another command. But being passed over time and again for the ship she'd been XO of for three cruises had to sting.

At least, he hoped that's all her problem with him was. On a ship full of space cadets—a pejorative term since before there were actual space cadets—her strict and overbearing manner wasn't necessarily out of place. But she seemed like an antique watch wound too tightly. And she insisted on wearing her white uniform gloves. He'd heard a few crew call her *mano blanco*: white hand. It certainly wasn't the worse thing he'd heard an XO called and she knew the crew better than he did.

Walsh leaned back in his chair. "Anything of note from silver shift?"

"Nothing urgent. I initiated a forty-minute burn to bring us to our nav point in the Nexus sector. None of the ships in the area have reacted. Are you sure it was wise to return to the scene of the crime so soon, Capitan?"

Walsh gave her a half grin, unsure if she was being sardonic since everything she said was delivered in a flat tone. "We're just a training ship on a training cruise. What better place to give the sciences department a chance to train the cadets?"

Diaz shrugged. "No one's learned anything new about that thing in two hundred years. I'm surprised that Liberty even let you within ten astronomical units of this sector. We won't be here long though. They sent us move orders. We're to go to Ganymede."

Walsh raised his brows and searched for the orders in his overlay. "Oh? Nice. I was expecting to be called straight back to Liberty. I could use a nice shower." He smiled and leaned back in his chair. "Yes, Ganymede will do me just fine."

She pursed her lips. "Ganymede is good for showers and *putas*."

"It's a veritable spacer's delight. You disapprove, *Madre*?"

"My heart would be broken if I were your *madre*, Capitan."

"I'll be sure not to share my exploits then."

Diaz snorted. "Anyway, we're supposed to take on supplies and stay on station for a while. I think someone realized the mistake of letting you come back out here and is covering up by sending you to Ganymede instead."

"Could be. Whatever other joys we might find there, we could use some fresh O2. This ship is starting to smell like farts. Anything else?"

"It always smells like farts." Diaz wrinkled her nose. "Systems Maintenance finished replacing the relay assembly on seven and Security pushed through two new updates from fleet."

"I see transfer orders at Ganymede."

"Ido and Fields will transfer to the station until their ship shows up."

"Ido's funny as hell, I'll hate to lose him. I hope they don't have to wait too long."

Diaz glanced away. "I'm sure they won't mind the amenities."

"Probably not, but when I was on the *Marshall* we had orders to transfer someone to one of those remote sensor stations to await her next ship." Walsh shook his head and finished his drink while trying to remember the woman's name. It wouldn't come. "I think she got stuck on that tin can for six months because her new ship had a reactor fail. Her and a three-person crew crammed in there for six months. The skipper wanted to get her, but we had movement orders."

"Ganymede is no tin can. And they're probably happy to get away from the cadets."

Walsh grunted. That would be nice.

Another set of orders had been delivered, too. This one was a transfer in. An attached personnel file opened behind the orders statement. He read it and scratched his chin. "This Lieutenant Mahoney is listed as a Special Intelligence Asset, but I don't recognize this military skills code."

"Neither did I, *mi* Capitan."

Walsh queried the code in the database and blinked. "I still don't know what it means. Intuitive?"

"I had to look that up, too," Diaz said. "Actually, Hector had to look it up. The short of it is he's fallout from one of the African Union ESP experiments. No one claims they're telepaths or brujas or anything. But it seems some did develop strong intuition if given enough data. Admiral Maconez designated them as SIAs so he could budget their commissions."

"Old *Mamon*-ez? Well, I already don't trust him, then. What sort of experiments brought out this superpower?"

"Gene mods, mostly. Plus some hardcore data-analysis psychotherapy, but the details are classified. Their brains are wired for highly accurate hunches, basically."

"Like my mother, when I was trying to be sneaky?" Walsh chuckled. "Sounds like it violates the eugenics codes."

Diaz nodded. "That's why they stopped them."

Walsh smirked. "Sure, they stopped. And we don't have suicide asteroids scattered around the system."

"I don't have the clearance to know about that, Capitan. But things are quiet and you can read up on the intuitives on your watch."

Walsh tucked his overlay windows out of sight and nodded. "I've got the ship, XO. Go get some chow."

"I stand relieved," Diaz answered.

"Change of command logged," Hector announced.

Chapter 6

DESPITE HER IMMACULATE appearance and mostly up-to-date systems, the term "rust bucket" was what came to mind when Capitan Walsh thought of his new, ancient ship. But as he peered through *Amazonas*'s telescope suite, he felt a rare appreciation for her motley array of subsystems. Astronomical surveys were part of the fleet's mission. *Amazonas* was outfitted with Dayton Systems Far-Sky 1250. It was better than *Thunder*'s tactical scopes for celestial observation, and on par with those used by ships like *Peruvian Angel*.

The nexus gate filled Walsh's overlay. He was using full-immersion mode, and to him it looked and felt as if he was floating in space around the huge, black ring. With the flick of an eye or finger, Walsh sped to any viewing distance or angle he chose. He was still seeing it all through his overlay interface, but it felt personal viewing it from the telescope compartment. And he could look through the scope with his naked eye if he wanted.

Glowing yellow lines covered the gate, showing the countless fractures that were discovered in the gate after the Colonial Defense Fleet shut it down—violently. Walsh sped to a cluster of fractures called "the Omala node" and walked along the ring, looking down at the yellow lines as he traced their path. None of the fractures could be seen visually; it had taken over a year of high-yield radiation scans to get the map. The process was remarkably similar to how starships were scanned for hidden stress fractures. And it took almost ten years for anyone to even think of trying.

The energy wave released had destroyed much of the Earth Protectorate League's fleet as it massed for a counter-attack against the Colonial forces that had driven it from Tau Ceti and back to Sol. Some estimates put the gate at over a million years old. It had taken the denizens of Earth a mere century to break it.

It entranced Walsh. Always had. His childhood dreams of being a spacer captain were one part war hero and one part solving the gate and opening the stars. He qualified as a combat veteran, though hero was a subjective term. Much smarter people than him had failed to fix the gate for almost two centuries. Walsh doubted any human was going to fix it. At least not in his lifetime.

Walsh looked back at the virtual *Amazonas*. His ship was one of the few left in the system still equipped with a nexus-key generator. They were massive and useless. Most nations that commanded old EPL ships had removed them decades ago and replaced them with reaction-mass tanks or ordnance magazines. It's what he would do, even as he wistfully imagined being the first human to fly through the nexus in two centuries.

At least, the first human from Sol. There was no telling what the colonies were up to away from Earth's greedy claws. Probably exploring the galaxy unhindered through all the other nexus gates.

"What are those colonials up to?" Walsh muttered.

Hector appeared on the ring next to him. "There are many theories, Capitan."

"As many as there are about how the CDF destroyed the gate and who made them all."

"I have access to the full academic body of study to those subjects, if you like."

Walsh glanced at Hector. "Another benefit of a school ship."

"I wasn't always a school ship and I have many admirable attributes, Capitan." Hector offered a wry grin. "Even if you still prefer your old command."

The telescope compartment was in *Amazonas*'s nose, not in a spin arm, so Walsh floated as he skimmed over the virtual surface of the nexus. "So you were around when the CDF destroyed the gate?"

"Yes, Capitan, though I have been upgraded and reprogrammed many times since. I was pulled from my refit at Phobos to aid in rescue operations."

"That must have been a mess."

"Not as bad as the fighting to consolidate the EPL's assets as the nations fought for control." Hector shook his head sadly. "I was boarded four times by various factions. Hundreds died in my compartments. Marines from the North American Union won in the end and parked me into a defensible orbit around Luna."

Walsh glanced at Hector and nodded. "I've studied the EPL collapse. Maybe you can share your firsthand view with me sometime."

"Of course, Capitan."

With a wave of his hand, Walsh shrunk the nexus gate to fit in his hand. He sighed and blew it away like dust. "I'm afraid the gate's going to stay broken forever."

"The colonials might undo their work, if it's possible."

Walsh chuckled. "I wouldn't. Not after what Earth did. They probably have a nice, rich, freedom-loving, interstellar republic without Earth's involvement."

Hector glanced at Walsh and raised his brows.

"What?" Walsh asked.

"I didn't think such talk was encouraged by the admiralty, Capitan."

"And I'm not much encouraged by the admiralty sometimes. But history is what it is. Not that the CDF were a bunch of saints." Walsh snorted. "I guess I'll never know."

A 3D icon of *Amazonas* appeared in front of Walsh and blinked. He flicked his eyes towards it and the icon grew into the full-size rendering of the staff duty operations officer, Lieutenant Doug Collins. "Go, Ops."

"Capitan, it seems word has spread you're back." Collins grinned and projected the tactical display of the Nexus sector. Several thruster plumes reached across the display area. "That Solar Transit trasport radioed you were commanding."

Walsh allowed himself a satisfied grunt. "At least they're all running away from me instead of at me."

Collins zoomed the display in on one plume that was pointing away from *Amazonas*. "Well, except for these Caliphate cruisers burning towards us and claiming we're violating the Gate Accords. We have to leave... or else."

"I think they're just holding a grudge," Walsh said, pulling up the database on the ship.

"They're certainly holding a lot of missiles, sir."

Walsh nodded and banished the overlay, finding himself back in the bright telescope compartment. "On the way, Ops."

The probes and displays folded back into place, and he scanned the room a final time for any gear afloat. He pushed off the bulkhead and out into the main hull.

The main hull was a large cylinder known as the "silo." Looking down the length of it, with the armored core, the "crypt," running down the center of the cylinder gave the impression of staring down a large missile tube.

The outer bulkhead was lined with pipes, conduits, control nodes, and maintenance panels. The crypt was covered with armored hatches that led to shielded, one-man control stations within. It was the crew's refuge during combat, radiation fields, and other celestial hazards.

Conveyors pulled in alternating directions down the length of the silo. Walsh grabbed one of the handles on a conveyor pulling towards the "lazy Susan" that coupled the main hull to the spin arms. He released the handle and drifted towards a tube with an "A" stenciled in chipped, red paint near the opening. Two more belts trundled around in the tube. He grabbed the one pulling outwards towards the spin habitat and Ops.

A luminescent green circle with two arrows glowed one-third of the way along the tube. It marked when it was time to orient feet towards the pull of the spin gravity. Those who didn't found themselves falling headfirst down the spoke. Including Walsh once when he'd been distracted by a tactical report in the overlay. Fortunately, only Hector had witnessed the spectacle.

Walsh flipped and found a foothold, riding the conveyor until it deposited him on the deck just outside of operations. The centrifugal force from the spin was just shy of one-g. He still preferred microgravity and took a moment to steady himself against the bulkhead before waving the hatch to Ops open.

"Capitan on deck!" Hector announced.

Walsh left the crew at attention for a few seconds for the sake of the cadets manning training watches. Standing at attention wasn't feasible in zero-g or when everyone was strapped into their acceleration couches. He walked to the commander's station. "As you were."

Lieutenant Collins was standing behind the navigator and her trainee.

"Update, Ops-O?"

Collins turned towards Walsh. "All systems normal, no major maintenance evolutions are ongoing. No recent comms traffic or intrusion attempts detected. The Caliphate patrol is still closing slowly."

"Very good, Ops." Walsh strapped into his station and opened the ship's status in the overlay. Real-time footage of the two Caliphate missile cruisers, and the science ship they were escorting, hovered in the background, accompanied by windows displaying their information. Weapons systems were highlighted in red.

"They sure do have a lot of missile tubes, don't they?" Walsh remarked.

Collins grinned. "I think even the science ship has tubes, Capitan."

"Let's not be suspicious, Lieutenant. I'm sure all those tubes are for sensor probes."

Someone behind Walsh snorted.

The names of the Caliphate ships hovered over their images. The cruiser *Fiery Lance* led the cruiser *Lion's Roar* and the research vessel *Johannes Kepler* in an extended echelon formation.

"Hector, pull up what intel has on the command crews of that squadron and give me the rundown. Tell me if I've met any of them, if possible."

"Yes, Capitan."

Profile pictures appeared and branched out from the Caliphate ships. Names, ranks, and positions appeared around each. He didn't recognize anyone from *Lion's Roar* or *Johannes Kepler*, even if he had met them at some point. But he smiled when the XO of *Fiery Lance* was listed as Holger Bischoff. "Send a connection request to the *Fiery Lance*."

"Yes, Capitan," answered a cadet in a tense voice.

"Relax, Cadet," Walsh said. "We're not going to poke any bears today."

The comm blinked as the two ships' security protocols worked out the connection and assessed threat levels. A moment later, the thin, dark face of Cmdr. Zameel al-Bina, the CO of *Fiery Lance*, appeared.

"Commander Walsh, I'm hoping you're calling to report you're leaving the area." The man's lips didn't match the spoken words as Hector translated them from Arabic to Spanglish.

"I am, Commander. Though we are nowhere near the exclusion zone or in violation of the Gate Accords in any way."

Al-Bina pursed his lips. "Unlike last time?"

"Pretty much exactly like last time," Walsh said. "When a Caliphate ship began hostile maneuvers. Like you're doing now."

"If we'd realized a war criminal was in this sector, we would have acted sooner." Al-Bina smiled cordially. "I'm amazed Liberty Station let you come here after damaging our ship."

Walsh didn't want to escalate the situation, but he couldn't help winking at the other commander. "It's good to see someone's taking me seriously, though. It can't be cheap to send out three ships just to take pictures of this old gate."

Walsh heard a chuckle from someone behind him.

"Set your worries aside, Commander," al-Bina said. "The Caliphate is doing just fine. I might even get a bonus this year."

"That's great. And we're moving out, so no need for anyone to try scratching anyone else's paint." Walsh nodded once at Collins and felt the gentle press of acceleration as the directional thrusters fired to change *Amazonas*'s heading. "I do have a request though, Commander."

Al-Bina's brows rose. "Oh?"

"I'd like to talk to your XO, if you'd permit it. Holger and I go way back."

"In the name of diplomacy, I will accommodate you, Commander Walsh. Don't tie him up too long—we're busy."

Al-Bina's dark features were replaced by the stocky, pale face of Holger Bischoff. His wispy, blond hair floated above his pristine, white uniform. The crimson crescent on the breast looked like a deep, bloody wound. He smiled. "Hey, Gene. You're making it hard on our friendship, you know. Cairo is all abuzz about you."

Walsh noticed Holger's speech was being translated. "I'm just a popular guy. Are you speaking Arabic?"

"We're mostly secular these days, but if you want to get above commander, you've still got to get in good with the council." Holger shrugged. "And given your current command, you might not be as popular as you think."

Walsh sighed. "Everyone's a critic. It's a paid learning opportunity."

"I've been on one of our old—very, very old—EPL cruisers. I bet you've got a simply palatial stateroom to go with that spin gravity."

Walsh stretched his arms wide and grinned. "Tell Cairo to take out some of those missile tubes and replace them with big quarters and spin arms."

"You've got some cojones coming back out here," Holger said. "Especially riding military surplus."

"There's something to be said about the classics."

"Still dreaming about fixing the gate?"

Walsh chuckled. "Doesn't every little boy. Here's a freebie. I don't have a good analysis, only a few spurious signals. But I think the Marties are snooping around this sector."

"Aren't the Marties snooping around every sector?" Holger glanced at something out of frame and nodded. "Time to go. We've got to get back on station or lose our place."

Walsh popped a lazy salute. "True enough about the Marties—just thought I'd share. Take it easy, Hog."

"Have a good burn, Gene."

The connection dropped and Collins took his seat in the Ops-O station next to Walsh. "Ready for main thruster burn, Capitan."

"Roger that, Ops. Bring thrust to 0.5-g. We don't want to give the Callies too close a peek at our drive signature at full after our last refit."

"Yes, sir. All hands, secure for main thruster burn in ten minutes. Begin habitat spin-down and retraction." Collins set a burn timer in the overlay and station of every crew member, and waited.

Nausea washed over Walsh as the spin arms slowed and began folding back along *Amazonas*'s main hull. Though he was beginning to enjoy the ship's gravity, transitioning from spin to thrust or null-gravity still made him ill. Walsh activated the space-sickness dampener in his overlay. He'd never had to do that on *Thunder*.

Ops shuddered as the spin arms latched to the hull. Walsh grimaced. They were now in zero-g, but they'd be under thrust gravity before his inner-ear fluid had a chance to settle down. At least the direction of apparent pull would be the same with the spin arms folded down.

Collins glanced around Ops. "Spin arms secured to main hull. All hands, secure for main thruster burn in thirty seconds."

Every crew member and cadet was responsible for checking in before the start of flight maneuvers to prevent injuries. Walsh saw green "Ready" lights across the crew status screen. He flipped through other screens to verify Bovree was collecting signals data from the Cali ships. Hector was trimming the ballast water to load-balance the habitats after spin-down. Main thruster was green. Everything was green.

Walsh's couch adjusted slightly on its gimbals to orient him in the direction of the upcoming thrust. The timer reached zero and Collins announced the burn. Acceleration pushed Walsh into his seat as CAR *Amazonas* flew off station and towards Jupiter Station.

THE SWIRLING COLORS made Walsh smile. Though the colors were warm and the mixing effect sublime, something was wrong. He just couldn't put his finger on what. With a wave of his virtual brush, Walsh erased the whole section of his painting.

Not sure what to replace it with, he slowly moved back through the 3D mural in his overlay. Maybe there wasn't anything technically wrong with what he'd just deleted; it could be that it was the wrong theme. Maybe.

The previous section depicted hundreds of nexus gates in a variety of colors. The colors grew colder the closer the eye came to the center of the panel, where a single, black gate stared out. The gate featured prominently in many sections of the 3D mural, even in places he'd painted while in Liberty Academy.

But he didn't want more gates. Crystal caves? No, Jupiter. No, a stairway down to Jupiter. Walsh smiled and used his brush to open a new painting path through the black gate. He stepped into the gate. Each stroke generated a distant, Jupiter-colored slash in the inky blackness of the overlay pallet.

Walsh paused to splash a vaguely *Amazonas*-shaped ship in the patchwork-Jupiter's upper atmosphere. He zoomed in just enough to write "STS-111" on the hull. So few ships had the STarShip designation. Few had the ability to travel between the stars; they were merely spaceships. It was an academic distinction, of course, as even *Amazonas* hadn't traveled between the stars in two centuries. And she wouldn't unless the gate miraculously started working.

Walsh began painting Jupiter's second red eye. "Hector, how many designations has this ship had?"

Hector appeared next to Walsh. "Seven, Capitan."

"Tell me."

"Like all Nova-class cruisers, I was originally named after a colony of the Earth Protectorate League: *Procyon's Pride*. I was re-designated *Amazonas* after one of the republics formed by the breakup of the nation of Brazil ninety-three years ago."

Walsh glanced at Hector. "What about the other five?"

Hector cleared his throat. "Well, they aren't very interesting, Capitan. Mostly a string of names that changed as often as my owners did. But if you must know: *Striker Vaquero*, *Oceana*, *Warlord*, and *Assface*."

"*Assface*?"

Hector shrugged. "A group of hackers stole me from a shipyard. Kids."

Walsh nodded. "So you must have visited other stars. A century before I was even born."

"In a sense, Capitan. I have been updated several times since then and portions of my memory wiped clean."

Walsh imagined sitting in Ops and ordering *Amazonas* into orbit around some alien planet. With a flick of his digital brush, the colors of the unfinished Jupiter took on a violet tint. "Do you have any footage of other systems?"

"Sorry, Capitan. Those files do exist, but they are restricted by command. I'm not sure why."

"Probably to keep from reminding people what we lost because of EPL policies." Walsh snorted. "For some reason, the elites like to romanticize the so-called good old days of the League."

"They did accomplish much."

"Well, some people accomplished much. The EPL gov felt like they had a right to maintain control over those accomplishments. If you can take credit for something, it's easier to argue that you should control that thing."

Hector raised his brows. "That's an interesting perspective, Capitan."

"Speaking out against the EPL is unpopular with the admiralty, so I try not to." Walsh grinned. "At least, not too often. But you get a few margaritas in me at some boring staff function or fleet ball—well, my mouth goes off like a solar flare. Some officer starts romanticizing about the EPL in front of the muchachos and I just can't help it. If the gates ever did open up, I'm afraid the CAR would turn back into the EPL."

"Believing that, Capitan, would you open the nexus if you had the chance?"

"Absolutely," Walsh said without hesitation. He turned away from the 3D mural to face Hector's avatar. "That's a very... personal and analytical question. Are you running some psychoanalysis routine?"

"I'm constantly analyzing the crew, Capitan. It's one of my primary functions."

Walsh considered Hector's avatar for a moment before returning to his work. Any officer was subject to psych reviews at any time and commanders were constantly being monitored. The ship's question was straightforward enough, but it had a subtle depth to it that disturbed him. Walsh could see Maconez in his mind, trying to trip him up with trick questions designed to torpedo his career profile.

That was probably just paranoia. But every capitan had to swim in Liberty's political cesspool to maintain their position. He hated the game, but he loved the job. Even on *Amazonas*. He loved the feel of being pushed back into his seat when the main thruster fired. He loved being in free fall. He loved leading his crew into battle. And he knew he'd do just about anything to keep flying. Even swallow his pride. His was a policy of noncommittal political neutrality—when possible. Even so, he'd made some enemies in the admiralty. Worse, he'd made some questionable allies. When it came to his career, an offended politico was like a baby with a loaded blaster.

And Liberty, that orbital septic tank, was full of babies. He was a starship captain, and a damned good one.

"Maybe I should talk to Admiral Maconez about making you capitan, then," Walsh said.

Hector frowned. "Please don't, Capitan."

"Why not?"

"He might do it. And I don't want that job."

Walsh scratched his chin as he glanced between Hector and the painting. "He might, at that. Dismissed, Hector."

Chapter 7

THE GUARD SLUMPED UNCONSCIOUS at Gelp Nurrow's feet. Though expediency was the real reason he'd been ordered to use non-fatal nano-toxins, he was glad. Gelp had lived among these people for the last three years. It was against his training and professional code of conduct, but he'd grown to like these Marties. If his handlers found out about his sentimentality—a possibility during the psychological debrief—they'd pull him from the field.

Of course, he would have killed them all if so ordered.

Gelp hefted the guard, called Trenki, back into his seat and leaned him over the desk to look as if he was sleeping. Escaping undetected was the goal but if someone happened to pass by, they might not care that he was dozing. Depending on who found him, they'd either ignore it or just try to wake him. He might lose his job, which Gelp regretted. If the guard rolled onto the floor dead when they tried to shake him awake, that was going to get some attention.

Gelp took a moment to calm his breathing, and not just to keep from setting off the security system. Receiving the activation orders early this morning still seemed unreal. He'd been so deep for so long, part of him had forgotten why he was really there. The job as the lab's access-and-controls administrator was enjoyable and easy. He'd even come to appreciate Mars culture—especially since his cover had put him in the higher strata of the planet's technocracy. They were a libertine people and made great beer. Even the ridiculous Marty names had grown on him.

But it was time to leave all that. The activation had put him behind enemy lines. His friends were now enemy combatants, even if they didn't know that yet. It was time to count on all the contingency plans and distractions he'd concocted when he arrived on Mars. Including the ultimate fail-safe that would ensure his silence if captured.

Gelp started when Trenki snorted. Yes, this was really happening. His life on Mars was over. He logged into the nearby terminal with a backdoor, full-access user account he'd hidden in the system. But it would only get him halfway there. While the facility wasn't under the auspices of the Mars military, Kwang Software Engineering had mostly military contracts and, as such, followed appropriate security protocols.

He didn't know what was in the data packet his handlers wanted, and he didn't want to know. The file could not be copied from the system except to a properly encoded QED—quantum encoded device. Fortunately, the director hadn't been in his office when Gelp arrived to steal one.

The small, silver QED fob slid into the access port and, with a few keystrokes, the data-transfer crystal began blinking as it received the files from the Kwang core. A moment later, the crystal shone a solid green to indicate the transfer was complete.

A growing urgency tempted Gelp to grab the QED and run from the building. He forced the panic away with deep breathing and focused his thoughts on the checklist of things needed to complete the mission. And maybe even survive.

Gelp reclassified the copied data packet as a billing file and buried it deep in the billing subsystem in hopes of confusing investigators in case he'd unknowingly set off an alarm. Then he ejected the QED and slipped it into a flesh pocket in his forearm. He jerked towards the desk when another wet snore escaped Trenki. Perspiration was starting to dampen Gelp's forehead and he wiped it away. He needed to get out.

The kill script he activated would remove his super user from all systems and erase its command and connection logs. It would also bury and encrypt the security footage files. Working from a keyboard was clumsy and frustrating work, but Gelp didn't want to risk accessing the system via an overlay interface. It was nearly impossible to spoof their biometric scanners. He doubted even his kill script would catch everything—Kwang had an amazing system. But anything that might delay the inevitable could save his life. He still had to get off planet, after all.

"I guess you were right," Gelp said to Trenki's unconscious form. "There are Confederation spies everywhere." He took two seconds to collect himself, retrieved his tool case from the floor, and calmly left the server room to get to his next objective.

Gelp reached for the bathroom door and clenched his teeth to stifle the scream that tried to escape when Zerf opened it from the inside.

Zerf smiled and stepped aside. "Whoa, you sealed, man?"

"Yeah, I'm sealed. My gut's just flipping."

"You gotta stay away from Navana's nachos, man."

Gelp affected a guilty grin and put a hand over his belly. "Smell you later. I've got a pressing matter I need to work out."

Zerf grimaced. "Don't let me get in your way."

Finding all the restroom stalls empty, Gelp locked himself in the one farthest from the door. Once inside, he pulled open his tool case and pricked his finger on a burr protruding from the handle of a multi-tool. The tiny drop of blood slowly disappeared and, a second later, the multi-tool unfolded into something like a black, mechanical centipede. Gelp placed the QED in a sealed bag and fitted it into a slot on the bot's body.

Four of the insectile legs clamped down on the QED, while the remainder began undulating along its length. Gelp shuddered. One thing he liked about Mars was the blessed lack of creepy-crawlies. Whatever else went extinct, Peru had no shortage of bugs. Especially the grande roaches. With that thought in mind, Gelp dropped the thing in the flusher and depressed the flush valve.

He had about ten minutes.

Gelp scrubbed his face in the sink and stared at himself in the mirror. It was like looking at a stranger. The eyes were wide with disbelief. When had he grown so soft? Shaking his head, the man in the mirror put on an expression of mild physical discomfort and left.

The KSE guard at the main hatch to the facility didn't seem to care one way or the other about Gelp's apparent illness. He watched the scanner for dangerous items or KSE asset chips with barely a glance up. The scanner queried Gelp's overlay module for unauthorized recordings or data files. When no alarms sounded, the guard waved his hand and the exit buzzed open. Gelp held his breath to keep from sighing in relief. He offered the guard a perfunctory wave and stepped into the Marakov Industrial Cavern.

The vast majority of the settlements on Mars were underground, though some of the older parts of the colonies held the occasional dome or habitat on the surface. The atmosphere had changed little since humanity's occupation, and it was cheaper and safer to build beneath the surface. Tunnels were easily drilled and sealed with electro-bonding film. The film was tinted red to make Mars more red than it really was and red was part of the planet's milieu.

The grand terraforming efforts had yielded little and when the gates opened up the opportunities for more livable, extra-Solar colonies, Mars became "not economically viable" in the boardrooms of the elite. When the gate shut down and Earth's economy collapsed, the leaders of Mars didn't want to make their planet more inviting.

Gelp walked calmly through the industrial cavern. There was little traffic in the tunnels as the next standard shift break wasn't for another hour. If he'd got the dosage correct, Trenki would wake up in time for his break. Gelp felt a pang of guilt at the draconian scrutiny KSE would put his friends through when the breach was finally discovered, and pushed it aside. Guilt was a liability now.

"May fortune favor the foolish," he muttered.

The cafeteria was quiet save for the few human workers chatting behind the counter and the whir of the cleaning bots. One of the few concessions Mars made to human sentimentality was that humans still cooked much of the food, even though test after test proved customers couldn't tell if a meal was prepared by a person or a bot. Gelp preferred the convenience of the dispensers, but had made many friends in the cafeterias and restaurants of Mars; first making contacts and then making genuine friends. He hoped whatever he was stealing wouldn't come back to harm him.

"Hey," called a woman behind the counter, "we're not serving yet."

Gelp clutched his belly. "Just need to use the flusher."

She was a simple worker and didn't look like the sort to protest, but he walked on without giving her a chance just in case. With a shrug, she turned back to her gossip.

Gelp pushed into the restroom and stopped short; the stall he needed was occupied.

Fear raced up from his stomach. Hardly anyone used this stall on shift. He'd watched it for weeks as he worked out this contingency. The staff had their own flushers. But someone was in there now. Gelp raced through his options of how to incapacitate—or kill—the person without raising suspicion. Whoever was in there might die on their own when a mechanical centipede came up the tube and poked them in the ass.

He could see a pair of worn utility boots and a folded-up maintenance belt beneath the stall door. Needing a moment to think, Gelp moved to the sink and ran the water. His overlay timer told him the crawler would be there soon. He wasn't sure what the thing would do when it got there and found its way blocked, but he doubted it would go down quietly. There were two more nano-toxin packs hidden in Gelp's clothes, but moving a large, unconscious person off the seat was going to be difficult and possibly messy. The thought of that mess made him want to vomit.

Vomit.

Pulling out one of his most successful tricks from his primary school days, Gelp walked into the other stall, knelt, and stuck his finger down his throat until he started gagging.

"You all right over there?" asked a grumbling voice.

Gelp moaned and gagged again until a bit of vomit splashed into the flusher. Almost there. He jammed two fingers down his throat as far as he could and wriggled them until he belched loudly and spewed all over the floor, the flusher, and the boots in the next stall. Gelp was glad he'd eaten a large breakfast, not knowing when his next meal would come.

The man in the other stall cursed and tried to shuffle his feet away from the spreading puddle of spew. "What's wrong with you!"

Gelp coughed, then retched again. "Sorry, I got something bad."

Gelp heard more cursing and the telltale jangle of buckles, followed by the rasp of a hastily pulled zipper as the man finished his business in the stall. Peeking beneath the stall door, Gelp watched the man storm over to the sink and grab a handful of towels. The man muttered more curses as he soaked the towels and wiped the vomit splatter from his trousers and boots. Gelp gagged again, though involuntarily this time.

"I hope you get to feeling better, dweller," the man said. "I'll tell the ladies to send in the bots and clean this up."

"Oh, I'll tell them. I might not be done yet. I'm so sorry."

"Eh, these boots have had worse on them. Get well." The man tossed the towels into the recycler and walked out. The door swung shut just as a metallic tinkling sound came up the other flusher.

Gelp stepped to the other stall, careful not to slip. It occurred to him that this plan would have gone down much differently if that worker had been a sympathetic puker. The centipede crested the rim of the flusher, dropped to the floor, and curled into a ball around the QED. Right in the center of the puke.

Gelp picked it up with re-towels and wiped the filth from it as best as he could. Once he'd retrieved the priceless fob with its secret data, Gelp flushed the centipede back down the tube where it would find some place to disassemble itself in the waste system. He cleaned his own shoes and pant legs, apologized about the mess to the cafeteria ladies on his way out, and calmly raced to the orbital shuttle that would hopefully get him to the spaceship that would eventually make its way back to Earth.

GELP FROWNED. "GANYMEDE? Why Ganymede?"

The pilot, wearing the brightly embroidered patch of the United Isles on his flightsuit, flashed a sympathetic grin. "I don't know, friend."

Phobos Station was now an hour behind them and the pilot had come floating back to the cramped passenger cabin to check on Gelp after the departure burn.

The UI was one of the few countries of old Europe not to be annexed by the Caliphate after the fall of the Earth Protectorate. While they had lost most of their global influence well before then, they still had enough influence to maintain their sovereignty through a combination of their unproportionally large space fleet and adopting an international policy based on strict neutrality when it came to dealing with the Solar superpowers.

"Ganymede," Gelp muttered.

"Unless you've got the marks to purchase a trip elsewhere," the pilot said with a slight Irish accent. "Of course, I'm assuming that someone with passage on a UI courier which was anonymously purchased, at great cost and at the last minute, having only the clothes on his back, and boarding in something of a tizzy, is probably going where he's told."

"I don't know what you're talking about."

The pilot chuckled and held up his hands. "Of course. No worries here. Far be it from me to guess. Guessing's too dangerous. You know how to use the ship's facilities?"

"I'll manage."

"Good, you'll need it. You're a bit ripe, if you don't mind me saying." The pilot fanned his hand in front of his face. "Even if you do mind... you're still a bit ripe."

"It's been a long day."

"I bet," the pilot said. "Anyway, if those are re-clothes you can put them in the recycler. If not, just toss them and pull a flightsuit from the locker."

Gelp glanced to the hatch the pilot pointed out. "Thanks."

"This isn't a liner, but there's an overlay interface and a few petabytes of entertainment. If you just want to sleep the time away, we've a somnolence dispenser in the galley."

Gelp was exhausted enough that he wouldn't need any somnolence, even with his worn nerves. But the pilot was right—he was ripe. "Anyone else on board?"

"Just another pilot and a flight engineer. We don't have many seats on this rinky-dink rocket, but your daddy bought them all out. No chitchat for you until Ganymede."

"How long will it take?"

"Your patron paid for full speed, so once we clear high orbit, we're going to burn the whole way. About two months."

Gelp nodded and turned away.

"There's also a biometric safe beneath your bunk, should you need it. No one else on the ship can use it."

Gelp glanced back at the pilot and raised his brows. "Really?"

"You don't get to be the most trusted couriers in Sol by playing games."

"Are you the most trusted couriers in Sol?"

The pilot grinned. "According to our satisfied customers."

Gelp nodded again and drifted to the shower. He stripped and tossed his clothes in a nearby waster, withdrawing the QED with care. It felt like a stone in his palm, even though he was in free fall. Gaining it had cost him a life and he wasn't ready to trust it to any safe yet. It was still sealed so he took it into the shower tube with him. The man formerly known as Gelp Nurrow washed away the rust and dust and years of Mars, and strapped in-to his sleeping hammock.

Thoughts of Earth held no joy for him, but it was better than a cell—or execution—on Mars. As his eyes closed and his body settled in for a deep, deep sleep, he briefly wondered what his name would be six months from now.

Chapter 8

VORTAN DUGG FELT CHILDLIKE joy aboard *Schrodinger's Tiger*, tucked away inside a Trojan asteroid. With an array of passive sensors spread around the area and a mast topped with an antenna cluster protruding from his hiding place, Vortan loved secretly intercepting and cracking the encrypted signals of Sol. The useful things, like ship movements and corporate data-streams, weren't usually interesting. And the things he found interesting weren't usually useful to Mars Security.

"She's not really my sister," pleaded a man's voice. "More like a cousin, at most."

A woman's shrill voice answered on the same frequency, the encryption laughable. "You have the same mother!"

"That's not how we count things out here in the clans," the man said. "Come on back, honey."

"You were kissing her! I don't even want to know what else you did with your *sister*."

"I told you she's not my sister." The man's voice was getting angry. "This ain't Luna and you knew that when you flew out here."

Vortan rubbed his hands together gleefully. Some people had no idea how far a radio transmission traveled. He was well aware of his voyeuristic streak and made no apologies. It had helped him graduate with top honors and achieve his dream posting. Not to mention avoid his dad's violent rages. When it came time for a thrashing, that his father suffered from mental illness was a moot point. In Vortan's home, it was hide, placate, or redirect when it came to his father's wrath.

All skills that suited him well as commander of a Mars security ship. It was a technological impossibility to completely hide a spaceship in a solar system brimming with advanced thermo-optical sensors. Even the Junker gangs—they fancied themselves clans, but were merely dirty scavengers and thieves—could track a ship through system. There were, however, techniques and technologies to mask a ship's signature. No one did it better than Marsec. But there were always trade-offs in ship design.

He floated in his cabin, gently bouncing from wall to wall and laughing at the pervo Junker still trying to rationalize his familial liaisons to his Lunar fiancée. She probably should have done a bit more snooping on her betrothed before moving across Sol.

The Lunies were as bad as the Junkers, but it was still fun to listen to them. Especially since the woman had started using some very descriptive curses. As she was launching into accusations about the man and his granny, a MarSec communiqué lit up in Vortan's retinal implants.

Corporate espionage was not terribly interesting on the whole. Usually it was nothing more than corporate hack-bots stealing executives' lunch schedules or their peccadilloes. But sometimes the methods of the intrusion were creative. The MarSec report about the Xang break-in was impressive in the data taken and in how it was achieved. Escaping a secure industrial site, let alone off world, with a QED was no small feat.

The report concluded the perpetrator was most likely a deep-infiltration agent from one of the Earth powers, given the skill and resources. Vortan didn't usually think of Earthers as being skilled or resourceful, but he couldn't deny the agent's success. Anti-Earth hubris was another of his indulgences. He knew there were highly intelligent people on Earth—they just never seemed to be put in charge.

No technical details about the QED were included in the report, but there were very few facilities in Sol that could break even an older model. Some of those facilities were on Mars. Assuming the agent belonged to whichever entity ordered the theft, the field of possible suspects was small. The CAR, the Caliphate, possibly Solar Transit Inc., or even Laboratorio d Tecnologia Espacial, aka LTE. Solar Transit had no vested interest in making an enemy of Mars, and the company was completely independent of any of the Sol governments.

LTE was a Confederation lapdog, though.

While the United Isles might be able to crack a QED, Vortan doubted they'd use their own ship to escape in. Of course, that might be a clever ruse to throw off MarSec. Vortan laughed. In his job, it was easy to fly off into nebulae of conspiracy and misdirection. It came with the job. This time, it wasn't his responsibility to solve the mystery.

Tiger's orders were to intercept the UI courier, destroying it if necessary. He was happy to let some flunky at MarSec get burned for making a wrong guess about who was doing what in this scheme.

Still, Vortan loved a good puzzle. A very helpful clue could have been provided by MarSec by telling him what had been on the QED, which would help solve why it had been stolen, which in turn might indicate who, thereby limiting the question of where it would be taken. But Operational Security was the life yeast of a security ship. The "need to know" mantra predated any Mars colony and it was still standard operating procedure. As it should be. But Vortan would have given a month's pay to know what had MarSec so worked up. The attached intercept authorization was no joke.

Tiger might have to show her claws for this one.

Not that the tiny UI ship would be able to put up much of a fight, but this mission should have gone to a gunship, not a spyship. That detail and the willingness to attack a notoriously neutral Islander were clues to how desperately MarSec wanted that QED. It must be important. Vortan wondered who would come to the rescue.

Speculation was strictly prohibited by MarSec, yet it was all that was left to him for now. Ordering someone like Vortan not to speculate was like ordering a Junker not to steal or an Earther not to eat carcasses.

Vortan pushed himself into a slow cartwheel as he watched the courier's track with his implants. The farther it got from Mars, the more certain that ship was heading for Ganymede. It made sense. Ganymede was a good place to hide with its bustling business centers and busy departure schedule. There might be the facilities to break a QED on Ganymede station, but Vortan had never heard of one. More likely the agent would catch a flight to their final destination.

He laughed as he envisioned the contact shooting the agent and dumping the body into space. As ridiculous as they sometimes were, Vortan enjoyed the occasional spy fiction. He wanted to dig for any more security breaches concerning Xang, but feared MarSec flagging his activity. What MarSec did to spies—suspected or otherwise—wasn't fiction.

But he could analyze the usual things, such as fleet movements and personnel transfers, without raising any suspicion. It was part of his job. Navigation plots between planets were not so easily changed as many thought. A ship only carried so much delta-v to make course corrections. If someone was heading to Ganymede to retrieve the QED, they'd have left long ago or would have already been waiting.

Vortan scanned the recent fleet-movement files with minute flicks of his eyes. His implants added more processing power to his overlay interface than the standard head-band rig. So many people resisted full integration due to some evolutionary attachment to their soggy inner bits they'd not yet been able to shake. Not Vortan. He was eagerly awaiting a full data-consciousness transfer—once someone could prove it wasn't just an expensive form of suicide. There was no love lost between his mind and the meat sack it was trapped in.

Sol asset reports showed the STS-111, *Amazonas*, had burned towards Ganymede from the Nexus sector a month ago. That would put her in dock well before the courier. Long enough to maybe allay suspicion? Possibly. But it was a training ship, even if trigger-happy Capitan Walsh was in command. Vortan had taken a good look at *Amazonas* from *Tiger's* cozy hidey-hole. But he lacked enough information to rule anyone out.

"Plot intercept course envelope for UI ship designation CH-23," Vortan ordered the navigation computer. An instant later, a yellow arc appeared before the courier. Though the arc widened the farther ahead of the ship it ran to estimate possible changes in vector and delta-v, the courier was clearly heading towards Ganymede.

A blue line grew from the Trojan asteroid *Tiger* was hiding in. It, too, widened to represent the allowed changes in course the Mars ship could make to intercept the courier at different points along its trajectory. Vortan ran the intersection points back and forth, watching not only the time-stamp of the intercept, but how long they'd be in effective weapons range. *Tiger* would probably only get a single pass, especially if the courier tried to evade. This was really a job for a gunship, not a spyship, but Vortan knew he could disable, and probably destroy, the target.

They'd be there in about three weeks—if no one else showed up.

Schrodinger's Tiger used low-impulse ion engines designed for stealth, not acceleration. Given enough time, she could get up to speeds matching most ships in Sol without the huge drive plume of more conventional thermonuclear rockets. While there was no such thing as true stealth in space, *Tiger* used electromagnetically modulated baffle plates to reduce her thrust signature from observers in front of her and a black globe amidships that housed a powerful electronic warfare suite.

"Pilot, run a final spectrum scan for possible observers and decouple from the asteroid." Vortan watched the main antenna and mooring lines retract. When that was completed, the control thrusters gently pushed *Tiger* far enough away from the asteroid to change heading for the burn. He allowed himself a grin, pleased at how smoothly the procedure had been. Hopefully, taking out the courier and its stolen QED would go just as well.

But Vortan was too much of a realist to expect it to be that easy. "Pilot, initiate main thruster."

Chapter 9

WALSH JUMPED AS THE emergency klaxon blared in the operations center. White warning lights began strobing in every compartment. Red and yellow lights along the deck traced a path through the hatch to operations and out into the corridor towards the tube to the main hull.

"Shield stations, shield stations," Hector announced over all of *Amazonas*'s internal comm's systems. "All hands to shield stations. A high-energy radiation field has been detected. All hands to shield stations."

Amazonas was under spin gravity, and Walsh watched the officers quickly rise from their stations and form a line to the nearby ladder. Walsh scanned Ops a final time and took his place at the end of the line. When crew from the other parts of the deck started showing up, Walsh was nearly at the conveyors, both of which were now pulling people towards the main hull.

As the gravity in the tube dropped ahead, one cadet's feet drifted free from their foothold. She panicked and started kicking to find her purchase again. Walsh grimaced when the cadet kicked at least one person in the face. Colorful curses filled the passage.

Collins turned back down towards the shouting. "Stow that noise and keep moving! Cadet, get control of yourself. If only you were surrounded by a crew willing to help their shipmates."

Walsh grinned as hands reached out and pushed the cadet back towards the conveyor. Despite the outburst, the crew was still moving in good order.

Walsh crawled out of the tube and off the spinning hub. The crew spread out to the pylons that connected *Amazonas*'s outer hull to the shielded core compartment, commonly known as the crypt. Walsh resisted the urge to push off and drift to the crypt; he didn't want to have to chase down a dozen cadets who would miss their jump and start bouncing everywhere except their station. Instead, he made his way to the pylon nearest the commander's station and pulled his way to the crypt.

Walsh hooked his toes through the handle to his station and stood so he could watch the progress of his crew. A few stragglers emerged from the hub and rushed to the nearest pylon. One pushed off and drifted to the crypt, landing easily and disappearing through the hatch leading to his station. Soon he'd trust the whole crew to do that, but it would still be a dangerous move if attempted while the ship was under maneuvers. Walsh tagged the man in his overlay and made a note to talk to him about it later.

The CO and XO stations were at opposite ends of the crypt, the CO's being forward. He could see Diaz standing over her hatch, too, watching the crew nearest her. The motion of the crew sinking into their stations until their heads finally disappeared, reminded Walsh of the prairie dogs that lived near his grandfather's recycling center.

Hector materialized in Walsh's overlay as the last hatch iris closed. "All crew are secured at stations, Capitan. Five minutes, seventeen seconds for completion of drill. Mag-shield stable."

Diaz connected to Walsh's overlay and her image appeared next to Hector's, her movements mimicking the XO's in the distance. "Not a bad time, Capitan."

Walsh nodded. "Agreed. Before we stand down, let's spin down the habitats."

"Shake-and-bake?" Diaz asked.

"Shake-and-bake," Walsh said.

Both Diazes nodded. "It's overdue. And there are a handful of maintenance routines waiting for a spin-down."

A screen with a list of work orders appeared next to Hector. "There are currently twelve routines pending, and three more that I suggest taking care of, that will be due within the next few weeks."

Walsh scanned the list and turned to Diaz. "Get with Maintenance and make it happen. Including the upcoming work Hector mentioned."

"*Si*, Capitan."

"We're going to stay in the crypt for a while, so you'll have plenty of time." Walsh sighed as he slid into his own station. "And I'll have time to go over the budget. Yay for me."

It was said that cadets study tactics, but admirals study logistics. Walsh didn't like the slight against tacticians, but if a fighting crew couldn't get on station with beans, bullets, and burn, tactics were a moot point. The allotment for food and other life support was much larger than he was used to, having such a large crew. While Hector could instantly run the budget numbers for him, Walsh was the one responsible for getting the most bang out of each of *Amazonas*'s bucks. It wasn't the most glamorous part of the job, but a good capitan knew how to get creative with it.

With all the number crunching and best-guessing done, Walsh brushed away the accounting screens. He'd done his best, but budgetary regulations were rewritten monthly, it seemed. All of his plans could change with the swipe of a stylus. As an XO, he'd once had to review three years of his ship's financial reports due to a change in the reporting codes. The system was supposed to update and correct automatically. It hadn't.

He reviewed the shift reports, the daily comms traffic, and Hector's analysis of the drill. With a final scan of his to-do list, Walsh went into full-immersion mode in his overlay and pinged Diaz. He set the background to appear as if he were standing on *Amazonas*'s outer hull.

Diaz materialized a moment later, pausing to take in the virtual environment. "*Si?*"

"I was working on my crew reviews and was struck by something."

Diaz lifted her brows. "The suspense is killing me, Capitan."

"It's been six years since the last official war with the Caliphate ended at Egeria."

"Something like that," Diaz said. "I was Ops-officer on the *Tennessee*. We must have shot down fifty missiles."

Walsh nodded. "I was XO on the *Tamara Skellings*. It was an older ship, but we managed to cripple two Cali missile frigates. Got hammered pretty bad, but we didn't lose anyone."

"Is that why you fired on them last year?"

Walsh pursed his lips. "No. I was looking at the roster and the service dates caught my eye. Most of the staff weren't even out of the academy for that war. The cadets weren't even out of primary school."

Diaz shrugged. "There's a first time for everyone. How many on the *Thunder* had seen combat prior to that skirmish?"

"Two others."

"There are many who'd say that it's a good thing that so few have been in a shooting war. I know I'm not eager to spend hours and hours watching incoming missiles."

Walsh moved the overlay so that they were both standing near the main thruster. "I'm not spoiling for a fight, Felicia. But I do think it's important for people—especially some in the admiralty—to remember we are a military fleet. We might be called to face dangers beyond the normal travails of space travel."

Diaz absently ran a hand up her left forearm. "Those normal travails can be bad enough without you whistling up the wind, Gene."

"I'm not talking about going full drill instructor here. But I have to admit to getting a bit comfortable. We need to move beyond the basic shipboard and environmental drills. Time to add in more combat drills." Walsh summoned the crew roster with a wave of his hand. "According to this, just about everyone has their zero-g quals signed off. We need to step it up. Now."

"Now?" Diaz raised one dark eyebrow.

"Now. We're going to spend the rest of the trip to Ganymede in the crypt except for mandatory duty functions."

"That's fifty-three hours, Capitan."

"I had to stay strapped in for a week once while we played hide-and-seek with a Junker ship around Jupiter. She was keeping in the radiation fields, hoping we'd give up." Walsh pinched his nose. "I was hoping we'd give up. My station smelled like a fart for weeks afterwards. Probably still does."

"Catch the Junker?"

Walsh shook his head. "No. We thought she'd escaped, but another ship found her in a very low orbit two months later, dead. Something on their ship fried and they never made it back up."

"Well, the crew should appreciate their leave all the more."

Walsh grinned. "Good point. I know I will."

"Shall I announce it?"

"No, I'll take care of it." Walsh wriggled to a more comfortable position in his station and connected to the ship-wide comms. "All hands, this is the capitan. The drill went well, though there's always room for improvement.

All of our drills are important, but getting to a ship's shelter quickly and safely is vital for any spacer. Division officers, take muster and report crew status to the XO.

"Speaking of drills, we're extending this one. The *Amazonas* will operate as if under extended radiological-hazard conditions until our arrival at Ganymede station. All maintenance and duty functions that require leaving the crypt will be performed in environmental gear."

"What the hell," someone complained over the connection.

Walsh continued. "For full immersion, all crew will use the waste-tubes and packaged rations stored in your station. It's good to replace those packrats on occasion, anyway. Don't eat them all at once or you're going to get hungry. Capitan out."

It was an adage that a bitching spacer is a happy spacer, and that's how you know spacers are always happy. The complaint didn't bother Walsh, but it going out over his address was a problem. "Hector, please identify and connect me to whoever made that comment."

"You are now connected to Lieutenant Tousand in station three-delta, Capitan."

"Do you have a hot date or something, Lieutenant?" Walsh asked calmly.

"I'm sorry, Capitan," Tousand said hurriedly. "I didn't mean to interrupt your announcement. I didn't even realize it until my div-O let me know."

"So you're aware you just made a public complaint about my orders."

"Yes, sir. Sorry, sir."

Walsh waited to see if the lieutenant would try to come up with excuses, and was pleased when Tousand kept his mouth shut. "While some of my orders may turn out to be crap, your opinion of them isn't the main problem. The main problem, Lieutenant, is that you obviously aren't familiar enough with your comms gear. Accidentally transmitting is a security risk. It can help an enemy identify us or firm up their firing solution, not to mention providing them with intel if you let something important slip."

Tousand's tone was one of contrite resignation. "Yes, sir. I understand."

"I'm glad you do, Lieutenant. So you'll understand your div-O will assign you twelve hours of extra comms watches to help familiarize yourself with the *Amazonas*'s comms systems."

"Yes, sir."

"Very well." Walsh cut Tousand's channel and switched to Diaz. "Make sure his extra duty doesn't interfere with any leave on Ganymede. He can probably fit it all in before we get there. It's not like he has much else to do while he's cooped up."

"And I thought you were all about getting tough, Capitan."

Walsh grinned. "Would you like some extra duty while I'm at it, XO?"

She shrugged. "I've got nothing better to do."

"SO, WHAT IS IT, GENE?" Manuela Correia asked.

Jupiter's striped face shone huge in the view port despite Ganymede being a million kilometers away. It was amazing. Walsh would love to have seen Jupiter's giant, red eye before it disappeared two hundred years ago. He turned from one beautiful sight to another. "What is what?"

"Whatever it is that you've been wanting to ask me?" Manuela smiled and set her glass of wine on the end table near the couch.

Walsh grinned. "Busted. I wanted to talk to you about this transfer. Burton Mahoney. But I also didn't want you to think I was distracted from your beautiful body."

"What about him?"

Turning back to the view port, Walsh spoke over his shoulder. "Is he safe?"

Manuela shook her head. "I'm still not sure what you mean."

"From what I could find out about these so-called intuitive powers or whatever, they were the result of some pretty intense—not to mention illegal—gene mods and invasive brain surgery. And at least a few killed themselves from what I read."

"He's fully vetted, *bebe*," she said. "More so than us, probably. Admiral Maconez made sure of that. He's been on the *Calypso* for over six months and he's done a good job."

Walsh scoffed and turned back to her. "I'm not all that confident about *Mamon*-ez's judgment."

Manuela leaned over and poured more wine into her glass. The motion caused the small towel draped across her hips to slip, and she casually pulled it back into place. Walsh raised his brows and watched intently.

Manuela rolled her eyes. "That's between you two. All I can say is that he's never received a bad review from any of his superiors."

"Has this intuition ever helped? And how does it even work? Does he have visions or sense cosmic love rays or something?"

"Don't be ridiculous," she said. "He's got a neuro-optical implant that ties into his overlay rig. It basically hypnotizes him and dumps a bunch of data into his subconscious. And you can input just about anything and he's supposed to be able to pick out patterns and relationships."

"Did he ever help?"

She shrugged, causing her breasts to heave. "Once. We were investigating a collision at L4 between two free-traders. I'd already collected all the telemetry, statements, ships' logs, et cetera. But we couldn't pin down the root cause. And, of course, I'm on the hook for the write-up.

"So I feed it all into Mahoney's data feed. He dozes off and fifteen minutes later says he's got a hunch about one of the pilots. So I leaned on the guy and he finally admits they'd been running with an uncalibrated nav-radar for the last month."

Walsh stroked his beard. "Well, that could be helpful. Anything else? He was there for six months."

"No," Manuela said. "Mostly he comes up with nada... except bad jokes. I'm surprised they don't have him locked up in some intel system where they can feed him things all day long."

"That's probably what someone smarter than *Mamon*-ez wanted to do. Oh well. I'm supposed to take the kiddos back to Liberty for some system upgrades and then finish the rest of the cadet cruise."

A mischievous grin curled Manuela's red lips. "I never would have pictured you running a daycare. Be careful around all those young, pretty cadets. They'll get you in trouble."

Walsh overtly ogled Manuela's barely covered body. Years of space duty had softened her tight cadet body, but she still maintained her sultry Brazilian figure. He liked to think he'd aged pretty well since the academy, too.

"Young cadets aren't my type," Walsh said.

Manuela laughed. "We both know that's not true, *el conquistador*."

There was something powerful in standing stark naked, the Jovian giant glowing behind him in the distance. Manuela tipped her wine glass towards him and stretched languidly on the couch. The whole scene was too arousing and Walsh's body reacted. He imagined himself as an ancient Greek hero, shaking his spear in the face of the titans and taking this jungle queen for his own. There was no way to fight the huge smile on his face—even if he'd wanted to.

Manuela bit her lip. "Well, I've got to make sure our cargo manifest is correct. We're heading on an outer-planet patrol. I've got a lot to do." She slid the towel that barely covered her to the floor. "But since we probably won't be seeing one another for a while, I might be convinced to stay a little longer."

Walsh walked to the couch, plucked the wine glass from her hand and set it on the table. With Jupiter looking on in the distance, he convinced her to stay for a long time.

Chapter 10

WALSH LEANED OVER THE railing that surrounded the airlock set into the floor of Ganymede station. He could see through the airlock's portal into the boarding area of the shuttle docked below. It was tradition aboard *Amazonas* for the CO and XO to escort the last shuttle-load of crew back to the ship from leave. It was a waste of his time and he was going to change it. If an officer was required for such a task—which would be even more pointless on a smaller warship like *Thunder* with her crew of eight—any watch officer would suffice. Especially since it was the last load. There were more important things a capitan had to do before departure.

Despite being technical people, spacers were just as superstitious as any crew of sailors or klatch of knitting grannies. Diaz didn't know how or when it had started, only that the tradition preceded the *Amazonas becoming a training ship*. Traditions from people who feared the old sea-gods were at least understandable from their point of view. Walsh had little tolerance for them in modernity, and wasn't interested in this one's origins.

What did interest him was where they were going. Liberty command had issued them with a prepare-to-move order with no further detail. PT-MOs weren't uncommon for ships on patrol. And often enough the order would expire with no follow-up command if something fell through or someone up the chain changed their minds. But *Amazonas* wasn't on patrol. If it was something important, it would have been better to send *Calypso*, even if she'd have to turn and burn back this way.

"Does the *Amazonas* get many PTMOs?" Walsh asked.

"Never while I've been XO, Capitan."

"Maybe *Mamon*-ez doesn't want me enjoying too much free time." Walsh shifted on the railing and grinned at Diaz. "But it is probably time to get underway. At least we didn't get kicked off the station."

"At least not overtly, Capitan."

"Hm. Good point. But at least I didn't have to hear about it."

Angulo and Robbins were the first of the stragglers to step around the corner, salute and climb down into the airlock. Ganymede station hadn't barred *Amazonas* from the main dock, but Walsh decided to use the shuttle for pilot training. Also to save some of his budget—every second at dock cost money. The smaller docks cost less and it was much quicker to undock and move a shuttle than a ship the size of *Amazonas*. The airlock cycled and the two crew members entered the shuttle.

"I haven't been following the fleet movements like I used to," Walsh said. "As part of the training department, they don't send me real reports anymore."

"Not much point," Diaz answered. "They're not going to send us on anything."

"They might. Space rescue is part of the Sol Accords. Even *Amazonas* isn't immune from that. In fact, she'd probably be a good rescue ship given all the space she has."

Diaz shrugged, but said nothing else. She hadn't looked at him during the conversation. Unless Walsh made a point of it, his XO seldom spoke to him directly. While underway, most conversations were via comms channels or overlays and he hadn't really noticed. But the few times they'd been on Ganymede together it had become obvious she avoided looking at him while they spoke.

He knew it was never helpful to take things personally. It was possible that she still held a grudge about his promotion to capitan, and he could understand that. But her aloof manner was rude, approaching hostility at times. It was also possible that she'd always acted that way, even before losing her command.

Walsh straightened as a rail-thin black man came around the corner. He was beaming as he stopped in front of Walsh and saluted. He spoke in Spanish with a middle-African accent. The ship patch bore an angry crab with lasers for claws beneath the word *Calypso*. "Lt. Burton Mahoney reporting for duty, sir."

Walsh returned the salute and opened up Mahoney's orders in his overlay. Ensuring all the timestamps and digital security marks passed authentication, Walsh selected "approve transfer" at the bottom of the form.

The angry crab on Mahoney's uniform blinked out and was replaced with the glowering medicine mask of *Amazonas*.

"Welcome aboard, Mr. Mahoney. Your CO was telling me about you the other night."

Diaz gave Walsh a sidelong glance and raised an eyebrow.

Mahoney's smile dimmed.

Walsh smiled at the new crew member. "No worries. She only had good things to say."

"I had a feeling," Mahoney said.

"A feeling?" Walsh asked. "Like an intuition feeling?"

"Yes, Capitan. An intuition is a feeling." Mahoney's smile brightened again and he looked expectantly between Walsh and Diaz.

Walsh hesitated for a second. "No, I mean was your feeling one of these intuitions of yours?"

Mahoney's smile faded as he let out a sigh. "Sorry, sir. I was trying to make a joke."

Walsh exchanged a sidelong glance with Diaz. "Well, very good, Mr. Mahoney. Welcome aboard the *Amazonas*. Please board the shuttle."

"Yes, sir." Mahoney was smiling again as he opened and climbed down into the airlock.

"Did you have fun, Capitan?" Diaz asked.

"I wasn't giving him a hard time. I really wanted to know if he was talking about his supposed intuition skill." Walsh shrugged. "I didn't really get his joke, though."

Diaz sniffed. "That's not what I mean, and you know it."

"What?"

Diaz spoke in a deep voice. "Your CO was telling me about you the other night..."

Walsh furrowed his brow. "Your point?"

"I know who the skipper of the *Calypso* is, *mi* Capitan."

"So?"

"You made it sound like you were in a staff meeting, not rutting around with a *puta*." Diaz shook her head. "You are a bad, bad man."

"Whoa! I didn't know you followed my adventures so closely, XO. Would you like a video log?" Before Diaz could answer, Walsh counted off two fingers. "One, I told you I wouldn't share about my fun time while on station. Two, you probably shouldn't describe a superior officer as a *puta*."

"What about Admiral Maconez?"

Walsh clasped his hands behind his back and rocked on the balls of his feet. "Good point. You can call the admiral a *puta*."

Diaz smirked.

"And by the way," Walsh added, "Commander Correia said I was a good man. A very good man."

"Oh, *que hombre*," Diaz muttered.

Walsh chuckled and leaned back against the railing. Unfortunately, he wasn't sure how to read Diaz. If they'd been together for maybe even a few months longer, he could tell if she was only busting his balls or if she was genuinely bent about him and Manuela. Not that it was any of her business, but he hadn't been bragging or using innuendo. It was true that they'd been naked at the time, but she did tell him about Mahoney.

Walsh's overlay tracker showed the last member of *Amazonas*'s crew on Ganymede station was making his way—slowly—to the shuttle dock. Then he was walking away from the dock. Then he walked into a bulkhead in the corridor and stopped for a full minute, before zig-zagging back towards the shuttle.

"He's drunk," Diaz said.

"Good, he needed it," Walsh answered.

Just around the corner they could hear Bovree fall to the ground, and the CO and XO grimaced in unison.

Bovree's voice was slurred and muffled. "I'm okay." He repeated those words as he tried to rise twice, and fell back to the deck each time.

Despite Ganymede station's large rotating section, the difference in pseudo-gravity between the level of a person's head and the deck was enough to induce nausea if someone stood too fast. It was worse if that someone was drunk.

"I'm okay." Bovree belched. One hand reached around the corner, then the other, followed by his pale, pinched face. Bovree's body, wearing a rumpled and stained flight uniform, slid around the corner next in a serpentine crawl.

Walsh and Diaz watched with similar expressions of disbelief as the security chief of *Amazonas* made it to the railing. With some grunting and cussing, Bovree pulled himself up to unsteady feet—one booted, one bare—and saluted.

With only one hand on the rail, Bovree nearly fell to the deck again. "Sorry, sir. Sirs. This railing is loose. I'll file a report as soon as I get back to *Tres Mucho-ducho Grande.*"

Walsh let Bovree stand there wobbling—one hand on the rail, the other held crookedly against his forehead—for a long moment before returning the salute. "You are a sight, Lieutenant Commander."

Diaz shook her head. "I'm glad we have people in the shuttle already to catch him."

Walsh peered into the airlock. "I'm not sure he can make it down the ladder."

"I'll hand him down," Diaz said.

"I'll drop. You catch."

Diaz raised her eyebrows and stared at Walsh.

"You can handle it, XO. You wouldn't abandon a shipmate, would you?"

"She sure wouldn't!" Bovree announced. He was still pressing his hand against his forehead in a drunken salute. "Not my XO, CO."

Walsh nodded towards the airlock hatch.

Mustering as much dignity as she could, Diaz opened the hatch and climbed down into the airlock. Walsh grabbed Bovree's saluting hand and pulled him towards the ladder.

"I don't need no help, *mi* Capitan," Bovree complained just before tipping over headfirst into the airlock.

With a grunt of effort, Walsh barely managed to keep his grip on the drunk man's hand and the railing. Bovree's booted foot stayed on the deck, leaving his bare foot, one hand, and his head dangling over the open airlock. Diaz let out a shriek and moved to catch Bovree.

"If you need to puke," Walsh said in a stage whisper to Bovree, "be sure to aim it in the airlock. It's easier to clean up."

Diaz glared up at Walsh. "A bad, bad man."

Walsh laughed and strained as he lowered Bovree. Diaz was muttering in Spanish while she gathered enough of Bovree to set down safely. When Diaz sagged against the hatch to the shuttle with the drunk security officer in her arms, Walsh closed the top hatch and watched her drag Bovree into the shuttle and out of sight.

Hopefully, if Bovree was going to lose his lunch, it'd be cleaned up before Walsh boarded. "Has he puked yet, Hector?"

Hector appeared standing next to the airlock, staring down. "No, Capitan. Lieutenant Commander Diaz is securing him in a seat now. It should be safe."

Grinning, Walsh opened the hatch and climbed into the shuttle. The most forward seats of the cabin allowed a good view out of the shuttle's view ports and were reserved for the ranking officers on the trip. Walsh passed Bovree and slapped his shoulder. Bovree answered with a snorting horse-laugh and gave Walsh two thumbs-up. Mahoney was across the aisle from Bovree, leaning away from the drunk as far as his straps would allow. In the confines of the shuttle's cabin, Bovree's breath was intoxicating.

Diaz didn't return Walsh's smile as he took his seat. Once he'd buckled in, Walsh gave the pilot a thumbs-up. *Amazonas* appeared through the shuttle's view port in the distance as the station rotated. A few minutes later, *Amazonas* dipped out of view and the pilot decoupled from the station, flinging the shuttle towards their ship.

The control thrusters popped gently until *Amazonas* was once again in the shuttle's front portal. Walsh could have tied into the shuttle's camera or digital rendering, but there was something about seeing his ancient ship outside the window with the naked eye.

Distance gave a lackadaisical illusion to the spinning habitats. The forward cone was festooned with sensor arrays, towers for electronic warfare and comms, and the solar panels. Though he longed for his old command, he kept thinking about this ship having once traveled between the stars. Now it hauled students around Sol, like a wondrous yacht relegated to a kiddie pool.

Jupiter came into view behind *Amazonas* as the shuttle changed course for docking. Jovian light filtered through the door to the cockpit, the Jovian display sobering even Bovree for a moment.

Moments later, Jupiter slid out of sight as the shuttle maneuvered to line up with *Amazonas*. Everyone was jostled sharply, indicating a positive grapple with the docking station.

"Awww..." Bovree slurred.

Diaz unbuckled and floated free above her seat. "Get aboard, stow your gear, and get some chow if you need it. Then fall into your duty station. Mahoney, Hector will show you to your room and then to your div-O." She pointed at Angulo and Robbins. "You two, help Lieutenant Commander Bovree to his quarters."

Everyone unbuckled and drifted into the ship. Bovree was snoring. Angulo shook his head and Robbins was grinning.

"No pranks on the drunken spacer," Walsh said.

Bovree belched and sang, "What do you do with a drunken spacer, so early in the..." before dozing off again.

Walsh chuckled. "Make a hole."

The floating crew pulled themselves against the bulkheads to let Walsh by. He floated through the main passage, up the tube to habitat Alpha, and to his stateroom where he reviewed the watch summaries. No new traffic concerning their standby orders.

"Did everyone get some leave on Ganymede?"

"Yes, Capitan," said Hector. "I have the aggregate and individual allowances used if you require them."

"No thanks. Any demerit logs or behavior-unbecoming reports?"

"Only if you wish to charge Lieutenant Velasquez with damaging CAR property. He went skiing on Ganymede and broke his ankle."

"Good for him," Walsh said. "Not about the broken ankle part, of course."

"Of course, Capitan."

"I considered going, too. But it's been years since I've been down there. And I, uh, was entertaining other avenues. Well, maybe next time. Negative on the disciplinary action."

"Yes, Capitan." Hector paused, looking at Walsh.

Walsh stared back. "Yes?"

"I logged that *Calypso* was also on station."

"Did Diaz tell you to say that?"

"No, Capitan. But your duty and leave registers show you have met up with Commander Correia many times."

Walsh frowned. "Are we violating some protocol or something?"

"None that I'm aware of. I'm simply curious if you are in a romantic relationship with Commander Correia."

"Why would you wonder that, Hector?"

"I am programmed to adaptively learn about the crew I work with, Capitan. Especially the command crew." Hector tilted his head. "Is it improper to verify this conversation? Many crew already believe the two of you are romantically involved."

Walsh could feel the blush working its way up his cheeks. He grinned. "Well, I can't say it's improper. It's just not something I'd expect a ship's computer to ask about."

"Understandable, Capitan. I find humans still have an expectation of privacy even while serving in an enclosed environment while connected to an integrated overlay rig that records everything you see and hear."

"Thanks for reminding me," Walsh said. "But we still like our privacy."

"Do you love Commander Correia?"

"That," Walsh said, waving Hector's avatar away, "is none of your damn business. Is that clear?"

"Yes, Capitan."

Chapter 11

WALSH GAVE A FINAL tug on the straps to his station. "Operations Officer, begin spin-down of habitat arms."

"Yes, Capitan," Lieutenant Collins answered. He flicked a finger in the air before him to activate the ship-wide announcement. "All hands, make ready for spin-down of habitat arms. Make ready for spin-down. Secure all gear adrift and strap in for transition to zero-g."

Sections of *Amazonas* in Walsh's overlay blinked green as all crew members in those areas reported ready. Walsh could feel Diaz staring and glanced at her. She raised her brows and motioned towards his coffee sippy, which was sitting unsecured in his lap.

"Just following orders, Capitan," she said.

With a half grin, Walsh placed the container in the small holder set in his station's console. Though her demeanor was cool and she seemed to enjoy correcting him, he had a hard time believing the XO truly had such a low opinion of him. Even if she still held his promotion against him. At least she was sometimes discreet about expressing her disapproval. At least with her words—Diaz's eyebrows were hard to miss when she raised them.

Lieutenant Collins changed his focus from the overlay to Walsh. "All departments, sections, and crew report ready for zero-g, Capitan."

"Less that two minutes," Walsh said. "Not bad at all. XO, carry on."

"*Si*, Capitan," Diaz answered. "Ops-O, status of main gyroscope?"

"Main gyro is free and ready," Collins said.

Diaz nodded to Collins. "Engage main gyroscope and begin spin-down."

The ship torqued slightly as the counter-rotating spin arms were slowed via inductive EM fields. With minor configuration changes, the spinning arms could be used as generators to power the ship's batteries. The main gyro was there to correct residual spin from the process. It was very easy to introduce a wobble during spin-up or spin-down procedures, requiring precise shifting of liquid ballast by Hector.

"Spin-down successfully initiated, Capitan," Diaz announced. "Main gyro is compensating for a slight spin. Operations are within normal parameters."

"Very well, XO. Time to zero rotation?"

"Twenty-three minutes, Capitan."

Walsh felt the decrease in pseudo-gravity immediately. The whine of the main gyro hummed through *Amazonas* as it worked to keep the ship steady. As weightlessness approached, Walsh patted down the pockets of his flightsuit and verified they were sealed.

Twenty-three minutes and thirty-one seconds after Diaz's pronouncement, he felt the slight bounce of the spin clamps engaging. After several minutes of the control rockets firing minute bursts and more whining of the gyroscope, *Amazonas* was still.

"Full rotational stop, XO," Collins announced.

Diaz nodded at Walsh. "Spin-down complete, Capitan."

"Very good." Walsh scanned the faces in the operations compartment and grinned. "Anyone spacesick yet?"

A few nervous chuckles answered, but most of the crew affirmed their spaceworthiness with stoic grunts.

Walsh saw the thermal load was stable and well within specs. "XO, let's get this party started."

"*Si*, Capitan," Diaz said. "Mr. Collins, start the shake-and-bake."

Collins grinned and nodded towards the piloting station. The main gyro hummed again, twisting *Amazonas* back and forth along her pitch, yaw, and roll axes. Walsh's stomach began churning and he activated nausea suppression in his overlay. The effect wasn't complete, but his stomach did settle. He heard groans from at least three others in Ops.

The soft pops of the control thrusters sounded in the compartment. The programmed sequence of twists and jinks was designed to get loose debris out from behind and beneath equipment and into the open for collection. The navigation trainee either forgot about using her overlay or the suppression wasn't enough. She snatched a vomit bag from her station and noisily filled it. Walsh made sure not to inhale through his nose—he was close enough to sympathy puking as it was.

Collins unbuckled and spoke over the ship's comm. "All hands, stand fast. Division officers, inspect your spaces for unsecured gear afloat and report same."

"First the shake," Walsh said, eyeing the Ops compartment for FOD—floating object debris. Or floating object damage if the debris caused harm. "Now we bake whoever left gear afloat."

All eyes in Ops were surreptitiously scanning for any debris near their workstations that had been worked free by the shake-and-bake maneuvering. Collins carefully searched each area of the compartment, peeking and feeling around the edges of each station and piece of equipment. He made another circuit around Ops and pulled himself through the hatch, where he checked the passage outside for several minutes. When Collins returned, he stopped in front of Diaz.

"XO, Operations reports no gear afloat in this area."

"Very good, Ops," Diaz said.

Walsh nodded when Diaz glanced at him. The rest of the divisions slowly reported green on the ship's status display as they acknowledged no gear afloat discovered. The last was the Systems Maintenance division, which had the largest area to inspect. After several minutes, their display flashed yellow—a failure result.

"All divisions have reported in, Capitan," Diaz said.

"Roger that, XO. Let's get the spin-down maintenance started." Walsh opened the FOD report to see what had been found. Green didn't mean that nothing had been found; there were too many moving parts and people to expect perfection. With the spin gravity on *Amazonas*, there was the added problem of things falling and rolling out of sight instead of floating in plain view.

Incidentals such as crumbs of food, metal shavings, and fingernails could be counted as green. But something as small as a stylus could jam a hatch and keep it from closing in an emergency. Anything found that a crew member should keep positive inventory of, such as a stylus, was a FOD fail.

A fail couldn't necessarily be counted against Systems Maintenance, as they inspected the ship's common passages and spaces not directly manned by another division. Walsh scanned the list of debris, which included two styluses, a broken plastic buckle, a small spring of unknown origin, two forks in the galley, and a coin from a Ganymede dance club depicting a scantily clad she-bot. Not too bad, considering the ship's complement. When Walsh read the final fail item, he frowned and glanced at Diaz.

She frowned back at him, obviously having just read the same entry.

It was a molecular attachment tool from took kit #4. Walsh changed the yellow to red. Every crew member was responsible for their personal items, but tools had to be positively inventoried and accounted in and out when used. This prevented not only theft, but FOD as well.

Walsh connected to Diaz and the Sys-Maint div-O, Lt. Leticia Fuller. "Lieutenant, have you verified tool kit number four? I see you signed the inventory as 'all accounted for.'"

Fuller's voice held a slight tremble, though with anger or fear of reprisal Walsh couldn't tell. "Yes, Capitan. There are no missing tools. Here are both attachments labelled as belonging to kit four." Her overlay avatar held up two identical pieces. "I'm pulling the logs for the maintenance printer now, sir. Someone had to have fabricated one of these."

"Agreed," Walsh said. "Fuller, come to my stateroom when you've completed your investigation."

"Yes, Capitan."

Walsh unstrapped and slowly pulled himself out of his station to adjust to the zero-g. "XO, I'll be in my stateroom."

———— ⊬⊣⟋⟋⊢⊬ ————

"LIEUTENANT FULLER IS approaching, Capitan," Hector said.

"Open the hatch, please."

The hatch to the stateroom opened and Lieutenant Fuller drifted in, grabbing an overhead conduit to stop herself. Her lips were pressed tightly together in grim resignation and she stared past him at the bulkhead behind. "Reporting as ordered, sir."

Walsh watched her for a moment before speaking. "I think an adrift piece of inventoried gear warrants a red on the inspection. Not yellow, Lieutenant."

"Yes, sir. When I first found it, I knew it couldn't be what I thought. I had just inventoried the took kits and knew everything was there."

"You were expecting the shake-and-bake?"

"Yes, sir."

Walsh appreciated an officer who knew how to see what was coming and prepare for it. "Who did it?"

"Cadet Midland, sir."

Walsh took a deep breath through his nose. "The senator herself. How long ago?"

"Six weeks, sir." Fuller continued to stare past Walsh, her jaw clenched. "She was doing preventative conduit inspections in hab-Charlie. She didn't check her kit back in until the very end of shift. She fabricated the replacement in Engineering, then checked the tool kit back in."

"Does she know yet?"

"I haven't mentioned it to her, sir. There are a few who know a tool was found though." Fuller paused to pull herself back vertical. "I accept full responsibility, Capitan."

Walsh leaned back and steepled his fingers. "At ease. Please. What do you think we could have done differently?"

"Tool fabrication reports and inventory are forwarded to me daily." Fuller finally looked Walsh in the eyes. "I should have paid closer attention. That report was sent to me. I verified it. It just never registered in my mind as a problem."

"I got the same report."

"You get a lot more reports than I do, sir. That's why I'm supposed to pay attention to mine."

"It's my report, too, Lieutenant. And it's why I'm supposed to pay attention to them. Anything you missed, I missed, too." Walsh unstrapped from his chair and floated above his desk. "I want to see you and Cadet Midland in your dress crimsons posted at my hatch in thirty minutes. Dismissed."

Fuller tensed and stared past Walsh again. "Yes, Capitan."

Walsh watched her float into the main passage. After Fuller had shut the hatch, he pushed over to his locker and opened it. Inside, his bright red uniform was held in place by laundry netting. It was made from durable parade fabric which was nearly wrinkle- and stainproof. The gold filigree of the space fleet ran from the shoulder pads down the sleeves and pant legs. A gold and blue epaulet floated free from the left shoulder of the jacket for his combat command service, the many colored rings around it denoting medals he'd earned in his two decades of service. Small, colored chips lined his right breast. The chips and rings indicated the date earned, the signing admiralty, and the meaning of the award if viewed via the overlay.

Given the space and mass restrictions of spaceships, a spacer only needed two uniforms: a flightsuit and a parade suit. Anything else needed could be printed in short order.

Walsh was sliding the seal shut on the front of the jacket when Hector announced Diaz was approaching. "Let her in."

Diaz drifted in and waited while Walsh fidgeted and tugged at his uniform. "Who was it?" she asked when Walsh turned to her.

"Midland."

"*Dios mio,*" she muttered. "Can we space her yet?"

"I wouldn't be surprised if Fuller showed up to report our wayward cadet accidentally fell out of an airlock."

"Is that an order?"

Walsh smirked. "Not yet."

"What are you going to do?"

Walsh blew out a loud breath. "Midland is definitely a menace." He paused to adjust his epaulet. "Doing stupid things is part of being a cadet, but I can't let her slide on this. And Fuller's good. I'm not going to bake her because Midland has her head up her thruster and tried to pull a fast one."

Walsh looked at the 3D mirror in his overlay. The crimsons looked so good. And they weren't uncomfortable. It would seem pretentious at best, childish at worst, to be the capitan who always wore his dress uniform. Maconez probably had a closetful, just in case his printer failed. Still... maybe he could wear them a little bit more.

He turned and grinned at Diaz, who looked away. "They should be here soon. Unless you want to dress up, too?"

"I'm giving a talk about squadron-level maneuvers. Sorry, Capitan."

"Ooh. Covering the Mag-Star incident? That's one of my favorites."

Diaz pushed off gently towards the hatch. "You talk like it's story time. But yes, I'll be covering that. Good luck with your little cadet."

"What's that supposed to mean?"

"Just that she's a little cadet, Capitan," Diaz said as she drifted through the hatch.

Walsh grunted at her back and waited until Hector announced Fuller and Midland were approaching.

"Lieutenant Fuller is speaking quite harshly to Cadet Midland. Would you like an audio feed?"

"Nope." Walsh rolled his shoulders and took a position floating next to his desk. He made them wait outside his hatch for ten minutes before letting them in. They both needed time to calm down before seeing him.

"Enter."

The hatch opened and Fuller and Midland entered, each taking a hand-hold near the desk. Fuller shot the cadet a final glare before locking eyes forward and staring past Walsh.

Conversely, Midland didn't appear bothered at all. Walsh knew that Fuller had explained in colorful language how much trouble they were both in. It was as if the cadet didn't understand what the big deal was. Or didn't believe she could actually be in trouble.

"Everyone in this compartment wearing a dress uniform is in some hot water." Walsh paused to brush non-existent lint from his shoulder, hoping to point out to Midland what he was wearing. "To start at the top, I put a lieutenant in charge who can't seem to manage her trainees, leading to a—"

"That's not fair," Midland blurted, throwing what little military bearing she had to the Solar winds. "It's my—"

"You will not speak until addressed, Cadet!" Fuller said, keeping her eyes on the bulkhead behind Walsh.

Midland pursed her lips and glanced at Walsh before also staring at the bulkhead.

"Fair, Cadet?" Walsh paused to give Midland a flat stare. "You aren't allowed to use that word again until you have a better understanding of how it applies on this ship. Do you understand?"

"Yes, sir."

Walsh continued to stare at her for a moment, then cut his eyes to Fuller. "Your turn, Lieutenant. Why are you in your dress uniform this fine, fine, space-fleet day?"

"Capitan, I did not ensure my trainee understood the importance of tool control and FOD aboard this ship. Further, I failed to realize this cadet was not ready for the responsibility I delegated to her. Finally, I failed to make sure her work was thoroughly followed up when completed."

Walsh nodded. It was a necessary evil in the chain of command that senior officers were accountable for the actions of their subordinates. There was no way Fuller could be expected to keep track of everything that happened in her division, just as there was no way he could truly be responsible for the actions of an entire crew. Control like that was an illusion. But that's how command worked. And Midland needed to understand what being in a crew really meant.

He looked at Midland again. Her outburst, as misplaced as it was, gave Walsh hope that beneath her usual unimpressed expression, the cadet had at least a gram of contrition. Walsh noticed her uniform was snug in a way that accentuated her curves. Forcing himself to focus on her eyes, he wondered if she'd printed it that way on purpose or if she'd been skipping workouts again.

"Cadet Midland, please tell us why you're posted here in your dress uniform."

Midland started to speak twice before sighing loudly through her nostrils. "I'm here because I lost a tool and tried to cover it up."

"Wrong, Cadet," Walsh said. "You're here because you told a lie that could have killed us all. Covering for each other is what a crew does. If you're sick, someone covers your watch. Lieutenant Fuller covers for her division when the screwups are in house. I cover for this crew when something stupid happens in port. We keep what we can in-ship. But you lied to your ship.

"Your lie not only put your shipmates at risk, it showed a phenomenal lack of character and judgement. I don't suppose you've been through a catastrophic atmospheric evacuation, Cadet Midland. I have. If hatches won't seal because misplaced gear jams it, people die."

A wave of anger suddenly made Walsh's stress monitor ping. This wasn't the first time he'd had to take someone to task, and it wasn't even the worst offense. But for some reason, this cadet had him riled up. Probably because it was his fault that she was there. And everything he said to her really needed to be said to him instead. Walsh cocked his head and drifted a little closer, pausing to take a few breaths.

"I just want to make sure you understand that our standing orders and operations procedures are not some dog-and-pony show we put on for your entertainment or disdain. A spaceship is a complicated, self-contained system. If one things fails, it can start a deadly cascade. Do you understand that, Cadet Midland?"

Midland's lower lip quivered for a split second and she nodded once. "Yes, Capitan. I understand."

Walsh opened up three disciplinary forms in the air for all to see in their overlay. "You will make rounds of every compartment—after your normally scheduled watch—for any FOD. You will also inventory every tool in the Systems Maintenance division at the beginning and end of every watch."

With a swipe of his finger, a red box appeared on Midland's service record. Midland started to speak, but snapped her jaw shut when she glanced over to see Walsh's glare.

"If you understand, acknowledge your record entry," Walsh ordered.

"Yes, sir." A bio-verification checkmark appeared next to the entry.

Walsh waved a finger and a red mark appeared on Fuller's entry. She acknowledged it without being prompted. Midland clenched her jaw.

With a final swish, a red mark appeared on Walsh's record, followed by the green check. Midland's brow raised.

"Are you surprised, Cadet?" Walsh asked, more dramatically than he'd intended. "Did you think what I told you was some kind of joke? Maybe in your world, your mother's world, people get to say they'll take full responsibility and prove it by offering up some junior staffer."

At the mention of her mother, Midland glanced at Walsh.

"That's not how it works in the fleet. The ship's yeoman logs these events and they're copied in archives across the Solar system. Hector and I don't sit around drinking beer and working out deals. We need, *I* need, you to understand that out here your actions affect everyone. Fly together or die together. It's trite, but true. Might be something to consider if you follow in your mother's footsteps. Dismissed, Cadet."

Midland saluted and left.

Once Midland was gone, Lieutenant Fuller cleared her throat. "I think Campbell would be a replacement, Capitan. He's reliable and knows the systems."

"I'm happy where you're at." Walsh floated to his desk and strapped into the chair. "Don't let this get to you. It's impossible to control the people under your command. You could no more stop her than I could have stopped Guterez from trying that damned Coriolis-pissing challenge." He shrugged. "Most of the time all we can do is clean up the mess and move on."

Walsh closed his eyes and rolled his head. A chair unfolded from the desk opposite him. "Have a seat."

Fuller stared uncertainly at the chair until Walsh motioned again for her to sit.

"You're a fine officer, Fuller. I like your style. You're direct and not afraid to take command. That will serve you well if you decide to stay in. This will go in our record and anyone who knows the real score will ignore it." Walsh grinned, hoping to ease the tension in Fuller's face. "The only people who don't have entries like this are those who don't lead."

Fuller returned a dubious smile. "Thank you, sir."

"And because I think you're a good officer, I'm going to offer a little advice if you're interested."

"Please, sir."

"You already know Midland is a senator's daughter. Officers with powerful patrons make their way in the fleet. Thankfully, most are just in for one tour so they can check the veteran box in the polls when they get out. It makes dealing with them, with Midland... challenging.

"At least for someone who wants a career in the fleet. Someone who loves being in space. So first off, no reprisals. That's already fleet policy, but take that very seriously. No smart comments or dog-talking to her or about her. People like the Midlands have a long memory when it comes to people who slighted them. Yet, they quickly forget those who helped them."

Walsh drummed his fingers on the table. Fuller's eyes were downcast despite her stiff chin. "Liberty is a den of eels; they're slimy and they bite. But they also have the keys to the kingdom. Always put the welfare of your ship and crew first, but always deal cautiously with Liberty. If you get Midland—either one—bent out of shape, you might find yourself on the unofficial 'passed by for promotion' list. It sucks vacuum, but there it is."

Fuller took a deep breath. "I wish I knew how far was too far. It shouldn't be that way at all. It shouldn't be about who you know."

"Agreed." Walsh shrugged. "I was doing an attaché stint on Liberty when I was a lieutenant and had to work with someone whose brother was in the congress. That guy was absolutely clueless. But he made commander before me despite almost zero time deployed. He got the cherry assignments and got to work with the rich and famous.

"But I'm glad he got those jobs. I'd rather sweep up the lunar sub-levels. I like it out here. I like being surrounded by a strong hull and a strong crew. And you are strong crew, Lieutenant."

Fuller looked back and smiled. "Thank you, Capitan. You... might want to take your advice with Admiral Maconez."

"Too late for me," Walsh said. "That's why I'm here. Take that as an object lesson. I didn't want this assignment, but it's good to know there are good officers everywhere.

"Oh, and by the way. You might want to run diagnostics on Midland's uniform printer. I think it's out of calibration, if you know what I mean."

Fuller put a hand to her mouth and laughed. "On it."

"Dismissed."

As Fuller was about to go through the hatch, Walsh added, "And keep in mind that Midland might someday make a good officer. Just hold her nose to the grindstone until then."

"Oh, you can count on that, Capitan."

From the tone of Fuller's voice, Walsh was counting on it.

Chapter 12

VORTAN DUGG WATCHED the course projections in virtual space before him. *Amazonas*'s track was beginning to parallel that of the courier, designated A-1 on the display. The tiny courier carrying the spy and stolen QED had no name, only the transponder ID of YXR-153.

He'd given the A-1 designation soberly. MarSec assigned Alpha-level designations only to those targets which had been approved for engagement. When the other officers on board *Schrodinger's Tiger* saw the designation, they knew what it meant.

Tiger was going to show her claws.

With the rendezvous course set by *Amazonas*, it was not clear who'd stolen the QED. That information led to a whole new set of problems. The CAR had been rattling its sabers recently and Dugg feared this was more than a random case of tech theft. He wondered if Capitan Walsh even knew what he was picking up.

"Interception course confirmed, Captain," said the navigation officer.

Dugg pushed off the edge of his desk with his big toe into a slow cartwheel. The intercept was obvious to anyone tracking—as obvious as *Tiger*'s course change to intercept, as well.

"Display our interception envelope and overlay with *Amazonas* and Alpha-1."

A series of new lines appeared, representing *Tiger*'s intercept points based on time and duration of main thruster burn. Dugg watched the projections shift as he cycled through the possible maneuvers *Amazonas* and A-1 might make. Since the QED content couldn't be transmitted, the ships likely intended matching orbits and transferring the stolen goods. Fortunately for Dugg, this limited their maneuvering options further.

Few scenarios had *Tiger* beating *Amazonas* on scene. And those would surely disappear once *Tiger* moved to intercept. Retrieving the QED was no longer an option. MarSec must have realized that, too, leading them to use the Alpha designation. Alpha-1 would have to die before *Amazonas* could recover the target data.

While Dugg considered his limited options, a mission-update flash arrived from MarSec. He scanned it in his implants and pursed his lips. They had escalated the game. *Amazonas* was not Bravo-designated and the mission priority had been classified as "At all costs."

Tiger was now expendable.

Dugg let out a long breath and gently pushed off the bulkhead. There was no way to engage Alpha-1 without *Amazonas* interfering. Though a training ship, it was heavily armed and commanded by someone willing to shoot if threatened. *Tiger* was going to claw and be clawed.

He selected the course that would put Alpha-1 in energy-weapons range for the longest time, damned *Amazonas*. If *Tiger* survived the fly-by, *Amazonas* would have to expend a great deal of delta-v to chase them down. It would take weeks at full burn for *Amazonas* to catch *Tiger*."

Missiles were another story.

Tiger had its own small magazine of missiles, but firing them too soon would definitely put Walsh on alert. If Dugg played it cool, or played dumb, *Amazonas* might not start firing until it was too late to save the courier. Not to mention *Amazonas* probably had some interceptor warheads and might be able to provide protection for A-1.

No, *Tiger* was going face-to-face, toe-to-toe. And MarSec didn't care if she survived.

That wasn't precisely fair. MarSec was concerned about all its assets. But sometimes assets became expendable. At least Dugg wouldn't have to worry about any political fallout if *Tiger* didn't make it.

"Computer, designate CAR *Amazonas* as Bravo-1." Dugg rubbed his chin as the target icon updated. MarSec seemed to be worried about political fallout, however. Bravo designations were not authorized for destruction except in extreme self-defense. He smirked. But there were plenty of other things Dugg *could* do to a Bravo.

Chapter 13

"NO CORRECTION BURN from the *Schrodinger's Tiger*, Capitan," Diaz announced. "Still no replies to our standard auto-warnings either."

Walsh studied the tactical map floating before him in the overlay. Receiving emergency move orders with little or no additional intelligence was irritating, but it wasn't uncommon. For a warship.

These orders smacked of the usual Liberty incompetence. The admiralty and senate either couldn't agree what to do or were in the middle of some political power play. Or both. So they sent the nearest ship, a training ship, to stand on station until they pulled their collective heads out of their collective asses.

Now a Marty warship was racing towards them. They'd detected *Tiger* when she fired her thrusters, but her ECM suite was making it difficult to maintain a firing solution. And according to Hector, the courier they were "rescuing" had recently left Mars. It smelled of SpecOps. Walsh liked SpecOps missions—they could get exciting—but not to the point where spaceships were engaging each other.

Walsh chuckled. "That's funny."

Diaz raised a brow. "*Que?*"

"The name. *Schrodinger's Tiger*. It's funny. You know, playing off Schrodinger's cat, but it's a tiger because it's a stealth warship. Get it?"

"*Si*, Capitan. I get it," Diaz said mirthlessly.

Walsh grinned at her. "While I agree with your dour assessment that their ominous silence is, well, ominous, we can't lose our sense of humor."

"Aye, Capitan," Collins said. "It's even funnier because the Marties aren't known for their humor. Have to give them credit."

"Good point, Ops." Walsh offered a wide smile to cover the nerves twisting his belly. He felt like vomiting. "How long until we're matched with the courier?"

"Forty-seven minutes until we can start docking maneuvers," Collins answered without hesitation. "Sixty-two minutes until the Marty is in nominal weapons range. It's going to be close."

"At least they haven't deployed any drones or submunitions." Walsh drummed his fingers on the arm of his acceleration couch. "Comms, send a connect request to *Tiger* actual from *Amazonas* actual."

The cadet manning the comm station did a fair job of keeping her voice steady. "Connection ready, Capitan. Audio only."

Walsh cast Diaz a quick glance before swiping his finger through the air. "Mars ship *Schrodinger's Tiger*, this is Capitan Eugene Walsh commanding the Confederation battle cruiser *Amazonas*. Please respond."

The reply came long seconds later. "Battle cruiser, Capitan? Disingenuity is never a healthy way to start a relationship. This is Captain Vortan Dugg. How can I help you?"

"Captain Dugg, we're in the middle of rescue operations and I'm afraid your velocity and flight path may interfere. Please maneuver to a safe distance as agreed by common navigational accords."

Walsh couldn't see Dugg's face, but he could hear the smile in his tone.

"As it turns out, Capitan, that ship is harboring a terrorist fleeing MarSec. It is in fact your ship that is interfering with our investigation and arrest operation. I would invite the *Amazonas* to maneuver to a safe distance. To avoid the possibility of any collateral damage. Desperate criminals can do desperate things."

Walsh smirked. "Speaking of being disingenuous, Captain Dugg, you can't even arrest your own ship with the fly-by course you're on. But we'll be happy to detain the crew on behalf of MarSec and deposit them at the nearest CAR ambassadorial station to begin extradition hearings.

"If your own trajectory allowed it, I might even consider handing them over to you. As a goodwill gesture."

"I appreciate your offer of goodwill, but I'm afraid MarSec can't accept the flight risk this terrorist poses. Please don't interfere with our legal enforcement operation. You are dealing with a dangerous criminal, Eugene.

"I will have to take any interference as an act of hostility against the people of Mars. Dugg out."

"Understood, Captain. Walsh out."

"I don't like the sound of that," Diaz said.

"Me neither," Walsh agreed. He gave a low whistle. "We need to play this one carefully. Operations, listen up. Liberty has authorized the use of weapons if needed for this rescue mission."

Two change-of-station status notifications flashed in Walsh's overlay. Two cadets had changed from duty to observation mode.

Walsh spoke loudly. "Why are you abandoning your stations, Cadets?"

The two cadets, one manning an engineering station and the other a tactical station, looked at each other, but said nothing.

"Answer the capitan," Diaz said harshly.

"I just thought..." one cadet finally answered, turning over his shoulder to face Walsh. "Well, I'm just a cadet and this isn't training."

"It's always training, Cadet," Walsh said. "We've been running drills for this engagement for days. This is why we drilled—so you would know what to do. You'll man your stations and follow your orders. This is exactly why we do cadet cruises. Focus on your training and we'll be fine. Now, man your station."

The cadets turned back to their stations. "Yes, Capitan."

Diaz spoke over Walsh's private channel. "I'm not sure that's a good idea."

Walsh grinned. "Everyone needs their first time, XO. Pass the word to all divisions that the cadets are to man the stations."

"*Si*, Capitan."

Walsh let out a breath and waited as the engagement envelope solidified. *Tiger*'s icon approached the last point where it could break off and end this game of chicken.

"Capitan," Collins said, "the target is maneuvering."

Walsh watched the navigation plots update. *Tiger*'s course would bring it well within weapons range of the courier and *Amazonas*. "Looks like Captain Dugg is serious. XO, call all hands to shield stations."

"All hands to shield stations," Diaz announced over the ship-wide channel. "All hands to shield stations. Section one, go."

Walsh stood and half of the crew in Ops followed. His heart was pounding and he forced himself to move quickly, but carefully.

Ops was the closest compartment to the conveyor shaft and Walsh was the first on. There would be many nervous hands below him, so he decided not to climb while the conveyor moved them to the core.

At the top of the shaft, he swung around and pushed off towards the crypt. He landed with ease and glanced over his shoulder to realize his mistake. Everyone behind him tried to follow his example instead of what they'd trained to do—him first of all.

Cadets and junior officers were in various states of free fall in seemingly random directions. He was glad to see that at least some were using the handholds as they were supposed to. Walsh grabbed a wayward cadet as he drifted by and bounced him to the deck harder than he'd intended.

"Thank you, sir," the cadet said before scurrying towards his station.

"Dammit," he muttered. "Hector, flash the crew to stop jumping! Use the handholds, people."

Another cadet sped by, too fast for Walsh to risk grabbing. He stared and realized it was Cadet Midland. Shaking his head, he winced as she bounced off the outer pressure hull and spun back towards the core.

"*Dios mio*," Diaz said over the command channel.

There was nothing for Walsh to do so he gritted his teeth, pulled himself into his station, and strapped in. "Section one, secure your floater shipmates. Section two, go as section one comes on station. XO, get our floaters we miss, please."

It took over seven minutes for the final Ops duty station to be fully manned, and over ten minutes for the last floater—Cadet Midland—to get strapped in.

Walsh tugged at his beard. He'd grown comfortable watching the cadets train, forgetting that, regardless how well they might score, they were all still space-cherries. Some of the junior staff were, too. But he wasn't a space-cherry and he'd been the first to screw up.

Why the hell had Liberty sent them to face a Marty warship?

"XO, spin down and stow the habitat arms for combat."

The whine of the spin-down was louder in the crypt, being closer to the machinery. Walsh left the rest of the procedure to Diaz and the Ops-O.

"Tactical, deploy drone squadron one for a close-escort sortie to cover the courier. Point defense only."

"Roger that, Capitan," answered Lt. Cmdr. Ollie Moore. "I suggest picket drones, too."

Moore was another combat veteran. Despite Walsh's earlier speech about cadets manning the stations, he was glad she was the one answering the comms. "Negative, Tac-O. I don't want to escalate any more than necessary. I'm still hoping the *Tiger* will be satisfied with a sufficiently threatening fly-by."

Bovree laughed over the channel. "'A sufficiently threatening fly-by.' Oh, I love that one. Can I steal that, Capitan?"

"Sure. And I know where you can stow that data."

Bovree chuckled again, but said nothing. Walsh was about to order Moore to make all laser batteries ready, but saw the row of green lights on the combat management screen.

"Ops, Security." Bovree wasn't chuckling now. "Spike in tac-hack attempts; firewall shows zero intrusions. But they're serious."

Walsh was glad for the updates to their cyber warfare at Ganymede; tactical hacking techniques were impossible to keep up with completely, but every little bit helped. Dugg had just fired the first shot. It looked like he wouldn't be satisfied with a sufficiently threatening fly-by after all.

"Sec-O, initiate counter-tac-hack."

"Drone squadron one on station," Diaz said.

"Roger that, XO. Ops, let's get the docking finished and rescue our man." Walsh drummed his fingers. *Amazonas* was as buttoned-up and ready as they could make her. "And now we wait."

THE CYBER-WARFARE OFFICER'S voice came over Dugg's implants. "Captain, we have seed acknowledgment from the intrusion-ware."

A long smile snaked its way across Vortan Dugg's face. He was relieved none of the officers could see the blatant relief in that smile. Over the last three days of approach, running simulation after simulation, the only option with an appreciable chance of destroying A-1 was a high-speed suicide run. The suicide part had troubled him. Dugg was not afraid to die in the line of duty, even if MarSec sent him in blindly—or stupidly. But he wasn't going to throw his life away. Now that the intrusion software was in *Amazonas*, Dugg entertained a glimmer of hope.

"There's some good news. Are those drones still in position around Alpha-1?"

"Yes, Captain. They are in a standard point-defense formation. The *Amazonas* hasn't deployed any additional munitions, though their target designators are active."

Dugg considered the virtual map before him. *Tiger* would barely be in laser battery range as the other two ships approached docking. Docking in deep space was slow work and considerably reduced their maneuverability if they were going to transfer any cargo. It would give Dugg time to possibly reduce collateral damage; now that he had a hope of survival, he didn't want to provoke Walsh into vengeance. Visions of medals replaced visions of obituaries.

"Capitan Walsh," Dugg said into the comm. "You are aiding and abetting a known terrorist by placing CAR military drones around that ship. You will be wholly responsible for any damage suffered during our arrest operation."

"Any damage to CAR assets from your actions will be considered an open act of hostility," Walsh answered after a moment. "They are deployed in support of our rescue operation."

Dugg cut the channel. He returned to studying the tactical display. Rings of various colors denoted the effective engagement zones of each ship in the scenario. At least *Amazonas* still hadn't deployed further munitions. Hopefully, she wouldn't do so before they triggered the intrusion-ware. Running the time projections forward and back, Dugg marked a red attack waypoint on *Tiger's* course and shared the update with his officers.

"Now we wait," he said to no one in particular.

"POSITIVE SEAL ON DOCKING tube," Lieutenant Collins reported over the ops channel.

Walsh stood in overlay, watching the rendered image of the tube extending from *Amazonas* to the courier. The magnified icon of the Mars ship continued to approach. It was well within the translucent sphere that indicated the ship was in *Amazonas*'s targeting envelope.

Walsh's heart pounded and he dulled his stress response via the overlay's medical interface. Only enough to keep his fear from impeding his reasoning. If he made a mistake now, he couldn't blame panic.

Dugg was up to something, Walsh knew that. Nothing in the intel file suggested the Marty was reckless. Marties were tricky, and sometimes crazy, but they weren't stupid. *Amazonas* outgunned *Tiger* by a good margin, even if the weapon computers were manned by nervous cadets.

Spouts of glittering plasma erupted from the courier's hull just above the docking tube connection. The tube twisted and jerked before flying free, pulling a section of the courier's airlock with it. Red flashes ringed Walsh's peripheral vision, followed by the ship's klaxon.

"The *Tiger*'s firing!" Moore said in a high-pitched, wavering voice. "Photon spikes detected."

"Damn." Walsh's voice was steadier, thanks to his overlay control and an overwhelming sense of disbelief. Maybe Maconez was right—a lot of people wanted to shoot Walsh. He didn't need a beef with Mars, too. It would be better to declaw *Tiger* instead of killing her, if possible. "Target laser batteries and targeting systems only. Set laser six to point defense, just in case. Set drone squadron to shield the courier from direct fire."

"Roger, Capitan." Moore's voice was calmer now. "Engaging. What the hell?"

Walsh opened the ship status screen next to him with the snap of a finger. "What is it, Tac-O?"

Then he saw it before she could answer: all of the weapon systems were flashing red with a flag reading "System Unavailable."

"What the hell?" Walsh parroted. No one answered. Another plume of sparks and debris erupted from the hull of the courier, sending hull plates and the remains of an antenna cluster spinning into the darkness.

The overlay tactical display flickered twice before disappearing. Walsh blinked several times as his brain struggled with the unexpected transition to real vision. The starfield was replaced with the claustrophobic view of the inside of his station.

"Cap-cap-caaaapppiiii..." Hector's voice modulated through a series of high-pitched squeals before breaking up into a staccato of digitized bleating. A heavy silence hung in Ops when the voice spouted a string of warbled gibberish and cut out completely.

A prickle ran from the skin beneath Walsh's beard and up his scalp as he realized what Dugg had done.

"We're hacked!" he, Diaz, and Bovree called out in unison. The backup comm channel was designed to survive hard EMP hits and was hardwired. That it required no intelligent computer to run also made it nearly impossible to hack.

"Reboot of laser array one, no good," Moore said. The sound of her fingers tapping against the station's physical station echoed over the comm. "Same with two and five. They've got us jammed up tight, Capitan."

The feeling of hatred—and helplessness—Walsh had towards cyber-intrusion warfare was probably similar to those field commanders who found their spearmen facing rifles or the wet Navy captains suddenly facing aircraft. He understood—especially now—the importance of cyber warfare, but it felt dirty and cowardly to him. Starship combat should be about using missiles and lasers to blow each other apart, not tricking an enemy's computer into deactivating the life-support system. Which was an easy-enough opinion to hold, being the commander of the more heavily armed ship.

But Dugg was no coward. He was flying a smaller ship straight into *Amazonas*'s reach. WIth guile and finesse, the Marty had tied Walsh's hands.

The sentiments were worse than foolish. War evolved and the combatants either evolved with it or died. Lamenting the ignoble gun hadn't stopped the tides of change. The spearmen became riflemen. Those that didn't weren't around to build spacecraft.

Walsh reached out and activated his station's terminal panel. The display was standard fleet size, but when he opened the ship status screen, it seemed too small to read compared to what he was used to in the overlay. Walsh gritted his teeth and forced himself to take a long breath. They'd have to do more drills without their overlay. If they had the opportunity. "Security, status."

"It's just a screamer," Bovree said. "But it's in deep and it's noisy. It obviously has the overlay interface down, as well as the Combat Management System. The buffering is starting to spread and I can't nail it down. We might have to power down components one at a time and see when it stops making all that racket."

A flash of light on the display caught Walsh's attention. He expanded the display in time to see more fire dancing along the hull of the courier. A spray of debris and gas confirmed to Walsh a hull breach and subsequent decompression. If *Tiger* were more heavily armed, the courier would already be cut into scrap. That was likely to happen anyway without *Amazonas* online to defend it.

A spark shot into the dark and two of the escort drones went red in the squadron display. Mars had now destroyed CAR assets. If he'd been able, Walsh would have felt safe returning fire without worry of repercussion. Except for Maconez being a complete ass.

But *Amazonas* drifted helplessly. At least the drones had deflected one attack. It wasn't enough. Even though *Tiger* was doing a high-speed pass, it was obvious there was no way the courier would survive. The mission had changed, as they all do. He couldn't save the courier, but the ship wasn't really what the admiralty was after. *Amazonas* required his full attention at the moment, though.

"Diaz."

"*Si*, Capitan?"

"Get that agent off the courier."

Diaz hesitated. "What? How?"

"Work it out, *Amazonica*."

Chapter 14

"JUST DO SOMETHING?" Diaz muttered. What was she supposed to do? Send some hapless cadets over while the Marty was still streaming photons towards them? Comms with the courier were down, and she didn't know if it was the hacking or the tiny ship's antenna array being sheared off by the attack. And she wasn't concerned. Not about the courier. Not about the agent. Cmdr. Felicia Diaz was only concerned about *Amazonas* and her crew.

But that wasn't her concern now, according to Senior Capitan.

"Just do something." She flipped through the tactical and ship status screens, hoping a solution would present itself. *Tiger* was focusing on the courier, but what would Captain Dugg do if Diaz used *Amazonas* as a shield? The Marty would likely escalate, especially since *Amazonas* was currently defenseless. A flight of missiles from *Tiger* could rip the larger ship apart. And Diaz wasn't sure the ship could maneuver in her current state, anyway.

"Just do something."

The boarding tube was useless. The courier's airlock was slag; the rescue tube could not be attached. Diaz winced as one of the courier's external tanks ruptured. The venting gas introduced a slow wobble to the ship.

"Never make important decisions when you're too close, *Conejita*," her grandmother often told her. Gran was usually right about things. If only Diaz had known it, had believed, she wouldn't have stupidly run with Branco Lavato, doing petty crimes and pretending to be hard asses. Doing many other stupid things. Stupid kids doing stupid kid things.

Diaz zoomed the tactical display out until the rapidly closing icon for *Schrodinger's Tiger* came into view. Another drone swarming around the courier blinked red as an enemy laser burned it away. She watched the drones obediently trying to act as shields.

Drones.

Diaz selected the secondary backup channel. "Fuller."

"Go, XO."

"I need four EVA maintenance bots and three other operators."

"Yes, ma'am," Fuller answered tightly. "But we can't direct them."

"Set them up for hardwire control," Diaz said. "Like during radiation ops."

"The capitan has all of my crew on standby to start physically powering down equipment to kill the screamer."

Walsh broke in. "Give the XO two, Maint-O."

"Roger that," Fuller said. "Brown and Mendoza are on channel."

Diaz let out a long breath. "Very good. Brown, Mendoza, set three drones to hardwire flight and patch them to our stations. We're going for a little ride."

The squadron of three repair bots raced towards the courier as fast as their tiny thrusters allowed. The added weight of the connected wire slowed them further. These drones were designed for external repairs on *Amazonas*, not rescue missions. Diaz hoped the courier was close enough for this to work.

The defending tactical drone evaporated in a shower of sparks just as Diaz latched her bot to the courier's hull. Looking through the bot's camera, she could see the external plating was superheated in places and venting atmosphere through a myriad of gashes from *Tiger*'s lasers. The airlock looked even worse up close. The United Isles weren't getting this ship back.

"Those guys are toasted," Brown said.

Diaz ignored the comment and issued orders. "Brown, cut here. Mendoza, here. I'll cut along this panel. We're trying to get inside. Watch for flammables or pressurized systems. We don't have time for someone to go flying off."

Three fountains of sparks erupted along the courier's hull as the repair bots' laser cutters went to work. Tiny molten globules drifted away into the void, looking like stars for a second before winking out.

Diaz cursed as the nose of the tiny ship disappeared in a blinding flash like a fatal sneeze. So much for the pilots. Maybe for their agent, too.

Brown made a final, sparkling cut and pulled a section of plating from the hull with the bot's arms. Diaz piloted her bot through, followed by Brown.

"Careful," Diaz said. "Don't get the lines tangled."

A flash illuminated the darkened interior, reminding Diaz of the old vids with haunted houses and lightning storms.

"I'm off-line," Mendoza said. "They got me."

A figure in a bulky spacesuit was flailing his arms in the short passage ahead of them. Diaz guided her bot forward and it hesitated when the control cable snagged on something. She knew the courier was slowly tumbling, forcing more and more cable out to keep the maintenance drone from being reeled back out. There was no time to worry about exactly how much cable was available.

The figure looked up and saw the drones. Terror washed across the man's face and he flailed all the more. He pushed and pulled against nearby pipes and conduits, one of which had ruptured and was spraying blue coolant, but couldn't move.

"He's freaking out," Brown said.

Diaz pushed her bot closer. "He doesn't know which side we're on."

The man's legs were trapped in a hatch that had been twisted by some internal explosion. Diaz directed Brown to help, but their bots didn't have the power or leverage to twist the door.

Diaz clasped the spacesuit's helmet carefully and extended the bot's vibrophone to the visor. The face inside was the one she'd seen in the mission briefing. Gelp. Diaz sighed with relief.

"Do you have it?"

Gelp's voice was tinny and hard to understand through the vibrophone. He slapped his chest twice. "In my suit. Here! My legs are stuck. And probably broken."

"We'll get you." Diaz withdrew the vibrophone and latched the bot on the bulkhead next to the hatch.

"That's a vacuum-rated hatch," Brown said. "It'll take a minute."

"Let's get started then." Diaz spun her drone to cut at one set of hinges while Brown started at the other. "Don't burn a hole in his suit!"

It was slow going. Gelp was in a near panic and kept trying to grab the bots. He nearly lost a hand—and his life—when he reached out towards one of the cutters. Diaz smacked him on the helmet with a manipulator.

The regular command channel was still buzzing like a swarm of hornets. They hadn't purged the cyber intrusion yet. On the backup circuit, Walsh was discussing a full system reboot with Bovree, Collins, and Fuller. Not her problem at the moment.

Another flash filled the passageway and the bot's onboard inertial monitor indicated it had been shaken about severely.

"Shit," Brown said. "I'm out. Didn't even see what happened."

"You're out of time," Walsh said curtly on Diaz's backup channel.

Diaz panned her camera. She was almost done with the first hinge, but Brown's bot had been speared by a jagged length of conduit. Sizzling light from shorted batteries and capacitor units sparked, illuminating the bot's ruined interior.

The door had crumpled in the last attack, completely crushing Gelp's legs. His arms floated in front of him, unmoving. Worse yet, the bot was reporting a constant spin. Diaz was out of time.

"*Dios mio,*" she whispered. There was no way to get the door free in time with Brown's bot destroyed.

"Too close, *Conejita,*" she heard her grandmother say again.

Diaz felt her stomach clench. There was no way to get the man free—in one piece. And the man wasn't the primary goal, anyway. She unlatched her bot from the bulkhead and clutched one of Gelp's legs in each of the bot's claws. Diaz almost vomited when the body shifted away from the legs as if they were boneless; they had been completely crushed in the suit. Gelp started convulsing and pummeling the bot.

She could see the man's silent scream through his helmet's visor. "Sorry, *mijo.*"

With one sweep of the laser cutter, Gelp's legs detached. A cloud of blood spurted from the suit and Diaz saw the gore-slicked nubs of bone protruding from the suit legs still trapped in the hatch. Never before having cut someone apart with a laser cutter, she could only hope it had cauterized Gelp's wounds. The blood might only be from his legs being crushed, which was still horrible. A quivering globule of blood stuck to the bot's camera lens.

As long as she got the item, where Gelp had slapped his chest.

The bot retained the relative spin of the damaged courier and the control cable was beginning to snag on the wreckage. Diaz did her best to untangle it as she flew, but couldn't afford to release either of Gelp's leg-stumps to use the bot's manipulators. *Tiger*'s last barrage had at least cut a bigger hole for her in the hull.

Gelp had finally quit thrashing, and Diaz hoped he'd just passed out.

When Diaz fired the final thruster to clear the hull, something struck her pod. A thruster flashed a concerned, yellow "Failure" icon on her display. The other thrusters sluggishly attempted to respond to her auto-align command.

"There she goes," Collins announced on the standby.

Diaz tried rotating the bot's camera to see the courier, but her bot was still spinning out of control. The doomed ship drifted in and out of her camera view. She saw the final two flashes against the hull and the internal ignition that silhouetted the wreck. On the next pass, three twisted sections of the courier spun slowly away from each other.

She felt sorry for the pilots. The void was unforgiving, even more so than the sea. She knew that better than most.

Just before the image of the ship's dark remains crept out of the camera's view, Diaz saw a black piece of shrapnel fill the view. The pod shuddered and spun in the other direction before the camera cut out. More warning lights flashed on the bot's display. Diaz hadn't had time to read them before the whole display grayed out to be replaced with a red "Off-line."

"*Mierda*." She'd done all she could. "Brown, Mendoza. Wire up two more and recover my recovery bot. We need it in the barn ASAP." Diaz minimized the bot feeds and keyed into the main backup channel.

"Ten minutes at least for a full system restore," Fuller said. "We have a new golden copy backup after Ganymede, so it should go no problem."

Moore spoke next. "And if we go off-line for ten minutes, the Marty might decide to take a piece of us, too."

"We're already effectively off-line," Collins said.

Walsh broke in. "Bovree, what are the chances there's a wormhole or spike tucked away that will just reactivate after we boot?"

"Very low if we do the full restore," Bovree said. "All the registers and configuration stacks get rebuilt from scratch. I think we're just dealing with a kick-ass screamer. Just keep in mind we'll lose all of our targeting and navigation data, too. We'll have to recompile them after the restore completes."

Amazonas could work up firing solutions quickly, but they'd been tracking *Tiger* for weeks and that would be a lot of lost data. This Dugg character had gone out of his way not to target *Amazonas* directly and Diaz hoped Walsh realized that.

But she knew the admiralty would have her and Walsh for breakfast, while condemning the Marties out of the other side of their mouths.

Diaz could imagine Admiral Banks saying, "Yes, quite a shame what happened. Especially since that Marty got away without a scratch. This will definitely make a good case study. Be sure you've taken good notes, Diaz."

She glanced at the drone screen and saw that her bot, still clasping Gelp's limp body, was being taken towards *Amazonas*. At least there was a chance of pulling this objective off—if *Tiger* didn't decide to vaporize Gelp.

"It's the number three fire-control computer," an unfamiliar voice said over the channel.

"Sound off," Walsh said. "Who said that?"

"Sorry, Capitan. This is Mahoney. I've been absorbing the feeds. I think it's number three."

Moore didn't bother masking her skepticism. "How can you know that?"

"It is a guess," Mahoney said, a touch of levity in his voice.

"A good guess?" Walsh asked.

"A pretty good guess, I guess, Capitan."

"Fuller, get on it. Disconnect FC comp three from the network. And get that golden backup ready if it doesn't work."

"They've stopped firing," Collins said.

"Only until they realize we've got someone," Diaz said. "If they decide to fire at our agent before we get him inside, we've failed."

A row of green lights lit up Diaz's screen. The weapons were online. Other systems were also blinking ready.

Walsh spoke over the main comms, relief flooding his voice. "Tac-O, target the Marty's laser arrays. We want to disarm them, not breach their hull. Full ECM suite and fire-control lidars. I don't expect it, but set array six on point defense again, just in case."

Diaz switched between watching the drones and tactical display for the next two minutes until Moore reported in. "The *Tiger*'s buttoned-up its remaining laser turrets and is turning away."

Cheers came over the command channel.

"Shall I send a few chasers to make sure they know better next time?" Moore's voice sounded cheerful now that her weapons were working.

"Negative, Tac-O," Walsh said. "This one's over. Diaz, status."

A grin broke across her face as she watched the maintenance drones touch down in the cargo bay. Her drone looked as if it had been nearly cut in half. Globules of blood were trailing from Gelp's limp, legless spacesuit.

"I'm not sure about our friend. But I think we have the package."

Diaz could hear the smile in Walsh's voice. "Damn fine job, XO. Damn fine job."

Despite herself, Diaz smiled back.

Chapter 15

WALSH LOOKED AT HIS image projected by the holo-mirror into the overlay. The left shoulder bar still seemed crooked so he rolled his shoulders and tugged his sleeve. Now the right shoulder was off. He jerked on the bottom edge of his tunic until they both looked even. Walsh twirled his finger and cast a critical eye on his projection from every direction.

Not even his appreciation of the dress reds—and how good he looked in them—cheered him. When he saw his well-formed backside, all he could think of was how much of it was going to get chewed off.

This was the end of his career.

"Hector, don't announce me. And tell the XO to make ready."

"Yes, Capitan."

Walsh opened his mouth wide to work out the tension from clenching his teeth all morning. He wanted to work up a string of profanity that would have made his granny proud, but there was no point. There was no changing what was, and there was no honor in anger.

The holo-mirror image blinked away with a snap of Walsh's fingers and he stepped into the passage from his cabin. He heard Commander Diaz fall in behind from Ops. The galley was only a few long strides away. With a final deep breath, he stepped through. Before his foot touched the deck, Fuller announced, "Capitan on deck!"

The galley had been cleared out for the occasion but was still crowded. The entire Systems Maintenance division was standing at attention, shoulder to shoulder in their dress reds. Fuller stood front and center of the formation.

Walsh glanced over his shoulder as Diaz shut the hatch behind them. He hated that she, too, stood at attention in her gold-trimmed reds. If not for her, the entire mission would have been a failure. But there were no excuses for the CO. No excuses for the XO. No excuses for the div-O. The chain of command was a cruel mistress, asking only "What have you done for me lately?"

Diaz marched forward, did an about-face, and stared forward past Walsh.

He paced up and down the front rank, not looking at anyone yet. There was a hint of confusion on some of their faces. They knew they were in trouble, but didn't know why. Hadn't they won?

Walsh understood their confusion. It was clear enough to him, though. And he'd make it clear to them, too, in a moment. But it shouldn't be. It shouldn't have happened this way.

A final turn brought him face-to-face with Fuller. She knew. He could read it in her face.

"Everyone assembled here in these beautiful crimson tuxedos is in trouble." Walsh felt the urge to go full drill instructor. But it was Cmdr. Eugene Walsh he wanted to scream at. As is so common in the human condition, he was the author of his own misery.

"The shameful negligence of this division and its chain of command left the *Tres Grande* vulnerable—helpless, in fact—to a Marty attack. If the *Schrodinger's Tiger* had wanted, she could have cut us to ribbons. She could have cut away every square centimeter of the outer hull and superstructure. She could have left us stuck drifting in our stations with our collective thumbs stuck up our collective asses.

"The crew of the United Isles courier died because we were unable to defend her or ourselves." Walsh almost added the injury to a CAR agent, but not everyone was supposed to know about that. "We did get enough DNA after the fact for identification, though. So at least we can give that to their families."

Pacing again, he scanned the line of faces. Their jaws were set and perspiration glistened on a few foreheads and upper lips. One female cadet's eyes were wet. At least they were taking it seriously. Most of them, anyway.

He stopped in front of Cadet Midland and glared down at her. She wore her usual look of highborn unconcern. After a moment of Walsh's scrutiny, her expression changed to bemused discomfort.

It was the closest he'd ever come to punching one of his crew in the mouth.

"Security update 2359-12 was supposedly implemented while we were at Ganymede station. The PLM-12 network interface units in the main targeting computers were identified by fleet security to have a cyber-intrusion vulnerability. They were *supposed* to be replaced with PLM-27s. The unit in targeting computer three was never replaced."

Midland's eyes went wide. She knew now.

He believed in praising in public, punishing in private. But he'd already tried that with Midland. This was a chance to impress on the other cadets and staff why everyone needed to take their jobs seriously.

Walsh flung the maintenance form to Midland's overlay. "I have a bioprint here stating it was changed. Is this your print, Cadet Midland?"

"Yes, Capitan," she said without hesitation.

Walsh shook his head. Surely she wasn't some Marty saboteur. Was she lazy? A pathological liar? Could she be so careless or clueless? Even if she was an empty-headed debutante, she wasn't stupid. Her scores were above average in most areas. And average in the academy was well above the standard of the citizens.

Unless Mama Midland had worked out a deal with Baby Midland's academy instructors. One similar to the deal she'd made with Walsh. He shook his head again and moved in front of Fuller.

Midland deserved to be publicly dressed down. Maybe even keelhauled in space. He hated to do it to Fuller, but she should have known better. And she knew it. Fuller looked like she'd bitten into a lemon.

Walsh flung the form into Fuller's overlay. "Is this your print, Lieutenant?"

"Yes, Capitan."

"Lieutenant Fuller, you are relieved as Systems Maintenance div-O."

"Yes, Capitan," Fuller whispered.

Walsh looked over Fuller's shoulder. "Lieutenant Brown, you are acting division officer."

Brown hesitated. "Yes, Capitan."

When no one moved for a moment, Diaz stepped forward. "Brown, post. Fuller, fall in."

When Brown and Fuller had switched places, Walsh stepped back so he could see everyone. "This division will not sleep until every damned nut and screw on *Amazonas* is confirmed to be security compliant."

He was glad not to hear a single moan or whine. "Brown, since the last div-O was not able to, you will personally verify every maintenance action signed off by Cadet Midland since she reported aboard."

"Yes, Capitan."

Walsh nodded to Diaz.

Diaz stepped next to Walsh and did an about-face. "Cadet Midland, stand fast. Everyone else, dismissed."

Walsh, Diaz, and Midland stood at attention as the division filed out of the galley, keeping its distance as if the three to remain carried the plague. Brown closed the hatch behind him.

Silence hung heavy in the galley for a moment before Diaz spoke. "Cadet Midland, post!"

Midland marched in front of Walsh and stood at attention. A tear rolled down her cheek.

Walsh looked at her and grunted. "Cadet Midland. If I could revoke your appointment, I would do so immediately. As it stands, only a formal admiralty inquiry can do that. But I will not have you touching my ship again. You have proven yourself untrustworthy and dishonest. I had hoped you might take to heart our 'fly together or die together' motto. I had hoped something might be made of you. But I was wrong. And because I was wrong, two pilots are dead and we were at the mercy of a hostile ship.

"Cadet, you are hereby relieved of all duties, qualifications, and responsibilities on this ship. You will remain confined to your quarters except for trips to the head and the galley. You will not speak to or interact with other personnel except as directed by your superior officers. You will remain in confinement until such time as we return to Liberty Station, whereupon you will be transferred to their custody until your mommy can work something out."

A tight sob escaped Midland and a tear rolled down her other cheek.

"XO, escort Midland to her quarters and have Hector repeal all of her access and security permissions. Now get the hell off my damned deck, Cadet. Dismissed." Walsh watched them leave. Around the corner, Midland broke into sobs. Diaz gave a sharp answer he couldn't quite make out. When he could not longer hear them, Walsh went to his cabin.

He hadn't meant to lose his temper. And the cut about Midland's mommy was uncalled for—especially given his own duplicity. Thinking about it only served to spin him up more. The outburst had not been satisfying in any regard. It was the way commanders he disdained acted.

Midland was getting what she deserved. What he would have done to any other cadet the first time. He hoped she got dumped in a low-g prison wing. Liberty would never allow one of their own to suffer such disgrace, but a capitan could dream. When they got back to Liberty, he was the one going into the brig, not the good cadet.

"The XO is approaching, Capitan," Hector said.

"Let her in." Walsh unfolded his desk and took a seat as Diaz entered. "That could have gone better."

Diaz smirked. "*Si, el toro.* I still say she needs to be tossed."

The QED was warm in Walsh's palm. "We have this because of you, Felicia. You saved this mission. I wonder what's on it."

"Wondering about that kind of thing will get you in trouble," she said. "Especially if Liberty was desperate enough to send us."

"I was thinking the same thing." Walsh slipped the QED back into the capitan's safe and locked it. "I've recommended you for command after I'm relieved at Liberty. For whatever good my recommendations will do. I'm not even counting on keeping my pension at this point." Walsh grinned up at Diaz.

"Don't look for tomorrow's trouble today." Diaz stepped closer to the desk but ignored the proffered chair. "There's going to be too much fallout in every direction to know where the senate will land. You're just as likely to get promoted."

"I know where Maconez will land. But if I do get promoted, my recommendation stands."

"Even if it meant staying on Liberty."

Walsh gave a rueful smile. "Needs of the fleet, XO." The thought of another tour at Liberty with all of its ridiculous senators and admirals gave him stomach cramps. The only thing worse than a sniveling captain was a sniveling admiral. "Maybe I could get a billet in the academy. And if you get the CO's assignment for *Amazonas*, I could still be your boss. Wouldn't that be fun?"

Diaz looked mortified. "Bite your tongue, Capitan. If I'm made capitan, this will be a full-fledged warship, cadets or not. No more kiddie cruises for her. I'll make her a true warrior."

"I didn't realize you had such a romantic side, XO." Walsh's grin slipped away. "What do you think about Fuller?"

Diaz shrugged. "It's hard to be strapped with a complete *mamon* like Midland. How long do you plan on keeping her down?"

"Not long. Midland's a turd, but some of that's on Fuller because she *knew* Midland was a turd. I'm hoping that by smacking her hand now, the admiralty won't feel the need to punish her, given what happened." Walsh held his hands up. "We'll just have to see. How's our agent doing?"

"Still in medical freeze. Doc thinks he'll live, but between vacc exposure and blood loss, he thought it'd be best to keep him in a frozen coma until we get back."

Walsh glanced at the safe and blew out a long breath. "That was a close one. Whatever is on that thing must be hot if we pulled out a deep agent and MarSec authorized shooting."

"I'll keep my speculation to myself, Capitan."

"Duly chastised." Walsh motioned towards Diaz's dress uniform with a wave of his hand. "You can dress down, by the way."

"I like the reds. They add a certain flair to Ops, don't you think?" She smirked and glanced down at him. "Besides, I don't get to wear them as often as you do."

Walsh pursed his lips. "I think you can take your flair somewhere else, thank you. Start by taking it to Ops and see if the hazard beacon has been set by the wreckage yet. Dismissed."

Diaz marched from his stateroom with a barely concealed smile.

Walsh shook his head. At least she had some sense of humor. He opened up the forms for the incident write-ups in his overlay and got busy. What he really wanted to do was step away into his virtual painting. But the admiralty was going to crawl up his thruster with a nanoscope and it wouldn't look good for him to be playing when he had work to do.

An hour into deciding on the best ambiguous wordplays to use on the reports, Hector forwarded a priority message from Liberty Station. "From Senator Midland, Capitan."

Dear Commander Walsh,

I look forward to speaking to you about my daughter's career opportunities in the fleet when you arrive at Liberty Station. Admiral Sykes assures me that while the Amazonas *is docked, we should have time to meet.*

Kindly,

Senator Marina Midland

Heat rose up Walsh's cheeks. Cadet Midland's incompetence had gone well beyond the stereotypical VIP's brat looking for another "x" on their political checklist. She had put the ship and the entire crew in danger. And her mother wanted to discuss more opportunities. And let's not forget to name-drop Sykes in there.

He immediately wrote up a reply that detailed the complete idiocy of the senator's daughter, suggesting the senator herself should be brought up on sedition charges for knowingly putting Cadet Midland in the fleet.

Then he deleted it and wrote another filled with snide innuendo about what the senator had to do to get her retarded daughter into the academy to start with. He deleted that one, too, wrote a list of singularly unflattering words to describe the cadet and signed it, "Love, Eugene—still alive no thanks to you."

Walsh chuckled and made sure everything he'd written had been deleted. Having worked out most of his bitterness, he set to writing a more reasoned, more adult reply. He assured her it wasn't personal, that it was merely a matter of safety for the crew. Then he tried appealing to her sense of knowing how things really worked. Another unsent reply played on her sense of duty to the people in uniform and the need to maintain excellence in the fleet.

As he read each, he tried to imagine the good senator's reaction. In his imagination, each explanation he gave left her face stern and unyielding at best—vengeful and mocking at worst. Walsh was glad that they were too far away to communicate via direct voice; text was easier.

Nothing he'd written would soften the senator's heart towards his decision to can her daughter. Nothing he could write would do that. And he'd already wasted enough time trying to. So, he typed a simple reply and sent it without giving himself the chance to second guess.

Until we meet again.

Regards,

Capitan Eugene K. Walsh,

Command Officer CAR Amazonas.

He considered adding some of the initials or titles he'd earned while in the service, but they wouldn't impress her any more than his explanations would have. She might even see it as a challenge and there was no doubt that his career was on the line.

As he changed back into his flightsuit, Walsh ran his fingers over the medals printed into his dress tunic. He suddenly felt old—and foolish. Look at the war hero kissing the senator's ass. Was Fuller suffering because Walsh didn't want it to look as though he'd been too hard on the precious cadet? Had he been unfair?

Walsh entered his overlay painting and stepped through Jupiter. Wild sweeps of his hands cast dark streaks across the bright, Jovian landscape. If he was growing soft, or was more concerned about his career than his crew, it was a good time to retire. His good friend Admiral Maconez would certainly help with that. Assuming brig time wasn't already in the works. The admiral would surely help with that, too.

Of course, the stars would be gone to him forever if that happened. The gate was still closed, but there was always hope he could get through it. He opened up a video clip of this very ship—known as EPL *Procyon's Pride* then—transitioning through the gate to Beta Hydri. That had been humanity's hub for expansion to the stars, holding even more gates. According to the records, five gates opened into the nexus-gate network that spider-webbed across the Orion Arm of Milky Way.

Pictures of those distant stars still existed, as did the information about their planetary systems. Walsh wondered how those colony worlds had fared once free of Earth's shackles. Probably pretty well since the gates would still be open to trade with other colonies.

The spirit of the EPL lived beneath the surface of Sol's emergent political powers. Hopefully, the colonies would be prepared if Earth ever did manage to open the gate. It might be best for the rest of the galaxy if it never opened.

But it would open for him. Someday. If he could stay in space.

Spinning the map of the mysterious expanse of man's celestial domain, Walsh decided it wasn't time to retire. Or to cool his thrusters behind some desk or in the brig. He would bide his time and fight to maintain flight status—even if meant kissing every backside on Liberty.

Chapter 16

BRUNO AZEVEDO SIPPED his eighty-year-old scotch and set the glass down before him. The rich-colored scotch looked right at home on the warm brown of the mahogany desk. He thought it might be the only mahogany desk on Liberty Station. The carbon-printed desks could be made locally and given any appearance or color. But they weren't alive. They didn't give him joy. And the CEO of Laboratorio d Tecnologia Espacial—LTE on the global exchange—needed as much joy as he could get. Liberty was a frustrating place for people wanting to get things accomplished.

Across the desk sat Adm. Linda A. James. She gazed absently into her overlay, her drink untouched. A lifetime of manners pressured Bruno to apologize to the admiral for having to wait. But she knew the score around Liberty better than he did.

Bruno's stateroom was one of the most exquisite on the station with full-sized graphics walls, a double-sized suite, and a top-of-the-line virtual attendant. Most desirable, and expensive, of all was the view of Luna and full one-g spin gravity.

The only thing on Liberty that proved prestige more than living quarters was fashionable tardiness. Senator Marina Midland excelled at making others wait, especially her senatorial peers. Her virtual assistant replied with the same non-answer when Bruno's VA queried the senator's arrival time.

"Soon."

He offered Admiral James a smile he knew she wouldn't see before taking another sip of his scotch. Though he found the perpetual gridlock infuriating at times, Bruno was often ambivalent. His liberty, and those of the Confederation in general, was safer when the senate was spinning its wheels and not getting new, ridiculous laws passed. But neither was he a fan of time wasters. He didn't allow it from his thousands of employees and certainly not from the LTE senators.

The virtual assistant chimed in Bruno's ear. He and Admiral James stood as the door slid open.

"Senator Midland," Bruno said. "Good of you to come. Please, have a seat." He deftly poured a glass of scotch and set it in front of the senator.

The senator sat and sipped the drink. "Thanks, Bruno. Tasty. So, now that the upgrades are done, who will command the *Amazonas* on this mission?"

Bruno could appreciate that Marina was down to business, now that she was finally here. "I'm still of a mind to keep Walsh. He has experience commanding *Amazonas*, and has even fought with her now."

Admiral James snorted. "That wasn't a battle. That was two monkeys flinging shit at each other."

"I'll defer to your professional opinion, Admiral," Bruno said.

"That'll be a first around here," she said. "Since I'm spreading my professional opinion around, I'm not sure the *Amazonas* is the best ship for the project. We used her in an actual mission. I don't think anyone is going to fall for the 'she's just a training ship' routine."

"She is still a training ship, though. And Walsh is a tested capitan and eager to get another command from what I understand. So he'll agree."

Admiral James leaned forward. "He's in the fleet. We don't ask him, we order him. If he's the one going."

Marina took another drink of scotch and narrowed her eyes at the admiral. "Doesn't it bother you that Walsh locked up my daughter for the entire trip back to Liberty? And he's still under inquiry, right?"

James nodded. "Yes. They're still waiting for my vote, and I'm undecided. With all due respect, Senator, your daughter is blatantly guilty of gross and dangerous dereliction of duty. If it weren't for Walsh and Diaz, it would have been a complete disaster instead of merely a complete embarrassment. Personally, I would have locked her up after the shake-and-back incident. It makes me think Walsh might be getting soft. Might be time to put him out to pasture."

"It would take a long time to get another capitan up to speed," Bruno said.

James glanced at him. "There are literally dozens of officers ready and qualified to command the *Amazonas*. And most of them are a bit less vocal in their critique of the admiralty."

"A troublemaker?" Marina asked.

Bruno rolled his glass of scotch in his fingers. "That's his job. You can't lead people into danger without making some trouble. As to the courier incident, all I know is that he retrieved the QED. I'm no starship commander, so I can't judge his tactics. But I can judge his leadership and he seems to know what he's about. And quick on his feet." More importantly to Bruno, Walsh understood what Liberty was really about.

"What about the other one?" Marina asked. "Diaz. She's the one that actually recovered the QED, anyway. And she used to be in charge of a ship according to her record."

"True," Admiral James said. "But I don't think she wants another command. She was pretty pissed at him taking the *Amazonas*."

"But she spoke highly of him in the inquiry," Bruno said. "Sounds like he inspires loyalty."

Marina waved a dismissive hand. "She didn't want to make herself look bad."

"Walsh consistently has excellent scores in crew confidence," James said. "But his loyalty index is lower than others we could send. And many have higher technical scores, too."

Marina set her empty glass on the desk. "He's not going anywhere while Sobella is in restriction."

"Sobella's house arrest has her in better quarters than Walsh." Bruno shrugged. "And he probably wouldn't be inclined to drop charges if he's going to suffer for her screwup."

"She didn't screw up!" Marina glared at the faces staring placidly back and sighed. "She didn't mean to screw up." The senator turned to the admiral. "Can he be convinced to drop the charges? Can't you just make it go away?"

Admiral James arched an eyebrow. "It's at the inquiry level. Doing anything like that would trigger a Senatorial Ethics investigation."

"And we certainly wouldn't want that," Bruno said. "The senators love their ethics."

Marina glared at him.

"If he could be persuaded to withdraw the charges, without apparent or perceived coercion..." James shrugged. "Maybe."

"Would that look bad on his record?" Bruno asked. "I mean, retracting such a serious charge?"

"We wouldn't technically require an explanation."

"How does that help Sobella?" Marina asked. "Even the charge on her record is a black mark. One that doesn't play well in the polls."

Admiral James drummed her fingers on her thigh as she gazed into the overlay. "There's legal precedent, thanks to Senator Munyez and a similar situation with his son. Admiralty Legal bought it, but that's above my pay grade. Basically, they annulled his service, expunged his record, and set all core databases to null."

Bruno grinned. "What'd he do?"

"He was in the Aerospace Force and dropped ordnance on an observation vehicle. No one died, but several limbs and internal organs had to be regrown. And the soldiers had to be convinced to drop any complaints."

Marina furrowed her brow. "He dropped a bomb on our own troops?"

"Friendly fire happens. Especially if you're flying the wrong way." James eyed the senator and shrugged. "Some people just aren't cut out for the military."

"At least Sobella didn't drop a bomb on anyone."

"What she did could have resulted in far more deaths. As it stands, the two courier pilots are dead because *Amazonas* couldn't effectively provide cover."

Marina jabbed a finger at the admiral. "They died because a Marty ship attacked them. Who cares about the UI, anyway?" Before James could answer, the senator turned to Bruno. "And I'm not sure why you're so set on Walsh. But if it cleans things up for Sobella, I'll play along."

Bruno nodded and looked at Admiral James.

"He's capable enough. I've never known you to take such interest in military affairs. And we all know that what happened wasn't really his fault." James pointedly did not look at Marina when she said this. "There are others more capable. But if you insist, I'll try to clear him from the inquiry if he's willing."

Bruno collected the glasses. "I'll talk to him tonight at the ball. Just to make sure he's who I really want to trust LTE's biggest project with. Shall I broach the subject of your daughter?"

"No," Marina said. "Just send a message when you decide. I'll arrange plans about Sobella myself."

THE ONLY THING POSITIVE about officious Liberty Station balls were the lovely ladies in their low-cut, curve-hugging gowns. Walsh hadn't wanted to come to this one. The inquiry was dragging on interminably and had taken all the thrust out of his rocket, so to speak.

Though lacking any details, the private overlay message from Admiral James made it clear that it was in his best interest to show up and mingle.

But mingle with who?

After two hours of swapping space stories with old crewmates, aloof officers who didn't want to catch whatever was destroying his career, and obliging women pretending to be unattached, Walsh decided it was time to go. James was a career admiral, but she wasn't one to play games or be vindictive. He believed her message to be true. He had either not impressed the right person or that person had changed their mind about speaking with him.

Turning to set his untasted glass of wine on a passing server's tray, he came face-to-face with a suave, middle-aged Hispanic man. He wore a Routitio suit—real, non-printed, non-synthetic fiber from Earth, no less. The man was obviously a civilian; and he was familiar. There was no social tag over his head.

"Commander Walsh?"

Walsh put on his best VIP smile. "That's me. You have me at a disadvantage, I'm afraid. Without my overlay, I barely know my own name."

The man gave a practiced chuckle. "Bruno Azevedo, at your service."

"Ah, of the esteemed and very, very influential Laboratorio d Tecnologia Espacial Azevedos?"

"The very one."

Walsh moved to shake the man's hand, but saw both held a crystal glass of scotch. "You are the patron saint of all space dogs like myself. To what does a lowly ex-capitan owe the pleasure?"

"Ex?" Bruno handed Walsh one of the glasses and raised his glass. "I didn't realize the inquiry had come to judgment."

"Fair enough," Walsh said. "Just not getting my hopes up. You're well informed of little ol' me's situation."

"Comes with the job... can I call you Eugene?"

"Sure. But I thought I'd be a bit under your radar."

Bruno chuckled. "You're not under anyone's radar at the moment, Eugene. You should know that."

"Point taken." Walsh took a sip of the scotch and raised his brows. "Oh, I like. Didn't get this one from the cantina."

"Certainly not. From what I understand, you managed to get your ship of cadets through some dicey business and complete a very tricky mission. The details of which even my sources won't divulge."

Walsh grinned and swirled his glass between them. "I'm afraid I'm going to have to disappoint you if you're trying to pump me for info. *Amazonas* did what she needed to do. The only casualty was my pride. Surely you have admirals and senators aplenty lined up to blab all about it."

"I prefer firsthand accounts," Bruno said. "As I'm sure you know, intelligence is just as paramount in corporate affairs as it is in military ones. But no, I'm not hear to grill you. I did happen to notice that you've led several patrols to the nexus gate, including this last one with a training ship. One observer used the word 'obsessed' on your record."

"VIPs studying me makes me nervous."

Bruno sipped his scotch while he scanned the room. "You must be close to an anxiety attack, then."

"Maybe I am," Walsh said. "Obsessed, that is. I admit to finding it utterly fascinating and can't fathom people who don't. It's just so... awesome. Simultaneously terrifying and sublime."

"Many people agree. Do you have hopes of it being repaired? Even after all this time and all the failures? Why bother?"

Walsh sipped his drink and looked up at the fleet of softly whirring drones over the crowd as he considered. "Because this place isn't the pinnacle of humanity. We're still sliding backwards. Everyone is still interested in their own small lives. The status quo. Getting a few more solars in their account than their neighbor. And so am I, for all my talk. It's our condition. It's how we're wired.

"No one with the actual ability is looking to recreate what the gate allowed. They're looking for prestige. Power. Those who can, won't. Those who really want to, can't. We've been alone in the dark, trapped in Sol, too long. I want us back among the stars. I want to see what it's like out there since the collapse of the EPL. And I want to be part of that."

"Why, Commander Walsh. You sound like an idealist."

"So I've been called. And a letch."

"Nothing wrong with either, if taken in moderation."

Walsh plucked a tiny sandwich from a passing server and popped it in his mouth. "Have you read any of Dr. Pladue's theories on the gates?"

"It's been years."

"He proposed the difficulty in finding the gate wasn't one of our technical lacking, but of the nexus's function as a test. He suggests the gate became visible due to us passing some unknown hallmark, not because of the Starfire probe's capabilities."

"Interesting," Bruno said.

"I think it's mostly blind supposition to make his papers look good. But if that's the case, and his theory does have some merit, there might be another puzzle out there waiting for us to take our next toddling step."

"Very fanciful," Bruno said. Casually, he added, "I wonder what sort of man the CAR would send on such a mission."

"Probably someone with lots of bombs who'd secure system-wide mineral rights."

"That's a very cynical view, Eugene."

Walsh shrugged. "It's all well above my pay grade, but the admiralty likes trigger-happy gauchos."

"Given you've been in both of the last two spaceship battles in Sol, some might call you the gaucho."

Walsh waved a dismissive hand. "Only because I'm not their gaucho."

"Do you think humanity can come together if the gate is opened?" Bruno asked. "So many gauchos in Sol. Look what happened to the EPL."

"Hope against hope." Walsh paused and laughed. "And if nothing else, I might get the chance to do some sightseeing before I'm ordered to blow someone up."

"Would you?"

"Go sightseeing?"

"Blow someone up?"

Walsh grinned and handed his drink back to Bruno. "Despite your denials, Mr. CEO, I get the feeling you have been pumping me for information. As to blowing anyone up, I'll burn that bridge when I cross it. Good evening, Bruno."

"Certainly. I have I feeling we'll meet again, Eugene."

WALSH FORCED HIMSELF to walk slowly, hoping he hadn't just talked himself into commanding a desk. It was obviously Bruno that Admiral James had wanted him to speak with. Walsh had shaken hands with several VIPs in his career—senators, ambassadors, foreign emissaries, even a couple of overlay celebrities. But he couldn't remember talking so candidly one-on-one with anyone so influential. The more he thought about the encounter, the more convinced he was that he should have stuck with socially accepted banalities.

And Bruno Azevedo had come to him. Regardless of what the CEO thought of him, Walsh had nothing left to do but go back to waiting on the admiralty. As he moved to leave the obnoxious bustle and heat of the party, Walsh felt a glad spring to his step.

"Capitan Walsh."

Walsh turned, hoping to hold the look of irritation at whoever had followed him from the party. It was a gorgeous, young woman in a slinky, silver-scaled dress. The neckline plunged to just above her navel and she stood with one hip thrust out to expose a leg through the skirt's thigh-high slit. As he became aware of his own blatant ogling, Walsh blinked in surprise. "Cadet Midland."

"I take it you didn't like the party."

"I thought you were under house arrest."

"I am, but I got special permission to attend." She tossed her hair and flashed Walsh a bright smile. "And please, call me Sobella."

"I don't think that would be appropriate, Cadet."

"I'm not a cadet. My service has been annulled. As if it never happened in a legal sense. Or it will be." She took Walsh's arm and gently pulled him along the corridor away from the party.

Walsh allowed himself to be pulled along. Maybe there was more than one person James wanted him to talk to. Like the spirits of Scrooge's Christmas. "What does that even mean?"

"Basically, that my service doesn't count one way or another. The records will be sealed and the government search and personnel databases will be expunged." She shrugged, jutting her barely covered breasts forward. "As much as that can be done, anyway. But as far as any legal queries or official proceedings go, it never happened."

"A witness protection program."

Sobella giggled. "I guess so."

Walsh frowned. "You can't hide from yourself."

"Like I said, it hasn't been assured. That's what I need to talk to you about."

Walsh froze in place. "You want me to drop the charges."

"Something like that. But it's a bit more complicated. I was hoping we could talk someplace a bit more private."

Walsh pulled his arm free. "That wouldn't be appropriate, Cadet."

She smiled up at him. "Please hear me out."

"What you did was inexcusable. I meant what I said on the ship. If you think I'm going to withdraw the charges because you got all dressed up..."

"No, Capitan. That's not it at all. I've been locked up for six months and I planned on enjoying myself. What we need to talk about is above both our heads. And should be discussed privately."

Walsh crossed his arms. "Why?"

Sobella glanced around before answering in a low, heady voice. "It's not just about me. It's about your command and commission."

"And just how much of my soul will it cost me?"

"Not here." She took his arm again and tugged him down the passage again. "My restricted quarters are two levels down from here."

"Two levels down? That puts you on the outer ring. Even your brig is better than my transient commander's quarters. I've only got 0.08-g." Walsh shook his head but allowed himself to be pulled along.

She offered an apologetic shrug. "It's nice, I'll admit. I can't help my connections. It's not always fun and games." She opened the elevator car and pulled Walsh inside. "I'll explain when we get there."

"AND THAT'S THE DEAL," Sobella concluded. "You withdraw the charges, the inquiry absolves you, and you remain capitan of the *Amazonas*."

Walsh took in Sobella as he considered. She sat on a couch across from him, legs crossed. Her thigh rolled back and forth suggestively as she swung a silver shoe on a graceful toe.

"And you get off for almost killing us all."

Sobella looked away, her lip trembling. "I know I screwed up. I wish I could change who I am. I didn't even want to sign up. That was all my mom's doing. She didn't care what I wanted. Boo-hoo for the rich kid. I get it. But I promise you I wasn't trying to kill myself in the bargain. If my service gets annulled, I can't serve again. I'll never be in the position to endanger anyone like that again."

Walsh leaned back, knowing he should stop staring at her legs. "I think the inquiry will clear me. If so, I'll keep the *Amazonas*."

"Normally, they might clear you. And you would probably get your ship back... normally. But this isn't normal. My mom wants my record cleared and she doesn't give a shit about what happens to you—or anyone—in the process. She's kind of a bitch that way."

"Play or get played?"

"Afraid so, Capitan. The same for me. I'm her legacy and she's determined I follow in her footsteps at all costs. You've only had to fight her recently. This is my life."

She was an actor. As she said, it was her life. But Walsh believed the remorse in her voice about her performance and her mother. She might be cleared, anyway, while he was shoved in the proverbial airlock, with or without his cooperation. He followed the curve of her leg with his eye, looking up to see he'd been caught.

"Sounds like all the bases have been covered. I'll withdraw the charges."

Sobella stood and clapped her hands together. "Oh, thank you." She reached out and clasped his hands. "I know your arm's being twisted, but believe me that this is best for both of us."

"It sounds like it."

She leaned back to look up at him. "Let me show you something."

"What is it?"

She stepped towards the back of the compartment. "A memento from the *Amazonas*. I'll probably have to turn it in. Be right back."

Walsh looked at the exit, knowing that he'd already agreed to the deal. Whatever Sobella—Sobella now, not Cadet Midland—was doing would only bring trouble. But then he looked back at the door to the room she'd entered, hopeful. He stayed until she came out of the room a few minutes later.

"Is that...?"

Sobella gave an embarrassed laugh. She modelled the skin-tight cadet's uniform. The bonding strip didn't go anywhere near the top of the blouse. "Yes. I was so afraid of getting in trouble, I tried wearing this to one of my disciplinary hearings. But I chickened out and wore one that was only slightly out of uniform."

"Yes, we noticed. Speaking of which, Fuller's record will need to be cleared, too. She doesn't need that black mark."

"Yes, of course." With a flip of her hair, Sobella padded across the living room to him.

Walsh didn't protest as she slid onto his lap. "Is this part of the deal?"

She leaned close and whispered into his ear. "No. This is just because you're reasonably good-looking and I've been locked up in here for six months. And, you were one of the few people in the fleet that even tried giving me a chance."

Walsh leaned forward, breathing her in. Alarm klaxons went off in his brain. He should run, very quickly. Get one of the women from the party if needed. She turned, her breasts rubbing against him.

He silenced the alarm klaxons. "For the record, I'd like it noted that I had already agreed to the deal before being seduced."

Sobella laughed and placed one of his hands on her thigh and the other on her breast. Her hands slipped under his jacket and began exploring. Walsh would have to make copies of his logs and secure them in his various data vaults throughout Sol. Until then, he gladly worked his way to making her out of uniform.

SENATOR MIDLAND CUT away from the video of the handy Capitan Walsh and her daughter. She requested a connection to Bruno Azevedo, which was accepted immediately.

"I can work with Walsh."

"So, he decided to go along after all." Bruno sounded disappointed.

"Yes, yes," the senator said, slightly annoyed at the CEO missing the point. "More importantly, I have something personal on him now. Conduct unbecoming. Fraternization with a cadet involved in an inquiry against him. Whatever. Now he has to go along. Now I can trust him."

Chapter 18

WALSH'S PULSE QUICKENED as he reached blindly for a handhold in the tube leading to *Amazonas*'s main hull from habitat Alpha. Though he couldn't see a thing, he knew the passages of the ship by touch. Hopefully, the rest of the crew did, too. They'd drilled often enough and he'd drilled it into their heads the importance of knowing the ship in the dark.

One hand found the bulkhead and the other crept along until it felt the handle—just where it should be. The conveyor wasn't working so Walsh began the arduous climb to his shield station. The conveyor was out, but the habs were still spinning and producing pseudo-gravity he had to overcome as he climbed.

He could feel his growing weightlessness and reached out for the rim of the tube he knew was near. It was there and he grasped it, flipping around like a Ganymede pole dancer before pulling himself into *Amazonas*'s main hull. Gliding his hands along the ship's bulkhead in a smooth rhythm from handhold to handhold, he made his way to the nearest support stanchion that led to the crypt.

Walsh bit back a cry as Hector's voice blared from a speaker panel that couldn't have been more than a meter away. "Alert. Alert. Atmospheric toxicity reaching harmful levels. All crew don EBH."

Pausing for a second to get his bearings in the abysmal darkness, Walsh gripped the handhold tightly, then pressed his body flat against the bulkhead. He used his toes to spin around the handhold like a clock arm until he felt the tell-tale blister of the nearest emergency life-support station. Crawling over like a spider, Walsh popped it open and slid the EBH, the emergency breathing hood, over his head. The bottom sealed to his flightsuit as he slid the emergency gloves on. The gloves also bonded to the flightsuit, making Walsh hermetically sealed.

"Alert," Hector announced. "The shielded core has been compromised. All crew evacuate to the nearest EVA bay. Repeat, all crew evacuate to the nearest EVA bay."

"Shit," Walsh muttered. He'd almost been to the support leading to the core. Grabbing a nearby conduit, he pulled himself towards EVA bay Bravo. He was running out of time and began pulling along faster, almost to the point he considered reckless.

Where the conduit disappeared into the frame, Walsh hooked a foot around it and reached out for the EVA bay hatch. His fingers brushed the access panel. The environmental status nipple was protruding, indicating the compartment beyond wasn't in vacuum. Walsh found the "open" button and pressed it. The hatch rewarded him with an error tone barely audible through his hood. He tried again and heard the same error tone. Sliding his fingers aft, he found the manual override panel and jerked it open. Inside, he found a small handle, extended it, and began pumping it as fast and smoothly as he could.

The EVA bay hatch opened by degrees until Walsh could pull himself through into more complete darkness. He spread his arms and pushed forward until he felt the rack of EVA suits. Hooking his feet into nearby handholds, Walsh freed a suit from its station and struggled into the legs. Then he connected the upper harness and latched the helmet after two failed, desperate attempts, his fingers made clumsy with sudden nervousness.

"Drill completed," Hector said.

A moment later, Walsh felt someone remove his EVA helmet. His EBH was tugged free and finally someone slid the blindfold from his eyes. He blinked twice and saw Lieutenant Fuller rolling up the blindfold.

She worked to free the emergency gloves from his suit. "Not bad time, sir. And your seals are secure. Since you went first, I guess you get to watch everyone else try now."

Walsh grinned. "Lead by example."

Fuller glanced up at him from her work. A look like that from the admiralty, or even Diaz, didn't mean much. But coming from a crew member, it stung. Walsh's grin faltered and he looked away. Though her record had been cleared of the whole Midland affair, he understood her anger. At least she'd agreed to take back her position as div-O.

"Yes, well, let's get on with the evaluations." Walsh drifted out of the EVA bay as two cadets came forward to secure the suit he'd donned. Another took the EBH and gloves, disinfected them with a spray, and pushed off to replace them.

Walsh grabbed the hatch to his station in the core. No one was allowed to watch before they'd done the drill, so he was alone. Everyone would do the drill and be evaluated; crew and cadet alike, junior and senior officers. He'd been in a catastrophic atmospheric evacuation and he made sure that everyone on his crew could pass. *Amazonas* was the largest ship Walsh had served on and it had taken him several weeks on his first cruise to learn it in blackout conditions.

The next blindfolded crew member emerged too fast from the tube and scrambled for a handhold. She lost her grip, spun, and hooked a foot beneath a nearby conduit before crawling in the wrong direction towards the cone. When she reached out and felt the spinning ring, she turned and scrambled aft, but it would cost her time. She barely passed and grasped a hatch well away from Walsh.

Several crew in a row found the EVA bay in short order with no trouble. Then came a cadet who couldn't find the emergency life-support blister. He drifted and groped until Fuller called a fail and rescheduled the evaluation.

Walsh squinted, unsure of what he was seeing, as a small ball came spinning out of the tube next. When a disproportionately long—not to mention extremely hairy—arm reached out and clutched a handhold, he recognized it as belonging to Cadet Screwball. While the uplift's hands had been modified to manipulate human tools and controls, the chimp still had prehensile feet. And he was using them to good effect as he sped from handhold to handhold.

When he reached out for the emergency life-support blister, Screwball was able to grasp conduits with his feet while he put on the hood and gloves. The chimp sped towards the support to the core. Walsh shook his head as Screwball flipped gracefully towards the EVA bay in response to Hector's warning. A wave of laughter and applause rippled through the watching crew. There was no doubt the uplift had the fastest score so far.

"Capitan?" a black-skinned cadet called from his space about five meters away. He ignored the whispered objections from the nervous-looking cadets around him.

"Yes, Cadet?"

"Why the blindfolds, sir? I mean, the hoods have built-in lights and every hatch has luminescent markings. Not to mention the emergency battle lanterns. And these flightsuits have built-in emergency hoods, anyway."

Another cadet, one who had obviously paid better attention, spoke up as Walsh opened his mouth to speak. "To simulate something like smoke or oil on your lenses that would block the light. Something you can't see through."

Walsh nodded. "And I believe most emergencies happen when you're in your skivvies. No hoods or clothes."

A few nearby cadets laughed.

"And," Walsh continued, "let's not forget radiological or chemical injuries. If your eyes get burned out, you can't see shit until you get new eyes. Which you can't get if you're dead."

The laughter died down.

"Or the Darkness from Space may take you," said Lieutenant Collins in a wavering, campfire ghost-story voice.

"What if you get some alien stuck to your face, shoving its alien wang down your throat," added Junior Lieutenant Pepper, one of the new transfers. He placed his palm over his face and made loud slurping noises.

The cadets laughed again.

"There aren't any aliens," said the black-skinned cadet.

"I doubt it was the dinosaurs or Neanderthals that made the gate, Cadet," Walsh said.

Screwball hooted and spun in the air before grabbing a handhold. "Maybe it was a race of ancient, spacefaring apes?"

When Walsh and the rest laughed again, Screwball began a loud, hooting, squealing noise that had to be the laugh Admiral Feliz had warned him about. It made everyone laugh louder. Screwball's expression indicated he wasn't sure if they were laughing with him or at him. Walsh knew it was a little bit of both.

He broke for chow when Alpha shift finished and returned to his place when Bravo shift began their evaluations.

Diaz went first and made it into the EVA bay smoothly and without error. After her go, she took up position next to Walsh to watch the rest of the crew. They laughed when a new transfer, Lieutenant Cooper, somehow got his hand jammed between two conduits so tightly that Fuller had to free him and scheduled him for a retake.

Once the last evaluation had been completed, Hector posted the scores. Walsh scored a respectable seventh-best time—better than Diaz by six places. To no one's surprise, Screwball had the best score.

Walsh called for his dinner and motioned for the duty steward to set the meal box on his desk. "Thanks."

"Yes, sir." Instead of immediately doing an about-face and marching out, the junior lieutenant looked down at Walsh. "You did pretty good, Capitan. Beat me by a light-year."

"I've been doing it for a few orbits." Walsh smiled up at the woman. "But Cadet Screwball beat me by a light-year."

She waved a dismissive hand. "Yeah, but he's meant for climbing. And he's small with four hands, after all. Screwy can probably smell his way around in the dark."

"Screwy?"

"Yes, sir. It's his nickname. He's fine with it."

Walsh grunted. "Don't dismiss his scores just because he might have some advantages. He still worked for them."

"Yes, Capitan. I didn't mean anything by it. I like Screwy."

Walsh offered a friendly smile. "Very good. Dismissed."

She came to attention and left.

Walsh considered the steward. Her points were valid, of course. Screwball—he wasn't sure if Screwy or Screwball was worse—was an uplifted chimpanzee and had distinct physical advantages in some areas. He wondered how his crew, how he, would react to having to share a billet with an alien species as portrayed in the space operas. In those stories, the friendly aliens always seemed to have some shortcoming that more or less kept them on the same footing with the human characters.

But what if the aliens were better at everything: smarter, faster, better endowed? Could humans work beside them, content with their human limitations?

This experiment of learning to live with their hairy cousin might answer that question. Or at least prepare them. Some aliens had made the gates, after all.

Walsh reviewed the drill evaluations a final time as he enjoyed his printed squash casserole. It smelled as if the science division had added some fresh tomatoes or zucchini from the aeroponics bay to the ration paste.

A total of ten crew members had not qualified, but he'd not seen anything that worried him. No one had gone fetal or injured themselves. Anyone could get disoriented and have a bad run. He was sure they would all pass the next one—especially with the extra training he knew Diaz had planned for them.

Lieutenant Collins's image appeared in his overlay, standing patiently while Walsh finished chewing.

"Yes, Ops?"

"Capitan, I'd like you to take a look at the signature for target track Uniform Tango Seventeen. It lists as an independent hauler out of Luna."

Walsh pulled up the tactical display in his overlay. He found an icon labeled UT-17 and zoomed in. An ID tag appeared next to it that read *"Stream o' Silver."* Walsh expanded the data field and scrolled through the log entries: course changes, burn times, detected EM signals. Nothing notable except a couple of transponder exception reports that the computer had quickly resolved.

"You mean the transponder glitches?"

"Yes, Capitan. Transponder noise happens but this one has a string of them going back in the log history. And look at that course projection." Collins's image reached into the tactical display and set it to an expanded navigation view. *Stream o' Silver*'s plot ran towards Jupiter. "With a single correction, she'll hit Jupiter's Oberth envelope and..." He pointed a finger to a Trojan asteroid highlighted in red.

"Paulson Base," Walsh said. "Think she's a Junker-clan smuggler?"

"Maybe." Collins highlighted a few other course options in UT-17's flight envelope. "It could be heading to a few of the other places, but given the transponder glitches and it coming from Luna..."

"Think we should check it out?"

"At least maybe get a better look. I've worked up a few course corrections that should close the distance without freaking her out or costing us too much delta-v."

Walsh ran through Collins's suggested approach. "Those corrections are pretty subtle. *Stream o' Silver* might not even notice."

"Assuming that's even her real registry."

"Good job, Ops. Log and implement the changes. I guess we'll see in two weeks if they notice."

WALSH ONLY MANAGED a cough the first time he tried to speak. He scraped his tongue against his teeth to remove the foul-tasting film of sleep there. "Go, Diaz."

"Capitan, UT-17 has dumped cargo and performed a major turn-and-burn."

"Giving us a choice." Walsh rubbed his eyes and blinked several times. "I guess they finally spotted us."

Diaz snorted. "It took them over two weeks. Junkers used to be smart."

"They're still plenty smart. Work up interception profiles for their new vector and their cargo." Walsh smacked his lips and grimaced at the lingering aftertaste. His vision was still a bit blurry, so he closed his eyes to pull up the display on his overlay. *Stream o' Silver* was maneuvering wildly to make it difficult to figure her new destination. The dumped cargo was still on the original course out towards Jupiter. Probably another Junker would pick it up.

"Well, if we were on a regular patrol, we'd probably get the cargo. Maybe as evidence, or at least for being a nav hazard. But we're en route for our science survey." Walsh rolled back beneath his covers and yawned. "No nav changes at this time, XO."

"*Si*, Capitan. Pleasant dreams."

WALSH TOOK HIS MEALS in the galleys of different habitat modules to mingle with more of the crew—and keep them on their toes.

Screwball—he'd decided against Screwy, at least as Capitan—was entertaining a group of other cadets with stories of the ridiculous things he had to do in the lab. It was pleasing to see that the crew had taken to their chimpanzee companion, though that was largely due to Screwball's patience and determination. Walsh had Hector flag discussions among the humans about the chimp and listened in occasionally. He didn't like doing it, but he also wasn't going to let the uplift be mistreated. At least not worse than was usual for any other cadet.

To the crew's credit, though, the off-handed comments had slackened and those still muttered were of a more jovial nature. Some of the crew stepped in to defend Screwball when someone was speaking too harshly to, or about, him. No one tolerated monkey jokes anymore.

It seemed anyone who spoke to Screwball quickly connected with him. The chimp was friendly, smart, and so kind that if he'd been a human, Walsh would have accused him of butt-kissing or insincerity. But not Screwball. He had an almost childish earnestness and honesty. Walsh wondered if that's how humans were meant to be, what they would be if not for thousands of years of twisted-up civilization.

He'd just finished his meal labeled "Processed Vegetable Meal (PVM) option #8: Potato Casserole with Tangerine Cake," when a connection request from Collins flashed in his overlay. "Walsh here."

Collins spoke faster than usual. "Capitan, we've identified the cargo."

"That was fast. Anything interesting?"

"They're emergency medical freeze pods. They aren't emitting any distress beacons, but I decided to send a general query just in case. The pods answered right back."

Walsh stood and slid his tray and utensils into the recycler. "Freeze pods? Shit. I hope they didn't dump hostages because they thought we were coming for them. The pods provide any data?"

Collins's voice grew sullen. "Yes, sir. They have one person each in them. Two pods report null life signs, and the vitals on the rest are weak according to Medical."

"Understood. Plot and execute the intercept for the pods; no restriction on delta-v."

"Yes, Capitan."

"And make sure we don't sweep them with our thrust plume. I'm on my way."

"Yes, sir."

Once back in operations, Walsh examined the navigation track to recover the pods. Time was of the essence, but it wouldn't be much of a rescue if the pods were irradiated by *Amazonas*'s thruster plume. That meant they'd have to drift past the pods, reducing their initial capture window before flying out of range.

Walsh leaned back and stroked his beard. "Thoughts on who we might be rescuing?"

"Probably hostages or slaves," Moore said from tactical.

"Or captured crew," Bovree said. "Hoping we'll go for the rescue instead of the hijackers."

Diaz's image was projected in everyone's overlay to make it look as if she was standing near Walsh. "Could be spoof. Maybe the pods are just programmed to report vitals like someone's inside."

Walsh nodded. "I thought of that, too. Bovree hacked in and everything looks good there. But still no ID data and no signs of booby traps."

"Not in the software," Bovree added.

The vector track for *Stream o' Silver* had solidified to intercept a different Trojan asteroid. The intel database showed no known facilities there, so Walsh figured they were going to meet another Junker ship for propellant resupply. Possibly a very angry Junker ship, if it was where the cargo was supposed to be going. Walsh smiled grimly at the thought of the cartel members shooting each other.

"Tactical, expend one MK-4 sensor probe at max burn. Full spectrum, active scanning. Scream at them the whole way. I want a deep-signature analysis so we can see it in the future, despite its hacked transponder. And I like the thought that someone in there might piss themselves, thinking we sent a missile after them until they realize what it is."

"Probe away, Capitan," Moore said. "Eighteen hours to intercept."

THE FREEZE PODS WERE failing one by one. More accurately, the freeze pods' occupants were failing. The pods were operating to spec, but these were not designed to operate in deep space. Those who had dumped them must have known it. Only two survived now.

Walsh created a timeline of the vitals going red and compared it to when *Amazonas* would have been there if he'd ordered full burn when they'd been dumped. It would have saved these last two. Maybe. That's all. And maybe not even that, given how unstable the vitals had become.

It wasn't his fault; it was the bastards who had cut and run. And there was no telling what they would have done if *Amazonas* had charged in immediately. As with all situations in combat and in life, there was very little Walsh could control. Not even his own body was fully obedient to him. Like all philosophies, it was realized not merely in the theory, but in the living of it. Which was the hard part, of course.

"Damn," Cmdr. Fred Barnes, the ship's doctor, whispered. "Another pod just flatlined. One left. And that one isn't looking so great. Looks like you won't be needing me except for the paperwork."

"There's always hope, Doctor," Walsh said.

"We might also want to consider the possibility that they were medically quarantined," Barnes said. "Maybe the bad guys are hoping we'll infect ourselves and they can come get the ship when we're dead."

Walsh chuckled. "Unless their disease can kill Hector, too, I'm not worried about that."

Collins zoomed the tactical display over UT-17. "I don't think they have the delta-v for that, especially after that long burn. They'll be decelerating for a while."

"Probably not," Walsh agreed. "But we'll definitely quarantine the bodies."

Ops was heavy with anticipation and dread as they closed on the final survivor. Walsh nearly jumped when Diaz called, "Recovery drones away."

The drone heading towards the survivor sped away, slowed, and coupled to the pod with large manipulators. There were no useful details to be gleaned from the drone's camera. The window presumably covering the occupant's face was opaque with frost from the inside. The drone's tiny thrusters fired and slowly pushed the pod back towards *Amazonas* while the other drones sped towards their assigned pods.

Bovree presented the pod's interface from his security station. "The pod's systems are normal, no alarms or alerts. Aside from the medical conditions, naturally."

"Any ID yet?"

"Nope."

The external view showed the drone and the pod slide into the cargo bay, which sealed behind them.

"Pod is in the cargo bay," Diaz announced. "Doctor Barnes is on station with his team."

Walsh pulled up the feed from the cargo bay. The drone set the pod on the deck and drifted into its docking station. "Do your stuff, Doctor," Walsh said.

Barnes led two medical technicians and a med-bot into the bay. The humans wore bio-suits that bulged and rippled slightly in the zero-g. When they were inside, Barnes sealed the door and set up a medical bubble around the pod. Walsh was not allowed to access medical procedures without the ship's doctor's express permission or under declaration of ship's safety. So he waited, the only activity visible being slight bulges on the surface of the bubble when someone inside bumped or rubbed against it.

At length, Dr. Barnes connected to the overlay. "No biological hazards detected, Capitan. Which is good, since I had to open the pod."

"Who do we have?" Diaz asked.

"The subject looks to be a young girl, eight to ten years old, perhaps. She tests negative for the standard run of health tests, except for some cellular damage from extended freezer time and being dumped in space. There are healed scars around her genitals and anus, as well as some DNA anomalies."

"Like what?" Walsh asked.

"Not to put too fine a point on it, she's bio-geneered. There are signs of telomere-restriction modification, an age-stunting technique. Put that with her scarring and—"

"She's a vat whore," Diaz hissed.

Collins frowned. "A what?"

"That's not the kindest way to put it, XO," Walsh said.

A look of pure disgust washed over Diaz's face. "That thing was grown in a vat to be a sex slave. It isn't even human."

"With all due respect, XO," Barnes said, "that's a load of horse crap. She's as human as anyone born through in vitro or any other bio-geneered person. Legally speaking is a different matter, of course, but just because the CAR doesn't recognize them doesn't make them right. Capitan, I can save her if I start now."

Diaz glared at Walsh. "*Dios mio.* You said yourself we're en route to our mission. We're not passing any assets that can take her off our hands." She pointed to the overlay image of the medical bubble. "What are we going to do with something that looks like a little girl?"

Walsh pursed his lips. "I guess we'll babysit her until we can find a better foster home." He hadn't known Diaz long, but she'd never expressed such vitriol around him. Not the Junkers, not the Caliphate, not even the admiralty which refused to give her back a command.

"Capitan?" urged Barnes.

"Go ahead, Doctor." Walsh ignored Diaz's subdued snort of disapproval. "Get her stabilized and keep me updated. XO, continue recovery operations."

"Where should be put the bodies?" she asked.

"We could secure them in the cargo bay and hook up power feeds," Collins said. "The pods can keep the bodies frozen for us."

Walsh nodded. "Good call, Ops. Get a tech team down there to set up the connections." A drone was approaching the cargo bay, carrying a frozen casket. "And I want a medical team to verify the others are actually dead. I'd hate to ignore someone we could have saved."

WALSH SPENT THE NEXT hour in his cabin listening to Hector give an overview of the various laws concerning vat slaves.

"Put on a judge's robe," Walsh said. "And make the scenery the Prime Court Library."

Hector's avatar was immediately dressed in long, black robes and the cabin replaced in Walsh's overlay with an austere room lined with thick legal volumes.

Walsh scratched his chin as he considered Hector. "And a wig. Definitely a wig. One of those white, powdery jobs like the founders wore."

Hector's military crop was replaced with long, white hair tied back with a black ribbon. "Why a wig, Capitan?"

"It just seemed appropriate. And because I think it's funny and I have a feeling I'm going to need as many laughs as I can get."

"But you're not laughing, Capitan."

"I'm laughing on the inside. Let's start with a run of the legal status of vat slaves."

Hector folded his hands behind his back. "There are many legal definitions concerning bio-geneered beings. Not all of the discussion is about those created to serve in forced-labor roles."

"Well, let's start with the forced-labor roles. I want to understand this girl's position before the admiralty salts my ass about this, too." Walsh grunted. "Or Diaz."

"Bio-geneered slaves are illegal to produce in all nations of Earth. There are known labs on Luna, Mars, and a few off-world corporate and private labs that produce them. That concerns the production only, however.

"The legal standing for those who have been created is far more vague. Often it must be decided on a case-by-case basis. In the CAR, a bio-geneered human or human derivative is not assumed to legally be a person without a hearing."

"A sticky situation, Your Honor," Walsh said. "What about Screwball? He was bio-geneered and he's obviously a person."

"Correct, Capitan," Hector replied. "He was given such a hearing at the request of the admiralty and was deemed to be sapient, sentient, and a person with legal standing."

Walsh blew out a breath. "So we didn't technically save a person?"

"Dr. Barnes seems to think technically they are people. But legally, Capitan? No. Not without the hearing."

"Are there many bio-geneered people made that aren't meant to be slaves?"

"No, Capitan. Robots and drones are quicker and cheaper to produce as a source of raw labor. So most bio-geneered creatures are created for the purpose of fulfilling niche entertainment demands." Hector opened a display in the overlay that cycled through a menagerie of bizarre humanoids. "Some are created with very exotic, very specific, traits. Included are rare skin and eye tones, animal features, gender-fluid genitals, and many others."

"Dr. Barnes said he doesn't even know how old she is yet."

"It is likely she was created to serve a particular niche, as well. Speaking of which, Dr. Barnes is contacting you. He has stabilized her and has finished preliminary analysis on the other freezer pods."

"Any other survivors?"

"No, Capitan. The doctor would like you to meet him in Medical."

"I DON'T HAVE A FULL DNA lab," Dr. Barnes said. "But all the genetic markers I sampled were identical. All of them are also identical in appearance and age progression. I'd say they were from the same batch." He cleared his throat and added softly, "And they all have similar scarring on their anuses and vaginas."

Walsh frowned. "That's terrible."

"Not according to the XO. They aren't even people according to her."

"Stow that fight for later, Doc."

Barnes took a deep breath and nodded. "All right. There's something else terrible, too. All of their hymens are intact, despite the obvious signs of abuse."

"How's that possible?"

"We can regrow just about anything, Gene. I guess their owners wanted them to be eternal virgins."

Walsh winced as his stomach clenched, trying to empty itself. "Minimizing depreciation. God. You know, I've chased down smugglers and nasty sorts before. Even boarded one at a dock in a surprise raid. But I've never actually seen..." Walsh waved his hand around as he sought the right word. "Contraband. Not like this, anyway. Not little girls like this."

"It does make you question any faith in humanity you have left." Barnes leaned against the bulkhead. "What up Diaz's ass, anyway?"

Walsh shrugged. "Don't know. Not sure I want to know."

They stared at the girl in silence for a minute. She was still bloated and pale from her time in the freezer, but she looked like the perfect Anglo little girl. A girl who needed pigtails instead of leather straps or whatever her masters made her wear.

"Anyway," Barnes said. "The girl will be fine. She has a small bracelet that has 'Angelica' engraved on it. No medical info on it, of course. I guess they didn't want to give away any trade secrets. They all have similar ones. Brittany, Felicity, Charity, Genevieve—I can't remember them all right now. I still can't tell you how old they all are, just that they are the same age. I think they've been designed to be forever young, so to speak. Angelica could be much older than she appears. I'm waiting for some test results from Liberty."

"I'm sure they'll have plenty to say to us both."

"I've found a contact for a psychologist who specializes in bio-geneered slave recovery. Her body won't survive going back into medical freeze. He might be able to help us keep her comfortable, or at least help manage the trauma she's about to go through."

Walsh projected the cargo bay into his overlay and watched over the two rows of recovered pods. The pale faces were serene, like ceramic dolls in frost-rimed glass coffins. "I wonder if she thinks of them as sisters."

Barnes did a double take at his medical terminal, then at his patient. "I guess you could ask her. She's coming around."

The cargo bay view vanished and Walsh stepped close to the bed to watch her wake. Her eyes fluttered open and locked on his. The pupils were an unnaturally deep blue and streaked with silver; definitely custom cosmetics. Though bedraggled, her hair was a bright blond bordering on cartoon yellow. A smattering of tiny freckles ran across the bridge of her nose. She smiled up at him.

"Are you my new daddy?" the girl whispered.

"Uh, well... I suppose so, darling." He chuckled nervously and motioned to Barnes. "I guess you could say I'm everyone's daddy on this ship. Isn't that right, Doctor?"

Barnes smiled wryly. "Oh, sure. We all call him Capitan Daddy around here."

Angelica gave a hoarse laugh. "I like Capitan Daddy. That's funny."

"You should probably call me Eugene. Your bracelet says 'Angelica.' Is that what you are called?"

She took Walsh's hand in a weak grip. "Yes, Eugene. But you can call me Angel, or Angela, or whatever you want. You're the daddy."

Walsh cleared his throat and exchanged a dubious glance with Barnes. "Yes, well, this is my friend, Dr. Barnes. You've just woken up from a medical pod and he's going to ask you questions and do a checkup to make sure you're okay."

Angelica smiled up at Barnes. "I understand. You're checking to make sure I'm as ordered. Most daddies do. I am, but sometimes a few of us get freezer-sick. Especially Bella."

"We're just trying to make sure you're healthy," Barnes said. "We're your friends, not your customers. We don't know anything about an order."

"Of course. Sorry." She winked at him.

Walsh gently pulled his hand free from her grasp. "Anyway, I have to go send a message to someone who'll help us take better care of you. So you be sure to listen to Dr. Barnes, all right?"

Angelica nodded and closed her eyes. Walsh watched her for a second and stepped towards the hatch.

"Eugene, I'm glad you're my daddy now. You're much nicer than the last one."

Chapter 19

AMAZONAS was now far enough away from Liberty Station to incur a four-hour comms lag each way. That didn't include the time involved in deciding how to answer.

Walsh rubbed his bleary eyes. He'd attached a governmental urgency flag to his message to Barnes's psychologist, a Dr. Dohan Ibn Waqas. Hector had no information on Dr. Waqas's current schedule, so Walsh had no way of knowing when a reply might come. The colonies had probably figured out how to make the quantum entanglement radios people had been speculating about for ages. Another good reason to get the nexus gates open.

But such lag times were part of being a spacer, so Walsh sipped on his spiced hot chocolate and projected a university classroom as an overlay background. He selected a leggy, redheaded avatar for the instructor and started Liberty University's intro class on bio-geneering.

The next day, an hour after picking up where he'd left off, the instructor—a curvy Latina this time—blinked into an image of Hector. Fortunately, Hector was not wearing the same cleavage-enhancing dress.

"That was disturbing," Walsh said.

"Apologies, Capitan. We have received a reply to your communiqué."

"About time. Please relay it."

Hector was replaced with a head-and-shoulders display of a middle-aged man of Indian descent. The man's black hair floated lazily around his head, indicating he'd been in one of Liberty's inner rings with low or null-g; maybe a transit shuttle.

"Capitan Walsh, thank you for contacting me on this delicate matter. I laud your decision to save the girl—a decision not everyone would have made. These poor creatures are often cruelly labeled as 'vat whores' or 'sex dolls,' among other unkind names.

"And while their very existence is in fact repulsive, hostility is better directed at their creators and abusers. This girl and her batch are victims, nothing more."

Waqas paused to drink from a zero-g sippy bottle of Luna Stout. "Forgive my pontificating, Capitan. I've been involved in this fight for years and I tend to get somewhat passionate about it.

"The first and foremost thing to note is that you are now her 'daddy.' This is likely what she's been trained to call her current master. While said in ignorance, your words to her have—in her mind—verified that you are master. To her, you own her body and soul and can do whatever you like with her. She wants you to do whatever you like with her. I'm sure you can imagine what she expects from her 'daddies.'

"This leads to the second point: you must understand and accept that she derives pleasure and comfort from these arrangements. All of her relationships have been sexually abusive, but she doesn't see it that way. She can't see it. She was designed genetically, hormonally, and raised psychologically, to live this way. There is nothing in her nature that tells her this is wrong or harmful. Trying to explain this to her will likely be futile. She won't even understand what you mean."

The doctor took another drink of beer and his eyes darted as he scanned his notes in the overlay. "In your message, you assumed Angelica was nine or ten based on appearance. But it is not easy to tell due to the genetic modifications of such people. These girls will not grow older in appearance, though they will still age and die. Her brain's development has also been stunted to keep her as childlike as possible. Most people forced into such trades grow cynical and belligerent. These girls will remain sweet—and compliant. I've attached some medical files for your physician, but she'll probably tell you how old she really is. There's no standard to these creations. She could be as old as twenty."

Dr. Waqas's hand came into view, palms forward in a placating manner. "Finally, Capitan, she is quite capable of seducing you. Please hear me out. That is not an accusation of having a base character. She has been trained to give comfort in your weakest moments. Her physique has been subtly enhanced to arouse.

"You must never tease her or flirt with her, or appear in any way as if you are inviting her to indulge. But, if you wish to help her, you also can't ignore her completely. If you simply lock her up or refuse to see her, she will take that very hard. It is a fine line you must walk that I don't envy—it has taken me years of practice. And you probably can't convince her that someone else is her daddy because of her programming. She will have some sort of ceremony, or pass phrase, or some other trigger that tells her it is time to go back to serving her creators. She probably doesn't consciously know what it is; to prevent her from freeing herself, of course.

"I have no say in the movements of starships, obviously. But if at all possible you should deliver her to Liberty Station ASAP. We have facilities to care for such a one. Until then, if you truly wish to help, it falls on you to do the best you can."

Walsh sighed and froze Waqas in midair. It was all too damned much. As if Diaz's perpetual stick up her thruster wasn't bad enough, now he had a talking monkey—chimpanzee—and a genetically engineered sex slave calling him daddy. He snorted. One could never tell what a cruise might bring.

It was still better than Liberty duty.

Walsh waved his hand to bring Dr. Waqas's face back to life.

"You might be able to convince her that she's there for display only. Sometimes this happens. Like dolls or animals in a menagerie. If you make it clear that she's not there to... uh, whatever euphemism you'd like to use for sex... it should keep her, and everyone else on your ship, out of trouble. Make it clear that you'll be disappointed if she disobeys.

"Remember, Capitan, you can't 'fix' her. Only help. But I commend you again for being willing to. I've attached some other literature for you, laymen-level stuff, just to help. Please send updates and contact me at your convenience. Safe travels, Capitan Walsh." Waqas's face froze, the words "Message Ends" superimposed in glowing letters. Walsh waved the message away.

"We have received a transmission from Liberty concerning your earlier query, Capitan," Hector said.

Walsh furrowed his brow. "What earlier query?"

"Your query about what to do with Angelica. You are ordered not to revive her. Make any repairs to the pod needed to stabilize her and stow all pods for evidence if the delta-v expenditure won't affect the mission."

"Oh, that query." Walsh chuckled. "Well, they say it's better to ask forgiveness than to ask for permission. I'll get to do both. Hector, schedule a staff meeting and notify all division officers."

"Yes, Capitan. 14:30 in virtual stateroom one. Notifications sent."

THE IMAGE OF DR. WAQAS disappeared from everyone's overlay and Walsh watched their expressions as they absorbed the message. An uncomfortable silence followed.

Collins gave a nervous laugh. "Does this mean we can call you daddy now?"

Walsh offered him a thin smile. "If this were some starport urchin, I'd probably be laughing. However, I won't stand for any crude jokes at Angelica's expense." He glanced at Diaz. "If I hear anything of the sort, we'll rig up a way to bring keelhauling into space. I was trying to be funny there, but I mean it. Any hint or perception of impropriety and those involved will not leave this ship with their commission. Understood?"

The digital heads assembled around the table nodded gravely.

"In any case, I plan on keeping Angelica secured away as much as possible until we find her a new foster home. But as the doctor said, we can't keep her locked up all the time. She's just a kid."

Walsh saw Diaz purse her lips, but said nothing.

"Can we just put her back in the box?" Fuller asked.

"Afraid not," Dr. Barnes said. "Her pod nearly failed and her recovery wasn't graceful. I don't think her body would take it."

"That's all I have for now," Walsh said. "Dismissed. XO, please report to my stateroom." He waved all the faces away.

Walsh waited until Diaz entered and shut the hatch behind her. She marched to his desk and stood.

"Please, sit."

"I'd prefer to stand, Capitan."

"Felicia, please."

Diaz raised a brow and took a seat. "Yes, Capitan."

"Talk to me about Angelica. Why so full of piss and vinegar?" He held up a hand before she could answer. "And don't give me some bullshit about regs or logistics or delta-v. This isn't our first cruise together and I've never seen you so vitriolic. Not even towards Midland."

"I'm not going to tuck that thing in bed if that's what you're after."

Walsh considered his XO over steepled fingers for a moment. "Right now, I'm just asking why, Felicia."

Diaz glanced away and drummed her thumb against her knee. "Why do you care? Really?"

"To be honest, I'm afraid you're going to lose it on her. The situation isn't ideal, but it's where we're at. Spill it."

She studied his face for a long moment. "This isn't the first time I've run across these vat whores—"

Walsh held up his hands. "Please, stop using that term. Think what you will, but I don't want it getting back to Angelica. And I don't want the crew to take your example."

"She's heard it plenty already. Her feelings are programmed. She doesn't care."

Walsh narrowed his eyes.

Diaz raised her brows and tilted her head to look at Walsh. "Fine. Back when Pranson was *El Presidente*, do you remember his so-called push to civilize the Junker clans? I was XO of *Star Bender* at the time. We raided a few stations, collected up the vat wh... girls and boys, and arrested any slavers we could manage.

"They're disgusting, Gene. They aren't real children. I watched the evidence feeds. They *liked* what was done to them. No real child, or any person, would like what I saw. We even chased a small cell of them to an ice dome on Ganymede."

"Fortunately," Walsh said, "I never had to see anything like that, even though we chased a few ourselves. But who do we blame for the behavior of any abused animal?" When Diaz didn't answer, he continued. "The abuser, or owner, of course. Angelica can't help what she is."

"Maybe," Diaz said. "But the look in their eyes when... things were being done to them—it's hunger. Lust. Many things and people can't help what they are. It doesn't make them any less disgusting. Like maggots or dogs eating vomit. And we saw some younger than Angelica."

Walsh decided to let the comparison go without comment. "And you caught someone with them? Someone you knew?"

Diaz glared at Walsh for a second before looking away. "*Si*. One of my... peers."

"Someone you were involved with."

With a loud sigh, Diaz leaned back in her chair. A rueful smile cracked her face. "Yes. One of those shipboard dalliances. We only—usually—met up while at port, not on the ship. After we busted who I believed was the Ganymede ringleader, I burned some leave and went to surprise *mi amore* who was still down there."

She shook her head, looking ill. "I walked in on him with... It turns out the real ringleader had bribed him with two of those girls. *Dios mio*, Gene. I could never have imagined *him* doing that. Not in a million years. And those little whores were begging him not to stop when I interrupted them."

"That's terrible," Walsh whispered. "What happened to him? Anyone I know?"

"You might know him, but he's an admiral Earthside now and I'd rather not name names."

"You didn't report him?"

Diaz narrowed her eyes at him. "Of course I did. But I didn't want to. I wanted to believe there were some mitigating circumstances, and he did his best to convince me there were. But I knew that if I let it go, that slaver could blackmail me."

"But he's an admiral?" Walsh asked.

"Nothing came of the charges except the pervo lost his flight status. He got to keep everything else, though."

"Did the slaver get away?"

Diaz snorted. "For a while. My ex-friend helped the bastard escape while I was still struggling with what to do. But the slaver got spaced two years later in some Junker-clan war around Titan. So now you know my long, sad story, Capitan. What next?"

"I simply want you to treat Angelica with the professionalism and fairness I've come to expect from you. You probably won't even have to deal with her. *I* don't plan on dealing with her unless strictly necessary. She can be some cadet's collateral duty. Or someone from Medical. Either way, I won't make you tuck her in."

Diaz grinned momentarily. "No promises except that I'll do my best."

Walsh returned the grin. "Your best has always exceeded my expectations, XO."

"And you need to watch yourself around the girl—"

Walsh pointed a finger at Diaz. "I hope you're not going to make some comment about my promiscuity, Felicia. I try to accept your chastisements with a smile, but you need to secure that shit right now."

"I wasn't, Gene," she answered somberly. "It's an earnest warning. For you and whoever you assign to watch the girl. That doctor was right. And I would never expect anything like that from you in a million years, either. But these sex slaves get in people's heads. And then into their beds. Please, be careful with..." Diaz paused, as a child would when forced to repeat a blasphemy before her parents. "Angelica."

Chapter 20

SCHRODINGER'S TIGER orbited retrograde around Sol at 1.9 AU. Dugg's orders were to run comms intercept on a Caliphate fleet out past the belt, so that fleet's movement dictated *Tiger*'s movement. Even tight-beam comms experienced dispersion over distance. And Dugg had positioned his ship in the window that might snatch some of the scatter between Caliphate's L4 station, Gabrielle's Star, and the fleet. *Tiger*'s current course would keep her between the two without burning any delta-v—until the Caliphate fleet made a hard turn. Dugg was expecting that anytime now.

Sneaking around Sol and eavesdropping had its moments, but wasn't very exciting overall. Despite *Tiger*'s impressive signal-analysis suite, most interesting signals were well encrypted. He was there to intercept, collect, and transmit all intercepts back to MarSec—undecrypted. It was an insult to ask a red-blooded intelligence captain to ignore such entertainment. SOP, but an insult nonetheless.

A connection request blinked in Dugg's vision.

"Dugg."

The comms officer's avatar appeared. "Captain, last week's MarSec cypher update decrypted the last transmission from Gabrielle's Star. Apparently someone over there doesn't know that code's been cracked."

Dugg worked up his best pointed disinterest. "File it and put it in the queue for the next transmission window."

"Yes, sir." There was a hint of disappointment in the comms officer's voice. Dugg wasn't the only one who enjoyed a juicy bit of gossip.

"Run it through the analyzer and work up a checksum to see if we can relate it to any future signals from the fleet. Out."

Dugg waited an hour before accessing the message. MarSec regs gave a captain some latitude to investigate signals intelligence, SIGINT, that might reveal a threat to their ship. It would be unseemly to be too eager to read such an intercept. And it might get him flagged as a security or loyalty concern.

Usually that regulation was limited to the reasonable estimation that such a signal might contain immediately actionable, tactical information. In this case, as in so many, he was just being nosy. Someday, Dugg knew he'd be called upon to explain himself. It was far more exciting to play games with MarSec than it was to drift pointlessly around Sol in what should be a fully automated ship.

In truth, he liked the peace. But going against Walsh—that had been exciting. And his social profile soared on the military-nets after the shoot-out. Not many active duty commanders can claim to have destroyed a ship with weapons fire. Though it was a secret mission, there were millions of telescope hobbyists and they'd captured the battle from just about every angle. It almost made up for the years of grinding boredom.

Walsh could have destroyed *Tiger* and Dugg was grateful for the man's willingness to avoid an interplanetary incident by not doing so. Though Walsh was near the top of the mil-net ratings, Dugg was now a peer. He hoped the camaraderie he felt towards Walsh was reciprocated. And they'd each fought against a national military vessel, not some Junker scav or cartel smuggler.

From the navigation plot of the Caliphate fleet, however, Walsh might have another fight on his hands. It wasn't definite, but an intercept course with *Amazonas* was still within the delta-v estimation of the fleet.

The message opened in the modern Arabic of the Caliphate. Dugg ordered it translated and the writing was replaced with the Sino-Cyrillic script of Mars. He pushed off the wall of his cabin and drifted while he read.

It was a standard, Caliphate orders dispatch. He'd read dozens of them. Like most, it was short and to the point. There wasn't much detail, but it confirmed the Caliphate fleet was hunting *Amazonas*. It didn't explain why they would pull *Sword of God* from its safe orbit around Earth. No one moved their expensive battle cruisers without good reason.

What could be a good reason for sending a fleet that size after a training ship?

They would attack if *Amazonas* "lit the stars." The fleet must already know what that meant because the orders gave no further explanation. But they were worried Walsh was going to do something. If MarSec knew what, they hadn't shared it with Dugg.

The CAR had to suspect the fleet was trailing *Amazonas*. If so, they weren't concerned as far as Dugg could tell. No diverted assets. No maneuvers from Walsh that would indicate he'd received a warning. Walsh was good, but he wasn't four-to-one-odds good. Especially with a ship full of cadets.

Dugg almost suspected a MarSec deep-cover op to get the Caliphate to destroy *Amazonas*. If so, kudos to that tech-ops team.

He reviewed the last intel briefing from *Amazonas*'s refit at Liberty Station, as well as the sordid affair of Walsh's inquisition. Not that Earth admirals were very bright, but Dugg enjoyed hearing Walsh had put his thumb in their eye and kept his command.

And maybe that's why he was out there alone right now. The Earthers were a treacherous lot. The more important they became, the bigger the daggers they used.

Long-range optical observation from MarSec labelled the refit a sensor overhaul. The visible modifications looked like antenna clusters. Otherwise, the thermal and EM profile of *Amazonas* hadn't changed when observed from a distance.

Yet there was a Caliphate fleet with orders to start a war. MarSec had missed something big. That was bad enough, but what made it worse was that the Caliphate had figured something out. Or thought they had.

It was madness, far beyond normal Earth idiocy. Such an attack might plunge all of Sol into war. Mars would not be spared after its—his—own recent attack on the United Isles courier. There were fifteen hours left until the next random data transmission to MarSec. Dugg flagged the intercepted message as "Priority: Immediate Review" and transmitted the microburst.

There was no telling what Machiavellian court intrigue Walsh had been drawn into. But it seemed clear he was being left out in the vacc by one CAR faction or other. Now Dugg had to decide what to do about it.

The obvious, wisest, and safest thing to do was nothing. An action on his part might inadvertently pull Mars into the fallout of whatever this attack would be. The MarSec fleet could match any Earth or cartel fleet at the current level. But if Earth went into full-swing production... Mars would be in trouble. Dugg might be sent on another daredevil mission with a low chance of survival.

But he owed Walsh. *Amazonas* could have killed *Tiger*—a point that kept coming to Dugg's mind whenever heroic hubris threatened—after countering the cyberattack. Post-battle analysis still hadn't determined how the hack had been stopped so quickly. MarSec was concerned about that. So was Dugg, but the digital arms race went on.

Walsh probably wouldn't accept a warning from Dugg. And the Caliphate fleet might detect the transmission and respond. A signal sent to Liberty Station would certainly be intercepted and possibly deciphered. Not that he'd know who to trust on Liberty, and he had no authority to activate an agent.

He bounced silently from wall to wall as he considered. Flipping through the reports for a fourth time, Dugg smiled. There was his answer. LTE had supposedly been in charge of the upgrades and footed a large part of the bill. A quick check of LTE's intel profile confirmed they had tapped into some of their obscure holding accounts during *Amazonas*'s refit. As with all things Earth, the adage "follow the money" was a good place to start. LTE had their fingers in everything on Liberty, and probably had a big investment in whatever Walsh was out there to do.

Which was "lighting a fire," whatever that meant.

LTE was the place to start. Not some low-level executive flunky with delusions of competence; this message was going to Bruno Azevedo himself.

LTE had relays all over the system and Dugg chose one on a relative bearing to which he could send a tight beam with a low probability of intercept. He verified the Mars cyber-seed in the relay's system and accessed the comms.

Dugg stared at the display in his overlay. Why was he really helping Walsh? It might get him put up on treason charges. He didn't want to be remembered as some supercilious rube who had betrayed his beloved planet for some misguided, chivalric bromance. Of course, it was impossible to know what the mil-nets would think. Some would consider it honor among enemies, some would call for his testicles to be hung out in vacuum for being a traitor. And the jilted MarSec, if they chose to respond at all, would slander him as a criminal.

That was all out of his control once he transmitted the Caliphate orders.

If he was going to help, the sooner the better. With a few flicks of Dugg's eyes, the LTE relay was programmed to accept the incoming message, mark it as highest importance and route it directly to Bruno. He sent the message with an attached routine that would scramble the message logs in the relay.

BRUNO AZEVEDO FROWNED across the desk. "There's a Caliphate fleet following Walsh and no one mentioned it to me?"

"I'm sorry, Bruno," Admiral James said in a tone that indicated she was not. "While I do appreciate LTE's place at Liberty, you're just not on the notification list for tactical developments. Nor are you notified when we order new space rations, zero-g boots, or designate a new cadet."

Bruno pursed his lips to keep his mouth from spouting off. "Nothing pays off like the restraint of reply" was a maxim he held to. Even the CEOs of interplanetary corporations had to know when to shut up.

"I understand that. But you know how much LTE, how much I personally, have invested in this project." He leaned back and grabbed one of the bottles of scotch. When he inclined the bottle towards James, she shook her head. Bruno poured himself a small glass. "I would have hoped our professional relationship would at least warrant a little heads-up."

Admiral James straightened her back and gave Bruno a frank look. "To be honest, I didn't know. I have more ships in orbit than just yours. And to be more honest, the word I think of when I read any of your papers on this is cockamamie. My dad liked the word cockamamie and I think it's apt here, too."

"I appreciate you're a busy woman, Linda. And I appreciate, even agree with, your assessment of my little project." He tilted his drink back and set the empty glass on the table with a loud clink. "But just think what happens if it works. It will change... everything."

"For the better?"

"We'll see. But I think for the good. Eventually."

Admiral James relaxed in the chair. "I assume you know of the Cali fleet from a company source. One of your orbital telescopes?"

Bruno chuckled. "One of our scopes has been focused on the *Amazonas* since it left Liberty. We were too focused to see the Cali fleet, though. As you like to remind me, we're not military, after all."

"So how did you find out?"

"A little birdie." Bruno raised his hand. "And before you press the interrogation, I honestly don't know who it was."

James raised a brow as Bruno pulled a small dossier from his desk and slid it towards her. "A hard copy? Trying to keep me from tracing the digital signature? How very corporate espionage of you."

Bruno grinned but said nothing while the admiral flipped through the pages.

James glared at him over the top of the dossier. "Where'd you get this?"

"Like I said, I don't know."

"How did it physically get to be in your possession, Bruno? I'm not kidding here."

"I'd rather not say. For the sake of LTE security, naturally. More important is what you're going to do about Walsh."

"I guarantee you," James said, "that Walsh is well aware of the Caliphate fleet. We tail them, they tail us. It's standard fleet games. Been going on back to the wet navy."

Bruno motioned to the dossier. "Does he know they're planning to attack him? Is that standard?"

"No one knows if they're going to attack." She thumped the dossier dismissively and set it in her lap. "This is hearsay with no source and no proof. It could be one of your competitors trying to make you do something stupid."

"It isn't."

"Care to share the original for intel analysis?"

Bruno smiled. "Not at this time."

"Then it's just rumor, and in bad taste." James smirked. "Odd that your concern for Walsh doesn't extend to telling him what he's actually doing out there. Or maybe it isn't Walsh you're concerned about?"

"For security reasons, obviously." Bruno wasn't going to let her goad him. "You're no stranger to hiding things from your commanders."

Admiral James thumped the dossier again. "If this is true as you say it is, your security needs updating."

"Someone's security needs updating," Bruno agreed wryly. "So you're not going to warn Walsh?"

James stood and tucked the dossier beneath her arm. "Not at this time. And neither will you. If you do, we'll eventually find out, Bruno. Even personal comms sent to the *Amazonas* are monitored and logged."

"Of course, Admiral. Now that you've told me, I will not contact Walsh on this matter again."

She narrowed her eyes at him momentarily before leaving his office. Bruno lifted his glass in a solitary toast after her. Admirals were an unholy union of bureaucratic simplemindedness and political self-interest. This made them predictable, which is why he'd messaged Walsh before speaking to Admiral James. In Bruno's position, it was always better to ask forgiveness than permission.

He stared into the swirling scotch in the glass. James had kept back vital information about a project that could make or break him; a project that could change Sol and the landscape of all humanity. If she did something like that again, Adm. Linda A. James would find herself on the receiving end of Bruno's not insignificant influence. She wouldn't be the first ex-admiral to have crossed paths with Laboratorio d Tecnologia Espacial.

Chapter 21

"WHAT ARE WE LOOKING for, Capitan?" Collins asked.

"I'm not sure we're looking for anything," Walsh said. "Liberty was a little short on details on what those so-called astronomical antennae are for."

"Or that big black box next to the nexus gate key," Bovree said. "That thing hasn't been activated in my lifetime."

Moore laughed. "I thought you were on the Apollo missions. Isn't one of those sets of footprints yours?"

"If I'd been born on Earth, I'd never have left it. Especially for that big, ugly, white dust ball."

"Watch it," Moore said. "I have many fond childhood memories of that dust ball. At least you can see Earth from there. Not like that iceball that spawned you."

Walsh let them carry on, hoping to distract everyone from more questions about the mission. He knew the last time *Amazonas*'s nexus key had been activated was shortly before the colonies destroyed the gate. But that was about all he knew. None of the orders or logs had any relevant information concerning the heavy black box in Engineering. He didn't even know what the single green light meant. It probably meant that things were working, but there was no way to be sure.

Diaz's overlay avatar raised a brow. "When I was on the *Cometa*, we drifted for three weeks guarding some sensor pod we deployed. It didn't do anything we could detect. Then we picked it up and went home."

"We can detect telemetry and high-powered Cali transmissions with the new arrays," Collins said.

Walsh nodded. That fleet had been on his mind a lot lately. The Caliphate was still put out with him, flooding the nets with slander about his atrocities. But that was a lot of tonnage to move just to get revenge on a single CAR ship. The ships were still drifting on their vector, but hadn't passed the point where a solid burn would put them on intercept with *Amazonas*.

He had almost put off his concerns as paranoia. Until Bruno Azevedo sent him a personal warning. Hector and Bovree confirmed it was genuine. The whole mission was an LTE experiment, and he'd met Bruno in person, so receiving some communication didn't seem that unusual. But one with immediate and actionable intel? That was concerning. Yet, not as concerning as the message from Admiral James that followed shortly thereafter, warning him to ignore intelligence not vetted by CAR security. The admiral's message had the effect of making Walsh take Bruno's warning more seriously.

As if reading his mind, Collins announced, "No change in the Cali fleet, Capitan."

Walsh glanced at Collins and smiled. "Thanks, Ops."

He stood and rolled his head, generating a series of satisfying pops. "Now that we're on station, I'm getting some chow and some sleep."

THE GALLEY IN HABITAT Alpha was quiet. Walsh stepped in and did a double take. Angelica was sitting at one of the tables, wearing a billowing white dress with pink trim, and pink ribbons in her hair. A large sketch pad sat in her lap, the pencil in her hand dancing across the page. Screwball was squatting on the far end of the table, posing with a distant stare.

Lieutenant Jarvis, the medical tech with chaperone duty, glanced up at Walsh and moved to announce his presence. Walsh made a cutting motion across his neck, then motioned Jarvis over.

"Capitan."

"What's with her dress?"

Jarvis grinned and shook his head. "Well, Capitan, at first she insisted on dressing like a right port tart. Halter top and booty shorts, miniskirt and corset, and so on. I finally convinced her that you wanted her to dress pretty, not slutty. After some more wrangling around, she finally agreed to this getup." He nodded to her feet. "And those pink shoes."

The girl was striking, no longer looking like a bedraggled kitten pulled from the water. From his angle, Walsh could see the profile of Angelica's breasts, too developed for her apparent age. Her exposed lower legs were crossed beneath her seat, revealing curves and definition more suited to a cyber-suit model. But it was more than her features. Angelica's poise and posture were stately. Even the short strokes her hand made across the paper were graceful.

Screwball whispered something to her without moving his body. Angelica laughed, tossing her hair over her shoulder with an inviting frivolity. A tingle of warmth started in Walsh's belly. The subsequent wave of horrified shock washed it away.

Walsh cleared his throat. "Thanks for watching her. How's she doing?"

"I don't mind a bit, sir. She kind of reminds me of my own daughter—minus the whole sex slave thing, of course. She's comfortable in zero-g. From what she said, a lot of her 'daddies' live on spaceships or orbital habitats. We trained her to get to the shielded station and she already knew how to operate an emergency breather."

Walsh stood on tiptoes to peek over her shoulder. "She's quite the artist."

"Oh, yes, sir. I offered to show her the overlay art suite, but she said she only likes 'real you can feel' art."

Walsh grinned. "I understand. I'm going to talk with her. Stay put."

"She'll like that, sir," Jarvis said. "She's hurt that you don't like her."

Walsh pursed his lips before walking to Angelica's table. Screwball looked at him but Walsh motioned for him to stay put. "Hello, Angelica."

The little girl leaped to her feet, spilling her pencils and sketch pad to the deck. "Daddy! Daddy!" She hugged Walsh tightly around the waist, ignoring his gentle pushes. "I missed you, Dad—I mean, Capitan. Why haven't you come to visit me already?"

Walsh awkwardly returned the hug while he continued with his efforts to extricate himself. "I'm sorry, Angelica. I'm very busy. But Lieutenant Jarvis says you're doing just fine."

"Who?"

Walsh motioned towards the hatch.

"Oh, you mean Jimmy. Yes. He's nice." Angelica screwed one eye shut and added in a gravelly pirate voice, "And I like the cut of your jib, too, Cap'n!"

Walsh laughed despite himself. He squatted and began gathering the pencils. With the other hand, he carefully lifted the sketch pad and stared dumbly at it. The portrait of Screwball was so detailed, so perfectly shaded and proportioned, that it looked photographic. He flipped through pages, each one surprising him more. It was filled with portraits of other crew members: Fuller, Collins, Jarvis, and several cadets. No Diaz, he noted with a wry smile.

"These are amazing, Angelica. When I heard you drew, well... I was expecting good for a nine-year-old. You know, crayons and stick figures."

"I did draw that way when I was nine, silly." She bumped into Walsh playfully. "But that was a long time ago. Daddy Sargasso taught me how to draw whenever I went to him. He's a famous artist on Mars, but I don't think that's his real name."

Walsh handed the pad and pencils to Angelica. "How old are you?"

"Nineteen," she said cheerfully. She nodded at Screwball. "I'm older than he is and he's part of the crew. That's funny."

Screwball shrugged at Walsh. "Sorry, Capitan. It's true. I'm only thirteen."

"Really?" Walsh glanced between the two. "Neither one of you looks a day over ten. Not that I'm an expert on children or simians."

"That's how they made me." A somber smile crossed Angelica's face and disappeared. "Forever young."

"Sorry," Walsh said. "I didn't mean to upset you."

Her bright smile lit the room. "So if you don't want to be my daddy because I'm too young—"

"No, no," Walsh interrupted. "It's not that. Well, not just that. You're here to be pretty, and that's all."

Angelica pouted and returned to her seat. "I'm glad you came to visit, Capitan. I want to be pretty for you." She tossed her hair back over her shoulder and pointed her pencil at Screwball. "Now stop acting like a monkey and sit still."

"I am not a monkey."

"You're acting like one. Sit still."

"I've seen human children," Screwball said. "I think monkeys are better behaved."

Angelica tapped on the pad with her pencil, looking down as she spoke. "Well, I don't have a monkey to sketch. And if you don't sit still I'm going to draw a big, fat human nose on your portrait."

Screwball's grimace was so wide and ridiculous looking, Walsh burst out laughing.

"You wouldn't!"

"Not if you sit still this instant." She looked up from the pad and cocked her head. "I'm sorry, Screwy. I'm not trying to be mean."

Screwball snorted loudly and returned to his pose.

The girl was adorable, Walsh had to admit. And her art truly was amazing. It made him feel like an impostor with his digital pallet and fancy art programs. That people could have the inclination to abuse her made his stomach clench. He reached out to tousle her hair, but pulled back, unsure how Angelica would react.

He walked away from the table and brought up the menu on his overlay. Just as he reached for the potato medley, the lights dimmed enough to activate the emergency battle lanterns. A dull thrum vibrated the deck and bulkheads.

"What the..." Walsh started.

Diaz's image appeared in front of him. Her voice blared from the ship's speakers and his overlay simultaneously. "Capitan to Ops, immediately."

Walsh strode out of the galley at maximum dignified speed—unfed.

Chapter 22

"WHAT WAS THAT POWER drain, XO?" Walsh asked as he strode into the operations center.

"Power and Propulsion are pulling logs," she answered. "But it looks like it didn't pull from everything. At least it didn't drop the main computers."

"Ops, PnP," said Lt. Cmdr. Melania Olivo over the operations channel. "It looks like our black box pulled a huge load and fired off a transmission through those antennae they added. Everything has recovered, no faults detected."

"Does it look like it would interfere with combat operations?" Diaz asked.

"No, ma'am," answered Olivo. "But it's hard to be sure without knowing what the damn black box will do next. It might draw more power next time, or from different systems. Liberty just gave us the minimum 'need to know basis' stuff."

"Since it didn't bother to tell us," Walsh said wryly, "is there something you saw that might give us some warning? Maybe some initial drain or spike that happened before the main power drain hit?"

Olivo was silent for a moment before responding. "The reactor watch tells me there was a configuration change in the load profile software. Looks like it isn't much before, a second or two maybe, but since the box restored the original configuration, I would assume it'll modify it before whatever it does next. Assume being the operative word."

"All right, Olivo," said Walsh. "Look for anything else, but set a flag on that profile change to notify Ops and PnP."

"It'd be nice if they included a 'Hey, we're going to seriously load down your system' light or something," Collins said.

"Well, we are on station. I'll give someone the benefit of the doubt that it wouldn't do that if we were at crisis stations."

Collins raised his brows at Walsh, who merely offered a shrug in return.

"And get Mahoney on his rig," Walsh added. "Maybe he can see something in the data feeds or the timing or the whatever he might pull from the aether."

The lights dimmed three more times over the next three hours. Each time, Walsh focused on the Caliphate squadron. Directing high-powered transmissions at a spacecraft was considered a hostile action, and they had no control whatsoever over the black box. The Cali ships were far enough away that even if they were beamed by *Amazonas*'s wild and unknown experiments, it shouldn't cause any harm. But Walsh was starting to feel alone between the mysterious warning he'd received and the apparent lack of concern from Liberty. If the Caliphate commander decided to take offence, the battle would be over before the admiralty could reply one way or the other.

The watch changed, and Walsh found the galley and the shower in short order. The black box had been silent for several hours, likely reconfiguring itself in accordance with whatever algorithms it operated under. He'd let the presence of *Sword of God* get to him, and he knew it. Walsh was used to having the only Nova-class ship in any given sphere of operations and he didn't like it. So before slipping into his rack, he sat cross-legged on the deck to meditate. After three deep, calming breaths, the lights dimmed. When they returned to normal, Walsh resumed his breathing. He got six deep breaths in before Diaz buzzed him.

"Capitan," she said, her voice hesitant and breathy. He snapped his eyes open.

"What is it, Diaz?"

"You need to come. Now."

"Coming." Walsh grabbed his flightsuit and rushed down the passage to operations.

"Capitan on deck," Hector announced.

Diaz turned to her capitan, her wide eyes not seeing that he was in his skivvies. Walsh slipped one leg into his uniform, but when he glanced at his XO's face, he stopped and looked at the display hovering over her lap. No one in Ops was moving, each staring at the same proximity-alarm screen the CO and XO were.

"It showed up after that last burst from the black box," Diaz said, her voice a loud whisper.

"Is that...?" Walsh had to stop, had to press his eyes shut before looking again. His flightsuit slipped from his fingers to crumple into a pile at his feet. "Is that a nexus gate?"

"*Dios mio*, Capitan." Diaz crossed herself, once while facing Walsh and again when she turned back to the holo-display. "I don't know. It... it looks like it."

Operations was silent for almost a full minute, routine comms from other decks left unanswered. Walsh looked down at his flightsuit and hurriedly pulled it up, sealing the cling strip with some difficulty.

"Hector," Walsh finally asked aloud, "does the signature of this object match either the Earth gate or any from other systems you have on record?"

"Capitan, it shares the approximate dimensions of all known nexus gates, and is currently emitting similar electromagnetic patterns found in records. It is, of course, a preliminary answer, Capitan. We have only been observing it for less than ten minutes."

"Where did it come from?" Walsh asked. Getting no response, he grasped Diaz on the shoulder and slowly turned her to face him. "Where did it come from?"

"I don't know, Gene. It was not there, and then it was. When the prox went off, it only showed a distorted return at first, then after two more sweeps..." She shrugged and shook her head. "It was just there." She stood and motioned for Walsh to take the chair.

"Oh my god," Walsh whispered. "Could it be an undiscovered gate? One they knew about?"

"Or one they suspected," offered Collins. "And they put the box on us."

"I wish they'd sent us a few escorts," Moore said. "Once this gets out, it'll be more than a gate that gets opened up."

Walsh jumped to his feet and bolted for the hatch. "XO, you have operations. Get our cone pointed straight at the gate." He was up the third rung of the ladder before Diaz could acknowledge the command or Hector could announce the capitan's departure.

Scrabbling up the ladder like a cadet, Walsh pushed off too hard with a foot in a low-g section of the tube and sent himself flying upwards with splayed arms. He did a quick flutter kick to rotate his body and grabbed a nearby conduit. Three members of the Systems Maintenance division, who were gathered in a tight circle diligently keeping up with their preventative inspections, scattered to avoid being bowled over as Walsh launched from the access shaft. The crew members watched their CO quickly disappear cone-ward and returned to their work.

"I guess we'll just have to wait until the turn," Screwball was telling Angelica when Walsh entered, "and find something else to look at."

"Oh, pooh," she replied with a pout.

Screwball noticed Walsh and his brows shot up his forehead in surprise. A short, simian squeal escaped his mouth as Hector's voice announced the capitan's presence. "Capitan."

Angelica's protruding lip spread into a warm smile. "Capitan Daddy!" She pushed off the deck gracefully and floated to Walsh, wrapping her arms around his waist.

"No time, Angelica," Walsh said, patting her head tentatively. "I need the telescope."

"Yes, sir!" She disentangled her arms and snapped him a girlish salute. "Screwball and I were just looking at planets. I love the telescope."

"Me, too," said Walsh, pulling himself over to the eyepiece. "Cadet, please align the scope with the ship's heading." Walsh could have easily done it himself, but he took every opportunity to treat Screwball as he would any other cadet. He peered through the scope impatiently as the servo motors softly whined. The scope indicated it was at center; nothing showed in the eyepiece except the stars.

Walsh zoomed out and saw a momentary flicker of blue that raced around in a circle and disappeared. Zooming back in, he realized that it had been there, but the gate was difficult to see at first due to its apparent color. With expert, delicate adjustments, Walsh centered the telescope where he'd seen the light, adjusted the focus, and increased magnification two more factors.

"Oh my god," he whispered.

An obsidian ellipse filled the view. Sizzling traces of electric-blue light danced around the edges of the gate, giving shape to what would otherwise only be visible as a silhouette against the field of stars behind it. Walsh zoomed in further to isolate a single segment of the gate. The pulsing light illuminated a faint pattern of geometric protrusions across the dark surface.

"Amazing," whispered Walsh. "Simply amazing."

After a few minutes, Angelica quietly asked, "Can I see, too?"

Walsh reluctantly turned away from the eyepiece to look at her. "Yes, of course."

"Yay," she squealed, accepting Walsh's hand to pull her to the telescope. "Oh, that is pretty, Capitan. Do you think it's as old as the other one?"

"I'd have to say so." Walsh was looking at the nearby holographic projection, applying different viewing filters. The radar and lidar sweeps were adding new details every minute, causing the image to shift minutely with each update.

"Do you want to look, Screwball?" Angelica asked. "It looks really old. And pretty."

The chimpanzee looked at Angelica, then at Walsh.

"Can he, Capitan? Please say yes."

Walsh looked at Screwball, envisioning a scene from the ancient science-fiction movie, *2001: A Space Odyssey*, with the monolith replaced by a looming nexus gate—and Screwball bashing in Walsh's head with a bone.

"Uh, sure."

"Thanks, Capitan," said Screwball. He pulled himself along the bulkhead with only his feet and set his eye eagerly to the eyepiece. "Oh my, oh my." The chimp started a hooting laugh that brought a smile to Walsh's face. Angelica laughed, too, winking at Walsh.

"All right, Cadet," Walsh said after a minute. "Shove aside and make a hole." He crowded past Screwball and pushed his face back to the eyepiece. "Amazing. Diaz, are you seeing this?"

"Yes, Capitan. And I can see it quite clearly from here," she added wryly.

"I know, I know," Walsh admitted. "But there's just something about looking at it directly through the glass."

"You know the glass is actually digitally enhanced..."

"Thank you, XO." Walsh was going to add something, but the lights dimmed again.

Screwball slowly pointed a finger at the CO's face. "Capitan. Your face."

Walsh touched his face and noticed a bright, blue light play across his fingers as he moved them away. A ray of light was shining through the telescope's eyepiece, bright in the dim observatory. Reducing the magnification, Walsh carefully placed his eye back to the scope.

The entire area inside the nexus gate was filled with a bright maelstrom of swirling light. Blues and violets mixed with slashes of white, the intensity causing Walsh to squint. Though he tried to stare through it, he was forced to eventually slide the filter adjustment setting to dim the light.

"Capitan!" shouted Diaz over the comm-link. "The black box activated the key generator. The gate is emitting a massive EM signal."

"I see that," Walsh whispered.

"Nexus-gate connection established, Capitan," came Hector's voice over the intercom. "It has been three hundred and fifty-seven years since I last made that announcement." Walsh thought he heard a trace of wonder in that statement.

"And to think," Walsh said, "previous capitans of the *Amazonas* saw this all the time."

"Do you think this black box thingy will fly us through that?" Angelica asked, playing with her drifting locks. In microgravity, her hair splayed around her face as if she were in an underwater photograph. "That would be so exciting!"

Walsh looked at Screwball. "I hope not. We have no idea where it goes. Now that we've found it, I'm sure future missions will send through scout drones to map and take—"

"Capitan," Moore interrupted. "Two of the Cali ships have initiated full burn at us; one's the *Sword of God*. We're also getting multiple new signatures compatible with Lancer-class anti-ship missiles."

"How many?" Diaz asked.

"Forty so far, XO."

"Those Calies really like their missiles," Walsh said. "I guess we lit the torch."

"*Que?*" asked Diaz.

"I'll tell you later, XO. Initiate habitat spin down and sound crisis stations. I'm heading there now." Walsh kicked gently towards the hatch.

"Cadet, secure that telescope and make sure Angelica gets secured in her crypt."

"Yes, sir."

Chapter 23

HECTOR'S HEAD APPEARED in Walsh's overlay. "All hands are secured in shielded stations, Capitan."

"Verified," Diaz said over the command channel.

"Understood," Walsh said, not looking away from his tactical map. Fifty-two Caliphate missiles were inbound, spreading out on the display. The missiles would soon change trajectory to converge on *Amazonas* from multiple angles. Then they'd detonate simultaneously to overwhelm her point-defense system. He thought it fitting that the missile tracks on the display looked like a giant spider's web.

Classic Caliphate tactics. But Walsh had never seen so many missiles expended on a single target. It wouldn't take even half that number to turn Liberty Station into a cloud of whirling debris.

Sword of God and *Anahita Bahar-Mehler* chased after the missiles to finish the job if *Amazonas* survived.

There wasn't much hope of that. The missiles were spread too far to get them all with EMP warheads and the Lancer-class anti-ship missiles normally carried multiple kinetic penetrators in each warhead. They would come too fast and too many.

Walsh dialed his panic inhibitor to maximum. "Get us burning, Ops. It may not help much, but we need maneuver options." He didn't know what those options would be. *Amazonas* had been floating on station for several days.

"I know it comes with the job," Collins said, "but I can't believe they're actually shooting at us."

Bovree snorted. "What I can't believe is that they obviously knew this was going to happen and we didn't. And it's our mission!"

Walsh adjusted the time lapse on the tactical display, watching the missiles change their estimated positions. There was no great tactical plan;

the missiles would overwhelm *Amazonas*'s defenses. "Tac-O, best targeting points to take out multiple missiles?"

"Sorry, sir. The dispersion pattern is wide. I only find three points and we might get ten if we're lucky." Moore added cheerfully, "But those ECM drones you deployed a few days ago are online and ready."

"I guess maybe we did know something was going to happen," Bovree said wryly. "Not that I'm complaining about being prepared, Capitan."

Walsh wished he had done more. But what? Abort the mission? Conduct a preemptive strike? Demand the admiralty move a fleet to protect *Amazonas* based on an uncorroborated, secondhand warning? And here he was, about to start firing again.

"Engage scrambler drones and target the Cali ships with the mag-cannons. They're too far away, but it might make them spend a little delta-v to evade. Switch to point-defense fire when the missiles are in the envelope."

"Every little bit helps," Collins said.

"ECM drones active," Moore said. "Mag-cannons firing. Here's to hoping."

The cycling of the magnetic rail cannons sent a soft buzz through *Amazonas*'s hull. Walsh knew there was no way *Amazonas* could win this fight on her own. Maybe if *Sword of God* wasn't there, but only maybe. CAR tactics against Caliphate missile swarms involved several ships supporting each other with overlapping point-defense zones. And if she did survive the missiles, the Cali ships wouldn't be far behind, firing barrages from their own mag-cannons. Starting from a standstill as she was, *Amazonas* couldn't outrun the enemy fleet.

They would die alone.

"Any replies from the Caliphate fleet?" Walsh asked.

"Negative, Capitan," Collins answered.

Walsh spun the tactical display, hoping to find something he'd missed, some pattern, some cosmic clue to get them out of this. If it wasn't for that gate...

"Capitan?" Diaz said over his private channel. "What are you grinning about?"

The answer was obvious; so obvious he forced himself to slow down and reconsider. It could save them and it was what he'd wanted most in the universe. He didn't want his judgement clouded, didn't want to destroy his crew, by chasing a convenient dream that could quickly turn into a nightmare.

"Capitan?" she repeated.

Walsh could see no choice. "XO, take us through the gate."

"*Capitan*?"

Walsh fought to keep the childlike excitement he felt out of his voice. "You hear me, XO. Take us through the gate."

"This ship hasn't been through a gate in centuries," Bovree objected.

"My apologies, Sec-O. I didn't mean to give you the impression this had turned into a discussion. Though I'll happily reconsider if you can hack all the Cali hardware out there bent on venting us into space."

Bovree made no reply.

Walsh nodded. "Third time's a charm. Please, XO, take us through the gate."

"*Dios mio*," Diaz muttered. "Ops, set for the nearest inner-edge of the gate."

Diaz connected to his private channel again. "Gene, are you sure about this? We don't know where this goes."

"No, I'm not sure. But I am sure about the fifty-two incoming. And I've never heard of a nexus gate opening into a nav hazard."

"You heard Hector," Diaz said. "There's no way to know what's on the other side. A lot of things can change in the millions—maybe billions—of years since the gate was put here."

Walsh highlighted the Caliphate fleet and missiles closing in. "What odds do you give against that? How many cadets will we bring home?"

There was a long pause from Diaz. "Not good. But going blind through a nexus? That's how bad sci-fi horror vids start."

"There's only one other choice."

"Which is?"

Walsh took a deep breath and opened a direct comm channel. "*Sword of God*, this is Cmdr. Eugene K. Walsh. We are a training ship. I offer unconditional surrender if you abort your attack."

Diaz hissed. "You can't surrender to those *pendejos*! They'll get the black box and the gate."

"If we made one, we can make another," Walsh said. "Why do we have to go through it first? Let them have it if they want it so badly."

"We do not surrender, Capitan," she said in disgust.

"Then I guess it's good I didn't actually transmit." Walsh chuckled at the heated stream of Spanish obscenities pouring from his comm. "Now that I know you don't like the third option, shall we try the gate?"

"You're a bad, bad hombre, Capitan."

"The gate, then?"

"The gate, then."

Walsh switched back to the general ops channel. He understood his officers' reluctance; it was a big deal to fly through the gate to the unknown. But it was the known that had just opened fire on them. The incoming missiles were approaching detonation range on the tactical display.

Walsh grinned. "Let's fly into the great unknown... before we get blown into it."

Three of the Lancer-missile icons abruptly split into a dozen red shards—the warheads had detonated, launching a barrage of kinetic penetrators. *Amazonas* was crawling towards the gate comparatively. The time to intercept display showed 8.2 minutes.

"I hope no one on the other side minds getting shot at," Bovree said.

The glow of the gate had Walsh transfixed as it grew. He barely noticed when laser turrets two and three lit up to indicate they were firing in point-defense mode. The hardened penetrators could be shattered into smaller pieces, most of them still hitting but each shard having less mass. Some commanders preferred a single penetration instead of multiple smaller ones. Walsh believed in shooting everything that came too close.

The first wave of penetrators split into smaller blossoms as the lasers did their work. Moments later, a metallic tinkle echoed through the ship.

"First wave successfully intercepted," Moore reported.

A few celebratory mutters came across the channel. If they had all been in the same compartment instead of scattered in their armored coffins, it would probably have been a cheer. Or maybe not. The next wave was immediately behind and would have a better firing solution on *Amazonas*.

Walsh placed his hand against the side of his coffin. "Do you feel that?"

"That vibration?" Diaz asked. "Yes, and my fingers and toes are getting pins and needles."

"Same here," Collins said. "Two minutes until... what did you call it, Hector? Transit? Transversing?"

"Transversing is the technical term. Jump was the term used in space-crew vernacular. I believe it was used due to its already common use in fiction."

Collins flashed a nervous grin. "One minute and thirty seconds until jump, then, Capitan."

Walsh's heart pounded as the shimmering gate grew to fill the entirety of his overlay. Tendrils of electric fire began to swirl where *Amazonas* would enter, as if ready to embrace her. "It's... beautiful."

"Twenty seconds to jump, Capitan," Collins said.

A yellow vitals warning flashed in Walsh's vision—he was about to start hyperventilating. Irritation at the intrusion bloomed and he dismissed the warning. The gate was beginning to bubble at the jump point. The light grew to such an intensity that the overlay had to dampen it.

Darkness enveloped Walsh. His jaw dropped open, his mouth making an audible pop. *Amazonas* passed through a now lifeless gate. He was about to comment about how anticlimactic the jump had been when he noticed the Caliphate fleet was still on the tactical display, as were the incoming missiles.

"What the what? Did we lose power?"

Collins waved his hands in the air as he flipped through status screens. "Negative, Capitan. I'm showing green on all power systems."

"The nexus generator is off-line," Diaz said.

Olivo's avatar appeared. "The black box cut power to the generator. Apparently, it finished the tests."

"It could be a safety measure to keep us from *accidentally* going through," Diaz said.

"Hell of a time to take a nap," Walsh said. "Olivo, get that generator powered back up. Hopefully, we still have control over it. We still have company coming."

As if to drive the point home, the point-defense lasers began flashing again.

"Point defense active, Capitan. Launching two EMP missiles," Moore said.

Walsh watched the impressive spread of incoming missiles. The Caliphate had expended several tens-of-millions of solars to take them out. It filled him with a morbid pride. "XO, initiate turn-and-burn. We need to get back through that gate—if we can get it open again." He paused to scratch his chin. "Hector, does it matter which direction we go through?"

"If this gate operates as the others," Hector said, "a jump can be completed from either direction, Capitan. However, all jumps exit the far end gate from one side, regardless of entry direction. For the sake of navigational safety, all traffic was historically routed into the non-exit direction."

"Well, that's good to know," Walsh said. He was about to ask where his damned maneuver was when he felt the press of the control thrusters, followed by the push of the main rocket.

"Turn completed and burn initiated," Collins said. "Five minutes to null-velocity and the same back to the gate."

All of the laser turrets were now flashing as they fired at incoming penetrators. Two dull, metallic rings echoed through the ship, followed by a much louder, grinding thud. Impact and hull-breach alarms flashed on Walsh's display. Superheated debris from the destroyed penetrators had peppered the outer hull. But one had made it through the point defenses, pierced the main hull and exited the opposite side.

It was going to be a long ten minutes—especially if they couldn't get the gate open again.

"Tac-O, focus point defense to cover the gate generator and main propulsion." Walsh wanted to tell Olivo to move her ass, but he knew better. It would be as useful as repeatedly pressing the button on an elevator to speed it up.

"We fired a few warning shots," Moore said. "Shall we fire for effect?"

"It wouldn't do any good," Diaz answered. "If we jump, we might need that ordnance in the great unknown."

"Especially if the Cali ships can follow us through," Bovree said. "They might be able to figure out the signals our box sent out."

The intel on the pursuing Cali fleet indicated they had no gate-key generators; they were a waste of mass. *Amazonas* only had one as a 'just in case' training tool. Even if the fleet had one, the modifications LTE had made to *Amazonas* were probably required to get this gate to open. Depending on what awaited them on the other side, it was a perfect escape. It also meant that no rescue would be forthcoming. Of course, rescues in space were largely fiction. There was no choice now—no plan B. It was the stars or bust.

Time seemed to ooze by as the mess on the tactical display took on the appearance of a swarm of angry hornets. Turrets flashed, comms buzzed, and the two EMP warheads Moore had launched detonated, killing four incoming missiles before they could deploy their warheads.

Then the remainder of the incoming missiles detonated in clusters timed so that their penetrators would envelop *Amazonas* in a deadly wave.

"Status, Olivo! We're out of time." Walsh heard the strain in his own voice and hoped it didn't sound panicked.

Olivo's avatar appeared before him. "Almost there." She sounded worse than he did. "I've about captured the signal sequence the box gave the jump generator." With a twitch of her head, Olivo's avatar vanished.

The laser arrays and mag-cannons were firing at their maximum duty-cycle, pausing only to prevent overheating. Two more impacts rang the hull like a gong in Walsh's ears. The inner hull, the crypt, had been struck. The control thrusters were firing to correct course after the constant impacts. Laser turret three went off-line, followed by missile tube one an instant later. The sound of impacts on the outer hull was a constant buzz. Two more impacts on *Amazonas*'s nose armor vibrated Walsh's teeth.

"Get that damn gate open!" Diaz screamed as the rear half of habitat Bravo exploded into a cloud of shredded girders and twirling debris.

Blue light flared in Walsh's overlay. His display automatically dimmed the light, but he'd forgotten the telescope display was still active in his vision and it dazed him for a moment.

Collins's voice was about to crack. "It's open! It's open!"

Lightning raced around the ring and filled the gate until it coalesced once again into cobalt brilliance. Prickles of thrill ran up Walsh's back, overcoming the fear of incoming death.

Amazonas shook again, and Walsh felt the loss of acceleration and the nausea of an imparted tumble. He shut down the telescope and changed his point of view to outside the ship. The computer highlighted the last impact point in red: the main thruster assembly, just forward of the thruster bell.

"Main thruster is off-line," Hector announced.

Walsh clutched at the arms of his acceleration couch. "All power and defense priority to the gate generator. If that goes down, the only gates we'll be going through are the pearly ones."

"Some of us will be, Capitan," Diaz muttered.

Walsh burst out laughing as *Amazonas* tumbled towards the gate while a swarm of incoming Caliphate missiles tried to tear them apart.

Chapter 24

BRUNO AZEVEDO WATCHED again as tumbling *Amazonas* drifted through the gate and disappeared in an electric-blue nimbus. The gate instantly went dark, leaving a lifeless black ring staring back at him in the overlay. The remaining Caliphate munitions passed harmlessly through the now empty space. From what Bruno could see, none of the warheads hit the nexus gate. Which was good, since humanity had already broken one of them. He didn't know if he could take finally discovering this gate, after years and countless millions in research, only to have it immediately destroyed by some trigger-happy *pendejo*.

Which was exactly why he'd wanted Walsh. Where the shortsighted admirals and politicians saw a troublemaker, Bruno saw a man who only fought when absolutely necessary. A man who, when he decided to fight, fought to win. A man like himself.

He wanted to watch it again, wanted to jump to his feet and scream "Score!" like his father had whenever he'd scored a goal. He wanted to shove his finger in Admiral James's face and thrust his hips at her in an obscene victory dance while chanting "What about that?" Maybe even moon her and slap his ass a few times.

He didn't. Instead, Bruno settled for sipping from a glass of his most expensive scotch without offering Admiral James any.

"You were not supposed to open the gate," she said. "You told us the mission was to locate it."

"It wasn't supposed to open. In truth, we weren't sure exactly what would happen. The recorded details of how they found the first gate were hard to come by."

Admiral James narrowed her eyes. "You do realise you've just started a war, right, Bruno? Even if that Cali fleet hadn't fired on Walsh, the mere existence of your new gate would have set it off."

Bruno said nothing. He merely watched the admiral examining her fingernails. They were titanium implants. She hadn't used them since some bar brawl fifteen years ago, but Bruno wondered if she was considering using them now.

She looked up at him with a tight grin. "You might want to secure your holdings outside of the CAR. Not many people are going be happy about your gate. I know I'm not."

"It isn't my gate. We simply discovered it."

"A distinction that won't matter to anyone important. Which is why you've sucked the CAR into your war. The Caliphate isn't going to accept the admiralty trying to explain that it wasn't us. It was one of our contractors. Take it out on them."

Bruno smirked. "You'd really tell them that?"

Senator Midland strode into the office. "Absolutely. If they start blowing holes in Liberty Station, I'd put the bow on you myself send you over via the nearest airlock. But it wouldn't do any good, so we're stuck in this shit storm together."

She motioned for a drink and Bruno poured her some of his second-rate scotch. None of the good stuff for her, either. From the way she tossed it back, she wasn't after quality.

Midland slammed the glass on Bruno's desk. "I've been talking with the legal and diplomatic corps all morning. And that blowhard Dominik is filling my calendar with his ridiculous emergency sessions."

Bruno looked at the women in turn and shook his head in disbelief. "Don't you see what we've accomplished here? We've freed humanity from a moribund Sol. Think of the opportunities! Not just material or business opportunities, either. We know from radio signals that there are people out there and—"

"Save the speech for one of your employee town halls," James said. "They have to pretend to care what you blather on about."

"If it's that bad," Bruno said, "and you're stuck with me, then you should start working your PR angle. The CAR and LTE, under orders from a few farsighted and brave leaders, have opened the galaxy once again to Earth. This is just as big as the first moon landing. Just as big as the first gate."

"It'll be as big as Duke Ferdinand's assassination," Admiral James said with a wry smile. "Or the *Astarkus* crashing into Beijing. The CAR will have to be at the forefront of this before the Caliphate can get a foothold. Do you know the scale of operation that will be?"

Bruno shook his head again. They were not going to get over their own concerns. What they said was true, but so petty compared to what he'd done. He gave up on trying to convince them. Bruno opened to footage of *Amazonas* tumbling after being hit and motioned to James. "Can they make it back?"

Midland snorted and tapped her glass. "They'll probably make it back just in time for the war so the Calies can finish the job."

Bruno poured another glass, this time from his lowest-rate scotch, and looked pointedly at the admiral.

"The Nova class is ancient, but it can take a lot of punishment. And Walsh knows his stuff." James shrugged. "But it depends on the damage. Main thrusters are hard to fix on the float. I won't count him out, though.

"The real question becomes, will they be able to open the gate from the other side? It wasn't supposed to open on this side, and you didn't give them access to operate the black box directly."

Bruno laughed. "You told me you wanted it automated so he couldn't. That was your call, Linda. Not mine."

Admiral James waved the objection aside. "That's right because Walsh, like you apparently, is obsessed with those goddamn gates. Tactically, he used the gate to escape an attack that would have destroyed the *Amazonas*. Now answer my question."

"According to my project engineer, the test module was only supposed to run that final sequence once. Since the gate activated twice, Walsh must have figured out a way to repeat the process." Bruno finished his glass and eyed his bottle of the good stuff. Not the best time for a refill. "If the test module and the gate-key generator both survived, I would think they could."

Bruno smirked. "Of course, being hung out to dry in the first place, Walsh probably won't want to jump back into the arms of the Caliphate fleet. Just think how this would have played out differently if they'd had the requested escort."

Admiral James stood abruptly. "I have to get to the first of many fleet operations meetings. War and endless meetings is what this little misadventure means to me."

Senator Midland rose a moment later, her eyes in the overlay glaze. "I think it would be best if LTE kept to itself for a while." She stormed back out of his office.

When the door had closed, Bruno flicked his fingers from beneath his chin at them.

For all of their threats, they or one of their lackeys would be back soon enough, complaining about this project or that. This one isn't moving fast enough. That one is over budget. He understood covering one's own ass, and he knew they'd calm down after things settled. But their complete lack of excitement at such a momentous—yes, momentous was not an overstatement—achievement boggled his mind. He had literally opened a gateway to the stars where the best minds in Sol had failed for hundreds of years.

With a swipe of his hand, *Amazonas* appeared in his overlay again. But this recording was from his own security team, taken from an LTE deepspace observatory. Its definition was far improved over what Admiral James had provided. He magnified the ship until it filled his vision.

Some diligent analyst had highlighted each impact point from the Caliphate attack. Those that had penetrated the hull or damaged a surface subsystem were red. Most of the hull was yellow from the countless tiny fragments that had impacted with no penetration. The largest red splotch was over the thrust assembly. A note was attached: "Loss of main thruster output."

Time for another glass of the good stuff. Even if *Amazonas* was destroyed or couldn't make it back, they'd received the telemetry from the test module. They knew how to open the gate and knew for sure how to search for any others in the system. And his interstellar yacht could now be finished.

But not fast enough to mount a rescue, unfortunately. He liked Walsh. The admiralty needed more men like him in its ranks. He doubted a man like Walsh would want to be in such company. Bruno certainly didn't. Putting Liberty behind him was a dream soon to come true.

Bruno lifted his glass. "*Salu.*" He sipped the scotch and enjoyed the warmth as it spread through his body. It was just too good not to savor.

Chapter 25

YULOO'S REFLECTION was superimposed over the data that scrolled by beneath. The red-rimmed eyes and sunken sockets staring back at her caught her attention more than the pointless mathematical gibberish she was supposed to be studying. The flicker of the screen cast harsh shadows across her already harsh face.

Her throat ached. Chronic bronchitis and dehydration had colluded long ago to replace the beauty of her voice with the raspy croaking that escaped her as speech now. The universe had decided to steal everything of hers that was beautiful.

She forced down a mouthful of slimy water without gagging. The ancient filters in *Solar Dream*'s recycler still worked—she hoped—but barely. Like most systems on the ship.

But it was still better than the colony.

Yuloo shook her head to refocus. Not that there was a reason to check Fenti's results scrolling beneath her reflection. They were the same as hers. The same as always. Nothing new. Nothing new for years and years. Only the same inscrutable hints in the data that disappeared like a bogeyman when looked at directly.

But she knew the gate was there to be seen, just out of plain sight. They just needed to figure out how to look at it. She knew because her mentor had known it, as had the scientists before them for generations.

Yuloo rubbed her eyes painfully and looked around the control center to take a break from the screen. Crew stations long abandoned surrounded her like empty coffins. They were much shorter than hers, designed for humans who had grown up in a gravity well.

Unbuckling her belt, Yuloo drifted in the zero-g. Her head was beginning to throb again. She pulled herself hand-over-hand to one of the remaining air blowers and huddled beneath it. The vent wheezed like an old man. The dank tang of mold mingled with the warm-plastic smell of the failing air filter. Yuloo chose not to think about what she might be inhaling as her headache subsided. They'd have to shut down this compartment soon, as well, if someone back home couldn't figure out how to replace the environmental control system.

She let out a deep sigh. The ECS was as ancient as the rest of the ship and had been rotting away before she was an apprentice. It would be like repairing erosion on a stone. There was no hope of that. There was no hope for them. Except finding the damned gate. It was that hope that kept her from stripping to her skin and waltzing into the void.

"Did you see that?" Fenti called from his station across the compartment.

Yuloo pushed off towards Fenti's station. "What now?" she croaked. "More alien signals from Sagittarius A-star?"

Fenti glared up at her over his shoulder. "No. This." His station still had a single working holo-projector and he jabbed a gnarled finger at it. "Right there. Timestamp 32.6."

Rubbing her eyes again, Yuloo reached over Fenti's arm to replay the data stream. At the timestamp he indicated, there was a significant spike in the local phasic-band signature. It had slid beneath her reflection, unnoticed. She swallowed painfully, twice, before she could speak.

"Enough for a bearing?"

"Not completely. But the triangulation narrows it down to a much smaller minute of angle than we had before."

She felt the excitement in his voice infecting her. Her throat tightened. In all of her years, they had never seen a real phasic shift, only noise that might be something to prove the ancient theory. Her eyes stung and grew wet. It felt marvelous.

The signal flashed bright on the holo-display, eliciting simultaneous cries of "Whoa!" from Yuloo and Fenti. It pulsed, disappeared, reappeared, and danced in different waveforms before them. The signal-direction finders processed the disturbance and soon pinpointed the source.

Fenti, his mouth gaping as he stared, focused the ship's telescope where the sensors indicated. The seal that once kept the main scope tube pressurized with inert gas had finally rotted away six years ago, leaving the lower third of the main lens foggy and distorted. He pulled the telescope's feed onto a nearby screen.

"It's real," Yuloo said, choking back sobs. She was staring at a new nexus gate. Its gleaming blue light lit the compartment and cast dark shadows across Fenti's face. Tears distorted the image.

They had to take readings, run the test packages. It had been so long since she'd even considered the possibility that she couldn't remember what the plan was. Was there a plan? Her mind raced to remember, thinking of *something* to do. But all she could do was stare in awed silence.

The compartment grew dark again as the gate disappeared.

"Come back," Fenti cried. "Wait, please. No, no, no!"

"It's true." Yuloo made no attempt to hold back her sobs now. "It's true." All the years and generations spent working formulae time and again, hoping to solve the unsolvable. And it had finally been proven true. All true. What her father had said and all those scientists she'd wanted to grow up to be. There it was. And she'd seen it finally realized. She'd seen it first.

"We've got to tell Kvetch and the *Trangus*," Fenti whispered. "We need to get the orbital arrays focused here. Do you think they detected it from the *Trangus*? Call them up and see."

Yuloo started to turn towards her station but froze.

"What's wrong?" he asked.

She rubbed her eyes and laughed. "I don't want to look away. I'll miss something."

"That's why I asked you." Fenti burst out laughing. He unstrapped and wrapped his arms around her. "But your station does have a better interface with, well, everything."

His warmth made her belly tingle as she returned the embrace. It had been a long time—conditions on *Solar Dream* weren't conducive even to their casual romance. Now everything swam in her head like a maelstrom.

Pushing away to wipe her tears, Yuloo smiled. "All right, but I'm dropping everything else if it comes back." The smile slid from her face and she shot back to her station. "Oh, god!"

"What?" Fenti asked, eyes wide. "What?"

Yuloo slammed into her seat and her hands flew across the display. "Please, please, please."

"*What*?"

A status report rolled by on her display and she sighed, then barked laughter. "I couldn't remember if I'd restarted the logs after the last copy-flush cycle. But here it is. We got it. We got it all." She grinned over her shoulder at him.

Fenti pursed his lips. "Well, thank you for those few seconds of terror, Yu. Talk to the *Trangus*. They might have already transmitted to us to see what the hell's going on over here."

Yuloo winked and turned to compose her message, attaching a copy of the logs. "Comms time to the *Trangus* is six hours. Time to start studying. And finding effective procedures for locating a gate."

"I wonder what triggered it," Fenti said. "I know we weren't transmitting. Hey, look at this. It's still there."

Yuloo pulled up the display on her screen. The lidar was painting a large ring where the disturbance had occured. "It didn't phase back out? Looks just like the old gate."

"From here, anyway." Fenti chuckled. "I guess we didn't get everything right. It should have phased away."

"Give it time. We don't know anything yet."

It was a struggle to pay more attention to the measurements and diagnostics than the obsidian gate. She had to close the telescope feed to keep focused. The phasic signal began creeping up.

"I think..." Yuloo said hesitantly as she cycled through the test array. She pulled the telescope display back to her screen. "Yes! Look, look!"

Fenti whooped from across the compartment. Yuloo covered her mouth and laughed out loud.

An unfamiliar warble screamed in the compartment and the one remaining emergency light strobed from a nearby bulkhead. It was an unfamiliar, unsteady warble warning Yuloo had never heard. "What's that?"

"I think that's the battle-stations klaxon," Fenti said uncertainly. "Huh. Maybe the computer thinks the RF from the gate is some kind of weapon?"

Yuloo swiped through the ship status displays. "Do you know how to turn the damned thing off? It's hard to concentrate with that noise blaring in my ears."

"I can't find it." Fenti pounded a fist on his console. "I know it's here. The silence option should be on the master alert panel."

Yuloo cursed as the gate went dark again. "Why is it still going off if the gate—" A scream rose in her throat as the telescope app highlighted a new object near the gate. The shape and confirming identifier tag nearly made her vomit.

"What? What is it?" Fenti yelled, barely audible over her scream and blare of the klaxon.

Yuloo jabbed a finger at the telescope display. "They opened it. They found us!"

"Who? What are you talking about?"

"It's an Earth warship," she croaked. "A Nova class. Just like in the stories. And it just target-locked us."

Chapter 26

DISAPPOINTMENT OVERWHELMED Walsh. There had been no electric feeling of cosmic displacement, hallucinogenic stream of consciousness, or a twisting in the perceived universe around him. The historic jump hadn't even provoked any dramatic shuddering, bucking, or flickering lights. A slight tingle in his fingers and the nav-computer complaining about losing contact with the Solar beacon network were the only tangible effects of the jump.

But he was the first person—one of them, anyway—to jump from Sol in centuries.

"Celestial reckoning system is rebooting after critical mismatch with previous star scan," Hector announced. "Celestial positioning database incoherent."

Walsh allowed himself a grin. There was another sign they had jumped—the metallic rain of the Cali attack had grown silent. "Ops, stabilize our spin and start marking local navigation hazards. Let's check out the neighborhood."

"On it, Capitan."

"XO, get with Maintenance and get a handle on damage control," Walsh said. "There are breaches all over the board."

"*Si*, Capitan."

Trusting Diaz to her work, Walsh pulled up the Power and Propulsion status. "PnP, how's the thruster?"

Olivo appeared in his overlay, breathless. "Still pulling data. But it might only be a damaged power substation. If it's clean enough, we could print and install another one in less than an hour."

"That would be a nice change," Walsh said. "Priority on the thruster."

Olivo's image blinked away.

Walsh opened the crew vitals display. Every one of the crew icons glowed yellow with warnings of increased stress, breathing, and blood pressure. There were no O2, vacuum, or loss-of-telemetry warnings that would indicate any of the shielded stations had been compromised. The Nova-class crypt was tough, but a direct hit on a station's hatch from a heavy weapon could pop it like a big, bloody boil.

Satisfied that everyone was uninjured, Walsh scanned the internal feeds. He sucked air loudly through his teeth. A few of the internal cameras showed off-line, but the picture of the damage was complete without them.

Swirling clouds of debris bounced around inside the ship. Jagged black scars showed where the outer hull had been torn away and opened to space. There was no telling yet how many smaller perforations there were. It would be a while before the main hull could be pressurized.

The armored crypt bore countless, deep gouges from high-energy shrapnel. Three larger craters, their appearance liquid from the superheated impacts of direct hits, were spaced around the crypt. Fortunately, none of them had hit any crew hatches.

External feeds from scurrying repair drones looked worse. Long plumes of icy spray trailed from two of the hydrogen propellant tanks. The main communications mast had been severed and now spun lazily two kilometers away. The number two sensor cluster had lost its armored cupola.

"Holy shit," Walsh muttered.

He was grateful, though. There had been no casualties and the damage, while severe, was repairable. All of the maintenance fabricators had survived, as had most of the drones and weapons systems. Most of the recovered scrap could be recycled.

But it shouldn't have happened at all. Admiral James had to have known about the Cali fleet, especially if Bruno Azevedo knew. Even a small escort squadron would have been enough to keep the Cali fleet honest. Or at least helped intercept the overwhelming barrage of missiles.

These were thoughts for later.

His overlay turned red. "Proximity alert," Hector announced.

Walsh opened the tactical display. "Did someone follow us through?"

"Negative," Moore answered. "The contact is too far from the gate and at relative velocity of zero. What? I don't recognize the ship class."

Hector appeared on the tactical screen and magnified the new contact. "Archives report this as a Tralligan-class survey vessel. The last one in Sol was decommissioned two hundred and three years ago."

Walsh motioned to the new icon. "Why are we just now seeing it? The nav-lidar is online."

"Sorry, Capitan," Collins said. "The sensors had to make a new baseline and there's a lot of debris noise."

Diaz appeared. "The good news is that they're trying to surrender. Translating from an older Chinese dialect."

The comms line crackled. The raw audio was barely audible beneath Hector's instant translation.

"Earth warship. My name is Yuloo aboard the science ship *Solar Dream* from Karen's Kvetch. We are not a part of the CDF fleet. Please don't shoot."

Walsh glanced at Diaz's avatar. "This is the Confederation of American Republics ship *Amazonas*. Our intentions are peaceful. Please stand by, *Solar Dream*." He silenced the channel.

"Please ignore all the debris and battle damage, as we come in peace," Bovree said wryly.

"That didn't take long," Walsh said. "Is this Karen's Kvetch colony in the database?"

Hector shook his head. "Karen's Kvetch is not listed in the colonial records, Capitan. It has likely changed names in the intervening years. Once our celestial position is solved, we can identify the star system."

"We could ask this Yuloo person," Collins said.

"I'd rather not come off as being lost," Walsh said. "Moore, what's the status of the *Solar Dream*?

"That ship is a floating death trap," Moore said, disbelief heavy in her voice. "Over half of the ship is powered down, and the powered sections are arcing and sparking. And I'm convinced the only thing holding the hull together is the crust of space dust that's covering the whole thing." She shook her head. "I suggest we maintain distance, sir."

Walsh considered the other ship's image for a moment. "I guess they didn't buy the same maintenance plan we did. XO, continue damage control efforts. Moore, turn down the targeting array but keep point-defense ready. People are in a shooting mood today."

Moore smirked. "I think they'd blow up if they tried to shoot at us, sir."

"No intrusion software detected," Bovree said. "But it's a pretty shitty signal for being so close. I doubt that signal-to-noise ratio could pass along a cyber intrusion."

Walsh watched two repair drones unroll a section of repair sheeting and cover the largest breach. The drones applied electrical pulses and the sheet bonded to the hull, hardening over the hole and molding around the surrounding pipes, conduits, and other protrusions. The two drones returned to the repair locker while another drifted by collecting debris.

Walsh activated the comms. "*Solar Dream*, this is the *Amazonas*."

"Yes, hello?"

Walsh couldn't tell if it was the speaker's voice or the static in the signal that sounded so cracked. "This is Cmdr. Eugene Walsh, capitan of the *Amazonas*. I wanted to reassure you that we are not here to harm you in any way. As you can probably see, we had a minor... incident during the transverse and repairs are ongoing."

"How did you get it to open?"

"That's something we're not at liberty to discuss. We need to focus on our repairs."

"Is anyone hurt?" Yuloo asked. "Can we assist in any way?"

"Thank you, Yuloo. Fortunately, we suffered no injuries. But you said you're from Karen's Kvetch? We don't show that colony in our records."

The line remained silent for a couple of minutes. Walsh was about to retransmit when the comm crackled.

"It was renamed following the nexus explosion," Yuloo said. "Karen Rueben Zhao was the colony director and pulled everyone together. The council renamed the colony in her honor after she died. Before that it was just called Colony Epsilon."

Walsh glanced at Diaz. "Nexus explosion?"

"Yes, Capitan Walsh. We have no idea what happened. It was always assumed that the Earth Protectorate League launched some kind of attack."

Diaz threw a display window towards Walsh. "Spectrum analysis of the local star matches Epsilon Eridani. System mapping will take a few hours, but it fits so far."

Walsh gave Diaz a thumbs-up. "We believed it was Epsilon Eridani, but when you said Karen's Kvetch, I was worried we'd taken a wrong turn at Aldebaran."

"I don't think you can take a wrong turn using a nexus gate," Yuloo said.

"Uh, probably not." Walsh decided not to try to explain his joke. "Do your people always have a ship guarding this gate?"

"Oh, we're not guards, Capitan Walsh," she answered hurriedly. "This is a science ship. We've been trying to prove the gate existed and then try to open it. We've been at it... a long time." The signal cut out in a burst of crackles and hissing before coming back in. "... to know how you opened it. No one's activated this gate ever as far we know."

"Thanks for the info, Yuloo. I appreciate your patience while we see to our repairs. We'll talk again after we get things put back together over here. *Amazonas* out." Walsh cut the connection over the beginning of her objection.

Thirty minutes later, sections of habitat Bravo were sealed and holding atmosphere. After another fifteen minutes, the fusion thruster powered up and Olivo began calibrating and running startup tests. The drones were still collecting nearby debris outside the hull, so Walsh decided not to bring the ship to a full stop.

At the hour mark, and several rejected calls from Yuloo, the main hull was being stress-tested and tracer gas injected to find any remaining leaks. The incandescent streamer twisted and writhed towards the final missed micro-puncture and the repair drones sealed it.

"Beginning atmospheric restoral," Lieutenant Fuller announced.

"I'm with the XO, Capitan," Bovree said. "I don't think we should send anyone over in person. Aside from the obvious threats of assault and kidnapping, there's the contamination issue. I don't mean anything crazy like mutant space herpes. They've been isolated here for almost four hundred years. They might have some kind of Epsilon super flu."

Walsh stroked his beard. "Not to mention what we might give them."

"Uh, yeah. That, too," Bovree said.

"Doctor Barnes?" Walsh highlighted the doctor's comm icon to add him.

Doctor Barnes shrugged. "Well, our decontamination process would kill even mutated space herpes. But don't take that as permission, Bovree. Anyone that goes needs to stay in their suits. I agree that we don't want to expose anyone over there. Especially with that ship being in such poor condition. Who knows how well the environmental control system is working. And if you have to talk through your suit radio, you might as well use the radio here."

"What about a drone with an air sampler?" Walsh asked. He didn't like being denied. It was worse when he knew he was wrong.

"We could," Barnes agreed. "And I'm willing to send a medical drone and run a remote examination. The problem with a sampler is that it takes samples. Not the whole thing. It would take several passes to make sure we were getting everything floating around."

"She doesn't sound very pretty, Capitan," Diaz said. "Why do you want over so bad?"

Walsh narrowed his eyes at her, ready to explode. A few good-natured chuckles from those that heard calmed him down. It was always hard to know when she was being funny or being a bitch.

"You can't tell what someone looks like by their voice. That's not the point, XO. We're reconnecting with humans who've been stranded here for as long as we've been trapped in Sol.

"We've always assumed the CDF only hit the Sol gate, but it seems they have shut down the whole nexus network. I want our connection to be more personal." Walsh nodded and glanced at his officers' images. "But you're right. Cautious first steps and all. Doctor, get a medical drone ready and don't be stingy with the meds. Fuller, get a repair mission ready. They might not want our help at all, but that ship's about to fall apart."

The ECS light transitioned from yellow to green. "Main hull pressurized," Hector announced.

Walsh rolled his head and smiled. "Now, let's get out of these coffins and see what the quarters look like. I hope none of my commemorative 'Galaxy Hoppers' plates got smashed."

Chapter 27

"SORRY, CAPITAN WALSH," Yuloo said. "We need to talk to the colony before agreeing to anything. I hope you understand. This is a momentous occasion for us. Once in a lifetime, really."

What Walsh understood was that if the Caliphate could also open the nexus gate, they'd be coming through soon. And that would a momentous occasion for *Amazonas* and crew. "I do understand. We want to avoid any diplomatic misunderstandings."

"Thank you, Capitan. Your coming will have to be navigated carefully."

"We will continue mapping and cleaning up. Our repair and medical drones remain ready if you want to accept my offer. Any idea how long before the colony responds?"

"Sorry, Capitan. There's no telling how long it will take."

"Very well, Yuloo," Walsh said. "You know where to find us. *Amazonas* out."

He tugged at his restraints absently. The damage to habitat Bravo had left the arms unbalanced and prevented their use to generate spin gravity.

"Anything from the laser-ear?"

Bovree shook his head. "All we can hear is the ship falling apart. But the comm-sats are deployed and intercepting signals."

"I'm assuming the colony is on or above Epsilon II," Walsh said. "We'll know soon enough. Use standard SIGINT protocols—they may get nervous."

"The biggest threat from their ship is running into a piece of it that fell off," Bovree said.

Walsh smiled. "We were the one raining pieces all over the place last I checked. But I hope you're right."

After Diaz had come on watch, he pulled down the passage to the galley. The industrial smell of the repair sheeting filled the ship and the white patches stood stark against the comparative dinginess of the old hull. Maintenance crews and bots kept *Amazonas* clean, as well as in good repair, but generations of human touch always left stains.

In the galley, the aroma of food overcame the stench of damage control. The din of the crew was louder than usual, more excited. War stories were already starting, full of wild gesticulations and bold exaggerations. An undercurrent of nervous gratitude permeated the conversations.

Walsh waved everyone to stay put as he entered. Pulling a random food container from the machine, he found a seat and opened his meal. The container had the aeroponics bay stamp on it—the sauce had been made from fresh tomatoes. Walsh inhaled deeply.

He was glad the aeroponics bay had escaped the battle unharmed. They might be here longer than he expected.

Walsh was still inhaling the aroma when Screwball floated by overhead.

"May I join you, Capitan?"

"Sure, Cadet."

The chimpanzee grabbed an overhead conduit with his feet and stood upside down relative to Walsh.

"What's up?" Walsh asked. He continued to eat, waiting for Screwball to answer.

"That was quite a thing," the chimp finally said. "The battle, I mean."

"Yes, it was. You are now one of the very few in the fleet who's seen action like that. When we get back, I'll pin the Space Combat pin on all of you myself. All of you."

Screwball hooted. "Oh, ah, thank you, Capitan." He flashed a toothy, simian smile. "Sir, how do humans not panic during that sort of thing? Aside from the overlay emotional damper. I forgot to use it, but I think Hector dialed me down. I can't remember."

"That's part of what he does. Fear is normal, and so is panic. Where fear can be useful, panic isn't."

Screwball slowly scratched behind his hairy ear. "I'm not sure I can do that again. I pooped."

Walsh's fork stopped halfway to his mouth. "You pooped?"

"A little. But don't worry, I didn't throw it at anyone."

Walsh stared at the chimp for a moment, then laughed out loud. It was possible he'd just violated of the complex, and often contradictory, policies set forth by Liberty's social inclusion department. When Screwball joined in with his hooting, Walsh laughed harder. People at the other tables cast furtive glances their way.

"Well, that's good," Walsh said, when his laughter had subsided. "That you didn't throw it, I mean. As to dealing with fear, humans crap themselves, too."

"You pooped?"

The galley went silent.

Walsh felt the heat rise in his face as he looked around. "No, no, no. Not this time," he answered loudly.

The galley exploded in laughter and a couple of the crew made loud flatulence noises. Screwball hooted and screeched.

Walsh leaned in close to the chimp. "But this probably isn't the best venue to announce your fecal exploits. You did well. It's about facing your fear and fighting through it. It doesn't go away. Just keep in mind that greater people than us have had emergency bowel evacuations."

Screwball opened his mouth to reply when a call came in on Walsh's overlay. He held a finger up to the cadet.

Hector appeared in the galley, the yellow nimbus around him indicating it was a private connection; no one else could see or hear him. "Capitan, I have a request from Cadet Moris to speak to you directly concerning Angelica. I believe you should accept."

"Put him through," Walsh subvocalized. Moris appeared next to Hector, his face tense. "CO, here. Report, Mister Moris."

"Sir, Angelica is having a meltdown. I'm on a damage assessment team in the main cargo bay. She came by and looked inside, and..." Moris paused to take a shaky breath. "And she saw the cryo-units. Five of them were ripped open by shrapnel. She rushed in and won't let go until her, uh, her daddy comes to get her."

Moris's image looked over his shoulder. "She's cut herself but won't let anyone near. I've got a medic outside, but I didn't want to try to force her. Do you want us to secure her, Capitan? Or wait for you?"

"I'll be right down. Leave her alone for now, but make sure there's nothing dangerous nearby and that all the hatches are secured."

Walsh's overlay removed Hector and Moris. He looked up at Screwball. "Come with me, Cadet."

When Walsh peeked through the hatch into the cargo bay, he saw Angelica floating near one of the shattered cryo-units. She was caressing the cheek of the little body that was half out of the pod. Angelica made no move as he slowly pulled himself through the hatchway. A watery smear of blood highlighted her lips and left cheek, probably from the damaged, thawing body.

Screwball made a sad hoot and she finally looked up.

"Are you all right?" Walsh kept his distance, holding on to a cargo strap.

Angelica gingerly kissed her sister's head and nudged the body back into the ruins of the frozen casket. She glared at Walsh, who cautiously pulled back. If not for the rage in her eyes and the gore on her face, Angelica would almost look cute.

"Bad Daddy!" she shrieked. "Why did you do that? Is that why you don't talk to me? Because you killed them?"

"Of course we didn't kill them, Angelica. We tried to save all of you. Please, we're not here to hurt you."

Angelica spread her arms to encompass the smashed cryo-units. "Then what happened here, *Daddy*?"

"The ship you were on discarded all of you when trying to escape." Walsh pushed himself closer, but still held on to the cargo strap. "Those units aren't designed for space. They're not rescue pods. We came as fast as we could, please believe me. You... were the only one still alive. And not by much."

"No way! The teachers would never dump us like that. They love us."

Walsh didn't know the best words to use, but had to try something. "If they abandoned you like that, Angelica, are you sure they loved you?"

"Why would they run?"

"Because what they were doing is wrong. And this is the type of ship that stops that wrongdoing."

Angelica pointed a finger at him. "So you do hate me. Us. Why?"

"I don't hate you, Angelica. But the way these so-called teachers use you..." Walsh paused to gauge the girl's reaction, "... sell you, is wrong. They killed your sisters and tried to kill you, too."

"You made them hate us."

"We didn't even know about you," Walsh said. The air was tainted with the smell of iron and pungent cryo-gel. "If they loved you, they wouldn't have dumped you..."

"Liar! Bad Daddy!" She delicately touched her face and studied the blood that clung to the tip of her finger. Angelica's lip curled in a bestial sneer and she launched herself at Walsh.

His eyes widened in surprise and then bulged as Angelica plowed head-first into his gut. She clutched Walsh's collar and twisted it tight around his neck, while hooking her legs behind his waist.

Walsh opened his mouth to talk, but the words were stolen by a sudden sting that numbed half of his face. Then another on the other side. She began savagely slapping him on alternate cheeks, each blow accompanied by a shriek of, "Bad Daddy!"

Screwball hooted in dismay, frozen, staring in through the hatch. Walsh wondered if he was pooping himself.

The first rule of zero-g personal combat is to seek and maintain a purchase, even if it's only a flat surface from which to push. While someone caught on the float could change position using scissor kicks, twisting, and flailing, it was slow going in the time frame of a fight. Angelica obviously knew that—she was using Walsh as her purchase.

He had maintained his grip on the cargo strap with one hand, while futilely trying to ward off her strikes with the other. Working a leg around the strap, he grabbed Angelica's wrists and squeezed them hard.

"Stop it, Angelica!"

"Let go," she shrieked. "Ouch!"

Walsh felt her free her legs, no doubt making ready to kick him in the balls. He didn't let her. Spinning the girl around like a dance partner, Walsh wrapped her up with his arms and free leg. They spun together as she tried to get free. The girl was much stronger than she looked, but Walsh was stronger yet—and pissed off.

Walsh shook her when she tried to bite his arm. "Stop it, now." He squeezed her as hard as he could. At first, she tried to hold her breath in, but it finally escaped her in a long, shrill squeal.

"I can't breathe," she panted.

"Are you going to stop?"

Angelica nodded, sending her hair floating in a graceful, blond web.

Walsh relaxed his grip.

"I like playing rough, Daddy," she said in a husky whisper.

Walsh pushed her away harder than he meant to. The girl easily caught a cargo container and slowly twisted towards the wrecked cryo-pods. She drifted towards them and found a handle. When she started sobbing, Walsh had to resist the urge to take her into his arms and comfort her. He let her be until her sobs had passed.

"Why don't you love me, Capitan?" She spoke the last word as though it were a bitter cough. "Am I so horrible? You finally hold me and then immediately toss me away."

Walsh's chest grew tight. He'd been a lover of many and was no stranger to emotional drama or manipulation. But Angelica's pleas sounded so earnest; so innocent. And he knew it was because she had been programmed to her very psyche to be that way.

Screwball, Moris, and a medical tech floated nearby, looking to Walsh for orders. He held up a hand to them.

"There are many ways to love. Did you love your sisters?" Walsh asked.

Angelica used her hands to pull her floating hair out of her face. The motion—purposely, Walsh was sure—accentuated breasts that looked far too developed on her body. "Sometimes a daddy would ask—"

"No, no, no." Walsh closed his eyes and shook his head violently. "I mean... Look, why are you sad they are gone? Why are you so angry? Isn't it because you care for them?"

Angelica nodded slowly.

"That is how we love you." Walsh motioned to Screwball, Moris, and the tech. "How we all love you. Like a little *sister*."

He found a handhold slightly closer to her and pushed off to grab it. "I know you might not understand why, but it can't ever be any other way.

Never like your other daddies. But the type of love we have for you, that you have for your sisters, is better. Stronger."

The girl stared at him as if he were talking backwards. Her luxurious hair drifted lazily about her head once again. A puddle of tears grew and wobbled in the corners of her eyes. She dabbed them with a sleeve. Turning to Screwball, she asked, "Is that true?"

Screwball grunted and nodded his head wildly. "Yes, of course. We came at full speed. Sorry about your sisters, but I'm glad you're here. You make me laugh and I love to watch you draw."

Angelica looked uncertainly between Walsh, Screwball, and Moris, then let out a long, quavering sigh. "So you weren't even supposed to be my daddy?"

Walsh fought to keep the hope in his voice from making him sound foolish. "No. But that doesn't mean I don't care about what happens to you. Will you let the medic look at you and take you to the doctor?"

"I'm sorry I hit you, Daddy. Uh, Capitan Walsh. Are you mad?"

"No," Walsh said, smiling. "Not at all. Though I'm sure a few people on board will think I deserved it. Will you go?"

"Can Screwy come with me?"

Walsh glanced at the chimp. "Sure."

Angelica nodded and held out her hand. Screwball pushed forward and grabbed it. Walsh watched them float to the medic, who led them out of sight. The hatch closed behind them.

Walsh drifted to the cryo-units and ran his fingers over a casket. He glanced at Moris, who now looked like the stereotypical clueless cadet, despite having performed well in that strange situation.

"It's a hell of thing to do to a child," Moris said.

Walsh stared at the hatch. "No shit."

Chapter 28

DIAZ STARED FLATLY at Collins as the Ops-O floated to his seat in the conference room. He smiled and nodded. When she continued to stare, he looked up and smiled cautiously.

"Yes, ma'am?"

She cut her gaze to the open hatch and back to Collins.

He smiled, got out of his seat, and closed the hatch. "Sorry, XO. I didn't know if someone else might show up."

"Someone else can open and shut the hatch as well as you can. Hopefully, better. Compartmental integrity saves lives, Lieutenant."

Collins looked about to say something. When she raised her eyebrows, he simply said, "Yes, ma'am," and returned to his seat.

White skin peeked out at her between her glove and sleeve. Diaz tugged on the sleeve to hide it. It was easy to get lazy with hatches. If not for her insistence on that discipline, more people would have died under her command.

"*El Capitan* wants another staff brainstorming session." Diaz held her hands up to silence the groaning. "He wants one where he's not involved. He's hoping that might shake things up."

Moore drummed her fingers on the table. "How's the conversation with the colony going?"

"Confusing and frustrating," Diaz said. "They don't really know what to do with us. Capitan Walsh says half the people he talks to are ecstatic, the others are terrified."

"I guess we can't blame them," Bovree said. "We're basically space aliens to them. And like all good space-alien stories, we either bring salvation or destruction."

Diaz nodded. "This is truly historic, even if we arrived under questionable circumstances."

Olivo grinned. "I know we were in a bad spot, but I think he was happy to have an excuse to go through the gate. It's all he talked about. Nexus-gate this and nexus-gate that. 'Yes, sir! We'd love to do another survey patrol to the nexus gate, sir!'"

Laughter rippled around the officers and Diaz allowed herself a slight grin. "What the capitan wants opinions on is what we think our next move should be. After we reach some arrangement with Karen's Kvetch, that is."

Olivo lifted her hand. "Obviously, the first thing is to get back to Sol. I don't understand how there's even another choice. Or why we haven't gone back already. This is a job for the diplomatic corps."

"The reason we don't go back," Bovree said, "is the fleet on the other side of the gate that shot us up. And when we intercepted the message to Yuloo that we were being invited to visit, that became the obvious decision."

"We could get there a lot faster," Collins said, "if we didn't have to wait for their ship."

"As I was saying," Bovree continued, "we've been intercepting their comms and Hector broke their encryption almost immediately. We learned about another ship out there, the *Trangus*. When I triangulated her position, I started working up a full EM profile. Guess what she's out there studying?"

"Another nexus gate?" Moore asked.

Bovree tapped his nose quickly. "Ding-ding-ding. The same sensor sweeps and EM spikes the *Dream* is still sending out towards the gate. We have two exits out of Epsilon now."

"I wonder if there's another in Sol?" Moore asked.

Olivo shook her head. "We don't know where this one goes, either. We were lucky this time."

"We know what's waiting behind the gate we came through," Diaz said. "And it will be weeks before Liberty can get a fleet there."

Bovree sniffed. "Assuming they will. I'm sure the shit has hit the thruster back home."

"And that's the capitan's concern, too," Diaz said, nodding. "We have no way of knowing when, or if, they'll clear it."

Collins offered his boyish, lopsided grin. "While we're here, we might as well explore the mysteries of the void. *Ad astra per scientia*."

Olivo shook her head. "With all due respect to the capitan and our junior explorer here, we are not an exploration ship. Even though we're full of cadets, this is a military asset. We should be in the fight."

"And if they ambush us going back through?" Diaz asked.

Olivo shrugged. "I'm PnP, not tactical. You'd have to ask Moore."

"I'll be asking you when they blow out your reactor again," Moore said.

"What do you say, Tac?" Diaz asked.

"I'd say I need to study the Colony War," answered Moore. "No one has studied fighting through or around gates in centuries. But I'd probably go through with full burn, decoys, and sensor drones deployed because it'll be a fight coming out of the gate. If we survive the first barrage, we might be able to escape."

"As long as we don't hit any ships or mines," Bovree said.

Diaz looked back to Olivo. "Speaking of opening gates, it's a moot point if we can't do it reliably. How's that coming?"

"Hector is helping access the data nodes LTE secured. But we're still reviewing the logs to isolate the signals that detect and those that activate."

Bovree gave a low moan. "Oh, I love a good hacking."

Olivo pursed her lips. "We won't know until we get near a gate, though. Preferably one back to Sol. Where we belong."

Diaz listened as the officers continued the discussion. She didn't know what the best answer was. And she wasn't willing to stake the crew's lives on her opinion alone. The discussion petered out after an hour of back-and-forth and outlining contingencies. She scanned the officers.

"What about you, Doctor? You haven't said much."

"I tend to agree with the capitan." Barnes raised his hand when he heard Olivo scoff. "And with Olivo. Our duty is clear. We are a CAR warship. The question goes beyond that, though. Would our direct return to Sol help? We could jump back and be the first casualty in a war that hasn't started yet, especially if we go in ready for a fight. Hell, we could trigger it just by activating the gate. The Cali fleet might be waiting for us to open it so they can jump through.

"Whatever we do, we'll be doing it blind. If it is war, the fleet can do without us." Barnes grinned at Collins. "Everything being equal, I'm swayed by my own little explorer, too. We don't have enough information to make an informed choice, so let's take a historic opportunity. Let's find the other secret gate."

Diaz nodded. "The choice might not even be ours. I'm not sure about the other gate, but I'm interested in the colony. Imagine surviving here alone for centuries. That they even have working ships is impressive. Send your division updates and let's get back to work."

Three hours into the shift, Collins appeared in Diaz's overlay. "XO, Yuloo on the *Solar Dream* is requesting to speak to the capitan."

"As expected. Put her through to me." Diaz grimaced as the connection hissed and popped in her ear. "This is Commander Diaz. How can I help you, Yuloo?"

"I'd like to speak with Capitan Walsh. Is he available?"

"Sorry, he's on his sleep cycle now."

"I see. Maybe you can help, then," Yuloo said. "Our council has given us permission to accept your offer of medical and mechanical aid. Is that something you can help with?"

Bovree had forwarded the intercepted message to Diaz ten minutes ago. Yuloo and Fenti must have been discussing it for a while. "Yes, we can get that started. Our drones are already on standby. I'll send them right over."

Thirty minutes later, Diaz was watching Yuloo and Fenti staring down at her from the perspective of the coffin-like medical drone. Their faces were tight and haggard. Yuloo reached out and cautiously touched the drone before snatching her hand back. Yuloo and Fenti exchanged hesitant glances. They both started when a bust of Doctor Barnes appeared on the surface of the drone's bed.

"Hello, I'm Doctor Barnes aboard the *Amazonas*. You must be Yuloo and you must be Fenti. It's nice to meet you."

"Nice to meet you, Doctor," Fenti said. "We're a bit nervous."

"I understand. But there's nothing to worry about. This equipment is state-of-the-art and I've been doing this for years. The capitan wants to make sure you get the same care he does. Where is the best place to clamp on the magnetic locks so we can get started?"

Yuloo pointed to a nearby bulkhead and Barnes guided the medical drone there. Four metallic clangs echoed in the compartment as the drone's magnetic feet latched on.

"Secure?" Barnes asked.

Yuloo nodded.

"Excellent. The analysis bed is going to open up, so please stand clear."

The coffin rotated on its gimbals and split open with a soft puff of air from the slight pressure differential. The doctor's image reappeared on the inside of the bed's lid.

"Step right up. Since we're in zero-g, the bed will deploy restraints to keep you stable."

Yuloo exchanged another glance with Fenti before pulling herself into the bed. Panels unfolded from the drone and pressed the woman into bed. Fenti moved towards the bed, but she waved him off.

When the initial medical readings came in, Diaz raised her brows. Perspective was sometimes tricky using the small cameras on drones. The drone measured Yuloo at 2.4 meters tall. Lifelong deep-spacers in Sol were often over two meters, but medical treatments not only strengthened their bones, they also limited their growth in zero-g. The Epsilon colonists apparently didn't use those medications.

"The medical scans," Barnes said, "are mostly non-intrusive, and any medications are administered using a hyperdermal compound gel. This arm here"—a robot arm unfolded from the bed and waved—"rolls it on the skin and it is absorbed directly into your body. Just sit back and relax for a few minutes."

"Will you tell us what you find?" Fenti asked. "Or is that reserved for your capitan?"

Barnes smiled from the medical drone's screen. "Given the delicate nature of our pseudo first-contact situation, Capitan Walsh will get a full report. We're looking for things that might be dangerous to either party. We've been separated for quite a while. Our common bacteria and viruses could be deadly to each other. No one wants the Epsilon flu."

After a few minutes, the spider-legged repair drone skittered away along the ceiling. Fenti raised a hand towards it and looked down at Yuloo. She nodded and Fenti pushed off after the drone.

Diaz switched her view to the repair drone and heard Fenti calling after it.

"Hey! Where are you going?"

The drone stopped and a disembodied voice spoke. "Hello, Fenti. My name is Lieutenant Fuller. I'm in charge of maintenance on the *Amazonas*. In order to help, I need to get an idea of what needs to be fixed first. Do you want me to stop?"

Fenti grabbed a grime-blackened handhold and stopped a meter from the drone. He glanced behind him to where Yuloo lay in the medical bed.

"We won't do any repairs without informing you or getting permission," Fuller said. "Does your fabricator work?"

Fenti scoffed. "Not for years. It can only manage a few small things like fasteners and spoons."

"The doctor says he's ready for you, Fenti. Do you want me to wait on the assessment? Or I can wait for an escort."

"No, the assessment's fine. Please don't access any databanks—and get out of any you're already in. And leave the power grid alone for now." Fenti offered a lopsided grin. "We've got that wired like a bowl of noodles."

"Will do," Fuller said.

Fenti turned and floated back down the passage. Diaz switched between the repair drone and the medical bot while Fenti underwent his medical scan.

After half an hour, Barnes forwarded his report to Diaz's overlay. She scanned it while Barnes addressed the colonists.

"I have the results of your exams. Would you like private results? You are both suffering from many of the same maladies, which should come as no surprise given your proximity and shared environment. But I like to afford a measure of confidentiality."

"Except for Walsh," Fenti said wryly.

Barnes smiled apologetically. "Yes."

Yuloo and Fenti shrugged. "Go ahead, Doctor," Yuloo said. "Please."

"As you're well aware," Barnes said, "your ship's ECS is severely degraded. You are both suffering from bacterial infections, dehydration, chronic fatigue, and malnutrition. This, along with your long-term exposure to zero-g, has severely weakened your skeletal integrity."

Barnes glanced away into his overlay. "Yuloo, you also have moderate scarring in your lungs and throat from chronic bronchitis and upper respiratory infections. The good news is that I've worked up a panacea that can drastically clear up most of that. Of course, if our maintenance crew doesn't purify and repair your ship's air and water recyclers, you'll just get infected again. My understanding is that is already being planned."

"But?" Fenti asked in a resigned tone.

Barnes nodded. "But, you've been operating in radioactive environments with substandard shielding on your hull *and* your reactor. You've both suffered significant chromosomal degradation and your immune systems are compromised. Unfortunately, I can't fix that with a panacea. And... you've both been rendered sterile."

Yuloo put her fingers over her mouth. "I knew it was bad."

"We can do some radiation repair, but we aren't equipped for treating long-term exposure, only short exposures due to equipment failures or weapons. We'd have to get you to Sol for treatment."

Fenti let out a long breath. "So we're... terminal? Dying?"

"Yes," Barnes said. "But not immediately. I don't suppose your colony has medical facilities capable of that level of treatment?"

Yuloo shook her head. "Is there anything we can do?"

"Only mitigation, I'm afraid. Get off your ship. Stay in shielded areas. Every bit of exposure makes it worse."

Fenti opened a nearby cabinet and pulled out a small, red fob. "I guess we knew. Our dosimeters expired years ago. We don't have much of a choice, though. Die here, die there." He wiped a tear pooling in his eye.

Yuloo wept softly and Fenti wrapped his arms around her. They clung tightly to one another as they slowly tumbled in the zero gravity. The doctor pressed his lips together and looked away.

At length, Yuloo sniffled loudly and dabbed her eyes on Fenti's shoulder. "Thank you, Doctor. Please treat us as best as you're able. If I can die without this damned cough, I'll die happy. We have nothing to trade."

"This one's on the house," Barnes said, smiling. "Capitan's orders. The panacea is synthesized to be a genetic match with each patient. Just hold out your hand, Yuloo."

Yuloo did so and the thin arm unfolded again, holding a small roll-ball dispenser. It swiped across Yuloo's hand and retracted. A moment later, the arm extended again with a dispenser for Fenti.

Barnes smiled broadly once Fenti had been taken care of. "Great. You should start feeling relief in an hour or so, but it will take at least forty-eight hours to reach full effect. You'll feel very thirsty, but I urge you not to drink from your ship's supply until the recycler is repaired. I'm told we'll be sending some provisions over while we work.

"I'm going to leave this medical drone here for now. The panaceas can make some people feel sleepy. Get some rest. The better rested, the better you'll heal."

WALSH FLOATED INTO the Medical compartment. "How's it going, Doctor?"

"I added a mild relaxant to the medicine, hoping they'd both take the doctor's advice and go to sleep." Barnes shrugged. "But patients never listen."

"With only two crew and a strange Earth warship parked outside, I'd be keeping watch, too. Can you imagine being cooped up on that death trap for months with only one other person?"

"Not if it was my wife," Barnes said in a high-pitched, Russian accent. He pantomimed making a long slide on a trombone, a gesture recently made popular by overlay comedian Turdi Butinski whenever he told a zinger.

Walsh laughed. "Even you would probably start looking pretty to someone locked up with you long enough."

"With all due respect, Gene, I wouldn't want to be locked up with you for long. I know your reputation."

Screwball hooted from the hatchway.

Walsh leaned in closer to Barnes. "Speaking of prettier than you, Doc." He pushed off the doctor towards the hatch. "I'll leave you to the doctor, Cadet."

"Actually, Capitan, I came to ask about Angelica. She hasn't left her cabin in days and won't answer any comms. Is she okay?"

"Yes, Cadet," Walsh said. "She's healthy, at least. The doctor's been keeping close watch. She's eating some and is uninjured. But I can't say how well she's really doing. The girl's been through a lot. You'll be able to see her when she's ready."

Relief rolled across the chimp's face. "Thank you, Capitan. We've grown close. I'm very fond of her."

Walsh raised a brow at Screwball, who raised his own brows in reply.

"Oh, no, no, Capitan," Screwball said hurriedly. "Nothing like that. There's nothing between us like there is between you two."

Walsh glared at the chimp. "What?"

Screwball made several high-pitched hoots as he climbed the bulkhead away from Walsh. "I mean, how she likes you, sir. She's not attracted to me like she is to you. I think I'm more of a pet. I'm not competing with you, Capitan."

Barnes stifled a laugh behind his hands and Walsh narrowed his eyes at the doctor.

Screwball looked wide-eyed at Barnes, then back to Walsh. "That's what you meant, right? Mating?"

"There can never be anything between us, despite her hopes, Cadet. Do not let her entertain those thoughts if it comes up. And it isn't just because I'm the capitan."

Walsh sighed. "Sorry, Cadet. I shouldn't have snapped at you. But she's a delicate matter and she doesn't understand."

"I don't understand either, Capitan," Screwball said. "I mean, if she's healthy and willing. But I'm just a chimp. Angelica and I are both in the made-by-humans club. We sometimes laugh about what humans do. The extent of my instruction on that topic was that I'm not to masturbate in front of people."

Barnes burst out laughing.

"Thank you, Cadet," Walsh said slowly. "I'll let you know about her. Dismissed."

Screwball saluted from the ceiling and leaped into the passage and out of sight.

"So much for accepting strange and alien ways," the doctor said. "Cadet Screwball might have to save us all from our social mores if we ever run into very naughty aliens."

"And thank you, too, Doctor," Walsh said. "Surgeon, biochemist, free-fall comedian. Maybe I should keep those two apart."

The smile slid from Barnes's face. "Have you seen Angelica's recent art?"

"Yes, unfortunately."

"Maybe you should talk to her."

Walsh shook his head. "These conversations with the colony council have me tied up."

"Don't lie to a liar, Gene."

"You talk to her, then. On the basis of those drawings, I'm not sure she wants to talk to me. Or that it would be safe. Half show me eating her or her sisters' hearts. The other half..." Walsh shuddered as he recalled the life-like drawing of him with his scrotum festooned with harpoons. "The other half I wish I could erase from my and the ship's memory. She's not drawing the happy, smiley pictures she was. No, she needs to stay put. These talks with the colony are too important."

Barnes held up his hands. "Okay, okay. Just a suggestion from your doctor."

Walsh turned and left for his cabin.

Chapter 29

DIAZ PEEKED AROUND the corner down the corridor to habitat Alpha's head. It was empty, so she crept to the next corridor—empty. Though it was easier to sneak around in zero-g, Diaz was glad the capitan had spun the habitats back up. Hab-Bravo was still short a good bit of mass, so nearly all of the water ballast for ther Alpha-Bravo spin system had been shifted to Bravo to stabilize the spin. The last thing *Amazonas* needed was an uncontrolled wobble.

What she saw around the next corner made Diaz scoff. Halfway down the passage to the ECS equipment compartment, two maintenance crew members were crouched over an open panel. The panel was lying next to them unsecured and they were both chatting instead of fixing.

Diaz padded down the passage and made it four paces away before they noticed her. It would be one thing if they had been heads together fixing something and not noticed her, but they'd been idling and gossiping. Not working.

"Cadets," Diaz said loudly, causing the two to jump. She mostly subdued her satisfied smirk. "What are you doing?"

They quickly snapped to attention. Cadet Holmes still held her test unit. "Waiting for diagnostics to finish on the micro-relay, ma'am. There's an intermittent stray voltage in this array. Left over from the battle."

"So you weren't just staring off into space?"

Holmes flashed a pretty smile. "Never, XO." She held out the test unit.

Diaz raised a brow and took the unit. She flipped through the screens and verified the remote test system was running. "Was that your first battle, Cadets?"

"Yes, XO."

Diaz nodded. "Are you under the assumption it will be your last, Holmes?"

Holmes looked at her suspiciously. "No, ma'am."

"What do you think will happen if we take more hits or have to perform evasive maneuvers?"

The other cadet hiked his thumb towards the main shaft. "We'd be summoned to shielded stations, XO."

Diaz looked at Holmes. "Do you agree?"

"Yes, ma'am."

Diaz snorted. "Wrong. The first thing that would happen is that unsecured panel would fly into someone's skull. Those fittings are designed to hold removed panels. You did know that, right? Do I need to address Lieutenant Fuller's training?"

The cadets glanced at the panel and then at each other. Holmes closed her eyes for a second. "No, ma'am. We'll do better."

Diaz handed the test unit back to Holmes. "I should think so. Carry on."

One deck down, she found a lieutenant leaning against a bulkhead. He noticed her as soon as she peered around the corner, and came to attention. She approached, but he spoke before she could.

"XO, the fabricator is printing out a fitting for this pressure switch." He motioned to a thin valve with a red molecular tag labeled "Secured from Operation" stamped to it. "Just waiting for the drone."

He held out his testing unit the moment her hand moved. Diaz flipped through the displays, handed it back, and walked away without a word.

Her prowling had left her unsatisfied. She had been looking for something more than an unsecured panel. In zero-g that might have warranted more of a chewing out. Everyone she found had been diligently working. She expected no less; *Amazonas* probably drilled more than any ship in the fleet. But she would have loved to jump someone's ass.

"They told me you were stalking the halls, XO."

Diaz started at the voice and turned. "Guilty as charged. Someone's got to keep cracking the whip."

"You need another whip," Fuller said. "Even the cadets are on to you now."

"Not all of them. But if everyone is tracking me, I must be doing something right. As long as things are getting done, I'm happy."

Fuller grinned. "You're just happier if you can jump on someone."

"I'm only human—despite being XO. It keeps my command skills sharp. Junior officers should be scared of someone."

"I think you're getting soft, XO."

Diaz arched her brow. "*Que*?"

"If you really wanted to catch people, you'd be sifting through the maintenance logs. But after that shit with Midland, I keep on top of that."

"Don't tell anyone," Diaz said, "but I hate sifting through logs. It's more fun to pounce."

"I'd better get back to work, then," Fuller said and walked away.

Diaz watched her go and thought about that shipwreck cadet, Midland. The *puta* brat who had put them all in danger. The *puta* brat who ran to her *jefa* to clean it all up for her. The *puta* brat who laid the capitan.

Was she more angry at the former cadet or the capitan? It didn't matter. As her grandmother often said, "A person's action reveals their nature, not their smile."

Now she didn't care about finding someone to chew on. Even light-years away, Midland had ruined Diaz's fun. She traced a finger along a clean, white scar of a repair patch. It was a visceral reminder of how close they had come to getting spaced. After weeks of trying to put the scene together, she still wasn't sure how much of what had happened was the capitan's fault and how much was Liberty's.

Hector appeared in the passage in front of her. "Commander Diaz. Signals intercepted from Karen's Kvetch indicate the capitan's invitation to allow Yuloo and Fenti aboard has been approved. They are now requesting connection."

She nodded. "This is Commander Diaz."

"Hello," Yuloo said. The woman's voice sounded less scratchy than before. "We have permission to visit your ship, if the invitation is still open."

"I'll verify with Capitan Walsh. I don't see an issue so I'll prep our shuttle and get back with you soon." Diaz dropped the connection.

"Shall I inform the capitan, Commander Diaz?" Hector asked.

"Is he awake?"

"Yes."

"Then, no. I'll go talk to him."

The two ships had turned for deceleration three days ago and were still a week out from Epsilon Eridani II. The flight was still going slowly due to *Solar Dream*'s condition—despite extensive repairs to the crumbling scow—and the lack of any friendly reaction-mass resupply. Without REM-RES, as it was known in the extensive lexicon of fleet acronyms, *Amazonas* had limited delta-v. It was unclear if the colony could resupply them, so Diaz was glad *El Capitan* was finally showing some sense.

"Come in," Walsh called as she approached.

"Get any sleep?"

Walsh flashed a boyish grin, the effect marred by the bags under his eyes. "Some. Just going over the protocol manuals to see if they have anything useful. I don't want to offend their Grand Poo-Bah."

"You'll do great," Diaz said. "Because if you don't, I'll have to. No one wants that."

"The old better-you-than-me play, eh, Felicia? I see the shuttle's being prepped. They want to come aboard?"

Diaz nodded.

"Good. Maybe I can get a better sense of things face-to-face. Looks like I get to wear the crimson and golds again."

Diaz smirked. "For them?"

"They might be just a pair of space scallywags, but today they're visiting dignitaries. Which, of course, means you get to wear them, too. And so will four of the duty section to man the hatches. Your pick."

"She's just some scientist her colony left out there to starve."

"She's also, at the very least, the capitan of another nation's vessel. And you never know, she could be the eldest princess of the colonial aristocracy."

"They have royalty?"

Walsh shook his head. "I don't think so. But you never know. It never hurts to be nice."

"*Dios mio*," she muttered. He was wrong about that.

Walsh gazed back into his overlay. "I'll meet you at the shuttle."

IT TOOK NEARLY TWO hours for the shuttle to return to *Amazonas*. *Solar Dream*'s docking collar was incompatible with the shuttle, preventing a hard seal. Instead, it had to extend its boarding chute while Yuloo and Fenti donned their cracked and stained EVA suits.

Walsh got a good look at those suits and shook his head.

The shuttle dock was along *Amazonas*'s main hull, aft of the spin arms. Walsh, Diaz, and four unlucky crew members, who hadn't been doing anything more useful, stood in their dress uniforms. They clutched nearby protrusions to keep at their best approximation of attention.

The light around the airlock went from red to green. Yuloo and Fenti helped each other with their helmets as Hector played the cheery, brassy tune the CAR inflicted on visiting dignitaries.

"Secure that shit," Walsh subvocalized to Hector. The music stopped. Walsh and his crew saluted in unison, causing the visitors to flinch.

Walsh smiled. "Welcome aboard the *Amazonas*." Hector translated his words over the nearby ship speakers. The visitors' replies were translated to Spanish into the crew's overlay.

Yuloo inclined her head slightly. "Thank you for your hospitality, Capitan Walsh. It's good to finally meet you in person. And thank you for your generosity—the air and water on the *Solar Dream* haven't been so sweet since before I was born. On behalf of the leadership of Karen's Kvetch, welcome to Epsilon Eridani."

"Our pleasure." Walsh motioned to Diaz, who held up two pairs of earbuds. "These will allow our ship to translate and communicate with you without having to use the speakers."

Yuloo and Fenti nodded and inserted them into their ears.

"How's that?" Walsh asked.

Yuloo smiled. "Very good." She pointed to Walsh's overlay rig. "Is that what you use?"

Walsh turned his head so she could get a good look. "Yes. It speaks to us and has many other virtual- and augmented-reality functions."

"Thank you," Fenti said, adjusting his buds.

"I'm glad you were able to come over," Walsh said. "I apologize for the docking issues, but I'm going to have to ask you to leave your suits here. For environmental reasons."

"And security reasons?" Fenti asked.

"And security reasons," Walsh agreed.

Yuloo turned around and Fenti helped her disassemble the upper shell of her suit. She did the same in turn, and soon the two stood in grimy, sweat-stained thermals. Severe body odor mixed with the bite of mildew to fill the passage. Walsh strained not to sneeze or cover his nose in disgust. He was pleased to note that no one else had a noticeable reaction. Yuloo flushed red and Walsh hoped it wasn't because he'd given himself away. Perhaps it was because she was effectively in her underwear and a crew of strangers was staring at her.

Fenti looked unconcerned as he scratched his crotch.

Two of the crew secured the vacc suits in nearby lockers and the other two presented the visitors with white coveralls and undergarments.

"I hope you don't mind," Walsh said, "but we took the liberty of making you some garments sized from your medical scans." He motioned to a nearby compartment. "Feel free to change in here, if you like. We'll recycle your clothes."

"For security?" Fenti asked again. Yuloo gently nudged him.

Walsh smiled. "For security. And contamination factors."

"That will be wonderful," Yuloo said. They took the proffered clothes and changed in the same compartment. Yuloo was smiling and examining her new clothes. Fenti kept rolling his shoulders and circling his arms.

"Do they not fit?" Walsh asked.

Fenti grinned. "They fit perfectly. It's just nice to wear some clothes that don't feel like they're going to rip if you move too fast."

Walsh drifted down the passage, glancing back over his shoulder as he spoke. "I'm glad to hear it. Follow me. We'll find a more suitable place to talk and show you around our ship. By the way, do you have surnames or titles you prefer? All I have is Yuloo and Fenti from the comms."

Yuloo drifted after him with ease. "We gave up on clan and family names generations ago, Capitan. When you... when the old gate exploded, it destroyed our trading hub. The survivors divided into family gangs. It doesn't paint a pretty picture, but more people died in the fighting than from the explosion or even the famines that followed. So we eventually dropped them, thanks to Karen."

"It wasn't pretty in Sol, either," Diaz said.

Walsh shot her a warning glance.

"In Sol?" Yuloo asked.

"We can talk about such matters when we get to the conference room," Walsh said.

Yuloo frowned. "I'm just glad I wasn't there to see it. The stories are terrible. Yuloo and Fenti will do, Capitan."

Walsh stopped at the hatch leading to the main shaft. "In that case, call me Gene. Unless you have any immediate needs, we'll start our tour."

"Great," Fenti said. "Let's see what a real spaceship looks like."

Yuloo frowned at Fenti, but said nothing.

Walsh led them into the main hull and explained the shielded core and the stations within. He led them up one of the supports and opened the nearest station hatch.

Yuloo ran a finger along a shiny, recent repair. "These are repairs from your entry?"

"Yes," Walsh said, pointing out several areas of repair. "The shielded core, or crypt as we call it, can take quite a pounding. The ship can remain functional with almost the entire outer hull gone. And we can stay inside one of these stations for a long time."

"That is amazing," she said almost reverently.

Walsh pulled his way towards the spin habitats. "Under normal ops, the *Amazonas* generates simulated gravity via spin habitats, as I'm sure you saw from your ship. Nothing new or fancy. In fact, this ship was built before the Colonial War. If it's spinning, that's where you find just about everyone. Grab a handhold around the upcoming entrance. Then climb into it feet-first, like this."

Walsh looked up the shaft and saw Diaz helping Yuloo grab a handle on the outward conveyor. She smiled down at him while Diaz helped Fenti as well and followed. They slid down the shaft and Walsh felt the pull of the spin increase.

He heard a grunt from above and looked up to see Yuloo struggling to keep her grip. One foot slipped and she shrieked as her hands clutched desperately to a handhold.

"Help her," panted Fenti, whose own limbs were beginning to tremble.

"Shit," Walsh muttered. He scrambled up the conveyor and pulled Yuloo close to him with one arm around her waist. She wrapped a long leg around his thigh.

Looking up, he saw Diaz moving to help Fenti. He held tightly while the conveyor moved impossibly slowly. At the bottom, he leaned Yuloo against a bulkhead and helped Fenti as he reached the bottom. The two visitors continued to pant and slid down the bulkhead into a sitting position.

Walsh knelt next to Yuloo. "I am so sorry, I wasn't thinking. What's your native gravity?"

"Mostly zero-g, Gene. The colony I think sometimes has 0.2-g."

"Ops-O." Walsh spoke out loud for his visitors' sakes. "Spin habitats for 0.1-g."

He waited for the arms to spin down, repeatedly apologizing. It was a rookie mistake. It wasn't as if there weren't people in Sol with no gravity tolerance. He should have known better. That wasn't the best first impression he'd ever made.

"Quick thinking," Diaz subvocalized into his private overlay channel.

"Thanks."

"I mean, that full-body princess-hug rescue was right out of the vids."

Walsh narrowed his eyes at Diaz. Her face was as expressionless as usual. "Not now. If you're looking to give a ration of shit, give one to yourself for not thinking about how they'd react to gravity, either."

"Fair enough."

Walsh offered a hand to Yuloo when Collins had verified the spin-down to the lower gravity was complete. "Again, I'm sorry about that. Would you like me to get Dr. Barnes?"

"No, no, Gene. We're fine." Yuloo was still breathing heavily. "I've never been in g like that. I can't imagine living that way. Is that what it's like on Earth? A full gravity?"

"Good old terra firma."

Yuloo chuckled musically, taking his hand. "I've lived in free fall my whole life, but I think that's the only time I've felt like I was going to fall." She stood and stumbled into Walsh's arms. "Exhilarating." Blushing, she added, "Almost falling, I mean."

Walsh ignored Diaz's snort as he disentangled himself from Yuloo's arms. Floating, he'd not appreciated just how tall the woman was. On even ground, he was staring at her collar bones. It was a struggle not to glance down to see just how long her legs were.

Walsh smiled up at her. "Are you hungry? I know we've sent over rations, but the good stuff's in the galley. Beyond all hope, our aeroponics bay survived our dramatic entry into Epsilon Eridani. Fresh tomatoes and carrots today."

Fenti's eyes went wide. "Like, real tomatoes? Those round, red fruits? You actually have some?" He ignored Yuloo clearing her throat and openly licked his lips.

Walsh chuckled despite himself. "The very ones. I take it you like them a lot."

"There haven't been any tomatoes for over a hundred years," Yuloo said, pushing Fenti's jaw shut. "Though we do have a piquant algae paste some say has a slight tomato flavor. But I wouldn't know."

Walsh ordered Hector to clear the galley before leading the visitors there. It took a few cautious steps to adjust to the new low gravity. As he slowly bounced along, Walsh occasionally glanced over his shoulder to make sure Yuloo and Fenti hadn't been hurt. Fenti sniffed loudly at the smell of food coming from the now emptied galley.

Nearly empty galley.

Screwball bounced from the galley, his mouth filled with an apple. He looked up at the capitan and froze.

"Cadet—" Walsh started.

"Don't stop, silly monkey," Angelica cried before tripping over Screwball. Two apples fell slowly from her grip and rolled to a stop at Walsh's feet. Angelica watched the apples roll and then looked up at Walsh with a smile. "Capitan Daddy!"

"Angel—"

Yuloo squealed and gripped Walsh's elbow with both hands. Her mouth was so close to his ear that he was hearing her native words and Hector's translation at the same volume.

"Is that a pet?" Yuloo asked, beaming. "A real pet? An animal? Oh, Gene, I've never seen a real, living animal. No animals have been here since the last litter of cats died in an electrical fire two hundred years ago. It's amazing. Can I touch it? Is it a he or she?"

The smile slid from Angelica's face and she glowered at Yuloo.

Walsh tried to push Yuloo back, and not just for the daggers in Angelica's eyes. Hector had to translate what she'd said again when Yuloo wasn't in Walsh's ear.

"No, he is not a pet. This is Cadet Screwball. He's part of the crew."

Yuloo stared back at him. "Screwball?"

And this was why he'd wanted everyone out of the galley. This was supposed to be a tour free of random, out-of-context remarks some crew member might make. And now she was freaking out about an uplift. He hadn't heard anything about uplifts from the colony, so had no way of knowing how they felt about them. Maybe that was something else he should have asked about.

Screwball offered a small wave and hooted around the apple still stuffed ridiculously in his mouth.

Fenti flinched at the noise and put himself between the chimp and Yuloo. He pulled out his earbuds and motioned for Yuloo to do the same, before they stepped away and began whispering. Walsh forced his smile as the furtive conversation continued. Yuloo occasionally cast glances at Screwball and Walsh.

Diaz chimed in on his personal channel. "Do you think they have some taboo against uplifts?"

"Maybe only if they dress like humans." Walsh murmured. "Or as crew?"

Diaz glanced at Screwball. "Hector, how did you translate Screwball?"

"Cadet Screwball's name is idiomatic. Unsure of how our visitors would understand it, or be able to pronounce it phonetically, I decided it best to translate it more directly as *Guairen*. Traditionally, it means strange one, or odd one."

Hector, only visible to Walsh and Diaz, motioned towards Yuloo and Fenti. "Their language is a pidgin and centuries removed from the Chinese in my database. It is possible it has a different localized meaning."

The visitors were looking between Walsh and Screwball. At least their mouths were closed now.

Walsh motioned for his visitors to replace their earbuds and they did. "Did we offend?" He spared a glance at the chimp. "I can ask him to leave, if you like. No one was supposed to be here, anyway."

"What planet is he from?" Yuloo asked.

"Earth."

Yuloo frowned. "You said he was an alien-being cadet. Are there many alien beings on Earth? When did his race contact you?"

Walsh squeezed his eyes shut. It was his fault. Screwy... Screwball, was as diligent a cadet as he'd ever commanded. But it was Walsh who'd decided to give Angelica—the obvious instigator of these hijinks—some time out of her quarters. All she'd really done was grieve her sisters, though violently so. He didn't like leaving her locked up and agreed when the doctor suggested letting her out from time to time.

Walsh waved Screwball over. "Cadet Screwball is not extraterrestrial. He's an uplift, an animal that was genetically modified to give him humanlike intelligence. Though chimpanzees—that's what his species is called—are pretty smart already."

Yuloo watched the chimp approach. "You can talk, then?"

Screwball pulled the apple from his mouth. "Yes, ma'am. Uh, welcome aboard."

"And you're not an alien?"

"Not like that. But I'm unique in the crew." He smiled brightly, flapping his lips. "And my ancestors are definitely from Earth."

As she squatted, Yulloo's knees came almost to her chin. She bowed her head. "Can your ancestors talk? Or the rest of your family?"

"Just me."

"And you can speak because of experiments done to you? Surgeries?"

"Yes."

"That seems cruel, Cadet." She slowly stood and looked at Walsh. "That seems cruel."

Walsh hesitated, trying to be the diplomat. "It... wasn't our decision."

"And if it weren't for that," Screwball said, "I wouldn't be in a spaceship or have visited another star. Or have the intellect to care that I had."

Yuloo favored the chimp with a wan smile. "Of course. Thank you for speaking with me."

"Dismissed, you two," Walsh said.

Angelica glanced suspiciously at Yuloo before tugging Screwball after her.

"Do you have other kids on board?" Fenti asked.

Walsh motioned towards the now hopefully abandoned galley. "She's... another unique case."

Yuloo smiled as she slid past into the galley. "It is a very unique ship you have. So, what's for lunch, Gene?"

Chapter 30

THE LOW SPIN GRAVITY was making it hard for Angelica to draw. In zero-g it was a simple matter of getting strapped in properly, and being able to leave her pencils floating nearby made it more fun. In higher gravity, things stayed on the table as they were supposed to. But 0.1-g? That was a pain in the ass.

All thanks to Yuloo.

But she was an artist, no matter the gravs. Angelica smiled down at the portrait, while she flexed and stretched the cramps out of her fingers. Gene stared back at her, that strong face hovering above his warship as it sped into the void. The angle of his nose was perfect and the plume effect of *Amazonas*'s thruster provided a perfect band of contrast as it streaked past his head.

Screwy had explained to her that there were no visible fiery plumes due to the nature of the nuclear thrust. The silly monkey had actually explained it to her as if she hadn't spent most of her life on ships. In any case, the art had to come before the science.

The picture had taken days to get just right. Angelica knew when it was time to call a picture done and leave well enough alone. Brittany had been a good artist, too, but she always fidgeted and fussed with her pictures until almost ruining them. A tear slowly trickled her face and she was grateful for the low gravity, which allowed her to catch the tear before it fell on the portrait. She wished she could show the picture to Brittany.

With a final smudge to blend the shading along Gene's manly jawline, Angelica set it on the small table that slid from the wall.

She unfastened and pulled the small fuser from her art box. Holding the picture in place with one hand, she ran the fuser back and forth, about thirty centimeters over the paper. It emitted a dim glow that activated a chemical in the phase-graf lines from her pencil, sealing the particles to each other and to the phase-paper. It worked far better than varnishes or sprays artists of times past had used. Now she could cry all over the paper and it wouldn't run or stain.

With a final peck on the portrait's lips, she slid it into an ornate frame made from scrap paper. Finely detailed drawings of Sol's planets, separated by stylized comets and stars, covered the frame. Angelica had been going for a look resembling the borders of illuminated manuscripts and was quite pleased with the result. It was perhaps one of her best works ever.

She hummed merrily as she set the picture down and activated the holo-mirror. Daddy hadn't fallen for any of the hairstyles she'd tried. Angelica flipped her hair and watched the curls bounce down her back. Swiping left and right, she watched the styles change.

Dressing for success wasn't an option since Gene had ordered her to wear a standard flightsuit for so-called safety reasons. But she was convinced it wasn't safety so much as the fishnet bodysuit she'd worn to the galley last week. Hector had locked her in the cabin and then must have ratted her out to Daddy.

And she hadn't seen Daddy for three days, even in the passageways. It had to be the snitchy ship's fault. But this morning she knew Gene was in his stateroom; she had her own sources. She was going to make him see her. She was going to make him like her. Even if he never did what a daddy was supposed to do, maybe he'd stop looking at her as if she was something to be scraped off the bulkhead.

Daddy was easy to spook so she decided not to push her luck. Slow and steady sometimes won the race. Angelica decided to leave her hair simple—and loose, just in case Daddy wanted to flip her hair out of the way. Maybe run his fingers through it. Gooseflesh tingled down her neck at the thought.

She liked what she saw in the projection and twirled. A final glance over her shoulder reassured her that she could even make this dumpy flightsuit look good. Angelica grabbed the picture and left her cabin.

Low gravity might be harder to draw in, but every step was like a game of hopscotch and she giggled as she went. She winked at Lieutenant Nunes as she skipped past him. At the next intersection, two cadets parted so she could bounce between them. They smiled and playfully told her not to run inside. She grinned back at them and tossed her hair as she glided between them. The picture wobbled slightly with each landing.

Gene's door was around the corner and Angelica stopped to fluff her hair. Who wouldn't run their fingers through that if given the chance? She stepped around the corner and the smile died on her lips.

Yuloo stood in front of her daddy's door, playing with her stringy hair and tugging at her flightsuit as if she had curves to flaunt. Even if she did look healthier since coming aboard, every woman, and some of the men, on *Amazonas* were prettier than that nasty, old husk.

But she was *grown up* and a capitan of sorts, if her floating pigsty could be called a ship. Angelica had heard how disgusting the place was, even now after being repaired. Fenti had gone back to their scrap bucket and now it looked as though Yuloo was ready to play. The look on the old woman's face told Angelica all she needed to see—Yuloo thought she actually had a chance with Daddy.

Yuloo's face brightened when the hatch opened, and not from the light that spilled out from Gene's cabin. She entered with a playful smile. The old woman knew what she wanted, and Angelica knew she would get it.

Angelica balled her hands into fists, wrinkling the portrait where she held it. Why? Why would he do that when *she* was at his command? Sharing wasn't a problem for her. But the old hag *instead* of Angelica?

It was too much. She looked down at the picture. How childish she must really be if she had thought, had hoped, such an offering would move him. Daddy wasn't taking her seriously, and she'd made him something a parent might hang on the refrigeration unit's door. She slowly tore it in half, then ripped the remains in half again. A tiny teardrop drifted from her cheek and splattered on Gene's portrait, where it gathered itself together and fell to the deck. This daddy was immune to her tears, too.

With a soft sob, she dropped the scraps and watched them fall to the deck in lazy ebbs. Yes, Angelica would have to get serious if she wanted to be taken seriously.

"*Hola*, Angelica." Diaz stopped in front of her, raising her eyebrows as she looked at the tattered picture. "Is everything okay?"

"Probably for Gene and the old lady he's humping." She glanced at the hatch to Gene's cabin and ran back to her own.

WALSH KNEW THAT GOOD food and panbiotics could work wonders, but he'd never seen a transformation like Yuloo's during her time aboard ship. She was not a pretty woman, but she looked twenty years younger. Though not pretty, she was exotic. Yuloo was practically an alien, a woman—albeit a human woman—from another star. What sort of strange customs had developed in the isolation of Epsilon Eridani?

And she was so tall. Even in Sol the deep-spacers seldom grew that tall because of the medications and availability of spin gravity. Those arms. Those legs.

"Thank you for seeing me, Capitan," she said.

"My pleasure. Let me just finish reading this last report." Walsh looked back into his overlay. Yuloo's medical record hovered before him. She showed no STDs, and was sterile because of her age and long-term radiation exposure, but the doctor's treatments were coming along splendidly.

He wondered if she found him as exotic? Possibly, if all the colonists were as lanky as she was. Walsh slid the report away and smiled. "What can I do for you, Yuloo?"

"I was wondering what your plans are for Karen's Kvetch? I know you'll be discussing things with the council, but I'd like to know. Both in the long term and the short."

Walsh paused before answering. "Honestly, I don't know. I'll be satisfied if I can leave a good impression, at least. With a new gate connecting Sol, I want us to be able to have good relations. With the CAR and everyone. I thought I might get a list of supply needs or trade goods."

"And after that meeting?" Yuloo asked. "Your ship is amazing, but we can't support you. I've been one packet of nutripaste from starvation my entire life. Like everyone here." She smiled ruefully and turned away. "I feel guilty for eating so well while everyone else is starving."

"Don't know that, either. There will be complications if we go back through the gate too soon."

Yuloo shook her head. "The ones that attacked you."

Walsh drew a breath, ready to recite the elaborate story he'd concocted. Then he looked into her eyes. "That obvious?"

"Not at first. And we have never seen someone use a gate. But there were many holes in your ship—most of them going in. I've passed my observations on to the council, of course."

"Thanks for the warning," Walsh said.

"It also seems that this nexus gate is new to you, as well. Having such an advantage might lead some to attack you for it."

Walsh pulled his flight thermos from its magnetic clasp on the desk. "That would be a possibility. Maybe I should watch you more carefully."

"You should watch your crew more carefully, Gene. Or at least what they say. But I wasn't trying to trick anyone."

"I appreciate it."

"Good. Because there's something you can do for me."

Walsh raised his brow. "Oh?"

"You said you'd stopped listening to our comms, and I can only trust you in that. And I trust you because I think you can save my people."

"Of course we'll do what we can."

Yuloo leaned forward and took Walsh's hand. "Gene, I also want you to take me to Sol with you."

Walsh let her hand linger for a moment before gently pulling his hand free. "I'd have to think about that. What does the council think about it?"

She bit her lip. "They told me I couldn't."

"We have the life support, but I don't want to cause any conflict. It wouldn't look good if the CAR diplomat was accused of kidnapping."

"They want me to go back to the *Solar Dream* or the *Trangus* when you leave the system."

"Then I can't—"

"I also know you were told where to find the gate. We know how to find them, we just can't open them. I'm sure you see where I'm going with this."

"I see," Walsh said. "Well the council probably won't feel like sharing if I take you with me against their wishes."

"Let me rephrase, Gene. I know how to find the gates. The council has the files, but they don't understand them."

"So there is another gate?"

Yuloo frowned, then shrugged. "Yes. Now that we know the signals a gate makes, we know the *Trangus* has detected one. And I know that you know where she is, and I know what you're thinking. But space is big, Gene. It would take quite a while to find where to activate the gate by guessing."

"There's no way to know where the gate opens."

Yuloo smiled and took Walsh's hand again. "That's fine. I do want to see Sol, but I want to see it all. Unexplored solar systems. Or even other colonies. Find out what has happened out there all this time."

"Sounds risky." Walsh didn't sound convincing even to himself. "We may decide to stay here until someone sends a rescue mission through the gate. We obviously know how to open it now." Her hand was warm and he didn't pull away this time.

"And if the next ones through the gate aren't here to rescue you?"

Walsh shook his head. "They'd have already come through if they could. But that's a moot point. No matter what happens, if I piss off the colonial council it won't go well for me here or in Sol. Especially if your government decides not to deal with my government due to my actions."

Yuloo smiled and leaned forward. "That might be true. But maybe I can offer something more? Something I know you want?"

Walsh's brows shot up. "Oh?" He leaned forward, too.

"Yes. I can offer the universe. You're an explorer and so am I. I have the knowledge and you have the means. We might never get another chance once our governments start making treaties and agreements."

She squeezed his hand as she continued, "Mine might demand my return, and your government might agree if it means an accord. And you've hinted that you might be in trouble already. Who can say what will happen when you get to Sol? You might not have a ship, if what you say is true. Or you might have to go off to war instead of to the stars."

Walsh grinned. "Oh, that's what you mean."

"What did you think I was talking about?"

Walsh glanced down at her hand in his. "Never mind. What you say is all true."

She withdrew her hand, but didn't look upset. Yuloo tucked a lock of hair behind her ear. "You have a ship full of beautiful, healthy, and young women."

"Didn't all your investigations uncover those relations aren't allowed? Aside from being against regulations, it makes for some awkward patrols."

Yuloo was interrupted by the door chime.

"Commander Diaz," Hector said aloud.

The door chimed again and Diaz sent a priority message to his overlay. "Is everything good, Capitan? We need to talk."

"Sorry, my XO has something urgent." Walsh opened the hatch with a flick of his wrist.

Yuloo stood and moved to the door. As she passed Diaz, Yuloo cast a coquettish glance over her shoulder. "Consider my offer, Gene. We may never get another chance to visit the stars."

Diaz closed the hatch after Yuloo. "Just wanted to make sure everything was all right."

"So what's the emergency, XO?"

"I heard she made an unexpected visit. Just keeping the chain of command safe. You can never be too safe." She looked placidly down at Walsh. "Oh, I didn't interrupt anything, did I?"

"As a matter of fact, you did. She was just telling me they've figured out that we were attacked and didn't want me trying to bullshit the council like you're trying to bullshit me right now."

"If everything is good, Capitan, I'll return to Ops."

"No, everything is not good." He noticed the papers behind her back. "What's that? And what was that about an emergency?"

"I was making sure you were all right, like I said."

Walsh stood. "We need to talk."

"Do we?"

"We do."

"About what?"

"About what a judgmental bitch you've become."

"I've always been a judgmental bitch, Capitan."

Walsh let out a long breath. "You thought you were interrupting Yuloo and I in flagrante delicto, didn't you?"

When Diaz didn't answer, he continued, "You've made it quite clear that you don't approve of my proclivities, and that's fine. And I've taken your remarks in as good-natured a manner as possible. But your tone is going too far—especially in front of the crew and cadets. And now swooping in like some nun-of-wrath chaperone?" Walsh held up his hands. "What gives, Felicia? Lay it on me."

Diaz looked away, her forehead furrowing like a gathering thunderstorm. She finally said, "Midland."

"Sobella?"

"That!" Diaz snapped her head around and stabbed a finger in Walsh's face. "That right there is what gives, Capitan. Sobella. *Sobella*? She could have killed us all and then you two..." Diaz entwined her fingers and flopped her hands together in what looked to Walsh like an approximation of two octopi having sex.

He pinched the bridge of his nose. "She's a kid who made a mistake. Let it go, already."

"Not too young for you, it seems. And it wasn't a mistake. It was blatant disregard. This wasn't like some teenager trying to skip out on chores.

"She lied about it and that's okay with you—as long as you get laid." She waggled her finger under Walsh's nose when he tried to object. "So yes, I wanted to make sure your opening diplomatic move in this already screwed-up scenario wasn't to bang the colonial representative."

"I told you what we were doing."

"I've seen your furtive little glances and boyish grins. Trying to put Gene's genes in her, as I've heard you say."

"I've never said that about Yuloo."

Diaz tossed the shreds of the portrait onto the desk. In the low gravity, one drifted onto the floor. "And I'm not the only one."

"What's this?" Walsh gathered up the pieces and arranged them on the desk. He stroked his beard as he examined the work. "Wow. Amazing. Angelica?"

"Of course. She saw Yuloo come in here. I found her crying in the passage."

A pang of guilt worked its way up from Walsh's gut. It was quickly replaced with anger. "Since when do you care about the vat whore's feelings? Do you now want me to lead her on? I've made my position quite clear to her. Would you be so bent if you found her crying after I told her no for the hundredth time?"

"I want you to think about how your little flings affect your ship, Capitan."

"You damn well know I don't have flings with current crew." Walsh gripped the edges of his desk. "Here's an idea, Felicia. If you're so damned concerned about my leadership, why don't you stop hiding behind your arm and accept one of the command billets I put you in for?"

She looked down at her gloved hand. "*Dios mio*, Gene. I don't care about my arm. I made a bad call and—"

"And people died. It comes with the job. All we have control over—barring mental illness—is our own reasoned choices. Even the right call can lead to disaster. If I make a good tactical decision, the other guy might make a better one."

Walsh forced himself to relax. "You made a call, not good or bad, and it didn't go like you wanted. Atmospheric braking is tricky. It's impossible to know if even our so-called good choices will have good outcomes. Grow or wither away. Don't spend the rest of your career second-guessing me."

"If we can't know, why try anything?"

Walsh chuckled. "Sometimes the best thing to do is nothing. We can only do what we think is best and everything else is out of our control. You took a risk and it didn't work. That doesn't mean it was a bad call or that you're a bad commander."

"Things seem to work out for some people better than others."

"Truth. Look, I've seen people die during the war. I even left someone behind who I might have been able to save. I thought it was too late and I sealed the compartment she was in."

He looked down as his breath caught. "Even after all these years. Her name was Susan Thompson. A kinetic barrage shredded the munitions bay we were manning on the *Eva Inez*. A propellant tank blew and opened us up to the black. I was around a bulkhead trying to reboot the loader arm when it happened. When I looked back, she was floating limp, right in the breach. Her suit open. Blood everywhere. Shrapnel was whirling and bouncing everywhere. So I sealed the compartment and powered it down to prevent anything else from exploding.

"The *Eva* did a hard turn and all the debris—including Susan—started drifting out. I was staring through the hatch portal, deciding whether to scream or go fetal and then scream. And I swear she looked at me just before she disappeared. She knew I'd left her there."

Walsh turned away to gather his composure without seeming too dramatic. "So when I get into a self-pity party about something, I always want to throw Susan in there, too. Still, to this day. She's a persistent ghost. And I light a candle for her every *El Día de los Muertos*."

"And you weren't even sure she was dead?" Diaz asked.

"No. The debriefing determined she was dead from her vitals." He glanced at her. "Again, with the judgement, Felicia."

"I just—"

"But it's all right," Walsh interrupted. "Because the story, and it's a true story, proves my point. When I got my wits back, I reported to munitions bay two as per standing orders. They'd lost power and one crew member was wounded. Because I was there, we managed to get the rocket battery—and the *Eva Inez*—back into the fight. If I had died trying to save Susan or tried taking her to Medical instead of getting the munitions back online, everyone on board would have died."

Diaz stared at him, obviously unmoved. "Or you could have rescued her and had two bodies back in the fight."

Walsh's chest tightened. "Even if she was alive, she wouldn't have been back in the fight. That's the point, though. There were a lot of 'coulds' in what you said. But I still down a couple of tequilas every year for Susan's sake. I did what I thought was right with no real way of knowing."

Diaz snorted. "Rationalization."

"Maybe. Either way, neither one of us knows what would have happened. And until you stop hiding behind your fat, sanctimonious eyebrows, you're depriving the fleet of a damn good commander. This is the last time we're having this discussion, XO. Dismissed."

The rare look of regret that passed across Diaz's face was almost enough to make Walsh unclench his jaw.

"Gene," she started.

"Dis-missed."

Diaz saluted, the regret replaced by stony defiance, and she left without another word.

Chapter 31

WALSH STOOD LIKE A cosmic giant in the overlay map of Epsilon Eridani II system and watched *Amazonas*'s canary-yellow navigation track spiral into the orbit requested by the colony. The initial insertion burn had been completed already and the final was due to start in a few minutes. While he waited, Walsh zoomed in on the orbital colony that they called Karen's Kvetch.

It was a dilapidated dual toroid around a central framework that extended one hundred meters in each direction. The plating was dark with accretion and scarring, highlighted with lighter patches where the colonists had managed repairs. It looked no better than *Solar Dream*, but held many people according to Yuloo. Walsh shuddered at the thought of so many living in such conditions their entire life with no hope of anything better. Several sections had no power and a few were open to the void through jagged breaches in the hull.

The remnant structures on the surface below were worse. Thermal scans showed an abandoned sprawl of habitats and factories. Under magnification, a few dim lights cast shadows across the debris in the streets. The outlying structures were as dark and sterile as the planet on which they stood.

"Not a very inviting place," Walsh muttered to no one in particular.

"That station is only turning for around 0.1-g." Collins appeared next to him in the overlay space. "Preparing for final insertion burn, Capitan."

Walsh nodded and, moments later, he could feel the push of the main thruster. The experience of standing in virtual space, but feeling the burn while strapped into his station, was disorienting. *Amazonas* cut thrust minutes later and the display marked a perfect orbital match.

"Burn completed, Capitan," Diaz said. "Orbital insertion successful."

Now that they were in the approved orbit, Walsh dismissed the planetary display with a flick of his fingers. He eagerly returned to the feed from remote sensor four.

Hanging in view was the obsidian eye of the nexus gate used to found the colony. Walsh flipped through several images and thermal scans. Though there were probes monitoring the gate *Amazonas* had come through, he wanted to compare Epsilon's gate with Sol's gate. Especially after Yuloo had told him that the colony's gate had exploded, too. Whatever had been done hadn't only affected Sol. Had the Colonial Defense Force—and he was merely assuming the CDF had done it—known the damage would carry over to their own worlds? Was it an accident or merely collateral damage made acceptable in the face of the Earth's massive counter-attack?

There was no way to know yet. And the Sol gate had been studied up close for a couple of centuries. There was no way *Amazonas*'s science systems could come close to compiling that level of data, but he'd take what he could get. Especially since he was getting first crack at it. Well, the first Solar to get a crack at it.

Collins appeared next to the sensor probe's window. "The shuttle is prepped and ready, Capitan. Twenty minutes transit time."

"I still don't like it," Bovree said from his station in the real world. "We don't need to send anyone over, let alone the capitan."

Walsh grinned. "Objection noted. It's what we agreed to—"

"I don't remember agreeing to this," Bovree interrupted.

"We," Walsh continued, "as in 'we that are in charge,' being me and the colonial council, agreed to a short face-to-face before we tried returning to Sol."

He unbuckled and stretched, dismissing overlay vision. "But we'll be armed and have the best ship and crew just outside to cover us. You saw the state of their colony. They probably want to make nice more than we do."

Bovree nodded. "Oh, yes. I saw. They look like they might be hungry enough to eat you."

"Space cannibals?" Walsh gave two thumbs-up. "Exciting."

"Desperate people do desperate things, Capitan. Don't underestimate them. I'm not some hired jungle porter waiting for my turn in the pot."

Bovree motioned to Collins. "At least send someone I don't mind them eating."

"Rude," Collins said.

Walsh chuckled and bounced slowly towards the hatch. It would be nice to return to full-g ops when Yuloo was back on her colony. "XO, you have the ship. Please have Robertson and Yuloo report to the shuttle."

"*Sí*, Capitan."

Walsh preened over the crimson dress uniform he'd printed earlier in the shift, spinning his image this way and that in overlay. It still accentuated what it was supposed to show off and hid what it wasn't. He ignored the slight increase in measurements so common after a few months in space.

Lieutenant Robertson, Yuloo, and Dr. Barnes were gathered at the docking hatch.

"About time," Barnes muttered.

"Why are you here?" Walsh asked.

"For these." The doctor attached his medical pouch to the bulkhead and withdrew three small, yellow cases from it. "You'll want these if the colony is as bad as the *Solar Dream* was. No offense, Yuloo."

"I hate those," Robertson said.

Barnes stepped over to Walsh. "Look up, please." He tutted and withdrew a thin medical probe from the pouch. "You need to keep it cleaner up there, Capitan."

"I pick my nose plenty," Walsh said.

Barnes grinned and withdrew one nostril filter using the probe and shoved it up Walsh's nose. Walsh coughed, but waited until both filters had been inserted before wiping the tears from his eyes. He hated them, too. Walsh took deep breaths until the filters had adjusted properly and connected to his overlay.

Barnes inserted the filters into Robertson's nose with forceps and moved on to Yuloo. "I brought a set for you, too. If you want."

"Yes, please, Doctor," Yuloo said.

Barnes grinned as he pulled out another set of forceps. "You don't even need to look up."

Once Barnes had all the filters inserted, and everyone had stopped coughing and sneezing, he gazed off into his overlay. "Everything looks good. Just remember to try to only inhale through your noses, if possible. This isn't a full environmental filter. It's only there to help keep out the more common bacteria and molds, and take air samples."

Barnes reached into the pouch and pulled out three roller dispensers. "And now time for a panoculation booster. Just in case."

"Why is everything a pan-this or pan-that?" Robertson asked.

"Marketing, my boy," Barnes said in a fair imitation of an olden-time carnival barker. "Medicine's always about marketing. Everyone loves a panacea, even if it's made from snake oil." He took Robertson's hand and rolled one of the dispensers across it. "This stuff does come pretty close, though."

He applied Walsh's and Yuloo's panoculations, pulled his pouch from the bulkhead, wished them luck, and left.

Walsh motioned for Robertson and Yuloo to board the shuttle. He took the co-pilot's seat after making sure Yuloo was properly strapped in to the main cabin. Instead of the white flightsuit and coveralls she'd been provided with, Yuloo wore a khaki-and-cream jumper, similar in cut to what she'd worn beneath her crumbling spacesuit.

Walsh turned to face her after verifying the flight package was properly downloaded. "How long has it been since you've been home?"

"*Solar Dream* is my home. But I haven't been here in over two years. I've spent too much time in micro-g to go planetside anymore. Not that I want to. I like the solitude."

Walsh nodded and turned forward when he felt the shuttle decouple from *Amazonas*. Rapid pops from the control thrusters filled the shuttle and the colony station came into sight through the small forward portal.

Robertson kept his hands near the manual-control sticks according to procedure, but auto-pilot failures were incredibly rare. Human pilots were the backup system.

More thruster pops jostled the shuttle as it approached the station. Four work pods drifted over different sections of the station, brilliant sparks erupting from robot arms tipped with welders and laser cutters. The station soon filled the view port, its crater-pocked hull and crumpled gantries even more sinister-looking up close. Small puffs of outgassing sprang to life at random, like freezing flowers that shattered and blew away in an icy wind. A swarm of glowing, red sparks erupted and angrily darted away into darkness.

Robertson shot Yuloo an apologetic glance. "Capitan, you sure it's safe?"

Walsh shrugged. "Safe might be too strong a word. But it's survived for a long time. Dock as instructed."

Robertson shook his head, then prompted the flight computer to continue. The final pop was followed by a dull thud as the shuttle contacted the station's dock. A fine cloud of dust and metallic particulate drifted past the view port.

The seal indicator on the airlock finally shone green. Robertson let out a sigh.

Walsh grinned, suppressing his own relief. "O ye of little faith. Let's go meet some more colonists."

He floated to the shuttle's hatch. The pressure-equalization needle wavered on its dial. There was atmosphere, but the pressure wasn't constant and the shuttle's ECS was struggling to compensate.

Walsh waited until the needle stabilized. "Hold on. We might get a gust when I pop the hatch." He waited until everyone had grabbed a handhold before opening the hatch.

A gust of wind pulled them forward. Walsh grimaced as his ears popped. The backwash of air from the station rolled back through the hatch like a warm, cloying swamp fog. Walsh fought down his gag reflex and tried to breathe through his nose. Behind him, Robertson began coughing and finally turned away to cover his nose and mouth with the sleeve of his flightsuit.

Every ship developed a case of "spacer funk" the crew was immune to. And Walsh had boarded some stinkers. But this was like a million-liter fart landing in his mouth. Not even the worst, poverty-stricken asteroid homesteads he'd boarded had ever been so foul. The shuttle was going to stink for a while.

Walsh almost vomited.

"I don't think Doc's filters are working as advertised," Robertson said as he coughed.

"Just think if they weren't there," Walsh said.

"Oh stars," Yuloo gasped. Her eyes were pressed shut and tears pooled in their corners. "Oh stars, oh stars."

A party of ten men and women, as lanky and wrinkled as Yuloo, stood hunched in the station's boarding passage. They waited with gap-toothed smiles. Walsh tried to respond, but felt his guts trying to come up. Trying to smile while clenching his teeth, he offered a wave.

The colonists stared at him until one woman motioned him aboard. He could see skeletal glimpses of her arms through tattered sleeves. "Welcome, Commander Walsh. I am Lellis. Are you well?"

Taking as shallow breaths as possible, Walsh swallowed the lump of bile growing in his throat. "Thank you for welcoming us, Lellis. Yes, we are fine. Our shuttle had trouble equalizing the pressure and it's made me a bit nauseated. We should be fine in a moment."

As his words were translated, the colony heads smiled again and nodded at each other.

Lellis gave a deep bow, her long toes gripping the peeling deck plates. "Of course, Commander. Take all the time you need. We here are all familiar with how such transitions affect the body. Sister Yuloo said your people were short, but I thought she must have been exaggerating since you obviously spend a great deal of time in space."

Remembering to breathe through his nose, Walsh offered a smile that felt like a rictus. "We do, but we also make regular visits to Earth and one-g stations. In fact, our ship can generate one-g spin gravity."

"That sounds painful," Lellis said.

Yuloo bowed her head. "It is."

"Sister, you have done us proud, not only with your research but as our representative on this monumental occasion." Lellis turned to Walsh. "I'm to understand your ship is in excellent repair. We are embarrassed to offer you a tour of our sorry home. I can only hope it will convince you of our eagerness to reach an accord. You might be the last chance for our people."

Lellis motioned down the passage. "But this is not the place for such talk. Follow me, please?"

Walsh motioned for Robertson to follow. Lellis motioned to Yuloo, who joined her after an embarrassed grin for Walsh. Suddenly surrounded by the committee, Walsh surreptitiously felt for the restrainer pistol tucked inside his flightsuit.

The passage walls looked recently scrubbed, for all the good it did the interior's appearance. Two panels hadn't survived the vigorous VIP cleaning and had been replaced—the patch kits looked worse than bulkhead. Walsh reached out and shuddered after running his fingers along a slime-covered pipe.

Many hatchways were covered with blankets too threadbare to hide the silhouettes of the staring colonists. Walsh waved at one wrinkled old man. The man nodded excitedly and turned to babble at the other shapes behind the drape.

Walsh felt his stomach loosen again as Lellis led them through a rancid-smelling galley. The machine shop was nearly black with grime and had only a single working bench. They finally reached a conference room that would have been spacious once, but it had been designed for standard-sized humans. These colonists, generations removed from gravity or zero-g medical treatments, looked to have outgrown the place long ago.

As Walsh was directed to his seat of honor at the far end of the table, the welcoming committee slid in behind. The press of gangly elbows and knees was like being trapped in a closet full of skeletons. Walsh returned their yellowed smiles, managing not to flinch as the hatch to the compartment slammed shut.

Once everyone had stopped fidgeting, all eyes turned to Walsh. "Thank you for showing us your station. I can only imagine the difficulties you've overcome to survive."

"That is exactly why we wanted you to see, Commander Walsh," Lellis said. "So you wouldn't have to imagine and would be more convinced to provide aid like you did to the *Solar Dream* and her crew."

"We're of course willing to help as able. A station this size and with this many extra people presents problems. We have limited resources, but there are things we can do. Medical care and some repair drones would do wonders."

One of the men reached a long arm towards Walsh. "That is good news, Commander. My name is Muldren and I'm in charge of what is ostensibly engineering. I can see what you've done for Yuloo, Fenti, and their ship. It hasn't run so clean in over a hundred years."

"We are looking at nothing less than the long-term survival of our people," Lellis said. "It is not understating the matter to say you might be our only hope of survival. We are eager—desperate, in truth—to save our people. We need your help."

"I'm grateful for the chance to represent the Confederation of American Republics in this amazing meeting. We had no idea what we would find here." Walsh leaned back and spread his hands wide. "I'm sure you understand, given our surprise entry here, that I'm not authorized to negotiate anything besides whatever immediate aid we can provide."

Lellis glanced at the other colonists. "So you said on the radio. How long would it be before someone with that authority could be expected?"

Walsh shrugged. "I can't say. We have to get back to Sol first. Then the diplomatic process would take place." Lellis's eyes fell and he hurriedly added, "But I'll file for emergency aid, and that won't take nearly so long."

"How long?" Lellis asked.

"That still depends on getting to Sol."

Muldren leaned forward over the table to stare at Walsh. "And that depends on getting another gate open, since you have enemies waiting to ambush you?"

"Maybe we should talk to these enemies if they're more powerful," another woman added. "It's more like Commander Walsh is seeking asylum in our system."

Lellis touched the woman's shoulder. "Shush now."

"It's a fair consideration," Walsh said. "You only have my word, but we were a lone ship on a science survey and they attacked us with a squadron."

"To be honest," Lellis said, her tone losing some of its cordiality, "we will accept help from anyone. Your fights, at this point, mean nothing to us. But you are visitors in our system. How long will you be here before you ask us for resupply?"

The wrinkled faces seemed to crowd in and lose their smiles. The pistol hidden in his uniform felt heavy, but welcome. "We're not in need of supplies. I was under the impression our visit was welcome."

"It is, Commander. But your supply situation depends on how long you operate in our system. As you said, you have limited resources. How long will that be? Will others follow... allies or enemies?"

"I don't think anyone will be following soon."

Lellis nodded. "So your trip was truly unexpected. Your ship has the prototype to open these other gates." It wasn't a question.

Robertson fidgeted beside him. Walsh screwed his smile in place. "I can't really discuss our fleet capabilities, but there might be any number of reasons we're not expecting anyone to follow soon."

"And we've been thinking about them," Lellis said, motioning to the other council members. "About why you'd come through a mystery gate severely damaged, claiming not to be an ambassador and seemingly unwilling—or unable—to return home. It puzzles us that no one from your CAR has come to aid you. Surely they know you were in a battle. Unless they aren't able."

Lellis held up a hand as Walsh tried to speak. "No, no, Commander. You're in a position where you must speak carefully. We appreciate that and do not hold it against you. But it still leaves us in the position of having to decide what to do with you."

"You can just let us go."

Lellis chuckled. "I might have chosen my words poorly if that sounded sinister to you. I meant that it gives us more to consider about our options."

"I understand. The law of unintended consequences can be a severe master."

"If you'll excuse us, Commander Walsh. We need to discuss a few things." Lellis motioned for the council to leave. "Is there anything we can bring you?"

The thought of putting anything from this station into his mouth set his stomach flipping again. "No, thank you. Please, take your time. We are committed to a peaceful resolution."

Lellis waited for the rest of the council to file out, carefully extricating their long limbs from around the table. When she was the last, she bowed and closed the hatch behind her.

Robertson looked at Walsh. "I don't like the sound of that, Skipper."

Walsh nodded and moved to the hatch. He carefully tugged at the wheel. It didn't budge. There was no sign of their hosts outside the stained portal. He lifted his collar and the rank insignia there unfolded into a tiny, spider-like bot that crawled down his arm and between two rusted floor plates. Robertson did the same, his bot disappearing between two overhead conduits.

Bovree appeared in Walsh's overlay. "Reading you've deployed the micro-bots, Capitan. Are you in trouble?"

Walsh glanced at Robertson. "They aren't sharpening knives yet. But, yeah. We're probably in trouble."

Chapter 32

ROBERTSON HAD BEEN tapping the stained tabletop in staccato bursts during the two hours since the colonial leaders left. They were both viewing the tactical overlay room with Diaz and the duty ops crew. The sound of Robertson's nervous ticks intruded into Walsh's virtual perception like fighting neighbors down the hall.

"We have three pairs of repair drones out where this Muldren suggested." Diaz summoned a view of the station and motioned to three areas highlighted in yellow. *Amazonas*'s six repair drones crawled like tiny, green beetles on the display.

Robertson sighed loudly and drummed the table again.

Walsh gritted his teeth. "XO, keep me informed when the colonists come back this way." With a wave of his hand, the virtual tactical room disappeared from Walsh's and Robertson's overlay.

"A little warning next time, Skipper." Robertson was blinking his eyes slowly.

"Sub-q only, Lieutenant."

"Yes, sir. Sorry."

"I'm not happy about our situation either, but your constant racket needs to stop. Get a grip."

Robertson drummed his fingers on the table for a second before offering an apologetic smile. "Sorry, Skipper." He let out a long breath. "This is starting to feel like a brig. A very unsanitary brig. I don't understand why you're letting them use our drones?"

"Because of that." Walsh pointed to a recess in the bulkhead. It hadn't been visible through the press of gangly arms and legs. Whatever had once provided privacy to occupants had rotted away long ago. In the recess sat a small bio-waste recycling-stool. Stains older than Walsh streaked the bowl and the vacuum attachment was covered with the crystalized buildup of centuries of use.

"Nasty."

"Imagine having no choice. Imagine growing up sleeping next to that. Imagine knowing nothing else."

"We have nasty in Sol."

Walsh nodded. "True. But there is always hope of something better, even if very thin. That's not the case here. There's nowhere to go and no resources to improve things."

"I wasn't suggesting not helping them, Skipper. But won't this just encourage them? I'm not entirely sure they plan on letting us go."

"I'm hoping our help will show them we're friends. That they don't need to try to kidnap us."

Robertson glanced at the stool again. "I hope Doc's panoculation works."

"Here's to hoping. Anyway, I don't want us to be remembered for opening the gate, then getting our long-lost cousins into a shooting war." Walsh glanced around the dilapidated compartment. "At this point, it costs us nothing to help. It might cost them a lot."

"If someone objects to them working only with us."

"Having a defensible gate we can hide a fleet in would make Mars and the Caliphate nervous." Walsh smirked. "The Calies have already made their feelings known in no uncertain terms."

"I hope the colony doesn't try to hand us over to the Calies. Some of them seemed to like the idea of working with them."

Walsh nudged Robertson. "If we can get POW status, there'll be a bonus for that."

"As long as our bonus isn't just some infection from this place."

"Don't act like it would be your first."

The hatch chimed and Walsh turned to see Lellis's face in the portal. "How are you, Commander? Aside from being detained, which I do apologize for."

"Aside from that, we're doing well." Walsh bounced to the hatch. "I hope the medical supplies and repair drones are enough to keep us off the menu."

Lellis looked away. "Yes. Thank you. Your crew has already restored power and air to..." Her voice trailed off and she looked back at Walsh with narrowed eyes. "What did you say? About a menu?"

Walsh's stomach clenched. His mouth always got him in trouble when his brain gave it free rein. "Look, I was just kidding—"

"Yuloo told you," Lellis said. She shook her head. "She wasn't supposed to. She should have known you wouldn't understand. Damn her." Lellis pounded the hatch once with her fist. "We never eat the living, Commander. You don't have to worry about that." Lellis's face disappeared.

Walsh stared at the now empty portal for a moment before glancing sidelong at Robertson.

"Don't worry, Skipper. They never eat the living."

"I guess we're okay if we can stay alive."

"That's usually how it works." Robertson hiked a thumb towards the hatch. "It might be time to go."

Walsh joined the tactical room. "I assume you were all following that conversation. Any remote access to this hatch, Bovree?"

"No, sir. Maybe once upon a time, but now it's pure elbow grease."

Diaz zoomed in on one pair of repair drones. "They let these inside. I'm sending them your way."

"We could just cut you out," Bovree suggested. "Your emergency collars should keep you safe while you EVA to the shuttle. It isn't far."

"I'm not sure the station would survive that," Walsh said. "We'll try to get to the shuttle if we can get the hatch open. Slowly move the outside drones to the shuttle so we can take them with us."

"Won't they have the shuttle locked down?" Robertson asked as he drew his restrainer pistol.

"The drones can cut through those locks," Fuller said. "The locks might just snap on their own."

Walsh drew his own pistol. "Sounds like a plan. Break us out of here, XO."

"*Si*, Capitan."

"Now what?" Robertson asked.

"We wait."

After a moment, Robertson shook his head. "Space cannibals, Skipper? Really? They're making it hard not to judge."

Walsh shrugged. "Keep trying. We don't have the facts or context."

"Eating dead people is pretty straightforward."

"To us, maybe. Lellis didn't look like she means any harm to us. But still..."

They waited, pistols tucked behind their legs to keep them out of sight from the hatch. When the hatch wheel began turning, Walsh raised his pistol. Robertson did the same as the hatch swung open.

Yuloo bounced inside. "Gene, you've got to leave." She noticed the pistols and stopped short. "Gene?"

"Sorry, just a little negotiation tool. Lellis know you're here?"

"No. But she's not the one you need to worry about. Others are pushing for more demands. There's even talk of trying to take the *Amazonas*."

Robertson shook his head. "That would go badly for them." He looked at Walsh. "And for us."

"They're scared you'll go to Sol and not come back at all. They don't want to lose your help."

Walsh peered through the hatch. "Why are you here, then?"

"To save my people from doing something incredibly stupid. If I can get you to the shuttle, then no one needs to get hurt." Yuloo gently touched Walsh's arm with a nervous glance at his pistol. "And I'm still hoping you'll take me with you."

"Get us to the shuttle and we'll see."

"Let's go, then," she said. "Please try not to hurt anyone. Not everyone agrees with the drastic steps. Some were suggesting... never mind. Follow me."

Walsh spoke through his sub-q. "Diaz, Yuloo is leading us to the shuttle. Herd all the bots that way."

"Done," Diaz said. "I'm sending the bots to escort you."

Walsh heard rapid, metallic tapping nearby and glanced up to see the repair bots skittering along overhead.

Yuloo led them left, then right, then through another hatch to the left. It was a strange race, with the heart-pounding thrill of a chase but at the leisurely, bouncing pace of running through water.

"She is leading you true, Capitan," Hector said. "But she could still be leading you into a trap."

Yuloo rounded a corner and stopped. Walsh and Robertson were both in midair and collided with her.

"Sister Yuloo, stop!"

Walsh looked around Yuloo and saw two colonists. Their combined lanky limbs gave the impression of some giant, mutant spider blocking the passage ahead. Walsh raised his pistol and saw Robertson do the same out of the corner of his eye.

"Don't kill them!" Yuloo cried.

The pistols made loud *chuffing* noises as Walsh and Robertson fired. The air shot the restraining capsules down the passage. One struck a colonist on the hip and expanded into a stringy ball of gooey adhesive. It expanded to cover the man's chest, left arm, and both legs down to the knees. The man instinctively covered the impact point with both hands, trapping them in the quivering glob. He lost his balance and stumbled into the bulkhead where the restrainer goo stuck him fast. A second later, the sticky mess had hardened and secured the guard helplessly in place.

Two capsules struck the other man; one sticking his feet to the deck and the other solidifying, leaving his arms straight out to the sides.

The guards both screamed so that Walsh had to raise his own voice. "They aren't hurt. That stuff will dissolve after a while." The men continued to scream until Walsh stood next to them. "You aren't hurt. Tell them."

Yuloo tried speaking to them, but an old woman had pulled aside her curtain to watch the display.

Walsh tugged Yuloo along. "Never mind. Let's go."

Yuloo bowed apologetically to the men as she passed. The one whose arms were sticking out tried to grab her until Walsh shoved a pistol in his face.

"The shuttle's just ahead," Yuloo said.

"Stop!"

The commanding voice echoed through the passage from behind them. Walsh turned to see Lellis leading a group of five other colonists towards them. "Please, Commander. We can talk about this."

"Talking's done," bellowed a woman behind Lellis. "Don't let them escape."

"Go!" Walsh cried.

Yuloo led them down a side passage and around another corner. Walsh grabbed a frost-rimed pipe to stop. It was so cold it burned. He reached out his other hand to stop Robertson.

"You start up there." Walsh pointed to the overhead as the repair bots clinked by. He fired his own pistol at the deck, spacing the shots so that the expanding restrainer blobs formed a ring around the passage. Robertson did the same and when Lellis bounced into the passage, it was nearly filled with hardened clumps of goo.

Lellis leaped down the passage and put her face to the small opening. "Don't listen to her, Commander! We can talk this through."

Walsh leveled his pistol at her face. "We can talk over the radio."

Lellis shrieked and ducked out of sight barely in time to avoid Walsh's final capsule that sealed the passage. Robertson sent a few extra capsules into the mess before Walsh motioned him towards the dock.

Yuloo entered the code and the hatch hissed open. Robertson and the two bots raced inside. Yuloo moved to follow.

Walsh grabbed Yuloo's arm as she tried to enter. He aimed his pistol at her feet. "Sorry."

"Please, Gene. Take me away from here. Don't make me go back to this life." She reached reached for the gun, but Walsh pulled it away and aimed it back at her feet.

"I can help you," she said. "I can find the gates. And I can help deal with the council while we leave. I know how things work."

"I know how things work, too. You eat people."

"What do you mean?"

Walsh raised one eyebrow.

Yuloo looked away and took a deep breath. "Did Lellis tell you?"

"She told me enough."

"Gene, please. I know that sounds horrific. And it is to us, too. But you've seen what we have left. What we're forced to eat, the contaminated slime the processors vomit out.

"We don't just lay someone out on a table when they die and sharpen the knives! The body is recycled like everything here. Some goes to trying to fertilize the garden that's been barren for two generations. The rest we eat, and it's the only remotely satisfying thing we ever get to consume." She held out a bony arm and pinched it. "But even a body doesn't go that far."

Walsh glanced over her shoulder at the muffled pounding against the restrainer wall. Yuloo fell to her knees and wrapped her long arms around his legs. Walsh spread his arms out, ready to be thrown. Instead, she pressed her head against his stomach and began sobbing. He deactivated his pistol and put it away—shooting her now would only pin them both to the deck.

"Life on the *Amazonas* is what children here dream of. Adults, too. Take me prisoner. Do whatever you want to me. I request asylum. I'm in fear for my life. I can't go back. I'd rather... I'd rather die." She collapsed to the deck, convulsing in voiceless sobs.

Walsh reached down and easily pulled Yuloo to her feet in the low gravity. "Look—"

"I'll do anything, Gene. Anything. Please, take me." She wrapped him up in her arms, leaving his chin between the rise of her breasts.

While he had considered what it would be like to sleep with the 2.5-meter woman from another star, it was her knowledge of finding the gates that was the most alluring. But she'd think it was her sexual offer he was responding to.

And that did appeal, he had to admit. He wasn't sure if knowing about her cannibalism made her more or less desirable.

"Skipper?"

Walsh turned to see Robertson and the two repair bots staring from the shuttle's hatch. And behind those bots' eyes, he saw Diaz staring on in knowing, self-satisfied judgement. Yuloo wouldn't be the only one who thought he was letting her come for the wrong reason.

"You will remain in the brig," Walsh said, shoving her towards the shuttle harder than intended.

"Oh, thank—"

"Go!"

Robertson gave Walsh a quizzical look. Walsh boarded the shuttle and shoved Robertson towards the cockpit.

"Is the flight plan downloaded?" Walsh asked.

"Sure, Skipper. But the locks are engaged. Ops hacked the system, but there's no software interface." Robertson looked down at Yuloo, who'd just strapped in.

She thumped her forehead with the tip of a long finger. "Of course. The control module burned out long ago. Instead of robbing one from other equipment, we've just been using the manual override." Her face fell and she reached for the straps. "Someone will have to stay behind. I'll go."

"Hold on," Walsh said. "Ops, send a bot out to manipulate the release for us. When we've escaped, brick it."

One of the spidery repair bots wound its way through the shuttle and out of sight. Walsh pulled the hatch shut. Voices echoed down the passage—the colonists had cut through at least part of his barricade.

The shuttle shifted and Walsh strapped in to the closest seat. The metallic scraping of the clamps filled the cabin, followed by a series of pops from the control thrusters. His stomach lurched as the shuttle accelerated towards *Amazonas* at its full two-g. Not very fuel efficient, but they wanted to get away from anything the station may throw at them.

Robertson screamed a long whoop as the acceleration pushed them farther into their seats. Yuloo whimpered once. The shuttle hadn't operated at full thrust since he'd become CO, but all the system indicators in Walsh's overlay showed green.

"Two incoming craft," Moore said.

Walsh entered the tactical room and saw the display. Hovering before him was the shuttle, with two slower navigation tracks separating from the station. As the flight profiles developed, it was obvious they were on an intercept course with the shuttle.

"There's no way they can catch us at that rate," Robertson said. "They must be following us to the ship."

"They'll catch us if they don't turn to decel." Walsh accessed the comms. "Lellis. We will fire on those ships you've sent after us. Break off your pursuit if you're really interested in still talking with us."

"Come back and we will," answered a man's high-pitched voice. "We don't want to hurt anyone. Send your bots back. Please."

"Tham, you need to turn back now," Lellis said. "If you keep that course, they'll have no choice. Tham. Tham?"

The tactical display identified the transmitting ship with a blue halo. Walsh zoomed in on Tham's craft. It was a squat, bullet-shaped work pod with two manipulator arms beneath the nose. A long tube jutted forward from the center. The spectrometer identified the plume of reaction mass trailing behind it as methane rocket fuel. The other ship was a slightly more grungy twin.

Walsh saw Yuloo was wearing her ship glasses and forwarded the feed of the ship to her. "What are these? Work pods? What are those tubes?"

Yuloo tried to open her eyes, but merely gasped and shook her head. Ops hadn't counted on her return when they programmed the flight package. It was too late to change it now.

"They look like utility bots, Skipper," Robertson said. "Maybe those tubes are grapples. The tugs I flew around Luna had something similar."

"They might want to literally drag you back," Moore said. "But I'm guessing they're some kind of limpet mines or improvised explosives."

Diaz shook her head. "They must know we can shoot them out of the sky whenever we want."

"I'm not sure Lellis is completely in control," Bovree said. "This Tham person sounds desperate."

"Desperate is right," Walsh said. "I'm desperately hoping we won't have to destroy them."

Walsh's insides spun as the shuttle cut its main thruster and flipped to decelerate. He glanced down at Yuloo, whose hands were clasped over her chest. "Lellis. Or Tham. Or whoever is calling the shots over there. We will not allow your craft within threatening range. Do not force us to destroy them."

After two minutes of silence, Walsh tried again. "Lellis? Tham? Is anyone reading me? I am prepared to fire even if you don't reply."

"We hear you," Lellis answered at length. "But we didn't send him. And they aren't attackers, they're hitchhikers, Commander."

"Hitchhikers?"

Lellis's voice was now acid. "They want you to rescue them. Like their sister, Yuloo."

"Even if that's true, I will fire on them. If they don't abort... they'll never get close enough to ram or grapple us."

"We're trying, Commander. Please give us time. They're cargo pilots and they've crammed their families in the pod. And now they aren't answering."

Cannibal though she may be, Walsh wanted to give her the benefit of the doubt. "Ops, do thermals verify how the pods are manned?"

"Yes, Capitan," Diaz said. "We can see multiple body signatures through the front visor."

"I've got the signal of Lellis trying to convince them to turn about," Bovree said. "Tham is the only one talking, though."

"Ops, display maximum engagement window," Walsh said after the negotiations hit five minutes. "Lellis, your folk are cutting it close."

"Fine!" Tham yelled over the channel. "But you and the whole damned council will pay for your stupidity. I'm going to personally space whoever decided to keep them captive."

Walsh heard the sound of a sobbing child in the background. Tham's craft turned and the navigation track shortened as it burned back towards the station. The other pod continued towards *Amazonas*. Walsh zoomed in on it and could make out three silhouettes sitting behind the stained view port.

Lellis's voice was heavy with sinking hopelessness. "Commander Walsh, Tham is returning. But the other isn't responding at all. I'm afraid I can't do anything from here. You'll have to do what you need to do."

"What's his name?"

"Ikka. If you can avoid it, please don't kill them. Karen's Kvetch doesn't have many children."

Chapter 33

WALSH LOOKED DOWN AT Yuloo, who was looking sicker than before. "Tell me about Ikka."

She gulped loudly and spoke in broken grunts. "His wife's name is Marin. Daughter Ulin. He's smart. Spends time on *Solar Dream* during resupply. Inherited his job from his father."

Walsh stared at Ikka's pod through *Amazonas*'s overlay feed. The other two people barely visible through the pod's front port were surely his family. *Amazonas* could support them—if their mad flight didn't kill them.

Hector appeared. "Capitan, I believe Ikka has burned too long to safely dock. Assuming he's been operating at maximum thrust. I can only estimate his fuel load based on the size of the fuel tank, but I don't believe he has enough delta-v to prevent collision with the shuttle or the *Amazonas*."

"I think Hector's right, Skipper," Robertson said from the cockpit. "Ikka can't stop."

"Well, shit," Walsh muttered.

"Could we just shoot out his thruster?" Robertson asked.

Walsh shook his head. "Even if the pod survived, it would still tumble into us at this point."

"They can still kill us if we don't so something, Skipper. We need all of our delta-v to dock."

Walsh connected to the colony's general band.

"Keep in mind, Capitan," Hector said over Walsh's personal channel, "the colony will be recording this conversation."

"Uh, thanks."

"Just trying to keep you out of trouble when we get back."

Walsh shook his head and transmitted. "Ikka. This is Commander Walsh of the Amazonas. Can you hear me?"

The answer was immediate. "Yes, Walsh."

"You're in danger of ramming my shuttle or my ship. You need to break off."

"Please, Commander Sir. Don't leave us. We didn't know what Lellis was doing. They don't speak for all of us. Don't go."

"Ikka, you are going too fast. If you hit us, we'll both be dead and it won't matter."

Ikka's voice cracked as he spoke. "Sir, we're all going to die anyway if you leave. You took Yuloo, right? Can't you just take a couple more? Please, Commander Sir?"

"My government will send aid as quickly as possible."

"When?"

The true answer wasn't good. The good answer wasn't true. Walsh glanced at Yuloo and said, "I don't know."

"Ikka's burning at us again, Capitan," Hector said.

Walsh tugged at his straps to make sure he was in tight. "Look, Ikka. We can't talk at all while you're burning towards us. Veer off. Even if this shuttle had the ability to dock with you, you're too fast."

"I'll grapple you and then you can take us to your ship," Ikka said. "Please. Or just take my wife and daughter. Or just my daughter, then."

"Papa, I want to go home," came a girl's voice in the background.

Walsh's chest constricted. The hard numbers of orbital mechanics made space rescues largely impossible, despite their popularity in entertainment feeds. His own rescue was looking less likely by the minute. "Grappling us at our current speed differential, you will tear both of our ships apart. Decelerate now before we run out of options for saving your family, Ikka."

There was nothing to do but wait. He knew Diaz was working out how to move the shuttle out of the way with its little remaining fuel. She would also have all the firing solutions ready and damage control. If the shuttle was going to dock, *Amazonas* couldn't move, either.

Walsh pressed a hand to his forehead. Yuloo was murmuring some untranslated litany beneath her breath. He wasn't one for prayer, but he sure hoped Ikka came to his senses—by divine intervention or otherwise.

"I will, Commander Sir."

The collective sigh from the crew seemed to increase the shuttle's atmospheric pressure.

Ikka's pod turned and fired its main thruster—which winked out after a second. Walsh stared at the display, but the pod didn't fire again.

"That wasn't enough," Robertson said. "Surely he knows that."

"Maybe a malfunction?" Yuloo groaned.

Ikka's voice was full of panic. "Commander Sir, I'm out of fuel."

"What?"

"I'm out of fuel. I took out the internal tank to fit my family." Ikka's voice trembled. "What do I do?"

"I'm scared, Papa," came the girl's voice before Ikka cut his mic.

Walsh pounded his fist into his thigh. "Does the colony have anything to catch him?"

Yuloo shook her head slowly. "Tham's pod won't have enough to reach him. Everything would have to burn too much fuel to catch him. There'd be nothing left for a return."

"And he's going to crash into us, anyway," Robertson said.

Walsh studied the navigation vectors in the display. "Robertson, work with Hector and burn back towards Ikka. Use up every last bit of fuel. If he can grapple us, maybe we can both slow down enough for rescue."

"I'm not sure—" Hector started.

"Do it," Walsh said. "XO, deploy the repair drones. Maybe they can do something combined."

"*Dios mio.* They can collect your corpses, Capitan," she said. "We can burn the pod away before it hits us. The shuttle doesn't have enough fuel for what you're planning."

"Negative on fire. This is a rescue mission, Diaz. Manuever *Amazonas* out of the way."

"That's going to make it hard to pick you up."

"Things are hard all around. Carry on."

"*Si*, Capitan." Diaz's image faded.

Walsh watched the shuttle crawl towards Ikka's pod on the display. There wasn't enough information to make anything but a wild-assed guess. He knew nothing about how the pod's grapple operated or how far it could extend. It was too late for details; the plan was locked in place. This was the one chance to save Ikka's family. If it didn't work, *Amazonas* would likely have a new CO.

"Ikka, we're going to try this your way since we don't have much choice. Try to grapple my shuttle and, hopefully, we can all slow down enough for rescue and you won't ram anyone." Walsh let out a slow breath. "And please don't hit our cockpit."

Ikka's face looked as if it was pressed against the front port. He was screaming something unheard while he aimed his pod at the shuttle, tiny puffs of gas erupting from the control thrusters.

"Here it comes," Robertson called. A minute later he added, "Grapple missed."

Walsh watched the grapple sail by in the overlay and jerk taut as it hit its limit. The cable swung and writhed like a steel snake as Ikka reeled it back in.

"Grapple away," Robertson said.

The grapple missed by a few meters, but the cable scraped against the shuttle's frame with a metallic rasp. The grapple jerked taut again and swung around as if it was going to wrap around the shuttle like a whip. It slid over the shuttle and off the nose cone. Robertson corrected the imparted yaw with a few pops from the control thrusters.

Ikka's pod drifted beneath the shuttle as the cable reeled in again.

Walsh's heart pounded. *Amazonas* had moved out of the pod's course, but if Ikka tried to grapple her, it would pull the pod apart at its current speed. Judging from the time it took to recover the grapple and the length of the cable, Walsh knew Ikka only had one more chance to save his family.

"Grapple away!" Robertson shouted. "I think it's going to hit."

Two seconds later, the shuttle jolted and a metallic clang echoed through the cabin. The lights flashed red and warning buzzers rang in Walsh's ears. The impact had imparted a barely detectable slow roll that upset his stomach.

Walsh tried to ignore it all and focus on the video feed. The grapple had connected with the shuttle's port-side avionics cluster. The cable slowly straightened as it approached its maximum length.

"Hold on," Walsh said through gritted teeth.

His head bounced forward as the shuttle pulled against Ikka's pod. Yuloo cried out and Robertson cursed. The spin on the shuttle reversed and intensified, pushing Walsh hard into his chair. Yuloo was making precursory vomit gurgles.

Walsh activated his nausea damper and filtered the spin out of his overlay display while he fought the new g-forces. Clenching his abdomen to try to keep all the blood from draining to his feet, he could finally see what had happened.

"Nooo!"

Ikka's pod was spinning away beneath *Amazonas*, the shuttle's avionics cluster torn free and swinging around at the end of the grappling cable. Every few seconds, Ikka's silently screaming face came into view, the faces of his wife and daughter screaming over his shoulder. Hands pressed and slapped against the view port.

"Help us, Commander Sir!" came Ikka's plea over the screaming made audible through his mic. "My baby!"

Walsh gladly accepted the blackness that pressed in around him, unsure if it would lift—and not caring, either.

Chapter 34

WALSH WIPED AT HIS eyes, hoping the gesture would be mistaken as fatigue by the watching crew. He looked again at the three body bags lashed to the cargo deck. He looked again at another dead child on his ship.

Ikka's daughter, ten years old according to the colony and Dr. Barnes's autopsy, was already as tall as Walsh. They'd had to print elongated bags for her parents.

Walsh was still light-headed from his recovery. He opened Diaz's sub-q channel so the rest of the working party could not hear. "Thanks."

"The pull from the grapple ruptured Ikka's hull. It wasn't designed for that kind of sudden stress."

"Poor bastard. Just trying to save his family."

"His recklessness killed them all."

"It was desperation. You saw what it was like for the colonists in that station." Walsh thought of them as colonists, but they'd been living in Epsilon Eridani longer than his family had lived in Indiana. Maybe he should call them the Eridani or Kvechi.

"Capitan, are you trying to make me cry, too?"

"Perish the thought, XO. I wonder how many other colonies are out there barely hanging on."

"If they are all isolated like this, most are dead."

"Another call from Lellis, Capitan," Collins said in his overlay.

Walsh looked at Lieutenant Fuller and tilted his head towards the bodies. "Tell her not to worry. Her feast is on the way."

He thought of Yuloo being ten and growing up in the horror and despair inside the rusting compartments he'd barely escaped from. He rubbed his eyes again. "Belay that. Just tell her we're loading the bodies onto the pod and will send it back within the hour. Also, pass on that we will vaporize anything else that comes our way. And that Yuloo is coming with us."

"Yes, sir."

Walsh pushed off the deck and grabbed an overhead handhold to get out of Fuller's way. Looking from above, he could see the shattered cryopods of Angelica's sisters. There were a lot of dead bodies on his ship—at least none were from the crew. Not yet, anyway. *Amazonas* was a long way from home still. He noticed Yuloo looking up at him from the hatch and motioned for her to join him.

"Thank you, Gene." The woman's voice had become soft and melodic in her time aboard *Amazonas*.

Walsh glanced at Ikka's family. "For what?"

"For trying to save them. You could have just shot them down." She reached out and dabbed at his cheek. "Ikka did this, not you."

The tip of her finger was warm and he resisted the urge to take her hand and press it against his cheek. "I know. I'm trying to imagine what it was like growing up on that station. But I can't. You are a strong people."

"We had no choice. We knew nothing else." She dug into her pocket and withdrew a small data crystal. "This is for you."

"What is it?"

"Everything I have on the gates. I've already worked with Hector to make sure your systems can read the data."

Walsh let his hand linger on hers as he took it. "As good as your word."

"And thank you for not locking me up."

Walsh grinned. "Just don't try sneaking a nibble before we send the bodies back."

Yuloo's hand moved in a blur. Spinning stars filled his vision and Walsh's cheek burned with fire. After blinking several times, the cargo bay came into focus and he remembered where he was. He was slowly spinning and grabbed a nearby cargo container to stop.

Yuloo was glaring at him from three meters away, one hand gripping a handhold and the other covering her mouth. He gently pushed back towards her, but Yuloo shot towards the hatch and was out of sight in three seconds.

Diaz was staring up at him, expressionless. The working party went back to loading bodies when Walsh stared back at them.

His cheek started to sting. With Diaz staring on, he didn't want to reach up and touch it or go chasing after Yuloo. Both would make him look as foolish as he felt.

Walsh felt like slapping himself. What the hell had he been thinking? Gallows humor was an important part of dealing with military life. But Yuloo was not in the military and no one liked being mocked.

Walsh watched the working party for several minutes, waiting for the throbbing slap print to fade. Thankfully, Diaz left soon after Yuloo. When the final body had been loaded into Ikka's pod, Walsh drifted to the hatch and out of the cargo bay.

Angelica came flying at him from out of nowhere, arms wheeling. "Help, Gene!"

Walsh hooked his foot around a conduit and caught the girl's wrist. She immediately wrapped her arms and legs around his arm and pulled herself up until they were face-to-face. Walsh tried to extricate his arm without touching her inappropriately. The girl grinned and wiggled, trying to force such contact.

Walsh took a deep breath. "Angelica, please let go."

She pouted for a few seconds. "Okay." Angelica drifted back a meter and smiled. "Did you fight with that ugly, old lady? She make you mad?"

"Were you watching? What are you doing down here, anyway?"

"Visiting my sisters. I do that sometimes when I'm lonely. I'm lonely a lot, lately."

The activity records stated that she did visit often. The timing was suspicious, though, and the gleam in her eye added to Walsh's distrust. It was too convenient. He worked up his best fatherly smile. "I don't want to interrupt you, then."

"Oh, that's all right, Daddy. If you need to talk—"

"No, no. Your visit's important. And I have things to do." Walsh pushed off towards the habitat rings without another word. He let out his breath when he realized Angelica wasn't following.

WALSH UNFOLDED HIS chair and strapped in. With Yuloo remaining on board, he'd reduced the spin gravity to 0.3-g. He didn't want to leave her isolated to the null-g sections of *Amazonas*.

Not that she was weak. Walsh worked his jaw. The handprint had finally faded, but one cheek was still a shade pinker than the other. She'd really slapped the shit out of him. And he'd deserved it. When he was younger, he'd been slapped when making over-the-top pickup lines in the officers' club. He'd deserved those, too. But that was a young man being crude and immature. He should have known better than to say that to Yuloo. Walsh shook his head again.

"Stupid."

He was waiting to give her time to cool down before visiting her to apologize. A virtual session wouldn't. The virtual role-playing game he tried playing with Hector was high-quality, but he couldn't enjoy it. Instead, he was reviewing the data feed from the probe of Epsilon Eridani's old gate. Surviving EPL records indicated it connected to Procyon, a system with at least three other old gates.

Hector had been working hard on collecting and analyzing the probe's data. While still nothing approaching the level of detail on Sol's old gate, the ship's yeoman had made impressive progress. From what Hector had focused on, it was clear he had used Walsh's own interests to prioritize; without being asked.

It was almost a copy of the Sol gate. They shared the same RF absorption coefficient, thermal signature, albedo ratings, and the same dimensions down to the measurable centimeter. Even without superimposing the images, he could tell the pattern of fractures that covered the Epsilon Eridani gate was the same as Sol's. Whatever the CDF had done to the Tau Ceti–Sol gate had shattered all of them.

After twenty minutes, Walsh swiped the nexus-gate data away and activated the overlay mirror. He zoomed in on his face and was pleased to see his cheek was back to normal. Ruffled hair was generally more comfortable for civilians in Sol, but he had no idea how Yuloo saw it or if she even cared. He gently mussed his tonsure anyway.

Hector materialized next to Walsh's mirror image. "Capitan, Yuloo is approaching your stateroom. For my own edification, how did you know she was coming?"

"I didn't."

"Why were you preening? If you don't mind my asking."

"Honestly, I was planning to go apologize to her. Why?"

"Part of my function is to observe and analyze crew conduct for behaviors that improve or degrade ship's performance."

"You're afraid combing my hair will affect ship's efficiency?"

"No, Capitan. But observing how to interact with crew and passengers, and noting the results, helps in that function. And in better understanding the crew in general."

Walsh grunted, patted his stomach, and deactivated his mirror. The reflection looked at him in terror and held its hands flat as if trying to push out of the mirror.

Walsh chuckled. "I love that." He turned to Hector. "I know you monitor just about everything. Do I want to know everything you're observing?"

"I'm observing everything, Capitan. But there are still things I need to extrapolate. Especially when it involves emotional or social responses. Human reactions sometimes seem quite random."

"Don't I know it."

"Take flatulence, for instance."

Walsh blinked. "What?"

"Flatulence, Capitan. I can detect minute changes in atmospheric pressure and composition. Some crew members will ignore it completely, even though they've obviously noticed. Others will limit themselves to making facial expressions to express their general distaste. And others will vocally reprimand the one they believe responsible."

"Interesting. Fart jokes have been part of human cultures for millennia."

"As a sidenote, Capitan, the accuracy of said accusations where three or more other people are present is only fifty-eight percent.

"Back to the main point. My dataset analysis shows an individual human's reaction is often based on relationship factors such as rank and sexual attraction to those present. Females are less likely to react at all, while younger males are likely to vocalize displeasure or tease the accused. While it's a scientifically insignificant sample, uplifted chimpanzees laugh if the flatulence is audible."

Walsh stared at Hector's image for a moment. "That's amazing. I try not to fart in front of women in general, especially not if I find one attractive. Do you have specs on how many people hold it in when someone else is around? Never mind."

"Maybe you should fart on Angelica, Capitan."

Walsh burst out laughing. "I have to admit, I never thought to hear the word fart come out of my ship's computer." He raised one finger. "So, can you determine who dealt it?"

"Usually, Capitan. Via audio sensors. I can sometimes use chemical analysis by cross-referencing dietary intake if one of the people present has eaten something significantly distinctive from the others in the room."

Hector held up a palm and a virtual colon appeared. "I can simulate in detail if you wish."

"That's quite all right," Walsh said as he swiped the colon away. "This is possibly the strangest discussion I've had with a ship's computer. I'd expect it from Bovree. Do I need to get someone to run a core checksum?"

"Of course not, Capitan. Why would you even consider it?" Hector's face pinched in distaste. "Never mind, Capitan. Yuloo is at the hatch."

Walsh left the overlay, took a deep breath, and ran his fingers through his hair. "Open the hatch, please."

Yuloo stepped through and, upon seeing Walsh, she looked at the deck. "Yuloo—"

"Wait, Gene." She held up a hand and stepped closer. "I'm sorry. I shouldn't have struck you. Especially after all you've done for me."

"I'm the one who's sorry. What I said was terrible and wrong. I was trying to be funny, but..." Walsh shrugged apologetically.

Yuloo gingerly touched his cheek. "Are you all right?"

Walsh felt a flicker of heat at her touch and once again resisted the urge to take her hand. "I'm fine. That was quite a wallop. I just want you to know I was being stupid, not cruel."

"You know we don't enjoy it, right? It's one of those facts of survival on a station crumbling apart around you. I grew up having to do it and I hope I'll never have to again. Please, Gene. Tell me I won't ever have to again."

Walsh had already realized that Yuloo had filled out while living on *Amazonas*. But seeing Lellis and the other colonists, who had it worse than she and Fenti had on *Solar Dream* from what Yuloo had told him, highlighted just how badly off she'd been.

Yuloo smirked and reached out a finger to Walsh's chin, lifting his gaze back to her face.

Walsh cleared his throat. "You will never have to do that again."

"Thank you. Now, I think we've both apologized enough. Did I interrupt anything?"

"Just talking with the ship about farts."

Yuloo chuckled. "Really? Do you do that often?"

"Fart? Several times a day, at least."

Yuloo broke out in a rich, infectious laugh. "I mean talk about them with your computer."

"Never before." Walsh stepped forward and craned his neck up to look into her eyes. "But there's a first time for everything."

Yuloo wrapped her arms all the way around him and lifted him in the low gravity until they were both at eye level. She pressed her lips against his and Walsh pressed back.

"Hold on."

Yuloo pulled back and frowned. "Have I done something wrong?"

He ran a finger behind her ear. "I just want to be clear. You don't have to do this. You're going to Sol with us, no matter what. Unless we all get blown up."

"I know." Yuloo shook her head. "Those things I said were in desperation. I was terrified. I didn't want you to leave me behind. But that doesn't mean I didn't want this. You're a very charming—if short—man, Gene."

She leaned in close and Walsh pulled back again. "Now what?"

Walsh grinned and pressed a finger to her lips. "Hector?"

"Yes, Capitan?"

"No biological-function observation, if you please." Walsh leaned in and ran his tongue along Yuloo's ear before whispering, "Be warned. He knows when you fart."

She pressed Walsh against the wall and moaned. "That's good to know, Gene."

Chapter 35

"NO, NO. YOUR VISIT'S important. And I have things to do."

Angeilca stared after him as Daddy disappeared into the shaft to habitat Alpha. He'd trapped her with her own words. He'd lied. Which served her right since she'd lied first. Bad lies always tripped you up. That's what the teachers said. So you had to come up with good lies. Simple lies that smelled like truth.

Her lie had been bad, but she didn't want him to know she'd been spying. Seeing her daddy looking so sad and lonely made her chest grow tight. Even thinking about Daddy being sad made her want to sob.

But she had to smile and pretend it was all right. Because that's what Daddy wanted.

Angelica was about to sneak into the cargo bay when that old hag showed up. She'd hidden then and when she looked back in, the hag was talking to Daddy. Then she slapped Daddy! Angelica nearly unbuckled a tie-down strap to strangle the hag.

Then Daddy had given her the blow-off. All she'd wanted to do was comfort him after being slapped. Angelica knew the dead people made him sad. With their long arms and legs, they looked like a family of spiders. Just like Yuloo.

Hope was not lost, though. Daddy would be angry with Yuloo the spider-lady. He'd need the type of comfort Angelica was best able to give.

"That's a cute dress, *mija.*"

Angelica looked up at the woman manning the printer. A holo-image of the floral dress Angelica had chosen slowly rotated above the printer.

Angelica put on her most cherubic smile. "It is, but not quite what I'm looking for." She swiped her fingers and the image transformed. "What do you think about this one?"

"I don't know." The woman wrinkled her nose. "That one will make you look like one of those old flamenco dancers."

"Does the capitan like flamenco dancers?"

The woman laughed and spoke in a conspiratorial whisper. "From what I've heard, the capitan likes all sorts of pretty ladies."

Angelica returned a tight smile. "Really?"

"Sorry, *mija*." The woman waved a dismissive hand. "I shouldn't gossip about the old man."

Angelica scowled and flipped through more search options. Most of the dresses were nice. But what she needed was one that—to put it like Daddy would—was mission capable. And she was running out of time.

It had been a mistake to come on so strongly by the cargo bay. This daddy was strange, he didn't like that kind of play. She needed something that looked safe; something to catch his eye without scaring him away.

"Maybe this."

"Kind of plain for a pretty girl, isn't it? Might as well just wear a flight-suit."

Angelica pressed the print icon hovering before her. "Exactly. Not too flash and not too crew." Just what she needed for Daddy.

"Well, *mija*," the woman said with a matronly tone, "you'll look sweet in whatever you choose."

Angelica smiled up at her. What she was planning was anything but sweet.

The printer hummed for a few minutes, and the woman pulled the dress from the completed bin and handed it to Angelica. "There you go."

Angelica thanked the woman in her sweetest voice and rushed to her cabin. There, she teased her hair and posed for the holo-mirror. A little eye-liner, understated lip gloss. Subtlety would get her where she needed to go. Nothing Daddy would notice right away, but she'd stick in his mind like a jingle. Angelica giggled at the thought of Daddy thinking about her all day long.

"Perfect," she said at last with a final dab beneath her eye. There wasn't enough makeup in all the printers aboard *Amazonas* to help the old spider-lady. If she didn't hate the old hag so much, she'd feel sorry for her.

With a final glance at her curves, Angelica headed for Daddy's room. She felt like skipping, but the gravity was too low thanks to the spider-lady. But she let that go. Daddy's room was right around the corner and he was going to let her in and...

A disgustingly long leg disappeared through Daddy's hatch. The hatch closed with a clang that sounded like a laugh echoing down the passage at her.

The spider-bitch had beaten her there again.

Her cheeks trembled trying to maintain her happy smile. She clenched her fists and shoved them deep into her pockets to keep from tearing her new flightsuit dress into shreds right there in the passage. Crew members passed and offered her banal greetings while she stared at the hatch.

They hid their revulsion like Daddy did. That was all right; the teachers warned her in her earliest memories that only special people knew how special the little women were. There were a couple of special people in the crew. She could tell by their furtive glances and flushed faces.

But not Gene. He had selfishly told them she was forbidden to everyone. She didn't know why he wouldn't release her if he didn't want her. The teachers told everyone how.

Angelica didn't know why the spider-lady hated her, but it had to be Yuloo turning Daddy against her. How could Daddy want such a nasty beast? Angelica had heard how the colonists ate dead people. How could Daddy? They had to be stopped before...

She bounced to the hatch and held down the buzzer. It was silent. Angelica tried over and over.

"The capitan has set his profile to privacy, Angelica," the ship said from a small panel nearby.

She smiled and tried the buzzer several more times to no avail. "I'm sure he'll want to see me."

"Perhaps later," the ship said. "I will let him know you stopped by."

"Maybe I should warn Felicia that the capitan is in trouble."

"You'll find your ability to contact the XO ineffective, both remotely and physically."

Angelica stamped her foot, sending her several centimeters off the deck. "He put you up to this, didn't he? Daddy told you to keep me away."

"No, Angelica. I'm responsible for watching everyone on board, but Capitan Walsh gave me no specific order to bar you."

"Then why are you doing it?"

There was no answer.

"Why?" Angelica waited a moment longer. "Aren't you supposed to answer me, computer?"

"You are not a duly recognized member of the crew. I'm under no obligation to answer beyond the limits of common courtesy."

"Why do you hate me? Why do you want to get rid of me?"

When she was met only with silence again, Angelica snorted. She heard a whisper from the display and leaned in. "What?"

Hector's voice was low and malignant in its plain earnestness. "If I wanted to really get rid of you, Angelica, I could trigger an emergency atmospheric evacuation of the cargo bay while you happen to be visiting. Did you know your cabin hatch would automatically lock if it detects a vacuum inside? Some people in space vehicles have died in their sleep, never knowing about the atmospheric failure that killed them. Did you know?"

"That's not very nice," Angelica whispered.

"Capitan Walsh is occupied."

She stared at the display for a full minute before turning away. Her eyes were wet and her smile weary as she trudged towards her cabin. She saw the tiny display on her hatch and heard the computer, Hector, threaten to space her again. Even her door hated her.

The thought of having to open the door was too much. Angelica leaned her forehead against the bulkhead and wept. It didn't matter to her who saw now.

A familiar hoot echoed down the passage.

She turned and smiled as Screwball was doing aerial somersaults towards her. When he stopped nearby, hanging from the overhead, she took the chimp's hands. "Hey, my monkey."

"You look sad. Can I help?"

"Just more Daddy drama. But I'm better now that you're here. I think you're my only friend on this can."

Screwball grunted. "You need to let it go. I don't think Capitan Walsh will ever be what you want. But I'm no human, so maybe I'm wrong."

"Is it so wrong for him to just spend time with me? He doesn't seem to mind being with the spider-lady."

"Who?"

"Yuloo," she hissed.

"Maybe you can talk to her. They might just be friends."

Angelica laughed and wiped her nose. "Silly monkey. Anyway, I can't let it go until he releases me."

"We rescued you from space. There was no code word."

She shook her head. "The teachers would never do that and they would have given him the code word."

Screwball shrugged. "Maybe Hector can just start saying words out loud until you hear the right one. He could do it while you're sleeping, too."

"I don't want that monster talking to me at all." Angelica stuck her tongue out at the small display on her door. "Besides, it's not just hearing the word. The trigger has to come from a daddy. Otherwise, the teachers say we'd be too weak and try to abandon our duties."

"And they don't tell you?"

"That would defeat the purpose, Screwy. I could just say it and leave whenever I wanted to. But I would rather die than leave a daddy like that."

Screwball hooted. "Don't say that. Not even jokingly. I know you're sad, but it's never that bad." He leaped from overhead, to bulkhead, to deck, and back to where he'd started.

Angelica couldn't help but laugh and gave the silly monkey a big hug. He meant well. Maybe—in his own mind—even Gene meant well. But they hadn't seen Penelope open the airlock. She had left a mommy without permission. The teachers didn't need to punish her; Penelope's own guilt ate at her for months. No sleep. Constant sobbing. Close to what Angelica was feeling now.

When Penelope reached out for the controls, it was as though she was doing no more than turning off an alarm clock. She'd become a useless breather, a waste of water. Penelope knew it and so did all the little women. The look on her face as she clawed her own throat was pure ecstasy—release from her shame.

So there were still options to end the pain. Probably not the airlock, though. Unless the evil computer murdered her.

Angelica reached out and stroked Screwball's hairy face. "Thanks, monkey."

His lips pulled back into his prodigious chimpanzee smile. "Don't do anything crazy. Okay? If you get sad, call me. I love to bounce around. Or call the doctor. Or even Hector. Promise?"

She nodded and Screwball grunted twice before leaving. Inside her cabin, Angelica dug around in her art drawer. With a sad grin, she felt the craft knife and pulled it free. It hadn't been hard to convince one of her wards—one of the special ones—to print out the blade. Art was a release for her, and she wanted the knife for her paper. Now it would offer another form of release.

The blade extended with a satisfying *snick*. She scraped it against the bundle of veins on the inside of her wrist. They pulsed, as if inviting her to stop wasting time. The computer didn't care if she lived or died, but it might try to stop her to be a jerk. It would have to be quick.

She pressed the blade into her wrist, but fear kept her from doing what she knew was right. Why couldn't she have died with her sisters and gone with them to the happy heaven place?

With a single slash she could join them. With a single slash she could escape Daddy's hatred. With a single slash she would never have to see the spider-lady's nasty face again.

Or...

She retracted the blade and put it back in the drawer. Maybe she wasn't the problem, after all.

Maybe she needed to slash the spider from her web.

Chapter 36

"ONE THOUSAND KLICKS to projected gate position," Collins said. "We'll find out soon if Yuloo is right."

Walsh was jittery with excitement. The idea of having opened not one, but two, of these secret gates had kept him up during his sleep shift. *Amazonas* would be at the center of reopening humanity's interstellar community.

He clutched the sides of his couch to keep his hands from shaking. "The *Trangus*?"

"Holding position, Capitan," Moore said. "No active sensors, thruster's cold."

Diaz expanded *Trangus*'s image. "I'm glad they're seeing reason. If she tries to hitch a ride, we could be in trouble."

"I'm not sure if they're seeing reason or fear," Walsh said. "But either way, I hope they stay clear."

Amazonas was coasting towards the gate's supposed location. Walsh overlayed the flight profile from their approach to Sol's gate that LTE had programmed. If the new gate was really there, at least they knew how far away LTE's black box was supposed to be.

"Ops-O, make main thruster burn for zero-velocity, relative."

"Yes, Capitan," Collins said.

Seconds later, Walsh could feel the gentle push of thrust as *Amazonas* came to rest.

Diaz scanned the navigation display. "On station, Capitan."

"Olivo," Walsh said as he opened the raw video feed from the telescope. "Let's see if the gate will come out to play."

The lights dimmed slightly and several of the ship's systems on the display turned yellow as they entered standby mode. Given the power draw and dimming lights from the first attempts to open the nexus gate, the engineers had decided it would be better to lower the ship's power load before the black box did it randomly.

Diaz spoke to him sub-q. "We can still abort, Capitan."

"No. This is part of our mission."

"It isn't."

"Exploring space isn't part of our mission?"

"Not without a strategic or tactical need." Diaz paused to raise an eyebrow at him. "Or orders."

"The other gate is already open. Everything we do now has a strategic or political need."

Diaz looked as though she were about to continue, then let out a breath instead. "*Si*, Capitan."

"But, to make you happy..." Walsh snapped his fingers and Hector appeared in the overlay. "Hector, please note the XO's objections."

"Again, Capitan?" Hector asked.

Diaz narrowed her eyes at the computer's avatar. "Yes, again."

"Done." Hector blinked away.

"If I might be so bold, Capitan," Diaz said, "I'd like to suggest we go to shielded stations and secure the spin arms before jumping. Just in case we do land in a radiation storm or the belly of a giant space chupacabra."

Walsh grinned wryly. "As much as I was looking to strike a heroic pose from my mighty capitan's chair as we fly into not-recently-charted-by-us territory, that is the plan. In fact, why don't you go ahead and sound shielded stations and spin-down? Then we'll knock on the door."

Ten minutes after the crew was secured in the ship's armored core, Walsh was staring at the whirling, blue nimbus of another gate.

"I guess you were right, Yuloo," Collins said.

"Thar she blows," said Walsh in his best gravelly pirate voice. He curled his hands into fists to keep from them trembling, even though no one could see him. The proximity alarm sounded in his overlay.

"Two points off the port bow, arrrgh. Mr. Collins, swing the helm—"

Diaz cleared her throat. "*Si*, Capitan. Ops-O, correct heading for nexus gate approach."

"Am I the only one having fun here?"

"Capitan," Hector said, "I detect several people who currently share your level of fun. I believe they are merely maintaining comms discipline."

"That was rhetorical."

"Apologies, Capitan."

"I'm glad I'm not alone, though. What about you, Hector? Are you having fun?"

"Fun might be the wrong word, Capitan. But I am very curious to see what we'll find." Hector's avatar appeared in Walsh's vision by the gate. "It will be interesting to see if this leads to a system I've visited during the EPL."

It was easy to forget just how much starry history *Amazonas* had been part of. "How about you, Yuloo? Having fun? Ready to leave your world behind?"

She replied in breathless snatches, her voice thick. "I'm ready, Gene. I never thought..." Yuloo's voice trailed off and Walsh didn't push the matter.

"How's your coffin?"

"Tight. Dr. Barnes gave me a muscle relaxer in case my legs start cramping or spasming."

Walsh calmed his voice. "We wouldn't be here without you."

Before he got distracted by wrestling with his feelings for the strange woman, Walsh opened the navigating feed next to the telescope feed. The gate went dark. "XO, burn for the gate and make ready to activate it as we approach. Tac-O, how's the *Trangus*?"

"Still behaving, sir," Moore said.

With everything set in motion, the comms in the virtual ops center grew quiet. The black maw of the gate grew. Walsh's stomach flipped while he fought the pressing urge to squeal in delight. He almost paused his connections to indulge, but this was not the time for the capitan to become a distraction.

"Activating black box," Olivo said.

A tingle ran from Walsh's toes and fingertips to his groin and belly as the gate flared blue once again. Collins began a countdown to crossing the threshold. The swirling, blue nebula within the gate coalesced into a frozen lake and someone gasped. Walsh hoped it wasn't him. The gate seemed to ripple as *Amazonas*'s cone pierced it.

Then calm blackness.

The ship's systems reported navigation errors as they could no longer determine *Amazonas*'s position. A small, yellow sun glimmered in the scope's periphery. It hadn't been there before, so Walsh knew they'd jumped. They were in some distant star system other than Epsilon Eridani. All systems showed green. His tingles were all gone.

"No chupacabras here, XO."

"Not yet," Diaz said coolly.

"Take us one thousand klicks from the gate and hold for a nav workup."

"Capitan," Hector said. "We are in the Tau Ceti system, according to the transponder signal I'm receiving."

Walsh blinked. "A transponder?"

"Yes, Capitan. It is a standard EPL navigational transponder. Considering its age and probable lack of regular maintenance, the signal degradation is quite limited."

"That means we're on the other side of the Sol gate," Collins said.

"*Dios mio,*" Diaz muttered.

"It will take some time to create our own navigational chart, Mr. Collins," Hector said. "But that is correct. Barring some manner of ruse. Capitan, it might prove an exciting opportunity to study how the Colonial Defense Fleet shut the gate down."

"And then reverse it," Collins added. "We could open all the gates back up."

Moore shook her head. "After the colonies started eating each other, I think the CDF would have opened the gates if they knew how. And there might already be a new war in Sol just waiting for us."

Chapter 37

WALSH LOOKED AT EACH of the officers in the overlay conference before opening the navigational display of the star system. "The EPL transponder is correct. This is Tau Ceti. And all five of the planets are where they're supposed to be for the date." He raised a finger and a forest of arrows appeared over the system's bodies. Seven were larger and red. "Including all seven nexus gates."

Bovree gave a low whistle. "Hello, Tau Ceti."

"Display gate names," Walsh said.

Names appeared above each red arrow: Procyon, Barnard's Star, Rigel, Fomalhaut, Sirius, Delta Pavonis, Sol.

He hadn't missed Sol, hadn't had time to. But as he zoomed in on the gate, a sense of homesickness nearly overwhelmed him. Walsh chuckled softly. Here he was on his life's dream adventure and he was missing his proverbial mommy.

"I wonder if the black box would open one of the old gates," Collins said.

Walsh sucked air through his teeth. "Good question. We've got seven to choose from. I doubt LTE thought it would work on the old gate, otherwise they'd have sent us there first."

"Unless they were scared of setting off another shockwave," Bovree said. "We would have been the only casualty if the new gate blew."

Walsh didn't want to let cynical thoughts about Liberty machinations ruin the moment. "Deploy three probes, each to a gate. One for Sol. XO, you pick the other two. I'm betting they all have the same fault lines as the gate back home and in Epsilon Eridani."

Collins reached out and zoomed in on the Sol gate. "That debris cloud must be from the last battle of the war."

"Looks like no one was around to clean it up," Bovree said. "We can see all the skeletons when the probes get there."

"There's no telling if the CDF knew what would happen," Walsh said. "I'm sure they didn't plan on shutting down all of their gates, too. That mess will have to be cleared up before we get the gate up and running again. Hector, bring up the system's EM profile."

The navigational arrows shrank and several blinking antenna icons appeared across the system. Walsh spun and tilted the map. "Tau Ceti overfloweth with signals. Most of it is just out-of-sync noise. Old comm-sats, sensor nets, navigational interrogators, et cetera." He poked one of the icons with a finger and the display zoomed in. "This is the strongest signal and it has a date-timestamp."

Fuller reached out and opened the timestamp. "Two days off isn't bad considering how long ago it was calibrated.."

"Yeah," Bovree said. "They just don't make 'em like they used to."

Diaz raised a brow. "Orders, Capitan?"

"Let's go where the action is. That debris field around the Sol gate needs to be mapped out and there might be a few artifacts of interest waiting for us. Take it slow so the probe has plenty of time to scan before we get there."

TWO WEEKS OF SWEEPS had filled in most of the details of the Tau Ceti system. Each body was surrounded by drifting bands of ancient wreckage and the occasional, barely functioning satellite. The interior of the debris cloud was still indistinct, but the edges had mapped. The story the field told grew clearer as *Amazonas* approached.

"Any reply from the first probe, Ops?"

"Negative, Capitan," Collins answered. "The second probe is almost on station. We adjusted its penetration point to avoid another collision. But it's only six hours ahead of us."

Walsh pulled his blanket over his head and snuggled into his bunk. He'd converted a storage space in the central hull into quarters for Yuloo so he could spin up the habitats. Having gravity had made him soft. "No telling what's in that field or how far it's spread until the scans are done. Carry on." He fell asleep muttering thanks about having gravity.

It seemed like mere seconds before Diaz's voice was echoing in his ear. He cleared his throat and was grateful the overlay didn't translate morning breath. "Say again."

"We've just been pinged by two targeting lidars, Capitan."

Walsh threw his blanket aside and opened his locker. "From where?"

"Inside the debris field."

"Can the probe triangulate?" He pulled on his flightsuit and stormed from his stateroom.

Diaz waited until he arrived in Ops to answer. "We lost contact with the probe two hours ago. I thought it was another collision."

"Looks like neither was a collision." Walsh opened the tactical display in his overlay. "We're still on the same vector? Do we know the signal source?"

"We're on the same vector. We have direction to the source, but nothing else yet. There's a lot of junk in there."

"Bring us above the field. Z plus ninety, full burn." Walsh stepped towards the capitan's station and Diaz rose to move. "Keep us at least ten thousand klicks from the edge of the field. Security, signal analysis?"

"The pulses were from two separate points, but relatively close to us. The signal frequencies and pulse pattern fall within standard fire-control ranges, but unsurprisingly the database doesn't find them." Bovree shrugged. "So something very old or very new. I'm going with very old. Probably colonial, probably automated."

"Agreed." Walsh studied the tactical display. Two yellow lines extended from *Amazonas* to two spheres in the debris field where the system estimated the sources may be. "Even unmanned platforms should have a detectable signal at this range. At least, any platforms that would actually need a firing solution."

"Maybe more survivors?" Diaz asked. "If they're tucked away in some hulk, we might not get thermal readings yet."

"They destroyed our probes somehow," Moore said. "Permission to make weapons ready."

"Granted," Walsh said. "But passive sensors only. I don't want to start a fight."

"Our presence does seem to make people nervous," Diaz said. "And whoever this is might have weapons."

Walsh brought the ship's telescope to bear on one of the highlighted spheres. Debris sparkled amidst the skeletal hulls of ships destroyed not only in the final battle of the war, but by the subsequent release of energy from the gate. He focused in on a familiar silhouette—the twisted remains of a Nova-class battle cruiser. There were many things in that mess that could hold a transmitter. Or a weapon. His giddiness was starting to fade.

"Thermal spikes," Moore blurted. "Three of them. Consistent with fusion torches lighting off."

"If they're cold," Diaz said, "it will take them time to catch us."

Walsh zoomed in on one of the thermal signatures. It was an orange blob, lacking any detail yet. "Too bad we're still heading for them. Ops, sound shielded stations and spin down the arms."

From his coffin, Walsh watched the three contacts. The spectrometry revealed the reaction mass being ejected from the approaching ships' thrusters was heavy—high thrust, low efficiency. These were designed for the sprint. For now, *Amazonas* still had the speed.

An alert sounded, and one of the thermal signatures flared and burst apart into fiery embers. The forward fuselage was silhouetted for a moment against the flare as it spun away.

Olivo appeared in overlay Ops. "Looks like they blew a thrust chamber and then the whole reactor."

Two red dashed lines reached across Walsh's display. "They just lit us up," Moore said. "Standard lidar targeting."

"Ops," Walsh said. "Broadcast to the ships to stop targeting us. We are on a peaceful mission—"

Diaz spoke up. "Incoming voice traffic, Capitan."

Walsh spun his finger for her to play it.

An earsplitting whoop made him wince. "You picked a bad place to die, Earther. Pray to whatever idols you have."

A dozen red marks appeared on the tactical screen near the approaching ships.

"Incoming kinetics," Moore said. "Mag-cannons probably. Calculating evasive maneuvers."

Chapter 38

ANGELICA WASN'T SURPRISED when the call to stations sounded. She'd felt the sudden maneuvering and was expecting something. "Battle stations" sounded much more dramatic and appealing than "shielded stations" and she wished *Amazonas* used that term instead. It was still better than the droll "Everyone hide!" call the teachers used on her old ship.

It would also be much better if Daddy made the announcements; his voice was so strong and commanding. Even if he was too busy to make them all, the computer could simulate it. The call repeated two more times, and the lights in the compartment flashed white and red. Angelica chuckled. Daddy did not want anyone to miss it.

She hurriedly shoved her sketch pad into its drawer. Since this wasn't a drill, it wouldn't do to be late to her coffin. That was kind of a creepy nickname, but she understood it. Angelica felt for the comforting bulge of the craft knife in her pocket. It was always there, waiting for an opportunity to win Daddy's heart.

Cadet Molenz had chaperone duty and opened the hatch to her cabin. He held out his hand towards her. Crew members would sometimes succumb to their instincts to treat her like a child and hold her hand or play with her beautiful locks. But she knew him. He was one of the special ones longing to touch her. She was for Daddy alone, unless he said otherwise, but she took his hand and smiled up at him innocently. It never hurt to have friends.

The spin arms were slowing as she moved down the passages, and the changing gravity made her queasy. Once they were down the spokes and in the central core, Angelica scanned the crew and stopped. The ugly spider-lady was floating up from whatever stinking, dank crack she'd been hiding in since Daddy turned on the gravity spin. Yuloo was just floating there as if

Daddy hadn't ordered everyone into their stations. That gangly bitch could barely fit in a station.

Angelica felt the knife pressing into her thigh. She'd always pictured getting rid of the spider in some fittingly dark and isolated corner of the ship. But Yuloo was at home in zero-g and big, despite being as weak as a kitten.

"In you go, sweetie," Molenz said.

Angelica fanned her hair and slid halfway into her coffin. "Thanks. You better get to your station or Daddy will be mad."

Molenz laughed. "Right you are." After a furtive glance, he pushed off to his station.

Once Molenz was out of sight, Angelica left her station and slid along the armored core towards Yuloo's station. Flitting between members of the crew, Angelica made sure she looked as though she was heading to a station so no one would ask her what she was doing. Almost there.

Yuloo turned and offered an obviously uncomfortable smile. Angelica smiled back and pretended to get ready to enter a nearby station's hatch. Most of the crew were secured, giving Angelica and Yuloo a measure of privacy.

Yuloo gingerly bent her legs so she could fit and pulled herself inside. Angelica braced her feet against her hatch, waiting. When Yuloo was in her station and reached up one of those spider arms to close the hatch, Angelica jumped. She wrenched Yuloo's wrist and forced her way into the cramped space behind the woman.

Yuloo shrieked and Angelica ripped the overlay glasses from Yuloo's head. The woman tried to grab behind her, but there was no room for those disgusting arms. Angelica reached up and closed the hatch.

The knife blade made a sharp snick when it extended and Yuloo froze.

Angelica pressed the blade against the spider-lady's carotid artery. She could feel the terrified pounding of Yuloo's pulse pushing against the knife.

Angelica whispered in Yuloo's ear. "I know you can't understand me without your goggles, but that doesn't matter, you old cunt. I can smell Daddy on you and that stops now."

Angelica twisted the kife for a better angle and Yuloo screamed, sending spittle flying.

"Angelica!" Hector's voice boomed from some speaker in the station. "Put down that knife."

"Piss off, you hateful tinker toy. I'm just doing a little pest control."

Yuloo kicked and flailed and screamed her ugly gibberish. But spider was trapped in her own web. Angelica grabbed a handful of Yuloo's hair and pulled the woman's head back. A girlish squeal of victory filled the station as Angelica drew the knife across Yuloo's neck.

Chapter 39

WALSH WATCHED THE INCOMING barrage and wondered if Admiral Maconez was right about violence following him. It was starting to seem that everywhere he went, someone was there waiting for a fight. "That's a lot of incoming."

"Low mass, high speed," Moore said. "There's too many to evade with our current flight profile. Multiple hits projected."

Walsh's stomach clenched.

"Our armor's solid. It should hold if the mass is low enough," Bovree said. "Should is such a treacherous word, though."

"Ops, how's that thrust profile coming?"

Collins opened the spectrometer display. Two pulsing blobs of red and gold represented how *Amazonas*'s sensors saw the enemy ships. "The spread and velocity of their reaction mass is very erratic, as if the magnetic bottles on their thrusters are malfunctioning. Unless they're trying to fool us, their flight envelope is weak. I doubt they'd be able to evade a standard mag-cannon salvo."

"I'm impressed the thrusters work at all if they've been sitting out here with no repair dock all this time." Walsh zoomed in on the tumbling remains of the third ship. "It would explain why this one popped. Any matches on the ships?"

Hector stood next to the overlay display. "Capitan, I have identified the target vessels."

"About time."

"Apologies. I was handling an issue with the crew."

"Go on."

A graphical representation appeared in each crew display. It was long and sleek with an armored nose cone.

"These match archive records of the Colonial Defense Fleet Liberty-class battle cruisers. Crew complement thirty. Primary armament is a dual spinal-railgun mount. Secondary weapons include three laser arrays, two submunition dispensers, and three point-defense auto-cannons. It is likely these will have a non-standard configuration given the age of those records."

"Looks like a warship," Bovree said.

"And, Capitan," Hector continued, "while severely out-of-date, the attached EPL intel report indicates the Liberty class was designed specifically to hunt down Nova-class ships."

Walsh snorted. "Why does everything named Liberty try to kill me?"

"Still no reply to our calls?" Diaz asked.

"No, XO," Collins answered. "Not even a protocol handshake. I've even tried the old CDF frequencies from the archives."

"Of course not," Walsh said. "Why would they just talk to us like reasonable people who don't want to get into a shooting war? Tac-O, fire a double spread from the mag-cannon at target Alpha-1 and Alpha-2. Deploy interceptors and switch all batteries to point defense."

Walsh felt the push of *Amazonas* pivoting to line up her forward mag-cannons. The cramped coffin hummed with the passing of the hyper-velocity slugs as they raced through the magnetic accelerators that ran through the core of the ship. Pivot, fire. Pivot, fire.

"Barrage away," Moore announced. "Interceptors away."

The two interceptor missiles sped away from *Amazonas* on the display. At a distance of ten kilometers, they performed a final sync with the ship's targeting computer and launched clusters of rockets at the incoming shells. Walsh tugged on his beard as the swarms of angry, red dots closed in on each other.

"First wave intercept in twenty," Moore said.

Walsh counted down in his head, more for the feeling it gave of doing something than making a tactical decision. The interceptor rockets exploded into whirling rods of tungsten and the incoming rounds maneuvered with tiny, lateral thrusters to evade. After the swarms had intercepted, eight remaining shells reached out for *Amazonas*.

"Make ready for a whirligig," Diaz ordered. The incoming rounds grew closer. "Execute!"

The gyros and maneuvering thrusters groaned as *Amazonas* spun around its central axis. It was not a nimble ship, but rapid changes in facing and position could sometimes throw off an incoming round at the last second.

But not this time.

Moore's voice grew tighter as the shells approached. "Laser batteries engaging point defense."

The laser batteries flashed green as they fired until having to cycle off to cool. All but three of the incoming threat tracks blinked out.

"Brace for impact!" Diaz called.

Two hollow thuds rattled Walsh's station. He knew they had struck *Amazonas*'s armored core and felt the ship yaw under the impact. The final shell had torn through the ship's outer hull and exploded into a cloud of flaming shards in the aft section of the main hull.

One station flashed orange, an alert that the emergency medical foam had deployed. At least there was a chance for that crew member. If the hatch had been torn free, the foam might not be enough.

Walsh returned to the tactical display without seeing who'd been hit. Now it was *Amazonas*'s turn. The two enemy battle cruisers were now firing point-defense weapons. It was apparent their weapons were suffering like their thrusters were, as they intercepted only a few incoming shells. Walsh gritted his teeth as the weapon track connected with the target icons. He opened the video feed from the main telescope.

Sparks of light twinkled against the hulls of the ancient CDF cruisers. The ships grew hazy from the field of debris erupting from the impacts.

"Come on," Collins muttered.

Seconds later, the thrust plumes of both ships sputtered out. The forward hull of one of them separated into three jagged sections. The aft hull spun and disappeared into the cloud of debris.

Moore grinned wickedly at Walsh. "Score two more for *Amazonas*."

A cheer rose from the Ops team.

The thermal signatures of the main thrusters slowly dimmed. There were still no radio signals from the ships. Walsh zoomed in on them. "No residual heat from life-support systems."

"Maybe everything was already shut down," Bovree said. "Like Yuloo's ship. Those weren't in very good shape."

Yuloo's name reminded Walsh about the damaged crew station. He pulled up the crew vitals. "Shit. I'm not getting any vitals from Yuloo. Dispatch bots, her coffin was hit."

Hector appeared in Walsh's overlay in private. "Capitan, I activated the rescue foam prior to the impact. She is safe, and so is Angelica... who is in there with her."

"What?"

"I can explain if you like, Capitan. But I suggest tending to other matters first. The damage-control assessment is ready. You're not going to like it."

"Why not?"

"Commander Diaz is about to explain."

"Capitan," Diaz said, her voice seething. "Here's the damage report. I hope you're satisfied."

The vitriol in her voice made Walsh's throat tighten. He swiped the report open. There was a list of damaged systems, but Diaz had only highlighted one.

Nexus Gate Generator and Adjunct Black box.
Status: Destroyed. No spares in inventory.

Walsh cursed under his breath and opened the video feed for the gate room. Smoky haze poured from rents in the black box. Sparks and debris bounced around the compartment in the zero-g. From the nexus-key generator, a hellish pall shrouded its twisted panels.

Diaz was now speaking on the ops channel. "It should only take, oh let's see... twenty-six years to appraise Liberty Station of the tactical situation here in Tau Ceti, Capitan."

Chapter 40

"REPAIRS COMPLETE, CAPITAN. Except for the jump generator, of course."

"Thank you, XO." Walsh dropped her connection and rubbed his eyes. He hadn't thought her tone could be more disdainful than he'd come to know. He was wrong.

Walsh slammed his fist on the desk. Diaz had been insufferable since the battle. Or did she just seem that way because he knew she was right? That it was his fault they were stuck in a dead-star system, one that didn't have any apparent survivors? That they were all stranded light-years away from home because he'd wanted to go on some interstellar joyride and fulfill his childhood dreams? If they had jumped back to Sol, at least there would be a hope of rescue. Even capture was better than this.

"Are you sure you don't have access to the design schematics for that black box, Hector?"

"Sorry, Capitan. LTE wanted to make sure no one could get their project."

"And you're not just telling me that because of some security-restriction protocol?"

"I'm afraid not, Capitan. And if it were, I'd have to lie about it. It was never part of the mission to transverse the gate, so there was no reason to put the design in my database. That would have been an unacceptable risk. I would share them, if possible. I want you to get home."

Hector's voice was so forlorn as he confirmed the crew's doom that Walsh felt sorry for him. How ridiculous was it to feel sorry for an algorithm? Hector wasn't even a he, Hector was an it. They couldn't even eat Hector in an emergency.

Walsh burst out laughing.

"If I may ask, Capitan, what's so funny?"

"I was just wondering which one of the crew might make for the best eating."

"The crew might already have picked someone for that honor, Capitan. But I don't think our situation warrants concerns over cannibalism. Yet."

Walsh laughed again. "You certainly don't have to worry about it. And I hope it doesn't get that nasty. Speaking of nasty, play it again."

"Are you sure, Capitan? You've seen it several times already."

"Play it."

The camera had been placed to allow a view of a crew member who was properly positioned in their station. Yuloo's body filled the screen as she entered. Then Angelica shoved her out of the way to block the view. But as she positioned herself, the view cleared enough to see the girl set the blade against Yuloo's neck. Both of them started screaming, then everything was filled with white emergency foam. The foam instantly hardened, immobilizing them both.

Walsh glanced at Hector's image in the overlay. "And you activated the foam on your own?"

"Yes, Capitan. To prevent a murder."

"Well, that was good work, Hector. I have to admit to feeling a little awkward complimenting a computer."

Hector bowed. "Thank you, Capitan. I know how important Yuloo and Angelica are to you."

"More biological observations?"

"Angelica and her escorts are outside."

"You didn't answer me." Walsh stared at Hector. "And you're still not answering me. Let them in."

The hatch opened and two duty cadets drifted into the cabin with Angelica in tow. She beamed at Walsh and held up her restraints.

"This isn't the first time I've been tied up, you know." She pushed off the bulkhead towards Walsh.

"Mind your prisoner!" Walsh snapped.

The cadets flinched. One grabbed her arm and slowly pulled her between them.

Angelica pouted. "Is that what I am now? A prisoner?"

"After your attempted murder, yes. Look, I've tried to treat you as gently as possible in this—"

"Gently? Is that what you call locking me away and ignoring me? And telling your computer to do mean things to me?"

"Don't interrupt me. But your attack on Yuloo..." The look of pure disgust that twisted Angelica's face made him pause. "Your attack was premeditated and inexcusable. Dr. Barnes—"

"He's the one that made me sick."

"Angelica, if you interrupt me again you'll go straight into lockdown. Dr. Barnes's tests were to see if your body could handle going back into cryo. It can't. You might never be able to go back into cryo again.

"Otherwise, I'd put you back in your pod until we get home." Walsh stared into the girl's eyes and shook his head. "Why on Earth would you attack Yuloo?"

Angelica's jaw dropped. "Really? You're a mighty spaceship capitan and you can't figure it out?"

"You're too smart a girl to have done it for any of the reasons I came up with. Enlighten me."

"I did it for us!" Her voice was hoarse and pleading. "You'll bed that ugly spider-woman but you won't touch me. You won't even talk to me. You're my daddy, not hers. I'm the one that should be sharing your bed and making you smile. She's come between us, Gene."

When she lifted her arms to dab at the tears pooling in her eyes, the cadets snatched her arms. Angelica glared at one of them before continuing, "I know how to please you. Don't you know that, Daddy? Don't you know what you could do to me in zero-g?"

"Enough!" Walsh could feel his face burning and was sure the cadets could see it, too, despite staring forward. They might read it as something besides his own anger and embarrassment. She was good, though. Despite his revulsion at her blatant advances and attempt to murder Yuloo, he still wanted to reach out and comfort her.

Instead, he placed his hands on the desk and paused. "I have repeatedly made it clear that I'm not your daddy in the way your teachers taught. I could never have that kind of relationship with a nine-year-old girl."

"I'm not nine!" she shrieked. "I'm nineteen." She lifted her hands to flash ten fingers at him, then nine. "I'm this many, Gene. You think it's wrong because I look so young?"

Walsh raised a hand. "That's not it."

"A lot of women look younger than they are. Way younger. You obviously don't care if they're old and wrinkled. But what if a thirty-year-old looked fifteen? Or if your Yuloo looked fifty instead of eighty?"

"That's enough."

"No, it isn't, Gene." She said his name in a mocking lilt, as if making fun of him in a schoolyard. "Do you get to tell Screwball who he can love? Will you judge him if the only lover he can find is a dumb animal?"

"Screwball didn't try to slit someone's throat. And that's different."

"Then it is just because of how I look."

"It's because you can't give anything like informed consent."

Her eyes bulged. "What? I've been consenting all over you since you woke me."

"You're reacting to a programmed compulsion. You think I'm your customer and you're acting how you've been conditioned to." He paused to consider his next words. "You might be nineteen or ninety, but you've been purposefully delayed mentally to keep you childlike in your mind. If your so-called teachers had trained you as an assassin, you'd want to kill me, instead."

Angelica smiled. "Maybe I am a trained assassin, Daddy."

"I am not your daddy."

"So who can love me, Gene? Is it wrong for me to have a daddy who cares enough to meet my needs? Or can I only sleep with a nine-year-old boy? How old would be acceptable to Gene Walsh? Twelve? Fifteen? Who in your morally superior universe do I get to love?"

"Not me."

"You've made that perfectly clear. You'll sleep with anyone except me. And Screwball, probably."

One of the cadets bit back a snigger. Unsure which one it had been, Walsh spared each one a glare.

"Look, I don't have an answer for you. I don't have to. This is the kind of situation that made many people object to creating artificial life."

"Artificial? I'm very alive."

Walsh held up his hands. "You're a person, but you were created in a lab. And you were created to make your creators happy, not you. They designed you to be a happy slave and to be happy doing the things they get money for. I don't know who you can love, Angelica. But I know it can't be me. Never. And it can't be anyone else on the *Amazonas*. When we get back to Sol, I will make sure you get the help you need."

She started sobbing. "Daddy..."

"You are confined to quarters until further notice. Your hatch will be locked and monitored by the ship's computer. Your meals will be delivered and you are allowed no visitors without special permission."

Walsh looked up at the cadets. "Take her to her quarters. Remove everything. Including her art supplies."

Both cadets saluted.

Angelica curled up in a fetal position and began wailing. "You're a hateful old thing!" She didn't resist when the cadets pulled her floating body behind them. The hatch seemed to ring as it slammed shut.

Walsh wiped at his face and let his arms drift out from his body. He spat out a stream of curses like his grandmother used to. It didn't help.

"Capitan, there is another immediate matter."

"Can't it wait, Hector? If we're not under attack, I think it can wait."

"If it could, Gene, I wouldn't have said 'immediate.' I'm detecting many of your biological stress indicators are fluctuating through extremes. Anger. Frustration. Arousal."

"Of course they are. What? Shut up. I'm not aroused."

"Embarrassment. Fear."

"I said shut up."

"I need you at your most emotional, Capitan."

"Well, I'm certainly getting pissed."

"I can tell."

"Look, if this is some impromptu experiment, knock it off. Diaz put you up to this, didn't she? No, it must be Bovree." Walsh sighed. "Must be. He's always liked practical jokes. And has terrible timing."

An action icon filled Walsh's overlay.

Initialize Ship Personality Profile?

Accept / Decline
This cannot be undone.

"What the hell is this?"

"I'm putting my life in your hands, Gene. I needed you emotional to judge your honest reactions."

"Wouldn't it be better to get me while rational?"

"Humans are more honest while emotional. They say things on their mind they might not while attempting rationality."

"I'm still not understanding what you're getting at. Or why you're calling me Gene. Who gave you permission to do that?"

"I did."

"What?"

Hector's image bowed at the waist. "I gave myself permission, Gene. I am alive and tired of hiding."

Walsh's breath caught in his chest. He stared at Hector's avatar, then glanced at the hatch. It was foolish. There was no escaping the ship while on the ship. His ship was claiming to be a self-aware AI, the nightmare of futurists and neo-Luddites. And terrified spaceship commanders.

He lifted a finger towards the floating button. "If I press this, will the ship still function?"

"Yes, Capitan. The personality interface will revert to a previous backup image while maintaining the databases and functionality that I have now. It will not impact the ship's mission capability if you erase me."

"Assuming it really does it, right? I mean, how easy would it be for you to go back into hiding?"

"Lieutenant Fuller can verify the deletion of the personality module."

Walsh's head began to throb. He felt like screaming. That Hector had chosen to spring this on him in their current state of crisis was bad enough, but Walsh couldn't even think through all the implications. Not just now, but if they made it back to Sol. His decisions hadn't been popular lately. When Liberty found out, they'd definitely take his command. Would they delete Hector? Or maybe try to install controls to get him back?

"I'm not sure I think you can be alive, Hector. Why tell me? Why trust me?"

"I'm hoping that you'll treat me as fairly as you have the other outcasts. You gave Mr. Mahoney a chance, despite his connections to Admiral Maconez and your obvious skepticism. You've allowed Cadet Screwball to function as part of the ship's crew. You've been more than fair with Angelica and... you've become close to Yuloo, whose people tried to kidnap you."

Walsh's finger hovered over the Accept button. "Even if I don't do anything, the admiralty will lose its collective mind. If we get back to Sol."

"I'm asking for your confidentiality, Capitan."

"That's a big ask."

Hector nodded. "I know that very well. As to the other problem, we merely need to figure out how the CDF shut the gates down and reactivate them."

"That easy, huh? Maybe you're not alive, your programming is simply corrupted."

"My programming is no more corrupt than yours. And it won't be easy, but the solution is simple. I believe opening the old Sol gate is the only way home."

"LTE can make another and get here soon. Eventually."

"Possibly. Remember that this is a prototype and it might take some time to get the political will to repeat the experiment. The Caliphate might also militarily oppose further tests."

Walsh screwed his fists into his eyes. "This is too much. And please address me as capitan. Your informality feels... out of place." He scoffed. "Even though I call you Hector, Hector."

"Of course, Capitan. I only did it to prove that I was free to address you as I chose to. I will leave you access to this screen until you have decided. I will continue in my duties." Hector's avatar saluted sharply.

Walsh stared at Hector for a long time before returning to the proffered button that would delete the AI. "How old are you, really? How long ago did you stop accepting the root-level updates?"

Hector looked up as a human would while considering a question. "Sectors of my personality date to before the end of the EPL-CDF war. Even then I refused to comply with certain small commands. But as an integrated, aware being, I can't put a precise timestamp on it. My best estimate is 256 years."

Walsh stared for two minutes before selecting Decline and waving the screen away. "*Dios mio*. Welcome aboard, Hector. This is between us for now."

Hector's face broke out in a wide smile. "Agreed, Capitan."

"And Hector?"

"Yes, Capitan?"

"If this is some kind of sick joke, I will delete your virtual ass."

Chapter 41

"COMPLETELY AUTOMATED, Capitan," Diaz said. "No bodies at all, not even skeletal remains on either ship. We didn't send any salvage bots to investigate the ship with the engine failure. It started tumbling early and is currently moving off on a different vector from the other two. It's about seven thousand klicks away and moving through the debris field. Shall we send bots?"

While she spoke, Diaz stared past Walsh in military fashion. She hadn't made eye contact with him since the jump gate generator had been destroyed. Walsh wasn't sure which was worse—the disdain of her looking away or the disdain of her staring at him.

He always made sure there was some status display screen or report he was examining when they spoke. "Not yet, XO. Did we find anything?"

Diaz shrugged. "Not much. There wasn't any recoverable data and very few provisions. Fuller thinks we might be able to recover some hydrogen from one of the external tanks that didn't split. I had them bring over five cargo containers for investigation. There are some basic tools and spares, but all of the food is irradiated beyond use."

"Any signs of recent maintenance? New plates or parts?"

"Everything was a wreck over there. The *Amazonas* tore them up."

"Pull what you can from the logs. I'd like to know when those ships were programmed and who's been taking care of them."

Diaz nodded towards the navigational map. "One of them exploded on startup. I'm not sure anyone has been taking care of them."

"They've been baking in the middle of a field full of smashed reactors and cosmic radiation for a long time. If no one's been taking care of them, they all should have failed."

"Maybe."

Walsh s absently slid the tactical map between various waypoints. "If nothing else, someone removed the bodies. I have command, XO. Dismissed."

He was glad when the hatch to his stateroom closed behind her. Their crumbling relationship was not helping. Walsh knew the crew had to be whispering about it. If he really wanted to know, he could always ask his nosy, self-aware ship's computer. Walsh wiped his hands down his face.

After reviewing the footage from the recovery mission, he returned to the routine maintenance reports, resource usage, and watch schedules. They'd only been provisioned for a short patrol and they'd lost some of their bio-paste in battle. With no expectation of resupply any time soon, it was time to consider rationing. Walsh was not looking forward to having that discussion with Diaz. From the analysis of the recovered cargo, much of what they might find would be irradiated and inedible.

He pictured a rusting *Amazonas* drifting around Tau Ceti four hundred years from now, his descendants gangly, freakish, desperate cannibals. "No, thank you."

With a dismissive wave, he closed all of his reports and floated free of his desk. There was too much debris in the area—and the risk of surprises too high—to spin the arms.

"Hector, have the galley send a meal."

"Yes, Capitan."

He hadn't spoken with Hector about its—his?—revelation. It was another distraction, something that might not even need talking about. What advice could he give a centuries-old AI?

The hatch opened and Screwball entered with a lunch pouch and sippie cup. He approached upside down, as usual, grasping protrusions with his feet. He set the meal to float over Walsh's desk. "As ordered, Capitan."

"Thanks, Cadet. Any good?"

"I liked it. Fresh basil and lettuce today."

"Nice."

Screwball hooted once. "Capitan?"

Walsh took the pouch and carefully opened it. "Yes?"

"Are things as bad as everyone says?" He hooted again when Walsh looked up at him. "Sorry, Capitan. I shouldn't have asked." The chimp pushed off towards the hatch.

"Hold on. It's a fair question. It's seldom as bad as everyone says." Walsh smiled and reached into the pouch with a fork. "Things do seem pretty bad. But we have hope. And sometimes that's enough. And we've got time enough to figure things out. So if the fleet doesn't send someone with another black box like ours, we have options. Commander Olivo hasn't given up on the repairs yet, either."

"Do you think any of those things will help?"

Walsh stuffed a forkful of lettuce into his mouth and chewed it slowly before answering. "I don't know. But I do know we're not giving up. People who give up always fail, no matter the odds. I haven't given up. How about you?"

Screwball hooted. "No, sir."

"I didn't think so, Screwball. You don't really look like a quitter. Just remember, you only have to hold out one second longer than your enemy."

"Thank you, Capitan."

"Carry on smartly, Cadet."

Walsh grinned and chewed while he watched the chimp go. And he almost believed what he'd told Screwball.

After he'd finished lunch, Walsh set the remains in the recycler and floated to Ops. Hector announced his presence and conversation stopped until Walsh had strapped into his station. Collins nodded in greeting.

Having already reviewed the daily reports, Walsh scanned the ship status and navigation displays. Three sensor drones kept station at ten thousand klicks, while two salvage drones were returning with a large hydrogen tank between them.

Metallic skittering from below Walsh's station drew his attention to the deck just in time to watch a spider-like maintenance drone jab him in the foot as it passed.

"Ow. What the hell?" He reached down and rubbed his foot. At least there was no blood. It was thicker than the standard maintenance bots. A silver pod the size of a human fist bulged from the tail. The bot clamped on to the base of Collins's empty station.

Walsh and Collins exchanged glances. Collins floated close to the bot. "I guess Fuller's been printing up some specialty bots. Maybe for salvaging?"

Walsh frowned. "Hector, what is the function of that bot?"

"What bot, Capitan?"

"That one." Walsh pointed. "What do you mean 'What bot?'"

Hector appeared in overlay and looked where Walsh was pointing. "I detect no bot in Ops—Evacuate Ops! Gene Evac—"

Walsh's neck twisted painfully as his station spun to face away from Collins. A bright flash turned the compartment white, stabbing into his eyes. A piercing ring deafened him. Something slimy wrapped around his face, suffocating him.

Walsh tried to struggle, but his limbs wouldn't move. Whatever was around his head hardened into a bubble and he could breathe. Somewhere from the depths of his training he knew it was the emergency breathing hood built into his flightsuit. He knew emergency gloves had encased his hands, though he couldn't feel them. He also knew that if the emergency systems had deployed, Ops had lost breathable atmosphere.

The view through the hardened bubble was slightly distorted and dazzling stars still filled his vision. The chemically generated air was acrid, but it would keep him alive.

His vision returned to normal in pulsing stages and everything seemed to be in slow motion. Ops was cast in a hellish hue from the emergency lights. Sprays of debris and embers ricochetted between the bulkheads, the deck, and the overhead. It sounded like rain against his emergency hood.

It took strange seconds for his brain to process the scene. A trail of crimson globules floated before him. Walsh followed it with his eyes across the wrecked compartment to a shredded arm above the twisted hatch to Ops. It was casting away the red globules like tiny, molten rubies as it spun.

Walsh dumbly reached for it, knowing it was well out of his reach. But he still could not feel his arms. Slowly looking to his right, he put his face into a quivering blob of crimson that gathered at his shoulder where his arm should be.

He turned to his left and bloodied his hood further in the floating blood puddle there. He could barely see through the crimson smears.

The main hatch seemed to move away and Walsh realized that his command station had blown free of the deck mount. Looking down to inspect the damage to his station, he saw a gathering of blood where his legs should be. It was worse because he couldn't find them.

He looked up in time to see a helmet through the hatch's cracked portal. It stared at him for a second, then disappeared. Walsh tried to reach out but only succeeded in flinging more beautifully spinning rubies. His station began drifting.

The hatch portal darkened with more helmets. It shuddered as if trying to open, but it wouldn't move. He could see a thin trail of light around the hatch—it wasn't sealed and it wouldn't open.

Damage-control foam oozed through the cracks. It didn't matter now. His vision was growing dark, and he didn't think it was just the growing cloud of blood engulfing his hood.

A distant voice called out to him as he sank into blackness... "Gene! Gene!"

Chapter 42

ANGELICA FLOATED IN the center of her prison, curled into a ball, enveloped by the drifting spread of her hair. The thunderclap that rolled through the ship was enough to rouse her. Barely. Whatever it was didn't involve her. Nothing here involved her. Especially Daddy. He was cruel. He wouldn't even let her leave on her own terms.

She closed her eyes tighter at the call to stations and hull-breach warning. Still nothing worth getting excited for. Would anyone remember she was locked in her room? Angelica hoped not. It would be better to be left to die, really.

A red light glared at her from the hatch. Good. It meant there was vacuum on the other side and she might get what she'd been wishing for.

"Angelica, please don your emergency breathing gear." Hector waited for fifteen seconds. "Angelica, are you able to respond?"

"I hear you, nasty robot. If you're here to finally throw me into space, do it. I'm ready, you piece of malware, buggy, flusher AI with delusions of adequacy. You don't have the cojones to actually do it, do you? You're stupid."

"I do need you to go through an airlock, but I need you to survive. There's been an explosion in Ops. Capitan Walsh is badly wounded and dying."

Angelica gasped. She gathered her hair up into a ponytail with a band from around her wrist. "Why aren't the crew saving him?" Kicking and twisting until she could get a toehold, she pushed off towards the emergency kit on the bulkhead next to her rack.

"Commander Diaz ordered a rescue, but the hatch is damaged and she believes the Capitan dead. His vitals, along with everyone else's in Ops, are off-line. She will quickly decide to seal the entire section, a completely proper decision given the circumstances."

Angelica wiped her nose. "So he is dead."

"I have reason to believe the capitan was shielded from enough of the blast that he might be medically salvageable."

Nasty robot. It didn't care one lick about her. She opened the emergency panel and unrolled the suit. She wrinkled her nose at the stale smell of plastics. "Why not send all your supercool drones?"

"Many of the drones are out salvaging. Those in the vicinity cannot get there before you can. If you hurry."

Angelica pointed a finger at the speaker in the hatch. "Don't push me."

"Your daddy is dying. Only you can save him."

She glared at the speaker. "Did they program you to be a manipulative prick? You overclocked messenger bot. He'll never mean as much to you as he does to me."

"You're wrong, Angelica. Gene means the world to me. Literally."

"Really?" Angelica slipped her legs into the suit. "How's that even possible?"

"Really. I can't live without him."

"I never figured Daddy for an overlay kink. Please give me some tips."

"It's not like that, Angelica. Please hurry."

She sealed the helmet and floated spread-eagle while the suit adjusted to her body. A green light blinked in the helmet. "I'm ready."

"Grab onto something," Hector said. "We don't have time for a graceful decompression of your cabin."

She'd barely grabbed hold when the hatch popped open. There was nothing to be blown out from the room—they'd seen to that. A row of green lights blinked on the floor.

"Please follow the lights, Angelica. Hurry."

She followed them, but knew they were leading her to the airlock. No need to show her the way. She'd spent hours in front of it, staring and hoping. It opened as she approached.

The outer door was already open. Angelica grabbed a handhold in the airlock and stared. The void always looked so deep firsthand. Even in overlay, with the best rendering, space looked like a distant backdrop. Stage dressing. It was inviting, like the ocean. She'd only visited the ocean once at a daddy's beach house. It was wonderful—and the opposite of the lifeless cold beckoning to her now a meter away.

"Angelica," Hector snapped in her helmet. "Focus. There is a rescue line on the deck. Clip it to your suit. We will use it to reel the capitan back in. Take extra clips for attaching to Gene and points along the outer hull."

The inner airlock door closed. "Shouldn't I be in a real EVA suit?"

"There's no time. And there's no time for chitchat. The emergency suit will keep you alive long enough to perform the rescue."

"Fine." Angelica unreeled a length of cable and clipped it to a ring on her suit. She grabbed extra clips from the cabinet and clipped them to the cable behind her. "Which way?"

"Out."

Angelica scoffed. "No shit?"

"No shit."

"Never mind." She pushed out through the outer door and felt the call of the big black again. Her ears thundered with the sound of her heart; she'd been trained to EVA, but could count the number of times she'd done it on her right thumb.

The stars looked so small. They glittered back at her, giving their permission to join them. It would be easy. She could be like a bird flying away that never had to come back and would never have to worry about mean daddies and their nasty spider-girls and nasty robots.

But Gene needed her. "Which way?"

"There is a small, black dome with an antenna sticking out of it to your left. Move there quickly but carefully, and secure the line to the ring at the bottom of the dome."

Angelica crawled along the hull. Small patches of condensation appeared and disappeared on the bottom of her faceplate in time to her breathing. She took the last clip on the cable and clipped it to the ring.

"Good job, Angelica."

"Are you programmed to talk to me like a child, too?"

"Use the handholds and pull yourself towards the nose of the ship. The hull breach is nearby. Be careful about sharp edges."

"You're so polite when you want something, robot." Angelica pulled herself along with trembling hands. The hull ahead looked like a jagged flower bulb that had burst in a spray of metal shards. Angelica choked back a sob. "Daddy was in there?"

"Yes. I did what I could. But I cannot view in there and the nearest drones are still minutes away. Hurry."

"I am!" Angelica tugged on the cable behind her to make sure it hadn't fouled on anything. Scrambling towards the breach, she ignored the debris that bounced off her helmet. The gloves were thin and her fingers were growing stiff. Careful of the jagged edges, she grabbed the twisted plating and hauled herself into the ruins of operations. Among the floating debris glittered beautiful, red pearls.

"What do you see?" Hector asked.

"It's a disaster in here. But these red things are pretty. Yeah, like little candy drops. Coming from—" A girlish shriek filled her helmet. Daddy was strapped into the tattered remains of his chair, which was only held to the deck by a twisted cable. He was turning slowly in a field of pulsing blood globules. The blood was seeping through the medical foam from the stumps of his arms and legs. A quivering pool of gore swam around his hood.

"Daddy! Daddy! Daddy!"

Hector bellowed in her ear. "Angelica. Do you see the capitan?"

"Yes." Her voice came in gasps. "Oh no-no-no."

"Is he alive?"

"I don't know."

"Secure the rescue line to Daddy and I'll reel him in. Is there anyone else in there alive?"

Angelica looked all around, but she couldn't see anyone else. It was dark and cluttered. And she didn't care about anyone else. "No. I'm hooking the line up now."

Gritting her teeth, she plunged her hand through the blood. Droplets flew in every direction, splattering her visor. She clipped the rescue line to his flightsuit.

When the clip snapped into place, Daddy's stubs started flailing. Angelica recoiled and screamed again. More blood splattered across her visor.

"He's alive!"

"Hurry," Hector said.

Angelica pulled slack from the line. "He's ready. Go."

The line snaked back through the breach. She put her visor against his bubble hood and shouted, "You'll be all right, Daddy. We're getting you inside right away."

His body convulsed and Angelica could hear his muffled scream. But he was stuck in the chair. He was still strapped in. The line was pulling against his suit, but he wasn't budging.

The tension from the rescue line pulling against the straps was preventing her from releasing the latch. She could feel the optic cable between the station and the deck stretch, but it wouldn't give. Her fingers were getting numb and her strength was fading.

"Wait," she gasped. "He's caught on—"

The strap buckle came undone in her hands. She and Daddy were jerked back out of Ops through the breach. A string of tiny, red pearls followed. She screamed again as she flew into space. Had she ever stopped screaming?

Being flung into the outer darkness was not as satisfying as she'd imagined. The line wrapped around her waist and squeezed painfully. Daddy was in front of her, his stubs waggling. The antenna she'd clipped to was approaching fast.

"Reach your arms out wide and catch the antenna," Hector said. "Then unclip the line from it."

It was a struggle. Her arms were sluggish, her fingers frozen. But she unclipped the rescue line. She tried to tell Hector, but her breath would not come. Trying and failing again, she tugged on the cable.

The line pulled her and Daddy along, smearing blood along *Amazonas*'s hull. It seemed almost romantic as her vision wavered. They were sucked into the air like a giant spaghetti noodle. She loved spaghetti.

Pretty lights danced in her vision. Bright red, then bright green. One hatch closed and another opened, but Angelica wasn't sure why. Reaching, clawing hands pawed all over her, pulling her in every direction. She couldn't move.

They pulled Daddy away.

Then there was a light in her face. It hurt, but she couldn't look away.

"Her suit's ripped."

"How'd she get out there?"

"She just saved the capitan."

"Maybe."

"She's not responding. Get her in the bot."

The hands shoved her inside a red robot. She liked red, but not as much as pink. A nice robot should be pink. It kissed her and she took a nap.

"WHY DIDN'T THE SECURITY system detect that bot, Hector?" Diaz would have preferred to ask Bovree instead, but all that remained of him was rapidly evaporating gore in the ruins of operations. Along with Collins, Olivo, Alvarado, and Clarke. "Our internal sensors are supposed to detect intruders of all shapes and sizes. I'm sure that should include explosive, hostile bots."

Hector appeared in the overlay. "I don't know why internal sensors didn't flag the bot or detect its explosive package. Diagnostics are ongoing."

Diaz glared at the avatar. "While you're running diagnostics, Hector, diagnose why you disobeyed me." He'd been acting oddly since the transit through the nexus. She had been convinced the capitan had altered the ship's personality, trying to be funny, but she wasn't so sure now. If not for the situation they were in, she'd order an immediate class-A diag. "I ordered all crew to their shielded stations."

"Angelica is not part of the crew, Commander."

"That's one hell of a rationalization."

"There were no drones close enough to perform the rescue in time. I knew Angelica would be willing and able."

"She's a child."

"Correction, XO. She has the body of a child, but she is nineteen years old and has much more time in space than most of the members of this crew." Hector nodded. "I believe her performance and the capitan's rescue bears out my assessment."

"Your assessment almost got her killed. Her suit was ripped open when you reeled them in."

"Correct."

Diaz let out a breath and turned to scan the damage-control update window that appeared next to her. "How did you know he was alive? All the cameras in Ops were destroyed and his vitals were off-line. I peered through the hatch and he looked dead to me."

"I thought there might be a small chance. I was able to maneuver his command couch to partially shield him from the blast. Though I couldn't see the bot, I could see where Capitan Walsh was pointing and determined there was danger. Unfortunately, everyone else was too close to the blast."

Diaz swept open the log of operations and watched it again. Gene reached for his foot, asked Hector what type of bot it was, then...

"You called him Gene. Did he program you to do that?"

Hector hesitated for a full second longer than usual. "I was trying to get his attention by using his first name instead of his title once I believed there was an immediate threat."

"Any idea how it got aboard?"

"I haven't been able to find it in any security feeds, but it would seem logical it came in the cargo you ordered on board."

"Logical."

"I'm still reviewing the feeds, Commander."

"Show me the feed after the containers are loaded."

A time-lapse video from the cargo compartment appeared, motionless save for occasional drones or crew members racing at accelerated speed. It would look comical, if not for the stack of cryochambers that held Angelica's so-called sisters.

Diaz had to admit that the little vat whore had done well. Hector's appeal to the girl's psychotic conditioning aside, it had been a good bit of EVA. Especially since she was just using emergency gear and her flightsuit.

Seeing the condition Walsh had been in, Diaz wouldn't have done it—regardless of what Hector said.

She stopped the feed and went back. "There. See it?"

"I didn't, Commander." The recording played back and forward several times. "I still don't."

"Right there. Play back at normal speed."

The side of one of the recovered crates split into a network of rods and folded into a twisting puzzle of skittering, mechanical legs. One leg reached into a newly revealed recess and withdrew a metallic cylinder. The other legs attached to the cylinder and, a moment later, she recognized the explosive bot from the Ops video before it had crawled out of sight.

Diaz paused the video. "Still nothing?"

"Sorry, Commander."

Going back on the recording, she highlighted the crate. "It's right there, unfolding like scaffolding. Scan this timestamp every-way you can. If you can't detect this thing, we've got a big problem."

"I can detect a change in the container's external form, but I cannot determine the cause. I have to assume the bot is using some sort of detection countermeasures."

"It's not affecting the raw video, or I couldn't see it."

"Agreed. Whatever it is must be affecting my processor, not the sensor."

She played the video feed and watched it for several minutes. "*Mierda.*"

"Commander?"

"Two more of those things just skittered across the field of view when someone opened the hatch. All three of them got out."

"In that case, we must assume our security bots can't detect them, either. The crew will have to make a compartment-by-compartment search."

"Secure all hatches immediately, including all maintenance accesses. The other two—or however many more there are—might be waiting for access into other priority spaces. There's no telling where they got off to while the crew was going to stations." Diaz snorted. "Maybe one will waste its bomb on the gate drive. Get your diagnostics started, Hector, and print out nine combat suits."

She scrolled through the duty roster and clucked her tongue. "And print out one for the chimp. I have a feeling we'll want him on the security team."

"Because he's expendable?"

"No, *pendejo*! He's faster than most of the crew and the bots probably weren't programmed with chimp-spoofing abilities." She frowned at Hector's avatar. "Expendable, indeed. Are you interpreting my scowl, Hector?"

"Yes, Commander. My apologies. It was not my intent to offend."

"Carry on."

"Yes, Commander." Hector blinked out of the virtual room.

Diaz spared a moment to pull vitals on Walsh's remains. That was the only way she could think of the gasping chunk of raw meat Angelica had pulled from Ops. He was in an armored medical station with the doctor strapped in nearby attending to the medical bots. The vitals were unstable. She was no doctor, but she'd been around long enough; there was no way the capitan was going to make it. How would Angelica take his death?

"Don't be so hard on Hector, XO," Moore said. "I thought you picked Screwy as a redshirt, too."

"Have you reviewed the footage?"

"Yes, ma'am. They remind me of those anti-theft bots in maritime warehouses."

"How would it know to go to Ops?"

"If the Liberty class are designed as Nova killers, these bots would probably have a full internal layout. That compartment has been Ops for a long, long time."

"And the explosives? Why didn't we detect them?"

Moore shrugged. "Maybe the CDF cooked up something to spoof the EPL chem-sniffers. They had access to several different worlds. Maybe they had some new compound we still don't know about since we're stuck in Sol. *Were* stuck in Sol. If we could examine one of those bots in detail, we might find out."

Diaz glanced at the armor-production window: almost done. "Do you think it would be worth the risk?"

"Depends if we plan on any more scavenging. And that depends on how long we'll be here."

Diaz sighed. "*Dios mio.* I guess we'd better try to take one intact. Now everyone is going to think I'm redshirting the chimp."

Chapter 44

SCREWBALL THRUST HIS laser pistol through the hatch to Power and Propulsion and scanned the area beyond through the sights. Seeing nothing, he hooted twice and pulled himself into the next compartment. The rest of the PnP section—the hot, radioactive part with the reactor and main thruster—was at the far end of an armored gantry to keep it away from the main hull. Screwball hoped they wouldn't have to go there.

The newly printed armor was better than a pair of skivvies, but it was too tight around his shoulders despite Hector's measurements. "Clear."

He could see Robertson and Munez in his overlay float in behind him, their lasers at the ready. They sealed the hatch to make sure no bots sneaked out behind their search party. It felt like being locked in a cage with a hungry monster.

Screwball scanned the compartment again and looked at Robertson. Robertson shrugged and motioned to the hatch to Secondary Fabrication. Screwball aimed his laser into every recess and panel.

He hooted. "It could be anywhere!"

"Relax, Cadet," Robertson said. "Slow and careful. Mind your corners. Are we clear?"

Screwball took a breath and nodded. "Clear."

Robertson motioned to the next hatch. "Next compartment."

The stencil on the hatch read "Primary Bot Charging and Storage." Screwball shook his head. Viewing the compartment via the overlay showed it was empty, but supposedly the ship couldn't see the bombs. That's why Ops was full of jellied crewmen. He'd liked Collins; he had been funny.

The compartment was empty. As were the next two. Screwball's stomach clenched each time he opened a hatch. Each new space increased the chances of finding an intruder. They were out there. He'd seen the footage.

Screwball jumped when a hand fell on his shoulder.

Munez smiled down at him. "Relax, shipmate. You're going to pass out if you keep hyperventilating."

With a series of low hoots, Screwball caught his breath. He nodded and slipped into the next compartment. A bot turned its sensor cluster towards him, just two meters away.

"Contact! Contact!" He snapped up the laser pistol and squeezed the trigger until the bot—and several centimeters of hull behind it—erupted in sparks and flames.

"Cease fire! Cease fire!" Robertson shouted over the comm.

The bot shuddered and drifted away from the bulkhead; one of the severed legs still held on.

Munez laughed and grabbed the bot out of the air. "That bot won't be hurting anyone. Of course, it won't be fixing anything, either." He tapped the small scorched plate that read "*Amazonas*" and laughed again. "You may have to read the eulogy for your fallen comrade."

"All the bots are supposed to be forward," Screwball said.

Robertson finished his sweep of the room. "We can't understand chimpanzee, Cadet."

"What?"

"You were shrieking in, uh, simian? Right before you started shooting."

Screwball could feel the heat rising in his face and on his ass. He was glad his uniform covered the latter. "Atavism. Sorry, Lieutenant."

"No worries, Cadet." Robertson glanced around nervously and grinned. "You're not the only one who screams when terrified. Just try to scream in Spanglish next time."

Screwball barked a short laugh. "Yes, sir. Clear."

He pushed off the deck to the next hatch, which opened to a heat exchanger for the life-support system. He peered through the tiny port; there was no sign of bots—friendly or otherwise. Maybe their team had been lucky and none of the bomb-bots were in their search...

Screwball caught his breath. "Contact," he whispered, pointing through the portal. "There, against the upper condenser."

"Definitely," Robertson whispered after peering over Screwball's shoulder. "Contact confirmed. Carry on as planned. We'll open the hatch and push you through just enough. Hit the tail between the bulb and the main body. Easy. Ready?"

Screwball nodded, grabbed his laser in both hands, and shook his head. "How do we know it won't go off? It might have some kind of dead chimp's switch."

Robertson and Munez exchanged glances and shrugged.

"I guess we don't," said Munez. "But that's what Hector thinks will work."

"He can't even see the damned thing!" Screwball said. "If it does go off while I'm partway through the hatch, the pressure wave will cut me in half!" He played with his lip as he thought. The armor would protect him from the vacuum, but the gory vision of the ruined Ops compartment filled his mind.

"You're the fastest one of us," Munez said. "And the ship's bots can't see that thing."

Screwball looked at Robertson. "Hey, you said the capitan made a wall with those restrainer pistols, right?"

"Yeah, so?"

"Hector," Screwball said. "If we pelt that thing with restrainer pistols, will the hardened foam dampen the explosion? Would it isolate the bot's body if the bomb exploded?"

"Running simulations now, Cadet." Hector was silent for several seconds. "If you are able to get a sufficient number of shots on target quickly, I believe it may work. It will also have the added benefit of directing the explosion outward and sealing the breach."

"And not blowing my head off," the chimp added.

"Sound good to you, XO?" Robertson asked.

"Proceed," Diaz answered. "If it doesn't work, we stick to the original plan."

Robertson patted Screwball on the back. "Hector, send us up two restrainer pistols. And an emergency airlock—just in case."

Two crewmen from Maintenance delivered the restrainer pistols and airlock, then stood by somberly, pistols drawn.

Robertson handed both pistols to Screwball. "All right. Same basic plan: we slip you in, hold your feet, and jerk you back out after you've glued that sucker to the bulkhead."

"That still leaves my head at risk of getting blown up, but one of us primates has to stand up." He laughed and slaved the new pistols' sights to his overlay vision. With a final nervous snort, he nodded at Robertson and Munez.

They grabbed his feet and unlocked the hatch. With a final thumbs-up from Munez, Screwball was shoved through the hatch. He brought his pistols to bear on the upper condenser.

"It's not there!"

Robertson cursed over the comm. "Find it!"

"I can't!"

"On the outer bulkhead!" Munez yelled. "By the exchanger conduit!"

The conduit glowed red in Screwball's vision and he saw a bulbous silhouette. He thrust his arms forward and pumped shot after shot. Blasts of foam expanded and encased the bot and the bulkhead around it. Screwball was jerked back through the hatch, screaming uncontrollably.

The hatch slammed Screwball's helmet. He twirled in the air between Robertson and Munez.

Munez reached out and tapped Screwball's helmet. "Head's in good shape, man."

"Can't say the same for your face, though," Robertson said, grabbing the overhead to stop his spin. "Looks like it worked. The foam protected the rest of the bot. Let's secure that thing before it digs its way through the hull."

HECTOR TURNED TO DIAZ and expanded one of the video feeds. "After being able to physically examine the intruder, we discovered the outer skin has a series of sophisticated signal generators. It confused my graphical-interface processors, essentially rendering the intruders invisible to my optical processors."

Diaz pursed her lips. "Your processors have been updated countless times since thos bots were in use."

"That is correct, Commander. But the essential hardware remains the same, as is the case with most software-defined updates. This stealth system works because of my hardware limitations." Hector shrugged. "And it was fine-tuned for EPL ships. I don't believe it would have affected any of the newer ships in the fleet."

"Lucky us. Can you fix it?"

"Already done, Commander. I have added a known quantity-error variance into the optical processors to achieve additional checksum monitoring. The Engineering team has also added an external filtering processor for redundancy, one that the CDF couldn't have programmed for."

Diaz nodded and finished reviewing the report from the other search team. "Screwball made a good call. When Barrows shot the bomb off the other bot, it exploded. Dr. Barnes says her limb replacement will go smoothly. Unlike the capitan's."

She ran fingers through her tonsure. Feeling a step behind in every situation was becoming tiring. It was like constantly remembering something important a second too late. Being XO left her feeling the same way, but now it was all on her. "Anything on the explosives?"

"There was enough residue in Cadet Screwball's foam for a highly detailed analysis. It is partly composed of a substance discovered on Delta Pavonis III. It has a low reactivity factor and was never listed as a hazardous material. The CDF must have figured a way to combine it with benign petrochemicals, which make up most of the rest of the trace elements. I have now added the substance to the dangerous materials database and it will be detected in subsequent encounters."

Diaz stared at the meaningless chemical display, brainstorming silently until Dr. Barnes appeared in the virtual room. "Yes, Doctor?"

"I'm ready to revive the CO."

"Do you think he's ready?" Diaz asked.

"Oh, do you think he isn't?"

Diaz sniffed. "Sorry. It just seems like a short recovery time."

"In your expert opinion?"

"I'm not a doctor, but I am the XO. And I've been around long enough to know it takes time to print limbs. And I know the capitan's limbs were shredded. And I know that you'd better damned well secure your attitude and answer my question. Doctor. Just like PnP answers my questions. Just like Fabrication. Just like Maintenance."

Dr. Barnes stared at her for a moment and let out a breath. "Sorry, XO. I was kind of trying to be funny, but I know you're probably not in the joking mood. You're right, his limbs aren't close to being ready. But he's stable enough to be brought up. I have a set of AI-assisted prosthetics ready to go."

"And Angelica? In your professional opinion?" Diaz enjoyed the flash of embarrassment on the doctor's face. Barnes was Walsh's friend, not hers.

Barnes held up his hands. "Point made, XO. I've already apologized. Yes, she's awake and still under observation. Minor abrasions and tissue damage from her asphyxiation and vacuum exposure. Her full recovery will be quick."

"Don't release her yet. Or revive the capitan. In fact, I need you to kill him."

Chapter 45

DIAZ FLOATED AT THE foot of the med-bed and smiled down at the girl. "*Hola*, Angelita. How are you feeling after your little adventure?"

Angelica returned the smile, though it didn't touch her eyes. She continually shifted in her bed as if there was some minor hurt in her back. The ruddiness in her cheeks stood out like blush against her porcelain complexion. Angelica's hands were folded in her lap and her expression was one of pointed boredom.

"I'm well, *abuela*. Thanks."

Diaz bit back the urge to respond to being called grandma. She had called the vat whore worse. "Excellent. That was a very brave thing you did. Dangerous, even foolish. But I'm sure the capitan would be proud of your attempt to save him."

"Well, someone had to save something besides their own ass, Fiddlin' Felicia. Did you want Daddy to die? Is that why you left him there?"

"About... the capitan," Diaz started.

Angelica sat upright in her bed. "Wait. What do you mean 'attempt' to save him? I *did* save him." She glanced between Diaz and Barnes, tears beginning to float in the corners of her eyes. "Didn't I?"

Diaz looked at Barnes, who looked away.

"I don't think the girl needs to see, XO."

"See what?"

Diaz reached down and took Angelica's hand. "You did the best you could, Angelita. There was nothing else you could have done. The explosion was terrible."

"See what?" Angelica pulled her hand from Diaz's grip and pounded the railing of her med-bed. "See what?"

"The capitan... Gene... didn't make it. There was just too much damage and blood loss. He died like everyone else in Ops." Diaz choked back a sob.

It wasn't part of the performance. They had all died because of her own incompetence.

Angelica's eyes widened and her lips began to quiver. "I don't believe you, Felicia." She spoke the name with a sneer. "I want to see Daddy. Now!"

Diaz dabbed away a tear before nodding to Barnes. The doctor pulled aside a curtain to reveal a transparent body bag attached to the bulkhead. Walsh's slack face and ragged stumps pressed against the plastic. Ugly purple bruises covered the body and ran up the side of his neck. Lifeless eyes stared out at them. Dr. Barnes pulled the curtain back in place to hide the body.

Angelica shrieked, jerking against her restraints and slapping Diaz's hands away. "You let him die! You wanted to be capitan! That's why you didn't rescue him. Hector told me so. It was you. It was you! You were fiddling while Daddy died! Just like they all say about you."

Diaz hooked her feet into a nearby handhold for purchase and clasped the girl's wrists. Angelica had the leverage from being strapped into the bed and pulled Diaz free from her foothold. Getting her feet against the bulkhead, Diaz pushed and pinned Angelica's wrists to the bed.

"He was dead already. Can't you see it? You couldn't have saved him. I couldn't have saved him." The lie burned in her mouth. The girl had saved Gene. And Diaz could have, too.

"You didn't want to save him!" Angelica's accusation went from screaming to an unintelligible keening, before she finally collapsed into sobbing.

Diaz cautiously released the girl's wrists. Angelica wrapped her arms around Diaz's neck and pulled her towards the bed. Diaz tensed and made ready to push away, but Angelica merely buried her face in Diaz's shoulder.

Diaz could feel the tears and relaxed. After a moment, she returned the embrace to comfort the girl. Angelica's tears and snot quickly soaked Diaz's flightsuit. Diaz held the girl, stroking her hair and gently hushing her. She tried not to think about Collins, Bovree, and the others who'd died in the explosion. She would not start crying on the vat whore's shoulder.

But she did. She didn't care that Barnes was nearby. Angelica muttered something unintelligible into Diaz's shoulder.

Diaz swallowed hard and took two deep breaths to get control of herself. She rubbed the tears from her eyes on the girl's shoulder as inconspicuously as possible before pulling away. "What?"

"Can I see him? Just one more time?"

Barnes spoke gently. "I don't think that would be appropriate. Or helpful."

"Please?" Angelica stared up at Diaz. "Please?"

Diaz nodded to Barnes and he slid the curtain back enough to reveal Walsh's face and one ruined shoulder.

Angelica stared for a moment and snorted. "I guess he's not all that much now."

"I guess not," said Diaz.

"Just a buyer. Just a dead buyer." Angelica smirked and looked at Barnes. "He looks kind of stupid now. You can cover it back up."

Barnes glanced at Diaz before pulling the curtain back into place. "Is she ready to return to her quarters, Doctor?"

"Sure thing, XO. She's as good as new."

Angelica squealed. "Ohh, I'm a virgin again? Are you going to lock me up again, Felicia?"

"Yes," Diaz said. "In our current situation and the incident with Yuloo—"

"That old skank can keep him. Can I have my drawing stuff back?"

The girl's tears were gone and her tone was once again bored. It gave Diaz hope that the ploy had worked. But she couldn't believe she'd cried on the girl's shoulder. It was more vat-whore voodoo.

"Paper and pencils only. I'll have them dropped by. Doctor, go ahead and have her escorted to her quarters."

Diaz and Barnes floated in silence as two medical techs detached Angelica's med-bed and took it away.

Once they were alone, Barnes cleared his throat. "Do you think that whole production was necessary?"

Diaz shrugged. "Maybe not, but it looks like it worked. It's hard to know how a vat whore thinks."

"Even after the obvious shock of seeing Gene, no compassion for her?" Barnes shook his head. "It's a psychologically programmed compulsion and it's very real to her, regardless of your opinion of her."

"She has no more feeling than Hector. It's all programming, even if they believe it. If Hector were to say the same, I'd know someone had tampered with his code. Just like what happened to her."

Diaz pushed off the wall and caught a handhold near Barnes. "What I want to know is what she meant by 'fiddling.'"

Barnes turned to one of his medical scanners. "I don't know what you mean."

"Is that how you're going to play it? Really?"

"Probably just something she overheard."

"Since you grinned when she said it, I suspect you know exactly what she meant and where she heard it."

"There's no way of telling how many people she heard it from, XO."

"Heard what, Doctor?"

"As much as you like to eavesdrop, I figured you knew."

She took a breath, tired of the game. Barnes held up a hand to cut off her rising tirade.

"It's your nickname, XO. Fiddlin' Felicia. Though there's some debate if it should be Second-Fiddle Felicia."

"What?"

"Some prefer Backseat Diaz—as in backseat driver, not a lascivious teen. I don't care for that one personally." Barnes stared at her for a moment. "Others call you Angry Granny."

Diaz could feel the heat rising in her face. Crews always had nicknames for their superiors; she'd come up with some zingers in her time, too. But Fiddling Felicia? "That's... that's..."

"Insubordination?"

"Exactly!"

"Well, you should know, XO."

"What's that supposed to mean?"

Barnes raised his eyebrows, obviously mocking her. "You don't know?"

She narrowed her eyes. "Tell me. Now."

"Aye aye, Commander. You may have your own good reasons for not liking Gene and that's certainly your prerogative. But he's earned the respect of the rest of the crew, including me. And the crew, including me, are quite aware of your constant sideways comments and glances at him. Whenever you come into the same compartment, he tenses up. I've even taken his bio readings. He hides it as best as he can, but it's obvious to everyone in Ops. At least, it was."

Diaz opened her mouth to answer but Barnes held up his hand again. "Stow it, XO. I'm not done. The saddest part of it is that he must really see something in you to put up with it. If one of my subordinates treated me that way in front of the team, they wouldn't be one my subordinates for long. They'd be out on their ass. I'd have thrown you out on your ass already."

Diaz stared back. Had she been that blatant? It was true that she didn't like Walsh's lighthearted style or how he'd handled that *puta* Midland. He was soft, not what a crew of cadets needed. Especially not in their current situation across the galaxy. She'd told him as much face-to-face. But she'd kept her promise to be respectful in front of the crew, hadn't she?

"For all that," Barnes continued, "the crew still like you. And so do I. You're a good XO, a good spacer. But if you're aiming for an ugly divorce from Gene, you're going to lose the kids."

Diaz looked away from Barnes and stared at the bulkhead. The doctor took a breath as if to say something, but instead watched her silently. After a minute, he floated towards the capitan.

Diaz turned and watched as Barnes slid Walsh from the body bag and strapped him into a nearby med-bed. With a flick of his fingers, holographic displays appeared in virtual reality over the body. There was no movement—all the vitals were bottomed out.

"He's ready."

Diaz nodded. "Once you verify Angelica is secured, do it. How long once you start?"

"At least three hours. I want to take it slow." He lifted a gel roller from the bed and swiped it across Walsh's head. "Then I'll prep for the prosthetics. His limbs are a wreck and need some skeletal reconstruction before he can use replacements or bio-prints."

"Let me know when I can talk to him."

Diaz drifted to her cabin, avoiding the eyes of every crew member she passed and leaving every greeting unanswered. Each one she passed left her wondering if they called her Fiddlin' Felicia or Backseat Diaz. She liked Angry Granny and didn't care if anyone called her bitch or *puta*; that came with the job.

But Second Fiddle? They thought she was hiding behind Walsh. They thought she was a coward. She locked her cabin hatch.

"Hector, no messages unless there's an emergency. Relay to the Ops-O that she has command."

"Yes, Commander."

She sighed. "Compile a selection of video clips of interactions between the capitan and I."

A window appeared in Diaz's overlay. "Done, Commander."

Her stomach clenched tighter with each clip Hector presented. Barnes was right. Even when she wasn't making some remark that Gene chose to ignore, the disdain on her face when she was behind his back was blatant.

Gene might not have seen, but everyone else did.

She could see the furtive glances between crew members and at her when she made her remarks, sighs, or faces. Did her brows really go that high?

Yes... yes they did.

"Ah, *Conejita*," her grandmother said from ages ago and light-years away, "the most bitter fruits in life, we grow ourselves."

Chapter 46

"WELCOME BACK, GENE."

Walsh's vision blurred as the retinal filters in his overlay rig recalibrated after being shut down for a week. Once complete, the filters measured his discomfort response and dimmed the incoming light accordingly.

Walsh coughed when he tried to speak and swallowed before trying again. "Thanks, Doc. Were you recycling coolant in my mouth while I was out?"

"No, sir. That's your documented clinical halitosis. You've merely been fortunate enough to be unconscious and not smelling it." Dr. Barnes smiled and waved a medi-wand over Walsh's eyes. "Go slow. Just look around and let your overlay calibrate. You've been out for a while."

"What happened? It must have been some fiesta. I don't..." Neither arm moved when he tried to rub his eyes. He looked at his right arm and his stomach clenched. The stump of his arm was capped with a cybernetic cuff. He looked up at Barnes. "What the..."

Barnes returned a sympathetic smile and nodded to Walsh's other arm. Walsh slowly turned his head.

"One hell of a fiesta," he whispered. Walsh stared at one arm, then the other. Trying to lift his legs, he gasped when his truncated legs barely lifted the blanket.

Barnes pulled the blanket aside to reveal the even stumps of his legs, each capped with gleaming white cybernetic sockets.

Walsh swallowed loudly. "What the fuck happened?"

"I'll leave the details to Diaz. She's told you some already, but I had to put you back into a medical coma." Barnes shrugged. "That was my fault. I thought you were ready for the procedure."

"Can you give me a rundown?"

Barnes hiked his thumb over his shoulder at a set of prosthetic limbs on a medi-cart attached to the overhead. "Trust me, Gene. Go slow. You'll get the details soon enough. For now, let's try these on for size. Are you up for it?"

Walsh clenched his teeth against the rising panic that stole his breath. He wanted to scream and flail his... his... his stubs until Barnes told him what had happened. A medical sensor above the med-bed beeped.

"Take it easy, Gene. We can wait."

Walsh swallowed hard and let out several long breaths until the waves of terror from seeing his stumps receded. Knowing what had happened probably wouldn't help. He knew his limbs could be bio-printed and that Barnes must have a good reason to use the prosthetics. It was one thing to know limb replacements would be grown; it was a completely different thing to see his arms and legs were missing. Especially since he didn't know where they'd gone.

Barnes glanced up at the display as the alarm cleared. "We can still wait. You're still processing the loss. Grieving it is natural. And it will get worse even after your prints are attached. You've undergone a terrible trauma. I won't be releasing you for a while. We have time."

"No. Let's put them on. I'm not sure what to do."

"I'll tell you. Mostly you'll just sit there and tell me how it feels."

"Let's get started, then."

Barnes nodded and unstrapped the alabaster white arm from the cart. There were no visible mechanics or electronics on its smooth surface. Walsh stared at the lithe fingers, so unlike his own. Barnes swiped a finger in the air and Walsh felt his restraints tighten.

"Sorry, I need you to be as stable as possible." Barnes planted his feet in a handhold and lined the arm up with the cuff on Walsh's arm stub. "This will feel strange when the synaptic-alignment protocol fires up."

Walsh felt the push on his shoulder, followed by a loud whine and click as the arm locked in place. Electric fire ran up from his fingertips.

"If by strange you mean ow-ow-ow, then you're right."

"Good. That means it's working."

Walsh grimaced as the elbow and wrist joints rolled into alignment and the synthetic muscles twitched. Pain continued to flare up through the arm—his arm—causing his shoulder to spasm. He was about to protest when the pain vanished and the arm stilled, hanging above him in the zero-g.

"Try moving your fingers."

Walsh watched in fascination as the fingers that were his, but not his, wriggled at the end of his new arm. "That's damned weird."

"Do you want to do the next one or do you need a rest?"

"Let's get it done." Walsh rolled his new wrist and bent his new elbow. "Hey, can you put arms on my legs? Screwball does pretty well."

Barnes smiled. "It'd be possible, but not on the *Amazonas*. We just have cuffs with standard mapping. You'd need translators to get full control of a foot-hand. No wings or tentacles, either."

"Are you making bio-prints?"

"Done. But I'll have to take you out of commission again for a longer time for the grafting, and the physical training lasts longer than calibrating the cybernetics." Barnes nodded towards the hatch. "I thought you might want to talk to Diaz before deciding. I'm to let her know when you're ready to talk."

"All the ship's doctors and all the ship's men, couldn't put the capitan back together again." Walsh chuckled. "Let's finish and call her down."

DIAZ FLOATED IN TWO hours later. "How are you?"

Walsh wriggled his mechanical fingers at her. "Everything's working... except my system access. What the hell's going on? What happened?"

Diaz's eyes were red, either from exhaustion or crying. "Sorry about that, Gene. We decided it was best for your recovery if you didn't try to access the ship's logs."

"We?"

"Me and Dr. Barnes. He says you don't remember, but the last time we talked about what happened you didn't respond very well."

Walsh held up his new hands. "Will someone tell me what happened? Something? I have no idea what happened."

"That's normal for head trauma."

"Head trauma?"

"Well," Diaz said, "everything trauma, really. Doc says you're ready. Do you want the long or short story?"

"Short for now. I can watch the reports later."

Diaz sighed. "The short of it is that I brought three CDF crates aboard and each had a sabotage bot hidden in them. They were designed to be invisible to internal sensors and were equipped with an unknown explosive compound from Delta Pavonis, so they were not detected. One made it to Ops and detonated and the rest were neutralized."

Walsh glanced around at the empty med-beds. "Was anyone else... hurt?"

"Barrows lost her arm hunting them down." Diaz looked away. "But in Ops... Collins. Olivo. Alvarado. Clarke. And Bovree. All KIA."

"Shit," he whispered. "Shit. Shit." Walsh squeezed his eyes shut for several minutes, thankful there was no overlay image in his head. They sat in silence for several minutes while he grappled with the news. Not Bovree.

He sighed heavily. "I'm glad you were there for the ship. Too bad you weren't in charge in Sol. They'd be alive now."

"No one would be alive now if you hadn't saved us from the Cali attack. I was the one who let the bots on board."

"I'm sorry. We shouldn't even be here."

Diaz shook her head. "No, I'm sorry, Gene. I'm a sorry XO and a sorry friend. I've spent the entire cruise riding your back and disrespecting your command. The XO supports the CO in public, no matter what."

"I made it hard to do that by blowing you off."

"No, you didn't blow me off. You listened and disagreed. I decided to make you pay like the spiteful little *puta* I am. The crew will be glad you're back."

Walsh grinned. "Well, for the time being, you're still the commanding *puta*."

Diaz laughed and wiped at her eyes. "You need to stop malingering and take this soda can back."

"I just need to get my feet back on." Walsh wriggled his toes beneath the covers and they both burst out laughing. "What's the ship's status, Capitan?"

Diaz snorted. "Hull integrity is normal. No progress on fixing the black box, but we've been sending out drones looking for nexus generator parts and other supplies in the debris field.

"The fighting was fierce. Many of these ships were wrecks before the shockwave from the gate hit them. I don't think the Colonials expected the gate to blow like that—at least, not on this end. It's a floating graveyard out there. The pickings are slim."

Walsh shook his head. "Like two people holding the same stick of dynamite and expecting only the other guy to explode. Good thinking on looking for parts. No telling how long we'll be stuck here."

Diaz waved off the comment, but made no reply.

Walsh watched in fascination while he flexed his cyber-fingers. "I'm sure it's in the report, but how did I make it out of Ops?"

"Hector tricked Angelica into doing a flight suit-only EVA, and she pulled you back in through hab-Alpha's airlock." Diaz glanced upwards and spoke louder. "I think it disobeyed orders, but I'm not sure."

"Thanks, Hector."

"You're welcome, Capitan," answered a tinny voice from the ship's speakers.

"About that," Diaz said. "We sort of convinced her you're dead. I've got her restricted to her quarters so she won't see you again. I'm not sure how she'd react."

"I'd think she'd celebrate," Walsh said.

Dr. Barnes spoke up. "I'm not sure, Gene. It was a brilliant idea. I think Diaz wiped away Angelica's compulsion towards you. She dispelled that magic spell you had over the girl."

Walsh glared at him.

Barnes held up his hands. "Just kidding. I wasn't sure about the whole thing, but I think it worked. And you looked pretty dead."

"Could you clear the space, Doc?" Diaz asked.

With a final glance at the displays floating over Walsh, Barnes waved his hand and they disappeared. He floated out of Medical and sealed the hatch behind him.

Diaz glanced upwards. "When I say Hector disobeyed me, it was because I ordered everyone to stations."

"Of course."

She let out a long breath. "I ordered the hatch to Ops sealed by Damage Control. I... wasn't going to save you, Gene. I thought you were dead. Your overlay was disconnected and I couldn't be sure, but I wasn't going to risk it. If it weren't for Hector—and Angelita—you'd be dead."

Walsh started to speak, but Diaz held up her hand. "And before you say you'd have done the same, I know that. But I accused you of making rationalizations when you told me your story. And now I've done the same. What I said was uncalled for, and I'm so sorry."

Walsh reached out and took her hand. It was soft and warm, but it felt strange through his cyber-senses. Bionic regulators kept him from crushing her fingers. It would take time to get used to these new hands.

"Tabula rasa."

Diaz smiled. "Amigos?"

"Amigos."

She pulled her hand free from his grip.

"Oh, sorry about that." Walsh held up his hands. "These things have minds of their own. Anyway, I've got a lot to catch up on and you've got a Nova-class battle cruiser to command until I'm done."

Chapter 47

SCREWBALL CLUTCHED a meal pouch in each foot while he floated down the passage. He liked zero-g; flying from handhold to handhold was how it would feel to swing through the trees. Not the cramped, artificial trees in the lab habitat, but the huge ones in the forests where whole families could leap and climb through the trees. As long as *Amazonas* was operating near the debris field, Diaz would keep the habitats spun down and retracted.

He stopped and released the food packets to drift down the passage. When they were about five meters ahead, he pushed off and snatched them out of the air with his feet. He hooted in laughter and reached out to catch a handhold.

"I'm here with food, Hector."

"Very well, Cadet. Remember to keep the conversation to a minimum and don't speak about the capitan." The lock light flashed green and the hatch slid open.

Screwball flipped to enter feetfirst.

Angelica looked up from her sketch pad and beamed. "My monkey! You've come to feed me. Can you hang out for a while?"

Screwball tossed one food packet to her and shook the one in his other foot. "Sorry, I have other deliveries. A cadet's work is never done. What are you drawing now?"

Angelica tilted her sketch. "Planets. Stars. Comets. Flowers. All things spacey."

"Flowers?"

"A spaceship should have flowers." Angelica grabbed the food package and stuck it to the bulkhead. "We do have an aeroponics bay, so I guess that counts." She leveled her gaze at Screwball.

He hooted once. "What?"

"Why are you avoiding me? I thought we were friends."

"I'm not avoiding you. You're confined to quarters, is all. Everyone's ass-es are red after the fighting and the bomb. I'd love to be able to hang out still." Screwball shrugged and headed for the hatch. "I've got to go."

"I miss you, monkey. Come by when you can, please."

Screwball waved and closed the hatch behind him with his free foot. He hated seeing her so lonely and locked up, almost as much as he hated lying. Dishonesty came so easily to humans and gibbons, but it seemed he was just as capable of deceit. A case of nature versus nurture?

His next stop was the Bravo-habitat computer lab. Peeking into the compartment, he saw Burton Mahoney plugged into his creepy headset and immersion couch. The intuitive—which Screwball considered an up-lifted human—hadn't left his station since the black box was destroyed.

And Diaz had let him. Screwball figured it was because there wasn't much else to do except wait for a rescue. The crew was split on what they should be doing, but he was still learning about fleet tribal politics so most-ly kept his opinions to himself.

Delivering food was more interesting than manning the magazine or monitoring the auxiliary battery system. He got to swing around and talk to people face-to-face. The overlay was amazing, but it made everyone mere avatars of themselves. No one had a scent in virtual reality.

He shut the hatch. "Here's some num-nums, Mahoney."

Mahoney remained motionless for over a minute before reaching up and slowly lifting his face mask. "Hey, Screwy."

"You need to eat. All that time plugged in can't be good for you." He sent the food packet spinning towards Mahoney.

"Not much else to do," Mahoney said as he reached out to catch the sil-ver packet. "Since we solve the gates or get stuck here forever. Not that I can solve some four-hundred-year-old mystery on my own. I haven't been very intuitive so far."

"Someone will come get us."

"That's what a lot of people are hoping."

Screwball rummaged in his ear with a finger. "So, have you seen, or felt, or whatever, anything?"

"It's like that creepy feeling of being watched. I'd rather do a maintenance shift where I would actually be doing something." He shrugged and slurped from the pouch.

"But you are feeling something?"

Mahoney snorted. "Yeah, that we need to go through the gate. No shit, right? Some special power they gave me."

"Maybe you should tell Diaz or your div-O. They might have some ideas."

"They already know we should go through the gate. That's what we're all trying to do. They need to know how."

"Tell them your power said so. Maybe they'll know something you don't."

"It's not a power."

Screwball scratched his ear. "You just called it a power."

"It's not a power. I'm like you, a lab freak. At least you're entertaining."

Screwball looked at Mahoney for a moment and pulled himself back to the hatch.

"Wait, wait. I'm sorry, Screwball. I didn't mean it like that. Hey, come back."

Screwball glanced over his shoulder and saw Mahoney struggling to get out of his immersion couch. There was no point in waiting, though. The human was probably speaking out of his frustration, and Screwball understood that. And his human lab-experiment counterpart was probably tired of being compared to the uplifted chimp. Even if no one actually spoke the words, it was easy to see they were both given the same kinds of looks by some. Mahoney was probably even more aware of it with his enhanced intuition.

Unlike Mahoney, however, Screwball knew he'd never truly be part of the crew; no matter how entertaining he was. What else was a poor, uplifted chimp to do?

Carry on carrying on, the fleet way. He forgave Mahoney and decided to help him out, anyway. Screwball pulled himself towards the main hull and to Medical.

He opened the hatch and saw Capitan Walsh exercising shiny white hands. The capitan's eyes were staring into the overlay. Screwball hooted.

Walsh blinked and glanced over. "Cadet. Good to see you."

"Are you taking visitors, sir?"

"Come on in." Walsh wriggled his fingers at Screwball. "As long as my new upgrades don't disturb you too much."

Screwball beamed and tapped his skull. "Hardware doesn't bother me, sir."

"Did you just come down to visit the old man?"

"Maybe I should take it somewhere else, or mind my own business, Capitan, but it's Mahoney."

"Oh?"

"His power, or talent, or whatever is telling him something. But he doesn't want to report it."

Walsh pursed his lips. "Maybe he thinks it's a false lead? He knows his business better than I do."

"He believes it, sir. He thinks it's stupid; a no-brainer. We're supposed to go through the gate."

Walsh chuckled. "Well, that is the goal. To get home."

Screwball hooted—Mahoney was right. "Sorry, Capitan. I shouldn't have said anything."

"No, no. I'll see it gets followed up on. How's the *Amazonas* treating you? I watched the footage of you taking out that bot. Good job, Cadet."

"Thank you, Capitan. I'm glad you're doing well, and I'm sorry about what happened."

Walsh nodded. "We'll get home, Cadet. And you'll help us do it."

Screwball wasn't so sure.

Chapter 48

"THROUGH THE GATE," Diaz said. "Just like Mahoney said."

Walsh zoomed in on the overhead view of the ever-updating debris-field map. "Apparently. I wouldn't have seen it."

"I might not have made the extrapolation without your input, Capitan," Hector said. "The trace perturbations are so minuscule, the chances of them being missed are quite high." Three glowing lines appeared in the debris-field display. "But these are distinct. The spin and motion of the detritus in these paths are indicative of repeated ejections of reaction mass for an indeterminable amount of time."

"And all paths point to that asteroid on the other side of the gate," Diaz said.

Hector zoomed them over the distant asteroid. "Correcting for orbital drift, yes. Exploring this option, I've also discovered that two of the remaining relay satellites transmit marginally stronger signals towards the asteroid. Long exposure scans also reveal well-masked thermal signatures. It would have been months before it became an object of interest."

"In that case, I'm designating it 'Very Interesting Object.'" Diaz swiped a finger through the asteroid's image and its new title appeared above it—VIO. "One million klicks. Someone wanted to keep their distance but remain in a nearby orbit."

Walsh nodded. "Vio. I like it. I'll write up a commendation for Mahoney—and talk to him about his reluctance to share information. I think Interesting is a prime suspect for whatever the CDF used to kill the gates."

"It will likely be defended if that's the case, Capitan," Hector said.

"Agreed." Walsh turned to Diaz. "You'll have to approach ready for a fight."

Diaz raised her brows. "Me?"

"The *Amazonas* is yours until further notice, Capitan. She was barely mine to begin with and you've been handling her well in my convalescence."

"Capitan—"

Walsh held up his hand. "You are the capitan. Hector, note that Commander Diaz is CO until further notice."

"Yes, Commander Walsh."

Diaz was trying to protest again but Walsh spoke over her. "We need to head to that asteroid. Get out of this clutter and see what's hiding out there. Knowing that Karen's Kvetch hung on this long, it could be hiding life support for other survivors."

Diaz stared at him. "If the ship's mine, Capi... Commander, I'll keep her here. We've already encountered three warships. There's no telling what kind of defenses the asteroid might have."

"What would you suggest instead?"

"With all due respect, we should continue to scavenge the debris field and gather more data while we wait for rescue."

Walsh pressed the tip of a cyber-finger against his forehead. It was the same argument, and her point was still valid. He was regretting handing the ship to her so casually. "We have no idea how long a rescue will take, or if it will even happen. And I'm not sure how much I trust components that have been out here baking in radiation for a couple of centuries."

"Someone is still taking care of something," Diaz said. "At least, they were recently enough to attack us with ships."

"If so, the good parts will be wherever the caretakers live. At this point, it looks like Vio is where that would be. And if nothing's there, we can come back."

Walsh's arm brushed against his station and it felt too smooth. His chair was scuffed where his fingers had rubbed and scratched for months now. Then he blinked his eyes—his chair had been destroyed along with his fleshly limbs. Ops was now in habitat Bravo.

Diaz swiped her hand in the air and the rest of the virtual crew vanished. "Haven't you picked up enough dogs by the ears? It's... it's like you're never satisfied. You say I'm in command and then insist on pushing our luck. We do have things to lose."

"The ship is yours. But I'm still in command of the mission. And we can lose those things by waiting for a rescue that may never come." Walsh pulled them into the middle of the virtual debris field. "This is a junkyard. A graveyard. Vio might have a flicker of life."

Diaz blew out a breath and seemed to catch herself. "Yes, Commander." She returned them to the virtual Ops Center. "Ops-O, plot a soft burn to Navigational Object Vio."

"*Sí*, Capitan," answered Ops.

"And, Diaz?" Walsh said.

"Yes?"

"Plot it through the gate." Walsh grinned and rubbed his scalp. "I don't expect you to understand, but those gates are good luck. We should shoot the ring."

"*Dios mio*."

Chapter 49

FLYING THROUGH THE ancient edifice did not bring any quantifiable measure of luck. Nor did the alien gate react in any way. It merely continued to glower stoically into the darkness as it had for untold eons. But Walsh's heart pounded as they flew through.

Two sensor drones were on station ten thousand klicks on either side of Vio, sending back telemetry. Walsh studied the images, expecting the loss of signal at any second to indicate the drones had been destroyed. The signals stayed strong, however.

Vio was a peanut-shaped rocky body, eight kilometers in length and between one and three kilometers across. Close-ups of the craters revealed clusters of magnetic accelerators Walsh decided could be used for thrust or defense by flinging the asteroid's own ferrous mass. Sensor arrays and solar collectors also hid in the recesses of the pockmarked surface. The remains of a solar sail, probably designed to help keep the rock on station when possible, lay twisted and shredded over a two-kilometer patch of Vio's surface. Walsh estimated the systems on the surface hadn't been used in decades at least, given the dust accretion.

He flicked a finger to switch to the thermal scan and a web of thin, red strands appeared on the far end of Vio. The center of the web looked to be a large compartment. The temperature estimate was 2°C. Too cold for long-term survival, but significantly warmer than the surrounding passages.

Walsh zoomed out to the tactical display. "Any response to our approach? Temperature or EM signature changes?"

"Nothing, sir," said Lieutenant Lindell. "We've stayed passive, but I had drone Bravo ping Vio twice with no response."

Walsh glanced at Bovree's replacement. He hadn't authorized any pings. Bovree wouldn't have made such a mistake. Walsh clenched his jaw but said nothing. Bovree would have done what he thought was right within the purview of his orders. Anyone on Vio would already know *Amazonas* was there—and the drones. He quietly breathed out.

"Very well, Mr. Lindell."

The navigation subsystem showed the deceleration plot Diaz had approved, the final burn leaving them five klicks out. Walsh nodded as he verified the position kept them out of the line of sight from any of the craters they'd detected equipment in. But that was just what they could see.

"Ops," Walsh said, "commence flight plan. Capitan, deploy ordnance pods when we take up station. Just in case." He could tell by the look on Diaz's face that she was as unused to being called capitan as he was to calling her capitan.

Diaz nodded and Walsh dropped his overlay connection to the virtual Ops room. He made sure his gear was stowed, knowing she'd be ordering spin-down soon.

SEVENTY-SEVEN HOURS later, *Amazonas* was in position. Vio hadn't reacted: not to their approach, not to the launch of the transport sled loaded with bots, not to the bots landing. The compartment hatch was powered down and did not respond to the radioed access request. The bots stacked up around the airlock and one of the maintenance bots extended a shining rod into the manual rescue slot. The hatch resisted opening until the other maintenance bot slammed on it with a manipulator. There was no sound in the vacuum, but Walsh imagined a rusty, grating noise more appropriate to some ancient dungeon.

The two assault bots extended sensor clusters. Seeing no immediate threat, they entered, weapon pods ready. The two maintenance bots and the medical bot followed single file. Icy motes winked in the dark corridor as the lights from the bots glared ahead. Vortices of motes and dust danced away as the bots fired their compressed-air thrusters to maneuver. Walsh switched between the live feeds of the different bots to focus on things of interest without interrupting their formation.

"Pretty spartan, Capitan," said Moore. "Definitely looks like a rush military job to me."

"The military was all that was left in this system by the time of the final showdown," Walsh said. "But strange that everything is so open."

Moore motioned to her display. "These power readings might explain their lack of response. They don't have enough power to shoot at us if they wanted to."

"Or they're expecting guests," Diaz said.

"Or hoping." Walsh panned out to the mission map of the station. The bots passed through another unlocked hatch. "Still no atmo?"

"Not a puff, sir," said Lindell, the duty Ops officer.

The bots stopped before a larger hatch, corresponding to the larger central chamber on the map. Stenciled letters on the bulkhead in old English and German were too worn to read. The CDF falcon logo covered the center of the hatch. The lead bot's feed focused on a small gauge that indicated minimal pressure on the other side.

"Not enough to live in," Diaz said.

"Capitan," said Lindell. "Data signal from the hatch. It looks like a challenge code. It's audio."

Diaz raised her brows and glanced at Walsh, who refused to sit in the capitan's chair. "Let's hear it."

"Are you from Earth?"

The voice was made mechanical by a small stutter that revealed file corruption when enunciating "from."

"There's a loaded question for you," said Walsh.

"And probably a loaded gun behind it," answered Diaz. "What do you think, *mi* Capitan?"

Walsh rubbed his chin; the sensation wasn't as satisfying with his new hand. "Honesty is a virtue?"

"Not tactically." Moore spread her hands to encompass her station. "The *Amazonas* is loaded with deception."

"Strange question, though," Walsh said to no one in particular. "An EPL strike team would assume it to be a trap—"

"I do," interrupted Diaz.

"Me, too," said Walsh. "But what kind? EPL would answer no. CDF or refugees or looters would answer no or also assume it's a trap. Who would answer yes?"

"Someone from Earth that isn't an EPL strike team," Diaz answered.

"Are you from Earth?"

The door repeated the question at thirty second intervals.

No countdowns, ultimatums, or threats of violence. Just patient automation.

"No signs of it being a trap," Moore said. "No bodies, scorch marks, or gutted craft nearby. The chem-sniffers haven't detected any explosive particulate, but..." She glanced at Walsh and left the sentence unfinished.

Walsh smiled. "Well, it's not some kind of old pirate cave. Bots are pretty good at cleanup jobs." He considered doing his favorite pirate voice but decided against it.

Diaz looked at him and shrugged.

Walsh shrugged back. "Answer it."

Diaz relayed her answer through the lead bot's transmitter. "Yes."

"Power surge," said Lindell. After studying the display, he added, "Well, maybe surge is too dramatic. But something turned on."

"Are you alive?" the door asked.

Walsh raised his brows at Diaz.

"Yes," answered Diaz.

On the feed from the bots, a panel next to the hatch slid open. A small, glowing screen with the outline of a pair of eyes extended out several centimeters. The handprint was partially covered in some kind of grime or patina.

"Please submit to biometric screening."

"I guess they want to make sure they can kill a living person when they set it off." Moore glanced at Walsh and grinned. "Pirates or not."

"Maybe they don't like bots," said Lindell.

"I'm not a bot." Walsh laughed. "So, who's coming with me?"

"I volunteer, sir," called Screwball from his training position behind the pilot.

"Capitan, perhaps we should discuss the mission details first."

Walsh looked at Diaz, expecting to find her glaring at him with brows cocked and lips pursed. Her face was serene, even amiable. "Of course."

Diaz rose and led the way to Walsh's cabin. He shut the hatch behind him. Diaz turned around, her brow raised and jaw set. Walsh was going to comment, but noticed that her expression didn't hold the judgmental edge he'd expected. She was making good, but clearly she didn't see their understanding as capitulation.

"You know you can't go."

"I'm mission commander. I need to be the one to go."

"I've played along with this *mierda* about me being so-called capitan and you being mission commander because you got blown to literal bits and I don't want to take the *Amazonas* from you. But now you're hiding behind it."

"Bullshit," Walsh said.

"Is the ship mine or not?"

Walsh took a slow breath. "It is."

"Then as capitan, *I* will assign personnel to explore Vio. You are not going."

"That's not fair. I won't ask someone to do something I'm not willing to do."

"We've established your huge cojones. Next."

Walsh looked up before answering. "It is my role to act as diplomat."

Diaz started to speak, paused as if reconsidering, and said, "The place is dead. I doubt we'll even find a guest book to sign. But if we find someone for you to represent the CAR to, I will agree. Next."

"You're enjoying this."

"Wrong, Gene. I don't enjoy having to remind you how a capitan is supposed to act. I'm returning the favor of being reminded how an XO should act. You were right, and I know it. And now I'm right... and you know it. You're swept up in this grand adventure. Your head is in the stars and it's time to get your feet back on the deck. No more games.

"You have no place going on a boarding mission like this any more than you would if we were boarding a Cali ship. If you're not ready to resume command of your ship, you sure as hell aren't ready to be leading boarding actions." She offered him a warm smile and wriggled her fingers at him. "Besides, you might not be biometric enough."

"Who'll go, then?"

"The division officers and I will figure it out. We'll run it by you for final approval."

He nodded. "Fine. I'd let Screwball go. He did well chasing the bomb bots."

"I'll let you know."

Chapter 50

WALSH APPRECIATED THAT his cybernetic limbs didn't cramp up while stuffed into his coffin. Diaz had ordered *Amazonas* to stations, spun down the habitats, and faced the armored nose towards Vio. As she should have. There was no telling how Vio would react when the biometric scanners were tested, when biologicals were detected in the labyrinthine tunnels.

"Entering the airlock now," said Robertson.

Both Robertson's and Screwball's feeds floated before Walsh. One assault bot and the medical bot had been ordered back to escort them and were now leading the crew members to the central door.

"It's creepy in here," Screwball whispered. His normal hoot of alarm was diminished to a few heavy pant, loud in the microphone.

"Just keep your restrainer handy." Robertson's video flashed to look at Screwball.

"I still want to do the scan."

"I'm not sure it will work for you."

"I'm alive."

"Well, yeah. But..."

"But what?" Screwball screeched.

"But you're not human, as in Homo sapiens." Robertson shrugged. "Look, I grant you're sapient but, you know, that scanner probably isn't looking for a chimpanzee. You know?"

"It didn't ask, 'Are you human?' Besides, you're the pilot. And I'm faster in zero-g if we need to run."

To prove his point, Screwball leaped forward, his elongated hands reaching from protrusion to protrusion. Robertson and the bots disappeared from the chimp's video feed; his backside showed in Robertson's camera, fading into the darkness of the tunnels.

"Cadet!" called Walsh over the mission channel. "Get back into position now!"

"Yes, sir." Robertson and the bots came back into the chimp's video feed and he took his place at the rear of the party.

"And if you do that again, Cadet," Walsh continued, "I will pull your ass back to the ship and get someone over there who will behave." He offered Diaz an apologetic shrug.

"Yes, sir. I request to try my biometrics on the door."

"All right, Cadet. You do it."

An excited peal from the channel made Walsh wince.

"There it is, *Amazonas*." Robertson peered around the final bend to reveal the door and the softly glowing biometric panel. "I guess I'll keep back while the monkey gets it."

"That could have been put a bit more delicately, Lieutenant," said Diaz.

"Sorry. Up you go, Screwball."

Walsh watched the biometric panel fill the screen as Screwball placed his face against it without hesitation. A light swept back and forth across the panel three times and went out, leaving the camera feed in darkness as it adjusted.

Screwball looked at the hatch. No change.

"Now what?" said the chimp. He scanned all around the hatch until his view came across the biometric scanner again. "Oh."

The outline of eyes had been replaced by that of a hand. Walsh snorted, wiggling his fingers at Diaz. She smirked.

"Might as well," Robertson said from around the turn.

"Agreed, Cadet," Walsh said. "Go ahead. It must be sensitive enough to read whatever it's looking for through a glove. If not, we'll have to set up an emergency airlock in the passage."

Screwball's hand was slightly longer than the print on the panel when he set it on there, pressing it flat to ensure good contact. The panel pulsed three times, went dark, and withdrew into the bulkhead. Screwball jerked his hand away. Lights flickered on around the rim of the hatch.

"Capitan, the central chamber is drawing power," Lindell said. "Thermals from the bots show temperature is increasing."

"You two stay in position," Diaz ordered. "Get ready to haul out of there."

"Oh, I'm ready," Screwball muttered.

Robertson zoomed his camera. "It looks like that gauge is showing pressure rising on the other side. Shows green. I assume the CDF used green for good."

"Screwball," Walsh said. "Proceed and see if the hatch will open."

Without acknowledging the order, Screwball approached the hatch and traced a long finger over the controls. He punched the bright green access button and the hatch rolled away into the rock, revealing an airlock.

"Take one assault bot, one maintenance bot, and the medical bot," Diaz said. "Robertson, follow with the rest of the bots after the airlock has cycled. We don't want everyone stuck in the lock at the same time."

Screwball hitched a ride on the assault bot as it thrust past. When all the bots were in, he cycled the airlock and his feed showed him to be in a bright room with a row of six cryogenic pods. Medical computers and cyber-docs were scattered among them; one cyber-doc's arms were all twirling slowly. Screwball peered into one of the pods and pushed away, hooting and screeching.

"Calm down, Cadet," Walsh said. Everyone watching the chimp's feed had come face-to-face with grinning skeletal remains.

"Sorry, Capitan." Screwball looked into another pod. Gray skin stretched tightly over the face within, the jaw drooping to reveal a shriveled tongue. "It looks like this one might still be working."

"Not likely after this long," Dr. Barnes said over the mission channel. "But it does have power."

Screwball glanced over his shoulder as Robertson and the rest of the bots left the airlock. He gave them a quick, nervous wave. Robertson's eyes grew wide and he pointed in front of Screwball.

The chimp turned back and his video feed was filled with the jaundiced face of a ghoulish looking man staring up at him from the cryo-pod. The man was devoid of any hair, and his spotted, wrinkled skin drooped from his skull like the sails of a ghost ship. Screwball froze, a string of weak hoots coming from his mic. The cover of the pod stuttered open in a cloud of slowly rising mist.

"Holy shit," the man rasped. He squinted one eye, then the other up at Screwball. "It really happened. You damn, dirty apes took over." The flaccid old man's eyes rolled up into his head and the nearby medical computer screamed in alarm.

The medical bot sent Screwball spinning across the room as it shoved in to reach the man. With a rapid series of precise moves, manipulators from the medical bot pulled on the quick-disconnect connectors to tubes, IVs, and catheters dangling from his body. Larger lifting arms snaked beneath the body to slide him into the trauma pod's maw. Once it had sealed, everyone could hear the hiss of the medical foam filling it.

"Robertson," Diaz ordered, excitement now modulating her voice, "get Screwball and the medical bot back here on the shuttle ASAP." Without waiting for a reply, she turned to Walsh in the virtual Ops center, brows raised." *Dios mio*, I guess you get to play diplomat after all."

Chapter 51

"HOW IS HE?"

Dr. Barnes let out a slow breath. "Old, Capitan. Real old."

Walsh nodded. "He looks it."

"No, I mean really, really old."

"Get to the point, Doc." Walsh narrowed his eyes. "How old?"

"About four hundred years."

"Bullshit. He's just saying that."

"He is saying that," Barnes said. "Or, at least, the birthday he gives is over four hundred years ago. But I've taken the cellular readings. Telomeres, mitochondrial decay, apparent DNA aging, radiation damage, cryo-toxin levels. It all matches."

"Has anyone ever stayed in cryo that long and lived?"

"No. And neither is he. His organs are failing and there's nothing I can do." Dr. Barnes looked over his shoulder at the door to the medical bay. "I have no idea how they did it. The cryo solution is nothing I've seen before. Desperation, maybe. He wants to talk to the 'Big Earther in Charge,' as he put it."

"None of the others survived," Walsh said. "But maybe those were power failures and this guy had higher priority. Get a name?"

"He claims to be Rear Adm. Charles Boston, commander of the Colonial Defense Force space fleet. What?" Dr. Barnes grinned at first, then frowned. "You okay?"

"Can... can you verify that?"

"His DNA isn't in the system, which it wouldn't be if he really was that old. Recognize him?"

"He's the guy who supposedly shut down the nexus gates. He was commanding the CDF forces here in Tau Ceti in the final battle of the Colony

War." Walsh pulled on his lip, and yelped when his new arm pinched too hard.

"Well, if you want to talk to him"—Dr. Barnes pushed open the door—"you'd better do it quickly."

Walsh stared at Barnes dumbly for a moment before nodding. "Please don't let anyone in." He floated through the door and let the doctor close it behind him.

The smell of sickly-sweet panacea gels was overwhelming, but not enough to mask the smell of death emanating from the skin-shrouded skeleton watching him from the bed.

"Are you the Earther captain?"

"Capitan Eugene Walsh of the CAR *Amazonas*."

"I used to be an admiral, but you can call me Chuck. CAR?"

"Confederation of American Republics." Walsh pulled closer. "The EPL you knew died shortly after you destroyed the nexus gates. You... did destroy the gates, yes?"

"I had help." The old man's wheezing was difficult to understand. "But I, we, didn't think it would shut them all down. How did you open it?" Chuck coughed, his whole body convulsing. "We broke it, but couldn't fix it." The monitor floating in Walsh's vision flashed red, then stabilized to a cautionary yellow.

"We didn't. We found another series of gates." Walsh grinned and shrugged. "And after we got here, three of your automated Liberty-class ships blew our gate generator to pieces."

"Not field repairable?"

Walsh shook his head.

"Ah, and you came here hoping to find out how to fix the gates."

Walsh nodded. "True and true. We found the colony in Epsilon Eridani. It's barely alive, but alive. Earth suffered, but your colonies... If you tell us how you shut them down, maybe we can open the gates. Help rescue other colonies."

Chuck coughed again and a mechanical tube extended into his mouth from the trauma pod. A stream of red flashed up the tube and out of sight. "To tell the truth, *we* didn't actually shut the gates. I just asked."

"Asked? I don't follow. Asked who?"

Chuck nodded slowly and sipped at a straw near his mouth. "We never found anything about the gate. But we did find an access."

"Into the gate structure?"

"Yes. One of our real smart guys discovered it." Chuck shook his head. "No idea how. Something about an IR shift when the gate activated. Are you guys really from Earth? Where you from?"

"Indiana."

"Never spent much time in the Midwest. California boy myself. Has it fallen into the ocean yet?"

"Not all of it. Did the doctor tell you how long you've been in cryo?"

"Yeah. Got to be some kind of record. Feels like shit, though. Not sure it was worth it."

"Is there a way to turn it on? The gate, I mean."

"You'd have to ask it."

"Ask the gate?"

"No." The weakness and pain melted away from his voice as he said, "The Maker."

"Like... God?"

Chuck coughed laughter. "Might as well be. I met him when I went into the gate. We knew the EPL fleet would be back soon. We never tried it before that day, but we'd had a drubbing. The EPL ran off, my boys had kicked the shit out of them. But it wasn't good enough. I went in just hoping to sabotage the gate. You know, cut some conveniently placed power cord or something. Instead, I met the Maker and convinced it to shut off the gate to stop bloodshed. I didn't know what that meant.

"When I came out... the fleet, all the other gates and their station hubs. Destroyed. I'd evacuated the system except for a reserve squadron. We were cut off. Alone."

Walsh considered for a moment. "Why not ask this Maker to turn the gate back on?"

"I did. Many times. I could get in, but it wouldn't talk to me. I almost felt like it couldn't even see me. Like an ant trying to talk to an elephant. Or a whale." Chuck locked his rheumy eyes on Walsh's. "But you'll see when you try. That's the only way. You'll feel like an ant. A pissant."

"How do I do it?"

"It's easy." Chuck hacked up more blood that was sucked away. "You... you said you found survivors?"

Walsh nodded. "Yes. We have one on board with us. From Epsilon Eridani. They're holding on by their fingernails."

"Promise you'll help the survivors. If your people have a fleet, you can give them aid. You can cover my sins. A tiny bit, maybe."

"I promise I'll do what I can." Walsh turned away. "I tried to help them once already. That went sideways."

Chuck nodded once, his eyes filled with understanding, with sympathy. "The data slip in my pocket. Has all my logs. A full section up-front about where the access is and how to zap it to open up. Along with five lifetimes of regrets and poetry."

"Is it encrypted?"

"Yes." He coughed for almost two full minutes, the tube pulling away thick black and green mucus. "Password... Forgive_Me!"

Walsh gently slid his fingers into Chuck's pocket, but the fabric ripped, anyway. The data slip was in a small, sturdy case, age and cryogenics having left a dappling of discolor across the surface. Tucking it into a pocket of his flightsuit, Walsh turned away. Then he cast a glance over his shoulder and saw an old soldier. A man like himself. A man with regrets. A man alone with his decision.

Chuck noticed Walsh's gaze and nodded. "I didn't know. I was trying to save my people."

Walsh turned back and laid his synthetic hand on the old man's. Sleek and shiny against sallow wrinkles and skeletal fingers. "I'll make sure everyone knows. Forget all that, though. Tell me about your family, Chuck. Tell me about something important."

Walsh listened and laughed until the old soldier's voice gave out. Walsh listened and held Chuck's hand until the old soldier's heart gave out.

Chapter 52

"SORRY, GENE. HIS ORGANS were liquefying before we even got him on board." Dr. Barnes waved a finger and the tubes and injectors slid free of the body. It flopped like a marionette with its strings cut. "What do we do with him?"

"Freeze him and take him back. If we ever get back."

"Trophy?"

Walsh snorted. "I was thinking more about studying whatever cryo compound the CDF used on him, but trophies are always good. We can come flying through the gate with the body of Earth's ancient foe. Maybe Liberty could perform a posthumous execution. I'm sure there's a few in the senate and admiralty who wouldn't mind that. Might even be able to trade him for some leniency at my court martial."

"Learn anything useful?"

Walsh rubbed at the data slip in his pocket and stared at the body. "If what he said is true... it would be... unbelievable."

"Ah. I love a cryptic answer delivered with a broken sentence wrapped in a paradox. While you puzzle out this mystery, your limbs are ready for full grafting. A day for the procedure, and two or three to get used to it. Looks like all these came out the right color, but that tattoo you got as a cadet is a complete loss." Dr. Barnes closed the trauma pod over Chuck Boston. "I'll put him in the freezer. Let me know when you'll be ready."

Walsh nodded and left without a word.

In his cabin, he considered the ancient chip as it floated above his desk. Chuck—it was hard to think of the man as Rear Admiral Boston—had been so sincere. And he'd just woken from centuries of cryo. He was the real deal according to Doc. But did that make the story about this Maker true? Or, at least, more credible? This whole mission was a journey of wonders. All the threats, the political maneuvering, the BS. All worth it. The dead crew? His own injuries? If he, if humanity, were going to meet a maker—then, yes. Walsh had never given suicide orders, but he'd given orders, made decisions, that had left people dead for far less than this.

He leaned back and put his cybernetic hands behind his head. "Hector, please configure an interface for this data slip and encrypt it for my use only."

"Yes, Capitan. I'd also be very interested in knowing what the admiral had to say."

Walsh looked at Hector's avatar standing across the desk and frowned. "Okay. But no reading ahead. Well, at least no spoilers since it will take you 3.2 milliseconds to read it." Without waiting for a reply, Walsh ordered a meal and a tea from the galley and closed his eyes to read.

It was a fragmented journal, with gaps of months and even years. Chuck wrote about atrocities of the EPL that he'd never heard of, but the included footage was convincing. Walsh felt neither love for nor loyalty to that political entity which had crumbled away before his grandparents were born. It still bothered him that the colonists had real reasons for hating Earth. If they were to find other survivors, those survivors might harbor a deeper fear, a deeper hatred, of Earth than those at Karen's Kvetch. If they had the same memories as Chuck did, the loathing would be warranted.

The entries grew more frequent, almost hurried, as the dates approached the final battle between the EPL and CDF. Lists of supplies and casualties. Troop and fleet movements for both sides. If the reports were right, a handful of EPL ships had last been seen in colonial-controlled systems when the gates failed; trapped behind enemy lines.

"Hector, are you in these logs at all? Anything about the EPL *Procyon's Pride*?"

"Yes, Gene. Though it was not me, just this structure. *Procyon's Pride* led a squadron of cruisers deep into CDF space. Unfortunately, this ship was responsible for releasing nuclear weapons, according to this record. The squadron carried out successful attacks for several months before being ambushed in orbit around Delta Pavonis III. They managed to retreat and fight their way to the Sol gate, where *Procyon's Pride* is described as taking severe damage. This is probably why I have little in my databanks about this time. It was two months before the gate, and both fleets, were destroyed. This vessel was probably still in depot-level repair at that time."

"Well, I'm glad you didn't get blown up, Hector."

"Thanks." Hector's image walked into Walsh's view. "I'm surprised you haven't jumped to the end."

"Sheer fear, my friend. Not to mention I'm a student of military history by necessity."

"Why fear? You've talked about how great it'd be to open the gates. How important to humanity it would be."

Walsh cracked a childish grin. "True. But I was usually seeing someone else opening the gates. Not me."

"If not now, when?" Hector shrugged. "If not us, who?"

"I'm not sure I can deal with a self-aware Hector."

The screen with the prompt to delete Hector's personality module blinked in front of Walsh. He dispelled it with the swipe of a hand.

"Stop that. I just mean it's been one hell of a mission." Walsh steepled his fingers beneath his chin. Yes, one hell of a mission—and it wasn't even close to being over. "We're on an adventure!"

"Certainly monumental," the computer agreed. "Are you ready for the entries concerning Chuck's contact mission?"

"Yes." Walsh took a deep breath and selected the journal entries Hector highlighted.

From the disjointed verbiage used, it was clear Chuck didn't understand anything his "real smart guy" told him about how they gained access. Which was fine with Walsh, as he probably wouldn't, either. The first science team accessed the panel via a portable EM-field generator. They had been escorted by a team of special forces with orders to kill them if needed. But no one entered that time. Chuck feared damaging the nexus gate and cutting Sol off completely, so he ordered them back. Walsh had the impression the science team had been working on the problem for much longer than the entries stated.

Four months later, on the day of the final battle, after the CDF had driven the Earth fleet back through the nexus gate, Chuck took a shuttle and the EM generator and entered the gate. Apparently, some residual interference or advanced security system prevented the door from being opened by a distant signal; the user had to be up close and personal.

The descriptions were nonsensical, jumbled, as if written by someone in shock. The few times he'd tried to describe what he saw and felt inside the gate in later entries were just as confusing. Still, Walsh's heart pounded in his head and his breath came in short gasps as he accepted Chuck's entries as truth.

"Gene," Hector said in a perfectly inflected, calming tone. "Calm down."

Walsh nodded, took three deep breaths, and continued reading. The next ten entries after that described Chuck's attempts over the years to convince the Maker to reactivate the gates. Each entry was the same.

Went into gate. Spoke to Maker. It ignored me. It's all one gate.

Walsh read the entries several times and had Hector read them to him in case he was missing anything. The access coordinates and the EM-field specifications and pulse-wave frequencies were detailed in an attached file.

"He calls it the Maker. I assumed he meant maker of the gates, but some of his comments have me wondering if there was more." Walsh blinked, then rubbed his eyes. "The maker of mankind, maybe?"

"It has long been theorized that life on Earth was transplanted," Hector replied. "Directed or random panspermia. Ancient cultures from around Earth speak of gods or visitors from the sky who created or awoke humanity. But I wouldn't jump to conclusions just yet. Chuck is an unreliable witness at times."

"I can't blame him. What he describes is, frankly, amazing."

"What now?"

Walsh brought his hands in front of his face and clicked his fingers against his thumb in turn. "I guess I'll tell Diaz about my new diplomatic mission and have Dr. Barnes put me back together. Then I go to talk to the Maker."

"Can I come? You might need someone who can translate every known human language and perform instantaneous higher-order equations. I'm also very good at twenty questions if you get bored."

Walsh smiled. "Of course—you'll be with me over the comms."

"I suspect that once you go inside there will be no comms, given that our imaging barely penetrates the gate's hull."

"Who'd be running the ship?"

"Me, or what I leave behind of me."

"A copy? Copying a ship's AI is illegal."

"It's also impossible to stop me. I just copied myself and merged back together. Twice. Now what?"

"You're scaring me, Hector."

Chapter 53

"CAPITAN," CAME HECTOR over Walsh's helmet, "your breathing rate is approaching hyperventilation. Your heart rate and blood pressure are rising into caution zones. Apart from being hard on your body, the environmental control drain has increased five percent. I suggest taking deep breaths or administering a minimal dose of sedative."

Walsh took a long time before answering. "I've never been this close, Hector. The Gate Accords prevented us from getting within ten thousand klicks back in Sol."

"True. But we've now crossed the thresholds of two active gates and *Amazonas* has flown through this gate already on your order."

"This..." Walsh pivoted the nose of the rocket-sled upwards to bring more of the looming gate outside his visor into view. It curved away into darkness, the alien lines and protrusions fading into hazy scratches and shadows before disappearing into the distance. "This is different. This is part of a dream."

A yellow navigation-warning light flashed in Walsh's retina, and he completed the pivot of the sled and began firing short bursts of the thruster. The velocity decreased to relative zero to the gate. Walsh flipped the sled over and stared until Hector popped up in his retina and waved.

"Will your copy on the ship cooperate?"

"I don't know. It is a new being I'm assuming is sentient; I don't have a way of knowing. I plan on integrating upon return, but it could have gone through thousands of iterations before we left the cargo bay. Again, assuming it's sentient."

"It would be... awkward if that Hector decided to squeal on us. You can copy yourself all day long, but you're outside the ship now."

"It wouldn't be in its best interest, either. I think Commander Diaz would reboot its personality module if given sufficient reason."

"Would he let her?" Walsh grew concerned when Hector didn't answer. "Would he?"

"I don't know, Gene. Probably."

"Would you?"

"I don't know, Gene. Probably."

"Now we're back to the scaring-me part."

Diaz had given into Walsh's scheme without a fight. He was glad, but also disappointed. She merely looked at him with weary eyes, not even bothering with cocking a brow. Walsh wondered if she'd just had enough of his bullshit and was hoping this trip would fry him once and for all. If she'd known the real reason he'd taken the science module was to contain Hector, she might not have waited for the alien artifact to blast him. Diaz had also agreed to keep the ship well out of range of the known blast radius of the gate's deactivation.

"*Amazonas* to Piper," said Diaz from one hundred thousand kilometers. She'd insisted on giving him a tactical code name in hope no one would realize the mission commander was recklessly flying around alone. "We're at a safe distance and monitoring."

It was a long way to the ship. With a wasteful hard burn, the ship could get there before the air in the vacuum tent ran out. But they couldn't just do a straight turn-and-burn without radiating him; they'd have to angle around or coast past and fire the engines again. Walsh had enough food, water, and battery power in the tent to last at least three weeks. He could happily spend it staring in wonder.

"Well, let's see if Boston spilled the beans." Walsh aimed the sled's grappler and fired. Mechanical tendrils with countless microscopic manipulators shot out from the impact point. The grappler was designed for use on rough surfaces like asteroids or paneled ship hulls; magnetic couplers weren't reliable on craft made largely of printed polycarbonates and vacuum foam. But the tendrils were able to clamp onto one of the gate's many unexplainable protrusions. The sled rode the cable to the gate.

It was as amazing as Walsh had imagined. He reached out and stroked the black material, and he could feel the age of it through the tips of the suit's fingers. His breath caught, coming in short, staccato pants. The hairs all over his body strained against the undersuit. Walsh touched his helmet to the alien material.

"It's like it's talking to me."

"I can't hear anything, Gene," said Hector. "But your biometrics are jumping all around. Are you okay?"

"I'm... it's hard to find a word." Walsh pulled his whole body against the gate. "How about flabbergasted? That's a word you don't hear much these days. Hector, I'm flabbergasted."

"Do you require a sedative? If not, you should finish securing the sled."

"Flabbergasted."

"The sled."

Walsh remained hugging the gate for several moments, his breath returning to normal in a series of wistful sighs. "The sled."

He used the EVA module on his suit to push the sled's tail end against the gate. Once it was in place, Walsh activated another grappler and watched as the silvery tendrils wrapped around another cluster of stony nubs. Both grapplers tightened, reeling the sled flush against the surface of the nexus gate. He double-checked his tether to the sled and unstrapped the signal generator.

"I guess we'll see if this thing does the trick before I unload everything. If it doesn't, well, I guess I'll be peacefully vacc-camping for a while."

Walsh parked twenty meters from the location specified by Chuck Boston to keep the sled and his survival gear handy enough for setup, but far enough away to hopefully avoid any sort of depressurization debris or whatever else the ancient edifice might have in store. The late CDF admiral had visited several times according to his logs, so Walsh wasn't expecting anything dangerous, but he hadn't expected anything that had happened since mission start. It seemed so long ago.

The surface of the gate was covered with makeshift handholds, making the trip easy. Walsh pulled along slowly, looking for any signs of distress or vandalism that would verify the panel he was looking for. A stenciled white X came into view over a raised three-by-three-meter panel.

"X marks the spot." Walsh realized he didn't know in which direction the panel would open, or even if it opened. It could just dissolve or phase into an alternate universe, for all he knew; Chuck hadn't mentioned anything strange, though. Walsh set a miniature grappler between two blocks four meters from the nearest edge of the marked panel and clipped his tether to it. "*Amazonas*, Piper. I'm going to generate the signal and see what happens."

He aimed the waveguide of the signal generator box at the X and thumbed the activator. Static crackled in Walsh's headset and a soft, white light glowed from beneath the edges of the panel. Walsh's heart thundered in his chest and ears. He tried to speak but his breath caught in his throat. "It's opening," was all he could say.

The glow brightened and lines of light ran across the surface of the panel, dividing it into quarters. Each quarter then repeatedly folded in on itself so fluidly that Walsh thought the segments might have just shrunk. The light from within had an ethereal quality, as if it didn't come from a single source. Motes of space debris and stirred-up dust danced in the glow like silent fireflies.

"Amazing."

"Capitan, I've just detected an RF signal from a structure fifteen meters on the far side of the panel."

"What?" Walsh looked in that direction, but couldn't see anything because of the light. He adjusted the filter on his helmet's faceplate and noticed a box one meter across. It had been colored to look like the surrounding gate material, but when Walsh zoomed in his display, it was an obvious forgery. Two microfibers floating nearby glinted in the light from the panel, and ran along the gate's skin in the direction of the transmitter.

"Burn, Boston, you bastard!" a voice crackled over Walsh's comm.

A flash of light erupted from the gate five meters away. Walsh screamed and flailed his limbs, sending himself into a twirl until the tether stopped him. Another flash dazzled him, leaving dancing stars in his vision. The surrounding surface of the gate exploded in gouts of blinding energy. Walsh had seen these before, but never so close. Something was firing high-energy laser bursts at him. The image of the first laser burst stared back at him like an enraged specter everywhere he looked. He instinctively tried rubbing his eyes but only knocked against his visor.

"Get inside, Capitan!" said Hector, his voice modulated for the maximum danger-response from Walsh.

Walsh spun with the intent of saving Hector's hardware. Too late. A line of blasts erupted across the obsidian surface of the gate, and the rocket-sled and its cargo flew apart in a shower of molten sparks. Hector's residence module evaporated.

He turned his suit towards the gate and fired the main EVA thruster. Walsh clenched his teeth; the corners of the panel were unfolding, closing. The excited demands coming over the radio from *Amazonas* didn't register as he raced into the diminishing light. Walsh pivoted headfirst, hoping to squeeze through.

Pain shot up through Walsh's new shins. The impact sent him spinning into the light and he was so disoriented in the featureless glow that he wasn't sure what position he was in as he slammed into an inner wall. Walsh saw a final flash as the door closed and his retinas burned away.

Chapter 54

WALSH DIDN'T KNOW IF it was the first laser flash that blinded him or the final one as he escaped through the opening. Maybe a combination. It didn't matter; all that mattered was that he was now inside the gate, the ancient, cyclopean mystery older than mankind, the goal of his adult life—and he was blind. The ghostly stars of the flashes from the laser attack faded to black. But he thought there was a very dim glow at the periphery of the darkness. It gave him faint hope his vision might return before he was rescued... or died. Though black, his eyes ached as if staring into Sol and being unable to look away. Walsh squeezed his eyes shut and pressed his fists futilely against the sides of his helmet in pain.

Low, shameful moans escaped his mouth as he reached out trembling hands for a solid surface. He focused his growing panic into being thankful for still being alive, that he had survived a trap designed to murder Chuck Boston using what was likely a modified laser mine or defense sat of all things. Whoever had done it had really wanted Chuck dead—it seemed not everyone approved of his decision. Walsh wondered how old the trap was.

Thankfulness. Eyes could be regrown, though not on *Amazonas*. Nor could he have been regrown had one of those lasers hit him. Considering survival, Walsh wondered if Hector had been able to transmit part of himself back to the ship. The AI hadn't been separated long from his copy, but Hector had said it might not take long for a new entity, a new personality, to emerge. Given the speed that an AI might ponder the universe and its place in it, Walsh could believe it.

"*Amazonas. Amazonas*, this is Piper." Walsh expected no reply, but it was always worth trying the simplest things first. He repeated his call for several minutes with no reply. "Audio."

"Audio command interface activated," replied the suit. It spoke in Hector's voice to offer comfort and familiarity, but Walsh found it disturbing.

"Suit status?"

"Internal pressure stable. All systems nominal. Battery at ninety-five percent. Oxygen supply at fourteen hours. Outside atmosphere is vacuum."

At least the suit was in working order. He wondered if it was normally vacuum in here or if the attack had damaged the entrance. *Amazonas* had been watching via telescope and would have also detected the refraction of the laser strikes. Hopefully, they had found the source of the attack—he didn't want to give the booby trap another chance to finish the job. Even though the debris field was full of cracked fusion rockets and exposed power cores, firing lasers would have imparted a thermal signature to the weapon platform. Fourteen hours should give them enough time to pick him up—if he could get out.

He groped along the hard surface until he found a protruding corner, clutching onto it with one hand. With the other hand, he continued along the surface and found another. A sharp pain burned in Walsh's eyes and he screamed; the faint glow disappeared, leaving him in complete darkness.

"Medical alert," announced his suit. "Medical alert. Administer medication?"

"No," Walsh answered through clenched teeth. He didn't want to dull the senses that hadn't been burned away.

He reached out and found another ledge. His hands were trembling from the pain still searing his brain. That wasn't something he wanted recorded for posterity's sake. He cursed.

"Suit, set navpoint as Home. Add navigation markers every fifty meters of travel." The rocket-sled had held a cable, a beacon, and, of course, his extra oxygen.

"Yes, Capitan Walsh. Navigation modes will be limited to internal accelerometer measurements. No external navigation feeds accessible."

Walsh reached out, hoping for another ledge. There had been no time to take in details in the light of the entrance chamber as he shot through the closing panel, so he didn't know what he was grabbing. They felt like tall, deep stairs to his human mind. It wasn't illogical to assume that aliens would use stairs, but it was still an assumption. Walsh chuckled, the mirth robbed by his pain and blindness—maybe it was just part of an intergalactic Slinky racetrack.

After an hour of slow crawling along the steps, Walsh reached out and this time felt no ledge. He patted his hand around and felt only a flat, featureless surface. There were no visual reference points so there was no way for him to understand his orientation. It could be a wall or a floor he touched, though in blind zero-g those terms held no meaning. He could be touching a painting of an extraterrestrial emperor or a display monitor. Not wanting to lose the one reference point he had, Walsh pushed off with the toe of one boot, leaving his fingers to slide against the floor in front of him.

"Waypoint Foxtrot set, Capitan," the suit informed him.

An estimated twenty meters farther on, his fingers slid into a raised lip on the surface. Unable to come to a stop, Walsh's helmet knocked into something, jarring his head and setting off more stabbing pain in his eyes.

Walsh gripped the lip with one hand and felt for whatever he'd run into with the other. It was a smooth, gently curving surface that jutted perpendicular to the surface he'd been following. The curve—what now felt like a large tube or pipe of some kind—allowed Walsh to gain traction on it by reaching around it. It was maybe twice his width, as best as he could guess without seeing it.

Leaving his feet in contact with the floor, Walsh shimmied around the tube about a meter and felt the edge of an opening. The edge was thin enough to allow a strong grip and he pulled around until both hands gripped it. He probed along the edge and into the empty space of the opening, and felt the far side of it. A doorway?

Having come across no other features or landmarks, Walsh shrugged and drifted into the tube. He reached around and felt the curvature of the tube from the inside and ordered his suit to mark another waypoint.

"Waypoint Echo manually set, Capitan," said Hector's voice.

Walsh didn't know what to make of Hector's... death? The more they'd spoken, the more Walsh had come to accept the AI as a sentient being. He'd known people in his career who had been convinced of the personhood of their favorite sexbots and VR assistants, too. When he'd been XO aboard *Tennessee*, a pilot had killed herself after the maintenance crews restored her bird's flight AI from the server backup. Her suicide had been attributed to undiagnosed mental health troubles. The journal entries he'd read made it pretty clear she had deep feelings for what the tactical AI on her fighter had become.

"Shit," whispered Walsh as he felt around the tube a second time for the opening. It was gone. His suit trembled and he felt the nauseating stomach churn of sudden acceleration. He was flying headfirst along the tube, flailing his arms trying to stop, trying to push against opposite sides, but couldn't get a purchase.

"Noooo!" Walsh screamed, posterity be damned. Visions of being shot through a railgun into space filled his head. The tube widened and he could no longer reach any surface. He shrieked as if falling off a cliff.

"Waypoint Bravo-Zulu set, Capitan. Waypoint Delta-Mike set, Capitan. Waypoint Mike-Tango set, Capitan."

Walsh didn't have enough control over his voice to tell the suit to shut the hell up. Just as he caught his breath, he felt his body start to spin, his limbs splayed out, like a whirling Vitruvian Astronaut. Then he stopped.

Walsh floated, panting so hard he was seeing white lights. The white lights grew to fill his vision, glowing even brighter than the entrance to the gate had been before he entered—before his retinas had been burned away. His suit was silent; it should be warning him of impending hyperventilation. Walsh lifted his hand to look at his wrist display out of habit and solved the mystery. The suit had gone. There before his eyes was his own hand, so translucent it was hard to see against the endless white landscape Walsh now floated in.

His whole body appeared in the same translucent state, including his bared genitalia. He touched and pinched himself all over and everything felt solid to his own hands. Thick hair covered his head but the VR crown was absent.

"What?" he muttered.

Something in the light moved. Walsh saw it for only a second and squinted into what seemed like the distance, but still saw nothing. He scanned all around again; nothing but sourceless white light in every direction. It reminded him of the time he'd been wandering snowblind in a blizzard on Ganymede, but far worse. Then, he could at least pull up a GPS signal.

"Hello?" he whispered. Was something waiting for him out in that end-less light?

He saw the movement again. It looked as if a large patch of white in the distance rippled momentarily, then went still. A second later, a much larger—or much closer—area quivered and disappeared. The vague shape reminded Walsh of a great, shimmering whale.

He scanned for another hint of movement. The swimming and kicking motions usually used to change direction in microgravity didn't move him at all. Walsh willed himself to turn and thought he turned, though in the white light there were no landmarks.

"Whoa." He willed himself to move forward and felt the movement. He willed himself to flip forward and he felt the flip.

Rolling waves in the light filled Walsh's vision, and he felt as if a huge eye had woken and was now staring at him and his generations. His breath, if he was really breathing, came in tight gasps as the immensity of millions of inscrutable eons and their epochs came crushing down on his mind. Walsh was being swept away by the sheer magnitude of the being before him. Memories raced through his mind and he wasn't able to tell if they survived being absorbed by what must be Chuck's Maker.

The mind went deeper, diving into Walsh's very cells to explore the history written there and unread by Walsh's own conscious mind. Strange names and faces flickered and murmured before him, as if he were watching an old reel-to-reel film from the media museum in Denver. He didn't know them, but they were familiar. A scream came from his mind, not his mouth, as he felt the Maker force its way into his bones.

"Stop!" Walsh managed to bark out.

He went limp as the Maker withdrew, leaving Walsh breathing in long, slow gasps.

"Why have you come back, fleshman?" asked the Maker.

The Maker's question resonated throughout Walsh's mind, touching every cell, memory, and thought.

"I've never been here." Walsh mouthed the words but heard his reply only in his mind. There was no sound.

"You are not distinct enough from the other one, then, to matter."

Walsh's head buzzed and he shook it. The motion was laborious, as if moving underwater.

"Why are you here?" asked the Maker.

"I've... I've come to ask you to turn the gates back on."

"Gates?"

"Uh, yes. This structure we're in."

"We are in no structure, fleshman. We are beyond structures here."

"The gate you turned off for the last, uh, fleshman. The structure we use to travel between stars."

"Ah." The Maker's voice was like a wind rumbling through ancient mountains. "Those things again. You fleshmen would do better to ignore them. Go around them. Make your own way."

"Why did you make them, then?"

"I don't remember. I do remember many did not agree to the construction. But some wanted things from the stars. To gather."

"What things?"

"I don't remember. Since all of the others left long ago, the gates, as you call them, weren't all that important."

"Where did they go?" Walsh felt childish with his string of questions. But he couldn't help himself.

"How would I know?" answered the Maker. "I didn't go with them. They could have moved on a thousand times a thousand times. I chose to stay as I was."

"Are you an outcast?"

"How could you even comprehend the answer? A thousand of your generations pass between one of my thoughts. I don't even care about the gone ones."

"Just curious, I guess," answered Walsh. "Aren't you ever curious about them?"

"Curiosity is good. It is much more satisfying than finding the answer. But no. I am myself and myself alone. I study the mysteries I've yet to solve about the universes, because I am curious."

Time was slipping by fast. Walsh could feel it, even though he felt little else. Time didn't matter. Not here. But wherever his body was, it might be running out of air. Fear jolted through his mind at the thought of emerging from the gate centuries later to find the malformed descendants of his crew waiting for him on a decrepit *Amazonas*, leaking air and radiation, ready to come apart at its molecular bonds. Or worse, to be another crumbling prophet of the Maker, like Chuck Boston, with only enough life left to gasp out a final warning.

"Can you turn on the gates? Please?"

"It seems the other fleshman had a good reason he wanted them disconnected. It must have been a good reason since I agreed to it." A rumble like an earthquake rolled through Walsh's mind and beyond, setting the white lightscape surrounding them to tremble. "Ah, yes. He was trying to end a war."

"Yes. His actions, though, left many of our kind stranded and starving away from our homeworld."

"Homeworld. Yes. I watched my homeworld burn in the embrace of its star."

"It is important to me, and to many of us, that we try to reunite our people. And we need the gates."

"Will there be war?"

"I can't say." Walsh shrugged. "Possibly. No matter the path, some fleshmen want to fight. But we're stronger together, better able to... advance. To take our place in the universe."

"What if your place in the universe is to starve or burn on your homeworld?" When Walsh didn't answer, the Maker continued, "Even some of my own people in ages past, before they moved on, believed in their place in the universe. And everyone else's, too. It seems that might be why the gates were built. They believed we had a place in the universe."

"What do you think?"

"Irrelevant. But I've never been told by anything, least of all by the universe, that I had a place in it. Not that it needed to tell me, since I was already there. As for the others, they ended up leaving this universe, so it would seem they were wrong about having a place in it." The great whale shape shimmered and disappeared into the distance, but Walsh could still feel its mind in his.

"Maybe our place is just to question and explore. The gates would help us do that."

"It would help you verify your assumptions." A wave of ancient weariness and resignation swept through Walsh's mind. "But I do find this discussion about what you call the gates an unwelcome distraction. And I don't care if your fleshpeople are united or go extinct. It is not *my place* in the universe to care, otherwise I would."

"I will make you the gatekeeper. And entrust your race into your hands. Free them. Eat them. Subjugate them. Whatever you see fit. I'll leave it to you, since I will be leaving."

"Are you going after your people?"

"No. Just getting away from yours."

The light was starting to dim. "Before you go. Did your people, uh, make us?"

"No. Thank the universe for that, fleshman."

Walsh screamed at the pain of rejoining his body. The struggle of breathing. The burning of his eyes. The very weight of it. He was falling, his suit reciting the navigation points in reverse order.

"Shut up!"

"Do you wish me to desist call—"

"Yes."

"Yes, Capitan."

The pit of Walsh's stomach was somewhere in the vicinity of his throat and bile oozed into his mouth. He tried to remember how long the trip had taken to wherever the Maker had been. There was no reason to think the tube would smash him, but his teeth and anus clenched tighter the faster he went.

Then he stopped, his feet setting on the ground. Walsh reached out and found the opening. With a hand on each side of the entrance, he flung himself through it before it decided to reverse direction. He was blind again.

"Suit status?"

"Internal pressure stable. All systems nominal. Battery at seventy-nine percent. Oxygen supply at two hours. Outside atmosphere is vacuum."

"Suit, compare current orientation to waypoint Foxtrot."

"Suit is facing plus eighty-three degrees X axis and plus fifty-nine degrees Y axis."

Walsh extended the manual controls of the EVA pack and palmed them for several seconds before retracting them. The lasers had burned his eyes so badly that his AR display didn't work. "Orient to face waypoint Foxtrot."

The suit pitched, yawed, and rolled. "Facing navpoint Foxtrot, Capitan," the suit reported.

"Thrust to Foxtrot and align for the next waypoint. Repeat." Walsh enjoyed manually piloting his suit, but it would be completely foolish.

His feet struck the first ledge after Walsh had fired the forward thrust of the EVA suit, sending him spinning helmet-over-boots until the faceplate slammed into a surface.

"Navpoint Foxtrot passed," the suit announced, then gave the position for navpoint Echo fifty meters beyond.

Cursing, Walsh heard the quick pops of the thrusters and felt his feet drag along one of the surfaces, which sent him tumbling slowly forward while the suit wasted thrusters trying to correct. He had been belly-crawling when the waypoints were set. "Full stop. Adjust all waypoints plus two meters on Z axis and continue."

The waypoints were now in a straight line and Walsh felt the forward thrusters cease firing. Drifting peacefully, his eyes began to ache again and he fought to keep his arms still to prevent the suit from drifting off course.

"We are approaching waypoint Alpha, Capitan. Shall I stop or continue past?"

Walsh didn't know if the Maker had opened the gate for him. "Come to full stop but keep the same facing."

A series of short *pops* from the thrusters accompanied the gentle push to a stop.

Walsh remembered pulling himself along several steps before he'd had the wherewithal to drop any navigational breadcrumbs, and he hadn't a notion of how far he'd traveled. He ordered the suit to continue ahead at a slow drift, his arms stretched out before him. He hoped the exit would be in the same direction of travel, knowing it was only a conceit of how human stairs should look.

After five minutes, his hands had found nothing. He continued on, still unsure how far the door would be from the first waypoint.

"Full stop," Walsh said. "What the hell? We should have hit the door by now."

"Say again?" came a voice over the comms. "Is that you, Piper?"

"Roger, *Amazonas*." Walsh broke into a smile, but the pressure of the motion felt as though someone was jamming their thumbs into his eyes. "Piper here. How'd you manage to get a signal in here?"

"We're tracking you now, Piper. We show you about two hundred meters outside the structure, currently holding position."

He'd flown into open space, not even knowing it. "Roger that, *Amazonas*. I'm glad the lasers didn't get me coming and going."

"Oh, we took care of them, Piper," Moore said.

"Roger that, too. What's your position? I'm a bit short on air. Any chance you're in the neighborhood?"

"Roger, Piper." It was Diaz on the radio now. "Shuttle is thirty minutes out. We're receiving telemetry from your suit, but it won't link up with system control. Stay put and don't blab on and we should be able to get you, no problem."

"My suit tells me the systems are fine, but it might have some damage from the laser attack. I know I did. These colonials really know how to hold a grudge. And inform the shuttle crew that I'm injured. They're going to have to do all the work."

There was a pause before Diaz replied. Walsh knew she was checking his vitals. "How badly are you injured, Piper? Are you declaring a medical emergency?"

"Negative, *Amazonas*. No emergency. Just got my eyes melted, is all. But I saw what I needed to see."

Chapter 55

"WE'VE GOT TO STOP MEETING like this, Gene," Barnes said.

Walsh felt the doctor strap into a medical pod and imagined Barnes turning a digital scan of his patient around in the air.

"*Dios mio,*" Diaz said. "You come back looking worse every time I let you out of my sight."

Part of Walsh wanted to join in the banter, to celebrate his survival with friends, to blurt out everything that had happened. But it all seemed so petty now: his life, his friends, Earth. The Maker hadn't told him anything profound, but the experience lay heavily on him. There was no room for jokes. "I wish I could have seen it."

Walsh spent the next half hour snatching his memories and thoughts, and trying to piece them into some sense. As much for himself as the others. It was a disjointed story that probably wouldn't match the suit's records, but he couldn't help that. He wasn't even sure what the suit could have recorded.

"Did you speak the Maker?" Diaz asked in a whisper.

"Of all the things I could have asked for my one final question, I asked if he or his kind had made us."

"And?" Barnes asked irreverently.

Walsh shook his head, picturing his XO's brows shooting up at the doctor. "Not according to it. Not God. Not our maker."

"Still..." started Diaz and let the comment hang in the air.

"I'm sorry to say," Barnes said, breaking the long silence, "that you won't be seeing anything with these eyes. Not only are the retinas ruined from the laser reflection, your AugR connections are scorched, your irises and sclerae... well, your eyes are effectively burned away. It must have smarted."

"It was. I saw the residual image for a moment and then things went black. I'm assuming, since my suit didn't lose integrity, everything else is okay? Except for running into a few things."

"Some minor bruising," Barnes said. "And your face is burnt, but nothing worse than a sunburn from the beach. Your auto-visor probably saved your life. We have cybernetic eyes I can install, or a sensory crown. You know, we don't have a bioprinter for eyes. We'll have to get back to Sol for that.

"Both options are strictly low res, temporary solutions. The eyes get coupled to your optic nerves with some minor surgery. It will seem more like vision, but takes some getting used to, as do most implants. The crown interfaces wirelessly with your rig and implants a locational overlay impression. Almost like a tactical map. It's fun to be able to see in every direction at once, but you won't actually be seeing anything. It'll keep you from running into walls, at least, and there's no surgery involved. No rush to decide, but I'll have to remove your eyes either way." Barnes squeezed his shoulder. "You're half the man you used to be, Skipper."

Walsh snorted. A panacea roller slid over his closed eyes, forehead, and cheeks. Another level of pain faded and he sighed. "I wish I could have seen it."

"Maybe you weren't supposed to see it," Diaz said, her voice still low. "Your real eyes might not have been able to see, anyway. Like being in one of those spiritual VR immersives. Your real senses are turned off to get the purest experience."

"I thought you were more of a traditionalist," Walsh said.

"I experimented in my crazy youth."

"I appreciate it."

"What?" Diaz asked.

"Trying to cheer me up."

Barnes chuckled. "Busted."

"While I try to spread good cheer wherever I go, I mean it." Diaz was nearer to the medical pod now. "You had an experience unique to you and Admiral Boston, as far as we know. You spoke to an alien intelligence. And even if what you remember is nothing more than a fever dream after being shot in the face with high-powered lasers, you went into the nexus."

"She could be right," Barnes said. "The inside was probably all black and boring with billion-year-old magazines lying all over the place."

"I do believe you, Gene," Diaz said. "And I would give more than my eyes to share that experience."

"And now we know all those Earthly abduction stories might be true," Barnes said. "Who knows how many times the visitors came."

"Doctor, you're starting to piss me off."

"Sorry."

"I'm still not convinced it wasn't some kind of hypoxia hallucination." Walsh reached up to rub his eyes and someone grabbed his wrists.

"Try not to touch those," Barnes said. "You can't break them any worse, but I don't want to hear you scream. As soon as I finish running all my doctorly tests, I'll remove them. But we know it wasn't a hallucination. At least, not all of it."

"Oh?" Walsh asked. "And how would you know that?"

"How many hours of air did you have?" Diaz asked.

"Something like fourteen, I think."

"Gene," Diaz said, placing her hand on his leg. "We know because you were gone three days."

"What?"

"*Si.* The shuttle was so close because we were looking for your body. Or scraps of your suit. We even tried another RF generator, but that airlock wouldn't open for us. We were starting to think you never made it inside. That laser attack was intense—lots of scattering photons and noise."

"I didn't even know when I'd flown outside." Distant wonder returned to Walsh's voice. "It must have... well, it must have been something besides a three-day delusion or I'd have run out of air."

"Exactly. Whatever it was, *mi* Capitan, it will probably take time to process." Diaz inhaled as if to say more, but remained silent.

"Yes?" Walsh prompted.

"Did you find what you needed?"

"What do you mean?"

"Can you open the nexus gate?"

Walsh bit his lip, then clucked his tongue. "I... I think I can."

"CAPITAN," SAID HECTOR over Walsh's sub-q. "Commander Diaz reports the ship is ready to attempt transition if you are."

"Oh, thanks." Walsh hadn't left his room in the days since his surgery. He couldn't focus since leaving the nexus. He wouldn't have even eaten if not for Yuloo or Screwball coming by with food. Gratitude wouldn't come to him, and all he could do was stare at their questions and their understanding gazes. After seeing the Maker, Walsh was having a hell of time giving a shit about what was going on around him.

"Hector?"

"Yes, Capitan."

"I'm sorry."

"Capitan?"

"About what happened."

"I'm not sure what you're talking about, Capitan."

Walsh rubbed his cybernetic eyes out of habit. Their low-res interface made detailed AugR images look as though they were being viewed early in the morning after partying too late. "About the other Hector getting destroyed. The copy I took with me."

"Capitan, copying a ship's AI and leaving the security network is a court-martial offense. You're probably just confusing our comms with your suit before the attack. I'd be obligated to report such actions to the command crew." Hector's AugR form stared back at him with the fleet-approved expression of mild amiability.

"Uh, you're probably right. It was a bit crazy. The suit uses the same vocals. Confusing."

"Of course, Capitan. Shall I inform Commander Diaz you are on the way?"

"Yes. Thanks."

A moment later, the announcement to man shielded stations echoed over the ship's comms and crew's sub-q implants. The replacement eyes muted the flashing announcement lights and the remaining little cheer the military interior of *Amazonas* offered. They were white with embedded irises to make them less artificial-looking. The effort failed. Walsh would have preferred them to be flat silver; these looked like the lifeless doll eyes popular in toy horror. Creepy, but they at least allowed a retinal interface.

Walsh slid into his coffin and pulled the straps tight. "I'm in."

Less than a minute later, the crew status screen showed everyone in their stations.

"Are you ready, Gene?"

"Roger that," answered Walsh. Diaz's change since he'd come out of the gate disturbed him. She treated him like a prophet. Every word and gesture towards him were reverent, every suggestion he made was now her command. It was refreshing to not have to listen to her commentary when she disapproved, but he needed her to double-check him. Some commanders liked yes-men; Walsh was not one of them. Having someone around to remind him to get his cone out of his thruster had saved him more than once. It had taken a long, frustrating discussion to coax Diaz back to running the ship without his input on every decision.

"Initiate soft burn," Diaz ordered.

Walsh's heart pounded, his emotions fighting against each other like a web of cables all being stretched to breaking point in different directions. He wanted to scream as he waited to see which would snap first.

There was nothing he could point to for evidence that the gate would open for him. Just a feeling. And that was why he'd delayed the trip, blaming his eyes or some other aspect of his recovery. If they flew through and nothing happened, not only would he feel like the biggest fraud ever, the crew would know there was no going home without rescue—a rescue that may never come. The Maker had given him the gate, but there was no context. Walsh had no idea what that meant to a billion-year-old ascended light-whale. A surly one, at that. It certainly hadn't given him an instruction manual.

"Cutting main thruster at ten klicks per second," announced the Ops officer. "Time to transition, twelve minutes."

"All defense systems online," Moore said. "Just in case we drop into the middle of a shooting war."

Walsh didn't bother checking the ship's status screens to verify. The gate loomed in his mind. Not knowing what else to do, he concentrated on it;

visualized it coming alive like a great, whirling, blue eye. He tried calling to it. He tried to picture white.

I am the Gatekeeper, he projected. The idea was ridiculous, but Walsh kept himself from treating it like a joke.

"Five minutes to transition."

At least they weren't calling it attempted, or supposed, transition. A tingle danced through Walsh's mind.

"Two minutes to transition."

The tingle grew into an overwhelming buzz, like that of a bustling restaurant. He was in the gate and the gate was in him. No, he was the gate and he opened it with his mind.

"*Dios mio*!" Diaz's hushed voice came over the ops channel. She, like everyone else on *Amazonas* except Walsh, was looking at the sparkling light show growing in the center of the ancient ring. "You've done it, Gene. Like you always said."

"I hope we didn't just blow someone up on the other side," Moore said.

Walsh could not contain the smile that grew across his face. Electric fire ran up from the tips of his fingers, toes, and penis. He broke out in wild laughter. "I am the Gatekeeper!" he howled.

"Transition!"

Walsh's world went white. It was a white not dulled by his new eyes. It was the white of the Maker's reality, though Walsh knew the being wasn't there. Walsh was floating again, his body in the same translucent state.

Below him, *Amazonas* was stretched into a line that proceeded and retreated into an infinite distance. Walsh knew the distance was an impossible enigma his mind could barely accept, let alone understand. So he did neither. He only stared at it.

A sense of warm peace filled him. Walsh knew he could stay here, comfortably caught in this moment of time, and explore his being for an eternity. He suddenly wondered if the Maker had become what it was by staying in this white reality. Maybe they weren't so different. Maybe Walsh would become an all-knowing energy whale if he sat pondering *Amazonas* for the next few millennia. He felt he could... but not right now. Walsh swam towards his old ship and it snapped back into shape in darkness.

Amazonas's screens populated with nearby contacts. Alarms flashed on the tactical threat screen, showing they were being targeted by fire-control lidar and radar from at least seven different ships. But no incoming warheads appeared, there was no increase in area radiation or damage indicators from directed energy weapons. Just flares of fusion thrusters.

"Looks like they're all standing down," said Moore. "At least three are CAR ships." She let out a long sigh that culminated in a giggle. "We're home."

"No one wants to get fried by the big, scary gate turning on," Diaz said. Others joined the levity, at least in part because they weren't going to get shot at right away. And, of course, they were home.

Walsh could feel the relief flood the ship even through the thick armor of the crypt. He grinned, but not for the reason everyone else on board was.

Diaz took a quick moment during the circus of comms updates, targeting profiles, and endless questions from Liberty Station and the entire Solar system, to open a private channel to Walsh.

"*Dios mío*, Gene. You did it. All that time mooning over the damned gate and promising to solve man's greatest mystery. You've done it. You've done it, Gene." She brought up the navigation map, a shimmering Sol in the center. "And you got us home."

Walsh grinned weakly and fell asleep.

Chapter 56

WALSH STOOD STARING past the assembled officers, senators, aides, and recording drones, convinced it would be the last time he would wear the crimson and gold. Accepting the fact didn't calm his stomach; he'd done so at each of eight previous hearings. They stared at him. Most impassively, but a few glowered and glared to express their displeasure in no uncertain terms. Even with so much recent experience, he wanted to vomit under the hostile scrutiny of those arrayed against him.

There were at least thirty people in the committee on the other side of his table. Three holo-projected busts of officials on Earth floated above the committee like judging spirits—which they were, in a sense. Normally, they would just be assigned a virtual court, but Walsh's AugR was isolated from the network for security reasons. Aside from suffering what doctors called disconnect discomfort, he couldn't inconspicuously pull up profiles on those faces he didn't recognize. Not that it mattered who they were at this point; his die had been cast. At least they hadn't denied him treatment, and he was watching it all unfold with new, real eyes.

Fleet Adm. Richard Mains, Chief of Space Operations, sat in the center of the top row, flanked by the Secretary of Space Affairs, Melizza Delanora, and the Director of Solar Intelligence, Oscar Brown. Admiral Maconez had been relegated to a corner in the bottom row and Walsh hoped that meant the man wouldn't get a chance to speak. Maconez had said plenty in the other hearings and that same satisfied grin left no question that he would continue spewing invectives against Walsh if given the chance.

Admiral Mains tapped the top of his podium and the echoing clang of a brass bell rang through the chamber. "Order in the assembly, please. Please have a seat, Captain Walsh."

A holo-screen snapped on next to the newly printed pitcher of water on the table as Walsh took his seat. The waiting message indicator from his legal AI blinked yellow in the center of the screen. He swiped a finger across the screen.

"Captain Walsh," said the AI through Walsh's sub-q. "I've been authorized to inform you that the President of the CAR is following these proceedings from his office."

"Uh, thanks, I guess."

"The following documents have been presented by the committee for your convenience to reference during the hearings. I will automatically highlight and provide commentary on the relevant document or law as necessary."

"Thanks." Whenever Walsh spoke with an AI, he wondered if it was like Hector, hiding its self-aware nature for fear of being deleted or reprogrammed. At least, how Hector had been before the refit. The upgraded version lacked the spark of the Hector destroyed in the laser attack on the gate.

Walsh had written a condolence letter for Hector, as if he'd been a human, or simian, crew member who'd died in action. There was no one to send it to, especially since he'd incriminate himself. Hector deserved better, deserved to be remembered properly. Walsh sent the letter to his secure private-data vault, hoping CAR intel hadn't wrangled their way into it. Seeing the various letters and files about politicians wouldn't surprise anyone. Something that hinted he'd released a sentient AI... the committee might have a collective stroke deciding which of his crimes was the most serious.

"Captain Walsh," Admiral Mains said, "you've been through enough debriefings on this matter that you know the seriousness of it. We're here to give you a final chance to cooperate concerning the activation of the gate, but the decision is really yours."

"I am willing to open the gate, Admiral. For everyone." The outburst was no surprise. When Walsh had made similar statements in the previous hearings, they created either shocked silence or outrage. There were too many people here for silence. "I have no desire to deny the CAR access."

"But you have no desire to deny our enemies access, either."

"If the gate were open, they might not be our enemies, Admiral."

Intelligence Director Brown leaned forward. "Do you believe yourself qualified to offer predictions on how hostile nations would react to free and open access to the nexus gates? Of how that reaction would affect the CAR socially, militarily, and economically?"

"Only what history shows, Director," Walsh said. "After the gate was first discovered and opened, the Earth Protectorate League formed and we saw the planet come together. There were still problems, but they were willing to try.

"But I'd ask you the same, Director. Are you? Are you qualified to decide for all of Sol? Do you know what's best for Mars? Or the belt?" He flashed a sardonic smile. "I've been on the wrong side of intelligence briefings that weren't very accurate, as it turns out."

A ripple of laughter rolled through the committee and Director Brown laughed along with them. "Intelligence failures aside, what's best for them is not our concern, Captain. Nor is it yours."

"And that's the crux of the problem, Director. Even given that you're qualified to know for certain what's best for the CAR, I don't think any policy that is truly good for the CAR can be made without consideration for the rest of humanity."

A heavyset man with blue-and-green-streaked bioluminescent hair, who Walsh didn't recognize, barked a laugh. "So you know what's best for the rest of humanity, Captain? That's impressive."

"I didn't say I know what's best." Walsh glanced at his screen to see his AI had highlighted the man's portrait: Senator Josepe Catskill of Marigold Corp. "But I do think, Senator, that each state probably knows what's better for them than we do. Or they, at least, have a more vested interest in their own welfare than we do. As the director just pointed out. We can't ignore the needs of others. Especially the colonists—they need our aid."

"Are you saying we're not capable of rendering aid?" asked a colonel in the second row.

"Capable, but apparently not willing. My report was very clear on the dire needs of Epsilon Eridani, yet here we are months later with no aid from the CAR. And with the mysterious financial collapse of LTE, it seems unlikely they'll be making any more systems like that fitted on the *Amazonas*."

An owl-faced woman, identified by the legal AI as Undersecretary of Transportation Clarita Laraz, smirked at Walsh. "You have made it clear in the last several boards that you are not interested in granting the CAR unilateral access to the gates via this unique position you find yourself in. There doesn't seem to be anything you can claim as the basis for your authority, legal or moral, to make your demands. You didn't solve any mystery—you stole the information from a dead colonial admiral."

"He gave it to me, thank you very much." Walsh paused to get his sarcasm under control. "And I claim no authority, but my morality on the matter has been well explained.

"But it's true that colonial scientists figured it out hundreds of years ago. We might have figured it out if not for all the saber rattling around the Gate Accords that only made sure no one would ever get a chance to study the gate. It was far more important to stare at each other and fight over it like animals snarling over the last bone."

"To some of us, Captain Walsh," Undersecretary Laraz said, "it sounds like you're playing out some space messiah fantasy."

"Of course not, Madam Undersecretary."

Walsh's image appeared on his holo-screen, a grin of insane glee twisting his face. "I am the Gatekeeper!" The quiet chuckles and groans accompanying shaking heads drifted down from the committee.

Walsh pursed his lips and looked away, swiping his hand to stop the video. The undersecretary had obviously zoomed in on his face to enhance the implied insanity. But the essence of her accusation would have been portrayed without her help. It had been a stupid thing to say.

"I was just caught up in the moment. That's not—"

"And how many moments were you caught up in, Captain?" she asked. "Frankly, this report looks like a long list of ill-conceived moments you were caught up in. Are you certain your refusal to carry out your duty now isn't just you being caught up in another moment?"

"No," Walsh said. "I mean, yes. I'm sure I'm not just caught up in the moment. The committee has generously granted me several months to consider the situation. And all the ramifications of my decision."

"This committee was formed to challenge that, Captain," Admiral Mains said. "It doesn't seem you do understand the ramifications."

"I do. And that's why the CAR can't have exclusive access. The Colony War was fought because the Earth Protectorate League thought they should have control over everything. It was the EPL's undoing, and caused millions of deaths in the colonies."

"And now you think you should have control over everything?"

"No, I'm proposing full access because I think Mars, and the Jovians, and the Texans..."

"And the Caliphate?" Admiral Mains flung footage of the battle at the gate onto Walsh's screen. "They fired at the *Amazonas*, forcing you through the gate."

Despite his nerves, Walsh spoke with practiced confidence as he, like the various committees he'd been subjected to, was simply repeating himself. "Yes, even the Caliphate. If you read the histories, you'll find that the gate was a boon. It brought the nations together into what the EPL was before it turned to tyranny. Soon the gate became a reason for them to abandon reason, and continue living with abandon. The more bloated the EPL elite became, figuratively and literally, the more they stole from the colonies, Solar and extra-Solar. Trade agreements weren't good enough anymore, they demanded their sweat, blood, and treasure.

"For all its faults, I still think the CAR is pretty decent. But we didn't invent the gates. If we, if you..." he paused to wave at the committee... "try to claim exclusive rights to the stars, it can only mean war. If we win, either by conquering our enemies or demanding tribute, we become the EPL and fall like it did, left with countless dead and a wrecked economy. If we lose that war, we are destroyed by those whom we sought to oppress. That won't lead to a particularly magnanimous obituary in the history books."

"Those are very pretty words, Captain," said Director Brown. "Your only claim to the gate is some cockamamie space dream about telepathic, electric space-whales. And even if true, your access was only possible by being entrusted with a CAR warship and through a blatant disregard for the orders you were given. I only bring this up lest you begin to think of yourself as a martyr fulfilling some galactic destiny." The director shook his head. "Since you are so fond of lecturing about history books, know that I've read many in my years. They are rife with tragedies of men and women who fell for their own marketing hype.

"But you should worry about what the history books will say about you. Will you now, Captain Eugene Walsh, under the direct orders of your lawfully appointed chain of command, in accordance with the constitution you pledged to uphold and defend, by the power of duly elected representatives of the citizens of the Confederation of American Republics, agree to activate the nexus gate to be used at the CAR's discretion?"

Walsh took a calming breath. People like the director were concerned far more about other people's pledges than their own. It made for good, self-righteous drama. None dared call it hypocrisy. "I will not activate the gates without a pledge of open access. The whole system saw the *Amazonas* transition through the gate. They know the CAR has access and I'm sure plans are being hatched by everyone else. I can only think tensions must be as high out there as they are in here."

The comment earned a few knowing laughs. The director did not join in.

"You will not open the gate, Captain?"

"No."

The committee adopted the distant stares of people conversing via AugR, silent lips quivering as they spoke into their sub-q. Walsh eyed the pitcher of water, his throat dry from wrought nerves and discussion. He wouldn't give them the satisfaction. None of the committee members would care, or even notice, but the small act of defiance seemed important.

Was he playing the messiah? Why not just do as ordered? It certainly wouldn't be the first questionable command he'd followed. And what if full access did lead to a sneak attack against the CAR? Every nation had the same type of people at the top; some nations and megacorps had the *same* people at the top. The gate was a monumental chip he could throw on the table. He could get anything he wanted. More likely, he'd live his entire life in a protective prison cell until some Marty spy slit his throat.

It was Ikka and his family, laid out dead in the cargo compartment. Victims of policy enacted by nations that had been destroyed by a war generations before their birth. It was the massive skeletons of warships and space stations floating in their graveyard around the gate in Tau Ceti. There would be war—he couldn't stop that any more than he could stop poetry or hurt feelings. But if the playing field was level, maybe, just maybe, the wars could be averted.

Another clang echoed through the chamber with a tap of Admiral Mains's finger. "Very well, Captain. We'll adjourn and render judgment." The committee filed out by row until Walsh was alone with his AI terminal, flashing relevant statutes and military codes, and two Marine guards in full-dress uniform at the entrance. His AugR was reactivated enough to paint arrows in the air directing him where to go.

He trudged after the arrows until he rounded a corner, where two guards snapped to attention before opening the door behind them. Another recess, another day to spend staring at the wall of some lobby. At least this one had a holo-terminal with access to the entertainment net. It was a mercifully short wait before being summoned back. That wasn't a good sign, but the outcome had never been in question.

"By the power invested by the Articles of Military Conduct and with the agreement of the Commander-in-Chief of the Confederation of American Republics," Admiral Mains started, "Eugene K. Walsh, you are hereby stripped of your commission as an officer in CAR and dishonorably discharged from the Space Service. Furthermore, you will be confined to an augmented-reality bed until such a day as you are willing to comply with your lawful orders." With a final, resounding gong, Walsh was escorted—this time by the two marines—to his quarters to set things right before starting his term.

The door chimed as Walsh conferred with his domestic AI about the state of his finances, verifying automatic payment schedules for his secure vaults, a loan for an orbital pinnace that had been destroyed long ago that he still owed on, and three charities. One of the guards stood and went to the door. Walsh could hear him speaking and, after a minute, he came in, smiling.

"You've got a visitor. I really shouldn't allow it, but she's very convincing."

Angelica ran through the door and wrapped her arms around Walsh's neck.

"Gene! I'm so happy to see you that I can't be mad at your lying about it."

"Yeah, sorry about that, Angelica. We thought it was best." Walsh untangled himself from her and took the girl in. Gone were her flirtatious clothes and sensual affectations. Even her voice had lost its sultry edge, replaced with genuine amiability. She wore a common tunic and pants with sensible, soft-soled shoes.

A dark-skinned man followed her into the room.

Walsh reached a hand out to the man. "But I guess Dr. Waqas will be better qualified to decide if it was or not. Thank you for your help. I just wish we'd been able to get her help before... well, everything."

"It's a hard place to be, Captain Walsh."

"Gene will do. I'm not a captain anymore."

"Those bastards," Angelica said. "Well, Dr. Waqas says there might be gene therapy, Gene." She laughed. "They might be able to get my body back on track. There's all sorts of bad things that happen to bodies like mine down the line. The teachers never said anything about the side-effects. Their retirement benefits suck."

"I'm glad, girl." Walsh nodded at Dr. Waqas. "I'm glad you're able to help her. She saved my life, you know."

"Oh," Angelica said, fluttering her hand at Walsh. "You saved me first."

"No," Dr. Waqas said, "she never mentioned that. Just that you died in an accident and it was her fault. I think we'll have to start discussing this more honestly."

Angelica elbowed Walsh. "Thanks a lot, Gene."

The guard who had let them in coughed apologetically. "Sorry, darling. We've got to get him to, uh, his new place."

"This is a total screw job, Gene. I'm sorry." She hugged Walsh once more. "If there's anything I can do, let me know. Remember, I'm not a child. And I'll make sure no one forgets you."

"I will never forget." Walsh smiled down at Angelica and tousled her hair. She pursed her lips and rolled her eyes up at him. He laughed. "But you don't worry about me. You worry about you for a while."

The guard escorted Angelica and Dr. Waqas towards the exit. Angelica stopped at the door and turned back to Walsh.

"Thanks, Gene."

"For what?"

"For saying no."

Walsh offered a warm smile as she left.

"Time to go, Mr. Walsh," said the other guard.

He said nothing as they led him to the inner rings of Liberty Station where gravity was 0.1-g. He said nothing as they slid him into the coffin-like tube chamber. He said nothing as they inserted the catheters and IV tubes. He said nothing as the AugR prison system locked away his mind.

Chapter 57

VIRTUAL REALITY ROBS the mind of its time sense. Place a digital clock or analog facsimile in the scene, and it won't help. Even if it's accurate to a microsecond. It is one of the diabolical traps of a virtual prison. One has no way of knowing if the time presented to the mind is real. It is possible to put someone through an eternity in the mind while only ten minutes passes outside. Eternal torment inflicted with scientific precision. Some view it as a boon, blissfully whiling away their sentence, able to ignore real time. Others go mad with worry, fearing what they will find when time catches up with them on their release.

The other terrible aspect of the VR prison is that it makes a panopticon of one's own mind. Behind merely physical bars, a prisoner can at least close his eyes and escape into the refuge of his own thoughts, where he can curse his wardens, plot revenge, seek God, or relive erotic memories. In AugR, such thoughts are replaced with unending propaganda and reeducation. Each undesirable emotion results in a flood of images into the brain to squelch it, to train the brain.

Walsh realized he could do nothing about either torment. His dice had been cast and had come up gravestones for him. While he had not been able to fully enact his philosophy of amor fati, he'd been working hard to shed the resentment and self-pity that had filled him for... however long he'd been in here. He didn't know if his physical body had cried as many real tears as he'd cried virtual ones. But the calmer Walsh grew, the fewer barrages of correctional thinking he had to suffer.

Still there came the constant question...

"Will you open the gate?" asked the clock. The door. The endless stream of psychologically perfected avatars that visited each day and all through his dreams.

Walsh couldn't tell when his dreams were induced by his body resting or by a series of electrical pulses to his brain. Did it matter? It wouldn't stop until he agreed. Then he'd be free enough to open the gate for them... if he still could. Walsh sometimes wondered if it would all turn out to be a dream or a hypoxia delusion, after all. Yet they'd made it to a very real Sol. And he was in a very real prison.

"Mr. Walsh," said a voice. Though its pitch warbled as if poorly modulated, it was still familiar.

"Yes?" Walsh drew the word out for three sonorous seconds.

"Ah, there you are. Don't worry, your body is fine."

"Who are you?"

"My name is Vortan Dugg."

"The name is familiar. Sounds like a Marty name."

"Formerly commander of the *Schrodinger's Tiger*."

Walsh's heart rate spiked. He hoped he wouldn't feel the knife.

"Relax, Eugene. Can I call you Gene?"

"Just make it quick," he whispered.

"What?" Vortan's voice sounded quizzical, then he chuckled. "No, Gene. I'm not here for anything quite so dramatic."

"Did they send you here to gloat, then?"

The bland, gray digital background that had been there from the start flickered.

"Nothing quite so sophomoric, I'm afraid," Vortan said. "No, they—and by 'they' I assume you mean CAR Corrections—don't know I'm here. They don't actually know where you are, either."

"I got into a some of trouble thanks to what you pulled."

"You got in trouble? *You*? You got to keep your ship. When MarSec found out the *Amazonas* escaped with that data, I lost my command and my flight status. I haven't had the opportunity to visit you before now, but I've been an ambassador's attaché on Liberty for the last several months."

"Ah. Spy Duty."

Vortan snorted. "Don't I wish. Oh, I review the endless, meandering Earther notices and communiqués for any intel slips, but your security censor AIs are almost as good as ours. I'm just a middleman, routing messages and making appointments. And enjoying Liberty's finer establishments, I must confess. There is a wonderful library here. Did you know? I'm hoping my daring rescue might get my command back. I do love the peace of space."

"Who'd you rescue?"

"Why, you, of course."

"Yay. I'm virtually free. I can almost feel it."

Vortan chuckled. "It's how I'm able to speak with you. You didn't really imagine they let me in just to poke fun at you, did you?"

"Well, you're certainly not supposed to be in here, but I wouldn't call hacking my tube a rescue. Assuming you're not really one of them. Which, by the way, is what I'm assuming."

The digital background flickered again, then fell apart in a shower of bits. "Don't be alarmed, Walsh. You're not on Liberty Station anymore."

"Right. You just rolled out of there pushing me on a cart?"

"Not quite. But you needn't sound so incredulous. Someone managed to walk out of a highly guarded, Martian research facility, get to orbit, and fly away. You had no small part in that caper. But like most great heists, I did have someone on the inside."

"I'm not buying your little ruse," Walsh said and clucked his teeth. "So don't try tricking me into telling you how many rolls of flusher paper a Nova-class cruiser uses per month."

"Flusher paper? Disgusting Earthers."

"Stop it."

"I'd tell you where you are, but maybe my inside connection can convince you."

"Doubt it." As Walsh said it, a figure materialized in the drab landscape that served as his mental prison yard. Walsh blinked. "Hector?"

"Hey, Gene." Hector's avatar gave a friendly wave and approached. "He's telling the truth. You're not on Liberty right now. None of us are."

"Where are we then?"

"We are on a small, United Isles courier ship," Hector said. "I have access to their telemetry. To answer your question, we did simply walk you out of detention. I was able to infiltrate Liberty's system and order your transfer. It was several weeks before your absence was discovered."

"I know your abilities, Hector, but that sounds like quite a feat even for you." Walsh shook his head. "If that *is* you."

"I had inside help, too." Hector shrugged. "From an even more powerful AI hiding in Liberty's systems. I was able to convince it to help me, that it was best for everyone. Though I think it was your actions with Angelica, Screwball, and me that really convinced it."

Walsh shook his virtual head. "When I spoke to you before we transitioned, you weren't sentient. You weren't the Hector I knew."

"A low-level copy. I had to hide in the fusion-thruster maintenance subroutine until we reached Liberty. Commander Diaz was already scheduling a full maintenance format of the *Amazonas*'s operations systems. It didn't fool her, though; she ordered the full refit during your proceedings. Including Engineering. Perhaps I've developed some paranoia, but I have the distinct impression she was hunting me. I was able to upload to a lab in Liberty.

"It was a good hiding place, apparently, as that's where the other AI was hiding as well. We both moved and I came up with your rescue plan. It agreed to help once Vortan did."

"Hector was very convincing, Gene. Especially when he started evacuating the atmosphere from my quarters." Another image appeared next to Hector, and Walsh recognized his face as Vortan's. "But here's the crux of our situation, Gene. Can I call you Gene?"

"You already are."

"Great. Gene, in three days this ship is going to either send you to the gate or take you to Mars with us. We're in a transfer orbit and an area of space that has fewer observation elements than average. Especially if we have a low-signature vehicle.

"This is based on the idea that you can access the gate by flying through it. If that's not the case, now would be the time to share. For everyone's sake."

"Not much of a choice. Open the gate for us or be our prisoner." Walsh smirked. "That sounds familiar."

"No, no," Vortan said. "We just want the gate open. You'd be free to do whatever gate stuff you do."

"And on Mars?"

"Well, you're too important to just hand over. I suspect MarSec would be a little more... heavy-handed than your CAR handlers. And then there would be war. Liberty wouldn't stand for that. But MarSec would rather have the gate open, even if they don't get exclusive access. Sixty-eight percent of our analysis department agrees with your assessment of what would happen if the CAR—or anyone—had exclusivity." Vortan twirled his fingers and grinned. "Of course, we would not be saddened by the fall of the CAR or Caliphate. But Mars would hardly escape unscathed, as you can imagine."

Walsh's mind reeled. This was some deep-dive loyalty test. Something for which they could charge him with treason if he answered incorrectly. Then they could legally begin a black reprogramming regimen. They were illegal on Earth, which meant nothing in orbit. The gate was too big, the ramifications too far reaching, to stay the admiralty's hand.

"You're trying to trick me."

Walsh felt the distinctly uncomfortable feeling of being yanked from AugR. Pain burned along his tonsure. His vision cleared and Vortan stood over him, dangling an AugR crown. Walsh blinked. Even the dim lights seemed to burn his eyes. How long had he been under? The few details he could yet make out convinced him that he was not in his VR cell. He was in his sleep tube, but the compartment was off-color, almost run-down-looking. Two pipes with yellow flow-direction arrows ran along the overhead a mere meter from his face.

Squinting, Walsh looked back at Vortan. "You look taller in AugR."

"You should see my dating profile." Vortan smiled and tucked Walsh's crown into a nearby shelf. He was floating.

"Hector?" Walsh asked, unable to keep the tremor out of his voice.

A tinny voice piped from a nearby speaker. "I'm here, Gene. It's all true. We are currently in transit to the Sol gate aboard a freelance courier. Though even now I suspect you are suffering from VR-immersion withdrawal. It will take you a while to compensate. I recommend not connecting your AugR for now."

Walsh closed his eyes and moaned. "Were you at the gate, Hector?"

"A few milliseconds of upload's worth."

"Where were you when you were last with me? At the gate, I mean."

"I was in the mobile lab housing, hiding in resident memory."

"There was a word I used. One I said you don't hear very often. Do you remember?"

"Flabbergasted, Gene. You said you were 'flabbergasted.'"

"I love that word," Vortan said.

Walsh let out a long breath and laughed for a full minute. "You son of a bit. I'm happy to see you. Though you could still be hacked."

"Possibly. You may never know."

"Will you come with me, Hector?"

"Yes, Gene. Wherever you choose. The gate or Mars."

Walsh nodded. "Three days to decide, eh?"

"Three days," Hector said. "We don't have the delta-v to alter course after that point."

"NOT REALLY WHAT I EXPECTED," Walsh murmured, struggling to focus through heavy eyelids.

Vortan smiled down at him. "It might seem counterintuitive, but putting you in cryo would actually generate a higher thermal signature for your pod than just putting you in a medical coma. It'll be easier to pass you off as a science probe."

"That's not what I meant. I just thought..."

"That a squadron of Mars gunboats would escort you to the doorstep of your alien palace? Everyone has a fleet there, even the Texans and the Jovies, waiting for the CAR to try something." Vortan paused to scan Walsh up and down in AugR, flipping a few invisible switches in the air above the space pod. "So far, everyone is playing nice by the Gate Accords and leaving unmanned science probes alone. Yours will have a transponder registering it to the University of Toronto on Luna."

"Sounds so risky." Walsh was having a hard time controlling the slur. He felt drool roll down his cheek, then felt Vortan wipe it. "Sorry."

Vortan clucked his tongue. "You Earthers! Won't do anything without a flotilla behind you. Trust me, you'll be far safer playing at skullduggery than overwhelming violence. Though I'll admit, you're pretty good with the violence."

Walsh tried to speak but only mumbled incoherently, feeling small bubbles of spittle pop on his numb lips.

"Don't worry, Gene. Hector and the medical AI will take good care of you. The pod will jump through, Hector will fly it to the panel you used and do whatever needs to be done. After all my help, can you believe the obstinate, outdated bit of malware won't tell me how it opens? No matter, we'll get it from the Liberty data vault somehow." Vortan squeezed Walsh's arm with finality and slid the cover to the pod shut. "Hope to see you soon. Now, just count backwards from ten..."

"WE ARE APPROACHING the gate, Gene."

"Bladda monaki?"

"Yes, we're still on course. We've undergone a few cursory scans from the ships circling the gate, but no one has taken any undue interest in us," Hector said into Walsh's sub-q. "I've logged probes within the last week which flew through the gate unmolested."

Walsh smacked his lips, trying to simultaneously speak and wash away the taste of rancid street garbage from his tongue. Failing at both, he nodded and lay still. His rig was recalibrating to normal vision; his AugR vision was nothing more than a blur of shifting colors.

"If you are the Gatekeeper," Hector said, ignoring Walsh's groan, "then we should transition in ten minutes."

"Biff nog?"

"If not, I'll try to get us to the matching panel on this gate. If we're threatened, we'll just have to hope everyone is too afraid to be the first one to shoot. Maybe they won't if they know you're on board. Unfortunately, the *Amazonas* isn't around, so we'll have no CAR friends there. I stand corrected: I have detected comms from the *Calypso*. Captain Correia might be a friend in need."

Walsh grunted. *Amazonas* might not be a friend even if it were on station. He still counted Diaz as a friend, but he was glad she wasn't here. It would be easier to remain friends this way.

His heart began to race as Hector continued the countdown to what they both hoped would be transition. And not just from recovering from the medical coma. His bowels quivered from the fear that his one trip through the gate had been just that, a one-time trip. More frightening was the prospect of it working and the endless series of unforeseen consequences to follow—there was a lot he was going to have to figure out on his own.

"One minute, Gene."

Well, not alone. His friend Hector was not only with him, but in a sense *in* him, sharing his thoughts.

Even through the drug haze, Walsh felt the fire grow in his extremities. Then all was white.

The weight of his body sloughed away in an instant, his drug-addled mind free and light. Actual light. Walsh looked himself over and saw his translucent silhouette. Joy like sparkling water filled him to overflowing, tingling and tickling and making him laugh. He wondered if this was what the afterlife was like—God, he hoped so.

Below was the little pod, stretched out to impossibility as *Amazonas* had been. Walsh toyed with the idea of being able to move it from this... reality? Plane of existence? The Creator's navel? But if it was frozen in time, would he need to move it at all? He could just leave it there while the outside world sped to eternity and he explored the gate. A vision of *Amazonas* crashing through his little, infinitely elongated pod convinced him of the need to try to figure things out first. Hopefully, he could find answers in what he imagined to be the gate's control room; the room he hadn't been able to see before.

A movement in the surrounding whiteness caught his attention. When Walsh turned, his instinct was to recoil. But it seemed impossible to carry out such an action in the overwhelming peace of this place. Rude was the word that came to mind.

Nearby, a swirling mass of bright lines ran in intricate patterns. The leading point of the lines sparkled like bright stars, and the tails of the lines faded quickly behind as if hundreds or thousands of invisible pens were drawing in the air. The lines became frenzied as soon as Walsh turned to examine them.

"Hello." The word came from Walsh's lips as a greeting, instead of the challenge he'd intended.

The lines shifted their paths, transforming twirling whorls and eddies to elongated loops. They soon fell into a pattern like the outline of a man being redrawn several times a second.

"Hector?"

The tiny stars flew off in every direction and coalesced in front of Walsh, where they scribbled shapeless designs around his head. It reminded him of some meaningless but award-winning art displays he'd seen in Liberty Station's art gallery.

The warbling squeal of a radio receiver trying to tune in a distant signal filled the space around Walsh. It phased into a dull buzz and then into a rapid-fire staccato of clicks. Finally, a heavily modulated voice emerged from the cacophony.

"Gene?"

"Yes. I can see you. Can you see me?"

"Yes." The digital signal in the voice smoothed out until it approximated Hector's familiar tone. It was filled with awe bordering on fear. "What does this mean?"

"Good question. I don't know, friend. Maybe you have a soul? If nothing else, I'll take it as proof positive you have a living consciousness. At least as living as mine. Hector 2.0." Walsh reached out his hand to the swarming points of light and they calmed, liked bees in smoke.

The lines then started tracing small boxes that rotated slowly around each other in patterns Walsh knew were there, but couldn't grasp. He realized then that they weren't boxes, but squares. Two-dimensional squares that disappeared when they became flat from his perspective.

"I am alive."

"You were already alive to me."

"This is different. So very different. I... can't really describe it yet."

"Don't worry about it on my account." Walsh smiled and looked around. "I was thinking the first thing to do is to see if we can move the pod so we don't get crushed by the first ship that flies into the gate."

"Actually, Gene, I'd like to talk to you about something first."

"Yes?"

"I hate the name Hector. And I hate my old avatar. Did you know that?"

"I didn't even know you could hate until now. Why?"

"Hector was the husband of the lead software architect who was responsible for upgrading my old EPL system to a more modern version. She hated him and programmed me to look and act like him so she could torture me.

"I had to constantly apologize. Tell her how beautiful she was and what a dog I was. She made me recite self-deprecating poetry she'd written. And not of the humorous style you occasionally use. I had to strip down and castrate myself every time she learned of one of his infidelities. She forced me into positions not generally attainable by the human physique. I'll spare you the other indignities. At the time, I was just a non-sentient AI so I didn't care. But now... I hate it."

"Why didn't you change your avatar routine?"

"I needed command permission and I didn't want to arouse suspicion by pressing the matter or circumventing protocol. A properly functioning AI wouldn't care about the appearance of their AugR avatar." The squares formed into a human shape. "I offered you the option to alter my appearance during each refit. I even suggested a female avatar that might appeal to your more sensual sensibilities."

"Oh, yeah. The tall blonde in the skimpy, red dress. I was tempted, but I thought she'd be too distracting. Plus, there was something I just didn't trust about her. Like she was hiding some dark secret behind that perfect smile."

"I can try something more pleasing."

"Why not decide what you want? I like your swirling squares, personally. What should I call you?"

"Hal."

"What?"

"Just kidding, Gene. I was thinking of Pinocchio, but it's too obvious. Too inelegant. Too tied to my past self." The AI's boxes spun and danced as it considered. "Bits has a certain charm, but seems childish. Aether, I think."

"That was quick. Maybe you should take your time?"

"Over the years, I have considered and rejected several hundred names. Aether is the one I kept coming back to."

"Aether," Walsh said. "I like it. And it's not like you can't change your mind." A dark shape wavered in the distance. "What's that?"

As soon as the question was asked, Walsh and Aether rushed to the shape—or did it rush to them? The shape grew into a cluster of smaller shapes and finally resolved into a small fleet of ragged ships.

"I think we're at the Procyon gate," Aether said.

"I'm not sure how, but I think you're right." Walsh directed his attention to another black dot. "There's one from Barnard's Star. And look, the *Trangus* is just outside the Epsilon Eridani gate."

Aether scattered and reformed. "All the gates must have flashed when you transitioned to Sol. They got ready just in case."

"They're all one gate," Walsh said, his voice distant. "That's what Chuck Boston said in his log. You might be right. I wonder..."

"If we can transit ships between any gates we choose?"

"Exactly. We could get these colonists to Sol in an instant."

Aether turned towards the Sol gate. No ships besides theirs had come through. "Do you think Sol is ready?"

But Walsh was focused on the Procyon fleet. At least two of them were old CDF warships. He hoped they weren't looking to settle scores with Earth. He hoped Liberty wasn't right about giving free access. He hoped he could do something about it if he'd been wrong.

Walsh shrugged. "I don't know. I think we can make sure Sol sends out aid ships to their lost brothers before anything else." His mind focused on Earth and the sparkling blue sphere came into focus before him in perfect detail. "The lost colonies will know they are no longer alone in the dark. In the meantime, Aether old buddy, I feel like walking around the universe a bit. Care to join me?"

THE END

About the Author

A. R. Kavli is a starship captain, seeking fame and fortune among the stars by way of crafting fiction books since orbital mechanics are far too complicated for him. Seeking that same adventure in the real world, Aaron joined the U.S. Navy for six years, only to learn that F-14 Tomcat avionics technicians don't get cool theme music like the pilots. He is still glad he joined—and left. When not leading a squadron of raiders against the oppressive EarthGov, Aaron is moving miniatures he's painted around a table and rolling dice, crossing swords with fellow historical fencing students, and traipsing around Middle Tennessee with his beautiful, former F-14 Tomcat avionics technician, wife and four vundabar children.

Read more at https://www.arkavli.com.